THE EXPHORIA CODE

THE EXPHORIA CODE

ANTONY JOHNSTON

PEGASUS CRIME
NEW YORK LONDON

THE EXPHORIA CODE

Pegasus Crime is an imprint of
Pegasus Books, Ltd.
148 West 37th Street, 13th Floor
New York, NY 10018

First Pegasus Books hardcover edition October 2020

ISBN: 978-1-64313-527-4

10 9 8 7 6 5 4 3 2 1

Printed in the United States of America
Distributed by Simon & Schuster
www.pegasusbooks.com

For Bill, Brenda, Percy, and Gwen

1

He wasn't really a mole. Not *technically*, and that's how he justified it to himself.

Of course, he didn't have any real choice in the matter. Not if he wanted to keep his job, his career, his pension, his family...his life. And what would his wife say, if she knew? If she knew where the money to buy their new car, her new clothes, their evenings in fine restaurants, came from?

The same money that had landed him in this current mess.

What he was doing was definitely espionage, he couldn't talk his way around that. But he wasn't actually working for the Russians; not in the sense that people meant when they said, "There's a mole in MI6," in those classic stories of British public schoolboys growing up to betray their country. He didn't work for an intelligence agency. Just another government man, punching his card and collecting his salary.

The only difference between him and anyone else on the project was that he was here, driving up a dark, tree-lined road in the middle of nowhere an hour before midnight, with a Toshiba SD card in his wallet. An SD card holding what were, *technically*, state secrets.

He wasn't even getting paid for them. He'd already been paid, for the other thing, and that had gone about as badly as it could have, so now he owed them. It was only fair, the Russian had said when approaching him months ago, that he repay his debt. He couldn't, of course. The money was spent. But the Russian expected that, anticipated it. People spend money when they have it. So the Russian would accept something else, instead. It wouldn't cost him a penny.

But it had cost him more than enough sleepless nights. Tonight, he thought, tonight would be the last one. It had to be, didn't it?

When the Russian first approached him, he'd asked if they could do the handovers at a café. Since coming here to work on the project he'd adopted a place in town as his regular lunchtime haunt. The sort of place guidebooks and low-budget travel programmes would prefix with "charming little", gushing about "local flavour" and "authenticity", oblivious to how being invaded by people from out of town — people like him — would chip away at that very same authenticity, until all that remained was a place where tourists went to take selfies and feel pleased with themselves for finding somewhere "so off the beaten path."

He just liked their tea.

The Russian had called him a stupid amateur, and insisted they meet at a secluded car park atop a wooded hill just outside town instead. He'd noticed on previous visits there was no cellular signal up here. Perhaps that had something to do with it.

He pulled into the car park, stopped the car, and turned off the headlights. There were no street lamps out here, and the sudden darkness left him momentarily blind as his eyes adjusted to it. A sharp rapping on the driver's window made him cry out in surprise. He still couldn't see, but as he opened the door he smelled familiar sour notes of alcohol and cheap German cigarettes, and knew it was the Russian.

And who else would it be, anyway? Nobody knew he came here for these meetings. Nobody followed him. For the duration of the project he was living alone, in an apartment on the edge of town, and on the Russian's advice had removed the complimentary GPS unit in his long-term rental car. On the way here tonight there had been one car that seemed to follow him from somewhere in town — he didn't notice it until they were on the outskirts, but it had definitely been there for some time — until the car turned off before they crossed the river, going in a completely different direction. After that he'd checked the rear-view mirror every ten seconds for the rest of the journey, but saw nothing.

"Good evening, Comrade," said the Russian, his accent as thick as the smoke he blew into the cool, dark air. "The stars are very fine tonight." He was right. This far from town, the lack of light pollution meant you could see almost every star in the sky, right to the horizon.

He shook his head all the same. "Comrade? You do know the Soviet Union hasn't existed for decades."

The Russian looked back over his shoulder with a thin smile. "Yes, of course. Absolutely." As usual, the Russian's car was nowhere to be seen. Either he parked it elsewhere, or he walked all the way here from town. Both seemed plausible.

He took the Toshiba card from his coat pocket and offered it to the Russian. The card itself held everything incriminating; if anyone looked at the mini-tablet it came from, all they'd find were photos of his wife and family, and an almost complete collection of Chris Rea music. He was just missing a couple of the early albums. One of the project coders had offered to 'torrent' them for him, which he knew was some kind of illegal internet thing, but that sounded too risky, considering what he was doing. The thought of his family made him protective and defiant, so as the Russian pocketed the memory card he took a deep breath and said, "I think now you've had enough."

"Excuse me, what?" the Russian frowned.

"I said, I think you've had enough from me. I can't keep doing this, someone is going to notice eventually. It's amazing I haven't been caught already."

"You owe us. And your debt is not yet repaid."

"It must be," he protested. "The project will be finished in a few weeks, you must have enough by now."

The Russian took a slow step towards him. He backed up against the car as the Russian held up the memory card between them. "I gave you many of these. You will fill them all, and then maybe we have had enough."

"You, you can't threaten me," he stammered, "I'm your, your only source, I know that. Without me, you've got nothing."

The Russian turned the card over in his fingers, its metal contacts gleaming in the starlight. "And without this, you are worth nothing…except perhaps the life insurance for your wife and children." The Russian leaned forward, snorting sour breath into his face, and something hard pressed against his chest, something lodged under the Russian's ill-fitting sport coat. He closed his eyes, trying not to think about what it was.

Something clicked. The Russian stepped back.

Nothing happened. He opened his eyes to see the Russian was holding the car door open for him. "You need rest. Go and have a good night's sleep. I will see you here again in three days."

He slid back inside the car and let the Russian close the door with a flick of his wrist. It started on the second attempt, and he drove away, back down the hill, not looking back. He didn't want to see the Russian watching him in the rear-view mirror, didn't want to imagine the hint of a smile on the man's face.

Just a few more weeks, he told himself. You've been doing it for months. A few more weeks and it would be over. The debt would be paid, and everything would go back to normal, because he only had this one thing to do, because he wasn't actually a Russian agent or mole.

Not *technically.*

2

"And what are your opinions on cryptographic mechanisms expressly designed to deny visibility to third parties, such as law-enforcement agencies?"

She caught a flicker of interest in the eyes of the casually-dressed young man sitting on the other side of the interview desk, and knew she finally had his attention. That was a good development for Miss Jane White, who'd asked the question, because so far the interview hadn't been going her way. Despite the cool, fully air-conditioned ambience of the room, she felt the back of her neck begin to warm, and pinpricks of sweat rose on her body. The interview room itself was spartan and anonymous, a deliberate choice to deny the candidate an opportunity to form too many ideas of whom, exactly, he was being interviewed by. The company Miss White worked for had never been stated, not even when Rob Carter, the young man sitting opposite her, had entered the room.

The job posting was itself obscure: *"Elite coders, interesting work, well paid."* It barely read like a call for applicants. To further the point, they hadn't posted it on the usual job sites, where CVs of the eternally hopeful masses piled up by the thousands, and algorithms seemed convinced that every listing that merely contained the word 'computer' was The Perfect Opportunity for the large subset of those masses who had the word 'computer' anywhere in their CV. No, Miss White had been very careful about where this job could be seen. Hacker board communities, unlisted IRC channels, anarchist email lists. Places that didn't advertise themselves, that you had to know to look for, that trolled newbies mercilessly until they proved their skills. Places that would ensure the people who responded, applied, and ultimately walked through the plain glass door of this red brick King's Cross building, waited in the distinctly logo-less lobby, glanced hopefully down the receptionist's blouse as she gave them directions, climbed the breezeblock stairs and, finally, entered this very room were exactly the kind of people Miss White wanted to see.

Curious. Driven. Excited by the prospect of clandestine work, hidden corridors of power, the potential to change the world.

Rob Carter ticked every one of those boxes, and more besides. Miss White (whose hair matched her name, her contrasting brown eyes conveniently focusing the young man's attention away from the rest of her face) had hoped all along he'd apply for the post. In fact, the moment Carter made contact, she rejected every other applicant and stopped answering further enquiries. Now here she was, opposite the very man she'd wanted to see, trying to get him to open up.

She fumbled with her pen, waiting for him to answer. If she fucked this up, her boss would be furious.

The interview had begun in a fairly standard fashion. They'd gone over his CV, even though Miss White had read it a dozen times, just to be absolutely sure he wasn't bullshitting about his talents and achievements. His self-taught coding skills, the game app he made while still at school, the trouble he'd got into for hacking his sixth form college's system and altering coursework grades. Dropping out of uni when he realised he already knew everything on the Comp Sci syllabus. Contracting on and off for game studios, contributing to open-source projects that focused on cryptography and zero-day exploits.

What he hadn't talked about yet — what Miss White was so keen to steer the conversation towards — were the projects that weren't so open. Carter had a strange habit of taking holidays in places with well established hacktivist communities, who then coincidentally released impressive new exploits and tech demos in the days after he moved on. That, ultimately, was all she cared about.

Carter narrowed his eyes. "So is that what you're doing here? Building stuff the law can't snoop on?"

"The balance between security and privacy," said Miss White, raising an eyebrow, "is a question everyone in the community must wrestle with these days. On which side do you fall?"

He replied with a lopsided smile. "Whichever side pays better."

Now she knew he was interested. Giles, her boss, had suggested she try to keep Carter's interest through less subtle means — "How about a tight blouse and a push-up bra?" — but that wouldn't hold for more than a few minutes. True, the hacker community was still overwhelmingly male, not to mention socially awkward. And Carter was better-looking than many coders she'd known, meaning he probably had less trouble with women, and maybe figured he stood a chance with Miss White. Truth be told, and under different circumstances, he probably wasn't wrong. Get a few double vodkas down her on the dancefloor of some dark subterranean club, and she wouldn't turn her back on him.

But in an age where eight-year-old kids knew where to find swathes of free online pornography, a flash of skin wouldn't keep Carter's attention for long. To really get him interested, you had to talk hacks. Dangerous, semi-legal hacks.

Her mouth was dry. She licked her lips, and her voice cracked a little. "Let's try a little thought experiment, then. Say a corporation is developing a new network protocol, and we'd like to see it. We know the identity of the project's deputy lead, and we have his home address. An inside source has also given us the specs of their central server, with several undisclosed script vulnerabilities. What's your attack vector?"

Carter smiled. "Holy shit, are you a front for the Chinese?"

Miss White half-smiled in reply. Enough to insinuate, not enough to confirm. She repeated, "What's your vector of choice?"

Carter leaned back and folded his arms. "Nah. If you know who I am, you know what I can do."

"You're evading the question, Mr Carter. Is that because it's beyond you?"

"Fuck off," he sneered. "You know it isn't."

Miss White looked down, made a note on her pad in silence, then looked back up at Carter. Waiting.

"Christ's sake," he said, rolling his eyes. "You go after the deputy lead. If you've got his ID and address, then you can get his phone number. He's probably in a credit card dump on a pastebin somewhere, so you match him up on that, and there's your new angle. Spend half an hour on the phone to Amazon to get into his account, use whatever you find there to crack his email, boom. Or maybe he doesn't bother to shred, so you dig through his wheelie bin and get the card from there. Same difference."

"Half an hour on the phone?"

Carter imitated a distressed customer. *"Oh no, my daughter made an account for me, and now I can't remember my password. But I can give you my date of birth, address, phone number, credit card number, can you just give me a new password so I can buy her a birthday present, pleeeeease?"*

Miss White smiled despite herself. "Fair enough. But this is all social engineering. Why not go straight for the corporate server?"

"Waste of time, it's probably done up like Fort Knox. Get into his email first, you're bound to find something on it. Everyone slips up, uses their personal email for company stuff. Why spend weeks trying to hack it when you can just walk in with the password?"

"So what you're telling me is that you're just a con man, not a real hacker."

Carter's forehead reddened slightly, and a muscle in his neck twitched. "They're the same thing," he said through gritted teeth. "And you still have to know what to look for. If you don't know what goes where, you're just running around breaking shit and setting off alarms. I'm not a bazooka, I'm a sniper bullet. I get in, locate the target, and get out without them even knowing they've been buzzed."

Miss White shrugged casually. "But you're not skilled enough to do the same with the script vulnerabilities? You're not familiar with *ZFlood*, or *MaXrIoT*, or *Bunker_Stalker*?"

"Of course I'm familiar with them," Carter snapped. "I wrote a couple of hundred lines in *ZF* 1.0, for God's sake, then did three bug fix releases solo. And I used *Bunker* on the DGT, because I was buggered if I was going all the way to Belgium just to grab a bunch of contract records."

Miss White put down her pen and stood up. "There you go," she said.

The door opened behind Carter. He turned, startled, as two broad-shouldered men in grey suits entered. Shocked and confused, he looked back at Miss White, but she was already leaving the room, sliding out of sight behind the security officers who'd been waiting to arrest him as soon as he admitted to hacking the EU Directorate-General for Trade in Brussels.

She shoved open the ladies' bathroom door and let it close behind her, shutting out the fading sounds of Rob Carter insulting her, her parents, her presumed sexual orientation, and anything else his rage could muster. She collapsed back against the door, short of breath, her head spinning as she threw the wig on the floor to reveal her dark hair.

Then Brigitte Sharp staggered to the sink and leant on it with all her weight, forcing her arms to keep her upright. She stared at the mirror, trying to work out what looked wrong, then remembered she was wearing coloured contacts as well. Her hands trembling, she slowly squeezed them out of her eyes and let them fall into the sink.

Somewhere at the back of her mind, Dr Nayar was shouting something at her. Something about her feet, the floor…

She kicked off the high heels, part of her Miss White disguise, and felt the cold, firm touch of the floor on her feet. Let her weight sink through her stomach and hips, down through her calves, her feet, into the floor. Let the world carry its own weight.

Ten. And breathe, and count. Nine. And breathe, and — the scent of hazelnut.

"Good work, Bridge. How are you feeling?"

She opened her eyes, not realising she'd closed them. In the mirror, the reflection of her boss standing in the doorway.

"Giles, this is the Ladies."

He looked confused for a moment, then dismissed it and continued, "You bagged him. Celebration time. I know it's against your religion, but do try and look happy."

The sting had been her idea, and it required a level of technical knowledge that only someone like Bridge could pull off. But she hadn't wanted to be the one carrying it out. She'd suggested Giles use someone from GCHQ instead, who could conduct the 'interview' and trap Carter into incriminating himself. Giles had put his foot down and told her to get over herself, go see OpPrep for a disguise, and spring the trap.

"Get over yourself" had stung. It was three years since the incident Bridge and Dr Nayar referred to only as The Doorkicker, and while she'd made a lot of progress, she still didn't feel ready.

Giles hadn't cared. "It's not even a real field op," he'd said. "All you have to do is sit in a room and ask him questions."

"You mean interrogate him," she protested. "Not the sort of thing they cover in basic at the Loch, is it? Get someone from Five, if you think GCHQ can't handle it."

"Five will put Carter in the net, but they can't reel him in. Just talk to him, nerd to nerd. I know you want to get back to OIT eventually, and this will be a really good step for you."

Operator In Theatre. The coveted SIS fieldwork status Bridge had gained, and lost, in the space of one week. Bloody Doorkicker. She shrugged. "I'm still in therapy. I'm not ready."

"Mahima says you are. You've improved more than you realise, and now you need to get back in the game."

Bridge scowled. "Oh, does she? Well, Dr Nayar's got her opinions, and I've got mine."

"Indeed, and you'd do well to remember which of those I have to consider when deciding whether to put you back on the list. Spoiler: it's not yours." Giles Finlay was exactly the kind of man who'd pull rank to win an argument, but she'd expected and hoped better of Dr Nayar. Bridge hadn't been to therapy since that day, and judging from her texts every week since, the doctor had no idea why.

Giles was also the kind of man who'd take credit for the operation to bag Carter, but Bridge had less of a problem with that. Let him deal with the Directors, the Ministers, the suits in their old school ties. He was good at politics in a way she never would be.

She was desperately thirsty. She hit the cold tap, bent down, and gulped at the freezing water. Her hands were still shaking, though less with each deep breath. She turned to Giles. "Can I take a day off? I've got some holiday carried over."

To her surprise, he barked a laugh. "Not getting out of the paperwork that easily. Go see the doc first thing — that's an order, by the way, no more avoiding her — for psych debrief. Then I want to see you back at your desk, writing this up. After all that, maybe we can talk about days off."

She opened her mouth to protest, but the look in Giles' eyes was clear. "Please don't tell me this is for my own good."

"I should coco. You'll thank me when you get your OIT back."

The door closed with a sigh as he left. Bridge looked up at her reflection and sighed with it.

3

```
T > By Jove, Ponty, I think I've cracked it.

P > cracked what

T > The ASCII art. It's a puzzle.

P > like how?

T > Like a code.

P > bloody hell
```

She retreated, as she so often did, to the shadows.

Or rather to 'Tenebrae_Z', one of her oldest friends, with whom she chatted regularly on a secure messaging server. They'd built it together, handcoded the whole thing from scratch, then piggybacked it on an admin machine somewhere deep in Telehouse North, the colocation facility in Docklands where dozens of service providers and internet backbone carriers routed their UK traffic. Bridge had been there once with her colleague Monica Lee, and Monica's GCHQ liaison Lisa Hebden, to observe installation of a hard routing intercept, but she'd never been by herself. By contrast, Tenebrae_Z had regular access. He was one of the privileged few with keys to a server floor, owing to his clearly important but never outright-stated day job.

At least, that's what he told Bridge and everyone else when they first met on Usenet, the now outdated and virtually defunct message board service of 'newsgroups' left over from the internet's early days. He certainly knew what he was talking about, and she'd run her own trace on the chat server to confirm it really did live somewhere in Telehouse. It all checked out.

But, despite being friends now for almost a decade, Bridge and Tenebrae_Z had never met in the flesh. She didn't even know his real name.

T > It□s not just on f.m.b-r. I found instances on other French groups, too. All low traffic, barely used. Every piece is 78 x 78 chars, all innocuous images like the ones we already found. Flowers, dogs, Michael Jackson□s face, etc.

P > which one

T > Which one what?

P > which face, he had loads

T > ROFL

To be fair, Tenebrae_Z didn't know Bridge's real name either. Everyone on the *uk.london.gothic-netizens* newsgroup knew her simply as 'Ponty', a silly play on her name and heritage. She'd come up with it on the spur of the moment when she first ventured into the deep end of the internet, graduating from the shiny, friendly web forum UIs inhabited by norms to the murky areas of pure text and command line interfaces. She'd been a fresher at Cambridge, then; black-clad, white-faced, and big-haired, with an inglorious social record and a teenage arrest for hacking. The last thing she needed was to screw up her chances of a First by using her real name to post to a newsgroup devoted to hacking and subculture.

In fact, what nearly sent her degree sideways was her second arrest. She'd cracked the university servers several times without anyone noticing, no big deal. But then one of her mathematician friends was approached by a faceless civil servant after a lecture, and gently asked if he was interested in a career of 'discreet but challenging government work'. The man left a card containing only a name and phone number. Figuring he must have been a spook, Bridge was determined to find out who exactly he worked for, to give her friend an edge. Some basic research on public websites led her down a rabbit hole, and she began to chip away at government servers, hacking into records and administrative databases. She got as far as discovering that the name on the card was fake, the phone number was real, and the faceless man appeared to be linked to Westminster Palace itself, before the police broke down the door of the house she shared with two other students.

After she was released on bail, a different but equally faceless civil servant approached her to make the same offer, with an added sweetener; they could make all this trouble with the law disappear, as if by magic. The only conditions were that she had to achieve a First, and to keep her nose clean from now on. It was all the motivation she needed, and Bridge still found it ironic that an offer to her friend, which he ultimately declined, had led directly to her own career.

SIS gave her a fully backstopped cover story to protect her family and friends, which she maintained in public spaces online. But on *u.l.g-n* her misdirection went even further; she claimed she 'worked in finance' and refused to say any more. Not that anyone asked. Almost all of the regular netizens used aliases, and those who didn't were cagey about what they did away from the safety of their keyboard. The group's specialist demographic meant much of the discussion was technical talk about hacking, coding, obstinate servers and idiot users, so it was understandable many wanted to remain anonymous.

Tenebrae_Z was more anonymous than most. All anyone on *u.l.g-n* knew about 'Ten' was that he was some kind of BOFH — *Bastard Operator From Hell*, online slang for a high-level admin doomed to work with idiot users — and that if his tales of weekends in the garage were to be believed, he owned a selection of very fast and very expensive vintage cars.

T > Found 14 images so far. Oldest dates back six months.

P > so random. any clue who's posting them?

T > Anon user, black hole email, obscured IP. That figures, if it's a puzzle. WHICH IT IS :-D

P > how did you even work out it's a code

T > That would be telling.

P > I AM NOT A NUMBER!

T > LOL. Actually, a number is what I decoded from one of the recent posts. A phone number.

P > \ (@ o @) / !!!

T > I called it earlier.

Bridge and Ten hadn't liked one another to start with. Their first proper interaction was an all-out flame war that split the group right down the middle, and just for once it hadn't been Linux vs Red Hat, or Vi vs Emacs.

Not long after she joined the group, someone — she didn't remember who, it had been yet another newbie who stumbled in, caused arguments, then disappeared — posted a rant declaring The Mission to be the apotheosis of '80s goth, as proved by the decline in Eldritch's work after Hussey's departure, and by the way, Fields of the Nephilim were a flour-filled bag of shite.

This was a red rag to Bridge's bullish and unconditional love of The Sisters Of Mercy, plus the lingering remnants of a pre-teen crush on Carl McCoy, thanks to her older sister's bedroom posters. It was her sister's record collection that had drawn Bridge into the subculture in the first place, starting with French 'coldwave' bands like Asylum Party and Excès Nocturne before diving deep into the UK import scene. When she'd later moved to England, she was shocked nobody had heard Mary Go Round's *Dark Times*, or Opéra de Nuit's *Invitation*, and talked them up whenever she could. Sure, most of this stuff had been released before Bridge could walk; but so was half the British music her new friends talked about.

She responded to the inflammatory post with the kind of withering disdain and righteous fury normal people might reserve for someone suggesting that Hitler had a point, and at least Mussolini made the trains run on time. To Bridge's disgust, Ten sided with the newbie, and for the next three weeks *uk.london.gothic-netizens* became the sort of place the *Daily Mail* would hold up as a poster child for why the internet was destroying modern society.

But over the course of thousands of words of intense argument about the definition of modern goth, the role of Bauhaus and Joy Division, the genius or pomposity (or both) of *The Reptile House EP*, the border between goth and metal, and whether Siouxsie and the Banshees were the last true post-punks or the first true modern goths, Bridge realised she and Ten had a lot in common. Not their specific tastes, which were almost diametrically opposed, but their attitudes to life, music, and most importantly hacking, were completely in sync.

They began private messaging, bitching about events and people on the newsgroup, occasionally helping one another out with tricky coding problems. After Bridge started working for the Service, she suggested they build an IRC server to keep their conversations entirely within their own control and untraceable. Ten went one further, challenging her to help build their own protocol, so as to keep it entirely unrecognisable to prying eyes, and offered to host it in a hidden partition of an admin server in Telehouse North. Nobody would notice a few tiny encrypted packets flying around the wires, and as they both used onion skin multi-node random routing to hide their true digital locations, even if the server was discovered there would be nothing to connect it to them.

P > what was it, like a competition winner's line?

T > Nothing so glamorous. Just a bloke. I said I'd got his message. He's here in London, we're going to meet tomorrow night.

P > WTF, you have no idea who he is

T > Well, he's obviously a massive nerd, so that shouldn't be a problem.

P > seriously Ten, who is this guy. could be a nutter

T > You're just jealous because he's going to lay eyes on me before you do ;-D

After they built the chat server, Bridge almost suggested they should meet in person. But something had stopped her — perhaps an instinct for self-preservation — and she never did. He never did either, and so they never had, and wasn't it maybe better that way? After years of chatting, bitching, and laughing, could either of them live up to the others' expectations? In Bridge's mind, Tenebrae_Z was a six-foot-tall young David Bowie with long jet-black hair and a penchant for tight leather trousers. She knew it was ridiculous, of course. But she was self-aware enough to know that if what she actually found was a five-eight guy with his roots showing, and a perfectly normal middle-aged belly that would stop any sane man considering leather trousers, it would inevitably feel like a let down. The only thing she knew about Ten's appearance was an upside-down Celtic cross that he wore, as some kind of private joke, that he'd once taken a photo of for the newsgroup. But it would take more than an almost-funny necklace to get over the inevitable disappointment of reality.

Likewise, while Bridge was by no means unattractive, it had been a long time since she backcombed her hair to within an inch of its life, caked herself in white foundation and black eyeliner, and pulled on a pair of spike-heeled boots. SIS insisted even technical analysts stay in shape, so she could probably still fit into her trusty old buckled leather corset, but it hadn't left the back of her wardrobe for years. Dyed black hair and the occasional silk choker were the only concessions to her younger days that Bridge could still get away with, and it was all a far cry from the image of Patricia Morrison's younger sister Ten was doubtless hoping for.

P > be careful, OK

T > My dear Ponty, the game is afoot! How irresistible to a man of my character!

P > jfc

T > I☺ll tell you all about it when I get back tomorrow night, promise. Signing off now.

P > cyal8r

She logged out and closed her laptop. For the last few weeks she and Ten had been following these seemingly random pieces of ASCII art — impressionist images made up of regular text characters arranged in a way that, when you squinted at them, they looked like a picture of something.

```
                                     bqjvzeshho/!:^
                               "%*./sA#H/!.oLhy+--syh$:s5
                             vnhFs-*.+yhesYY1sy/`.-o@sylAh#
                           #+-^.-/s##kys5ss..y+sd0+o.mdhyAHep
                          0mdsqrRqV+/X+sssd0+/^r-HKiqyh4so@+yg8
                         yhso     +!A#Hyscdo7ys5xh3haPX0KsoGZeWe
                         /A $     D+o     y#o!Cgsz       OR   GqJ
                        91 P3     9scV2DJA$5m5iBNEs:^I:o++o    syX
                       Ps- 4  Ø+o@7B$Ui7OhM?h]oAR8FdXHhQis+O     0o+
                       yo  $dQIsHSmpc1xZ%MJBybZ[f^.:+shhs-tx     `hs
                      xS#kyqL$w8oe4K4laspy!:/+0gghsWMb7adxiqzTS3ss+o
                 Cgyso/+dm$gcys+oC+PY+di!hmOVhazec-Øshybschl8xT-/++o
               so/-:axS+d        'h4so@ycpZemdu92GDdpeVUhhyo@o+xBtd
             w7(y%XPAgD   y$D:/jTlPeH4!x60Dy58#Sm:Sdy2yXPhddRu6T1LBdh
            jhysO0oxnz+++og3xu5H4Y?6MB-os+/+!WN/:zO0omwmAX\ntCGJTSnZy
        O0Scjs18-:ofRxJ2XY/-?$+osyhmdOaDekS:dA#Hydpø+8:/o+O0soD2Uz24U8B
      Mjr!1:oys+4uWxOTD&uzxKKJoZCeSd%(huifjVo/+o@xnzØEz0rN2OxD4+n/+o@sy]k
     gycw+N!N/:;/sy)h%!3xatCHwsm8hfo*xZcplCbhVD5oo9AEtS(s4:/og8yo+/:yuxGgT
    U9Nd[#]hhyysCgyho+o@/+-Øox95NtNxnz+B7vHJP$.kl+syhyomqcZ2Q+oyf][hrVo*2j
   MzlxjrEymJ"HbIxNy9U52X746WR-EMCJSuxexy081MX77k9eUvjyIjyGVF$ae1E7Ke5A5G\d
   yO2/UJcfj6ae2HvcrzMYx=R8#iGdf2zD4p0eDdE#!rSE4SpDQ3Iy38??neo4j6gSQUXK!UVH
   $BnDZnyJzsbgLpBxmk+)ueIDFy6!Vddr[TnSeqy1k$es8\JRlyO24vbskxLss4RuvCYEuz[r
  jIkaNSj5SEOAG67/Mcv=OTson%hqOKM&*Uf1028I3Vw4lptAjRCfG?bNA2Fyw7RTLxa$QnvJh
 +diagFVNdv0o58B$5kgcT/r85SkVxn84s!zhDenxmESxv5teFA94IF89UWb531lQVhMa=4IY5#
s7TR7e2eP$t9FRik%n4bJASP$lg\fbqTWK!4g04w]cA5EXN!PnLhmxmTNa7Tl!YQzvc7zUmuy2I$
06OQecKEVPLKT9JvM@3w0s0iQDM!kKPvPHUiakH0cNdxoHwW2mdL9lz5gMmMjIc*Au1U1r+/8co
xRns/.$/x+nsYhkL7KO!3xhyhmzafahyhvnh4mysCgsTFN9b!-//oD2y3IUxQs5sUulax$hxh!A
   Vo£y#c0yhd!!o:-=x0._.\x-of][hhyssg8ØFVcBzo-Ø++!WN//FpofY+++sO0oWVqwj3@
    dpøsyhYGAExLbFuv!./ssD2yhso+x/+oHdEc5ICldkxd^.:+-ØsnOjs6:j86Ts.amrzzF
    KOHB8o48LTjRg786q9RHCX8I9RiMbG6mZK2oOyxh3]b[so+UmOuxLDG     VqCe^-/+o
    @5ys[yXPyVh6/o@so/+xH/CemV3U8Cgh##dUqj3x]Ffys?syhmd[h]Wrw3s-:+s_o+O0
     ouE6Ez/=5yX   Ph3sEu2Xx2RXD!yhuw     IY4e9HV41`:oswbTh5i3Wbt1PZIWtv
     5e7v:-$!./    +s3Mso@xEthYUjF6IM   nxqF1NRe5o/-!'.djt9G8s36d0sosqc
      65aYq9fB@d[ovdrido++rmpmyo@-Øsso//+OPI7co+msjcdzb+/:+sYF$x/+o
      o36ss6B2P45OAsyyf]ioD!dIdoopDm2lwpme5nq1KWfHlsXq-
       peo0bO0/:-6JNHbGc5UcKKT6NaIDu1ju692o@s#eg
         xhjbywlo##ysO0oEEgDNhdxh3!/-$-shF
           dhyso@+    AS*0 6 188 D16   A
```

Someone was posting them, one every couple of weeks or so, to an obscure French newsgroup. Who? And why? They didn't know. There was never any follow-up, never an explanation. But now, somehow, Ten had figured it out. Found more pieces of art that had been posted in other newsgroups, and decoded one of them to find a phone number. Now he was going to meet the man behind them.

Bridge's mind drifted back to something her mother had told her as a child, about a treasure hunt, where an artist had made a solid gold hare brooch covered in gems and buried it somewhere in England… *Masquerade*, that was it. The artist then made a puzzle book of surreal paintings, which contained a hidden code leading to the brooch's location. Bridge's mother had shaken her head at the silly eccentric English as she recounted how the whole country went quite mad for a while, trying to solve the mystery and find the treasure. But Bridge was so fascinated by the idea that her father bought her a second-hand copy of the book during a work trip to London, and she spent a happy summer trying in vain to solve the puzzle.

Thinking of it now, it seemed like an old-world geocaching puzzle. Maybe this was something similar for the online age? Posting random pieces of ASCII art in obscure places, in the hope that someone tenacious enough would be compelled to dig into them, and figure out the code? It had been done before in the form of Alternate Reality Games, or ARGs. But ARGs were normally big PR operations linked to movies or videogames, and neither Bridge nor Ten had been able to find any announcements about it here, in France, or in fact anywhere else online.

They'd only stumbled across the images themselves because she was still subscribed to *france.misc.binaries-random*. Once it had been a good source of French jokes, memes, and photoshops, and was a comfort blanket for the small part of Bridge that remained nostalgic for her childhood, growing up in Lyon, and even the infuriating habits of her French mother. But traffic had slowly dropped off as spambot posts took over, and for years now the group had been an endless stream of garbage. She wasn't sure why she was still subscribed, but she was, and looked in every so often to see if there was anything interesting. There wasn't — until these strange, random posts of ASCII art began to appear.

Bridge finished her tea, yawned, and headed for bed. Tomorrow night was dinner with her sister and the girls, and she was looking forward to it. But she knew she'd spend the whole evening impatient to get back online, and find out if Ten had dug up their very own golden hare.

4

"Adrian!"

Bridge couldn't breathe. She stared at Adrian's body as his jacket slowly, ever so slowly, changed colour from desert camo to a dark, rusty crimson, spreading out from the bubbling wound. She couldn't, wouldn't, couldn't look away.

"Yop tvoyu mat!"

The guard's surprised shout wrenched her back into the cold, dry room, but things seemed to be moving at half speed. Slow enough for Bridge to finally take a breath, her survival instincts kicking in, and move. She raised her pistol, turned one-quarter into the sight line, squeezed once, twice. The guard fell, his trigger finger spasming, spraying semi-automatic three-shot pulses into the surrounding racks. Servers exploded in showers of electric colour.

The other guard was still shouting, firing indiscriminately.

"Stupid fucking doorkicker," she muttered, and fumbled inside Adrian's jacket for what he called his 'ICE' grenades. Slick and wet, her fingers slipping over them, struggling for purchase. They were in the middle of a desert, why were the grenades so wet?

ICE. In Case of Emergency. Like now, like this emergency, right here.

Adrian's little joke. Adrian's blood.

Bridge's sense of humour, silenced by the hammer of bullets.

5

"You seem distracted this morning. What's on your mind?"

Bridge stared into her coffee, only half-hearing Dr Nayar's question. Last night had been a bad one. The same episode over and over, reliving Adrian's death, helpless to save him, unable to prevent it. No, that wasn't true. She knew that. What she didn't know was, why now? She hadn't suffered a Doorkicker nightmare in months, yet this morning she'd woken up sweating like a goth at the beach.

"You don't have to talk, Brigitte, but if you don't tell me then I can only make assumptions, and I'm sure they're worse than the truth. Family trouble?"

Dr Nayar's tone was soft, friendly, comforting. Everything about her was comforting. Her lightly aged skin, her soft brown eyes, the gentle grey streaks in her gently styled hair. Her office, in a corner of the SIS building at Vauxhall Cross, was soft, quiet, and comfortable. The whole package, designed down to the last detail to put intelligence officers — men and women trained to be permanently suspicious, alert, verging on paranoid — at their ease.

She often wondered how many of her colleagues came in here, sat on this oh so comfortable sofa, every day, every week, to unburden themselves and ensure their psych evals were up to date. Surely not that many. Prior to the Doorkicker incident, Bridge had only encountered Dr Nayar during her interview and selection process, and that had been in the Doctor's regular Marylebone offices, which were well appointed but not quite so comfortable. Here, though, she had an entire corner office to use whenever she needed.

Even Giles Finlay didn't have a corner office.

But over the past three years Bridge had come to know every inch of this room, this comfortable sofa. Every other day at first, then every three days, then once a week, then monthly — until she argued with Giles before the Carter mission, and discovered Dr Nayar had betrayed her trust. This was her first session since, but while Giles had undoubtedly briefed the good Doctor on the sting, she hadn't mentioned it, or Bridge's absence.

"No, my family's fine. I'm having dinner with Izzy tonight, Mum's still in Lyon, Dad's still dead." Her father had passed away long ago, while Bridge was still a teenager, but she half-hoped Dr Nayar would rise to her flippancy.

No such luck. "Do you think about him a lot?"

"Dad? All the time. What kind of question is that?"

"When was the last time you spoke to your mother?"

"Last week," Bridge lied. "She's fine."

"But you're not. What are you angry about?"

"How long have you got?" She fixed Dr Nayar with a stare. For a moment she was fourteen again, glaring defiantly at her mother from under a fringe carefully cut to seem like it had been achieved without a care in the world, and bracing herself for an unbroken string of French expletives.

Dr Nayar sipped at her cup of tea. "Giles tells me you still don't think you're ready for another bash at OIT."

"I'm not. I nearly threw up yesterday."

"Nearly, but you didn't. I've seen the tape, and I thought your performance was excellent. You did exactly what you needed to, and no more, without seeming at all outwardly nervous." Bridge didn't know what to say to that, so stayed silent. "Brigitte, I think you're ready to take the next step. It's completely natural that you'll be nervous at first, and honestly, I'd be concerned if you weren't. But I'm just as confident you'll overcome it. I'm going to formally advise that you're ready for OIT."

"I had the nightmare again last night."

Dr Nayar paused mid-reach for her reading glasses. "The whole incident?"

"Just the part where I got my partner killed."

"You know that's not what happened. Adrian Radović was an experienced officer, and the senior operator in theatre. It was his job to assess the risks."

"And my job not to freeze up when someone pointed a gun at me."

Dr Nayar sighed. "A relapse is unfortunate, no doubt. But this is the first time in…" She consulted her notes. "In four months that you've had this nightmare. That's a really good sign. I wonder what triggered it now?"

Bridge shrugged.

"Well, do come and talk to me if they become more frequent. It's possible the anticipation of getting back in the field will trigger an anxious response. Again, perfectly natural, but I'll want to stay abreast of it."

They'd danced this waltz many times before, and Bridge knew every response the Doctor would give, just as she in turn must surely know what Bridge would say. But this time, she was changing the steps. "I don't think I should go back on OIT."

"As I said, I know you don't think you're ready. But your own actions demonstrate otherwise."

"I want you to take me off the list completely."

Dr Nayar paused for a moment, then said, "Brigitte, if you don't get back on this horse now, I fear you may never ride again."

"Good." Bridge stood, picked up her leather jacket from the back of the sofa, and walked to the door. "Tell you what, make it permanent. If I can't trust myself, how can I ask another officer to?" She tried to slam the door on her way out, but it was rigged to close slowly, ruining the effect.

6

The child had seen the man before, in the market. There were always a lot of people there, but he was very sure it was him, because of the way the man looked at the child's mother. The same way his father sometimes looked at her, though not very often these days, since everything changed.

Now the man was in his father's bedroom, but he wasn't looking at the child's mother in the same way. He was shouting, in that very quiet fashion grown-ups sometimes had when they didn't want other people to hear. But the child heard, because the teachers had sent everyone home from school today. His teacher said the pandas were coming to ruin the school, but that didn't sound right. He'd seen pandas on the television, and they seemed nice. They wouldn't ruin a school.

That was what the teacher said, though, and the children were sent home. He played with his friends for a while, until he got bored of running around the streets, and he went to the shop. But his mother had already left to do housework, and the child made a sad face. His father ruffled his sandy blond hair, told him to get a grip, and sent him home to help her with the chores. He set off, but had no intention of telling his mother what his father had said. He hoped she'd let him read a book in his room instead.

He heard the man whisper-shouting when he entered the house, and at first he thought maybe it was the new friend they'd made when everything changed, the man who never smiled.

Instead it was the man who the child assumed was only friends with his mother, because he'd never seen the man say hello to his father. Not even after the man met his mother that time in the market, and kissed her on the cheek.

The child's mother began to cry. He peeked through the doorway and saw the man from the market get out of bed and start to dress. He was still whisper-shouting at the child's mother, and she was still crying, and suddenly the child was too upset to stop himself from bursting into the room and hitting the man over and over and screaming at him to stop hurting his mother but the man was too big and strong and he threw the child against the dresser and things fell off on top of him and then the man stomped out of the house and his mother was shouting at him and crying at the same time and everything was horrible.

Months later his parents would be dead, and he would learn the truth.

7

"Ciaran, did you nick my pen? The lightsaber. It was here yesterday."

Ciaran Tigh looked up from his screen on the other side of the tiny Cyber Threat Analytics room. There were only three desks in the CTA unit office — one each for Ciaran, Bridge, and Monica, who was currently in a briefing — yet it was still too small for them. Bridge had once stood in the centre of the room and swung a two-foot piece of string around her head, just to test the theory about dead cats, and it was a pretty close thing. Almost took out the holiday calendar on the back wall.

"First, what would a *Trek* man like me want with a lightsaber? Second, how the hell can you tell?" Ciaran's desk was immaculate, a sanctuary of order, precision, and calm. Every notebook squared off, every document tray in alignment, every pen and pencil arranged in parallel and accounted for.

By contrast, Bridge's desk was, well, a contrast. She liked to think it reflected a creative mind, and was working on a desk-tidiness-correlation theory about *Star Trek* fans like Ciaran vs *Star Wars* fans like herself, although Monica's desk (somewhere in the middle, not as neat-freak as Ciaran's but tidier than Bridge's) threw the whole thing for a loop. Monica preferred *Aliens*.

Besides, where everyone else saw nothing but a mess, Bridge saw a system. She might be the only one who understood it, but she was the only one who had to, and she always knew where everything was. Except, at this precise moment, her favourite pen.

She stood at Monica's desk, scanning the surface, but it wasn't there. She knew it wouldn't be. Why would Monica need to take someone else's pen? Why would anyone need to? This wasn't high school.

Ciaran had resumed reading, already lost in the morning's wires and scan alerts from GCHQ as they scrolled up his screen. Bridge returned to her own desk and flopped in the chair, which belched an ergonomically-designed pneumatic sigh in response. "Only ten-thirty," she sighed. "How much worse can today get?"

Giles entered, smiling. "Bridge, there you are. Broom Eight, please, in five minutes."

Without looking up from his monitor, Ciaran smiled, but said nothing. She scowled at him anyway. "Will I need to take notes?" she asked, opening her pen drawer. "Only I've — *ah*." Her lightsaber pen stared back at her.

Giles, still in the doorway, shook his head. "No notes. Problem?"

It took all of her self-control not to slam the drawer shut.

8

The drone came rushing toward them over the airfield, buzzing like an angry wasp.

Some observers cried out, but Air Vice-Marshal Sir Terence Cavendish remained motionless except for an imperceptible sigh. This was all part of the display, designed to put them in a heightened state and get the heart rate going, so they were more inclined to gasp and be impressed by the drone team's feats today. Not that Sir Terence didn't want everyone to be impressed, including himself. The programme was under his purview, and if the boffins could pull off what they promised, the RAF would leap from zero actionable capability to the forefront of active engagement drone technology within two years. That was a noble goal, and made it worth sitting through these interminable slide shows, meetings, and demonstrations. He just wished it didn't require quite so much *theatre*.

As he predicted, the drone pulled up at the last moment. It buffeted the crowd with the thrust blowback from its single rear rotor, giving the crowd a close-up view of the *X-4* code number stencilled on its side before ascending to turn and resume its regular path. Sir Terence made a mental note to give the pilot a talking-to for getting quite so close, then turned his attention to the targets and missiles on the ground.

The missiles were a standard four-by-two array, rear-mounted on a jeep for mobility. Not that the jeep would need to move today, as it wasn't the target. The focus of this demonstration was at the far end of the airstrip; a cluster of cars, a dozen blue models surrounding a single red one.

A klaxon sounded to signal the start of the final exercise. First the drone carried out some impressive, but standard, high-speed manoeuvres. Everyone knew drones had no onboard pilot by definition, but Sir Terence found it often took an extra moment of enlightenment for non-RAF personnel to truly understand the capabilities made possible by that omission. No pilot meant no concerns about g-forces, oxygen pressure, inertia, or indeed any life support systems whatsoever. It meant the craft could turn on a sixpence, as it was doing now — changing speed, direction, and altitude in ways no human pilot could attempt, much less endure.

But the manoeuvrability display was a minor part of the demonstration. That was for the hardware boys to show off, to prove they could make drones as capable and impressive as anything America had tucked up its sleeve.

The drone righted itself out of a barrel roll, turned, and made its final approach to the airstrip. The jeep lit up as it fired a single ground-to-air missile at the drone, a green-tipped 'dumb' rocket that streamed a fuel trail in its wake. The drone easily took evasive action, banking right, and the rocket passed harmlessly by, flying on into oblivion. But two more missiles had already been fired, and these bore white tips — the mark of 'fire and forget' self-guiding weapons. The X-4 dodged and weaved through their paths, even as they made their own automatic flight adjustments, slowing and turning to re-seek their target within seconds. But unlike a manned vehicle, the drone could fly just as fast as the missiles, and it soon became obvious they would run out of fuel before catching it.

Of course, that was assuming the remaining five missiles didn't slow it down first. They fired simultaneously, bathing the jeep in a glow of hot exhaust as a mixture of white and green tips sped toward the drone. One dumb rocket almost winged it, but the X-4 rolled at the last minute, flipping its wing out of the attackers' flight path while diving to avoid the high path of a self-guided missile. The sky filled with fuel trails, obscuring the view, but this was also part of the demonstration. A human pilot would have been flying blind in the middle of such chaos, but the drone's 'eyes' were made up of dozens of sensors and cameras that 'saw' straight through the fog of battle.

Nearing the end of the airstrip, while still taking evasive action from three remaining self-guided missiles, the drone fired its own weapon. A single rocket soared out from under its wing, aiming for the cluster of cars. The red car exploded in a ball of flame, leaving the surrounding blue cars untouched. Bullseye.

The drone continued on, performed a loop, then flew to its landing zone at the far end of the airstrip and came to rest. Behind it, the chasing missiles dropped to earth as the demonstration team aborted them.

An impressed silence fell over the airfield, quickly followed by enthusiastic applause.

Anyone not versed in the project might have thought they were applauding the human pilot controlling the drone from a nearby bunker; that the live fire part of the exercise was another hardware demonstration, to show off the drone's responsiveness to its remote pilot. But the pilot had done very little. In fact, after the opening aerobatics display, his only action had been to activate the evasive manoeuvre autopilot, and trigger the payload release. The evasive action itself, dodging and weaving to avoid the barrage of missiles, and the corrective targeting required to bullseye the target car while engaged in those manoeuvres, were all calculated by the drone's own software. It was all part of a new and highly advanced system for which Sir Terence had been assigned responsibility.

Exphoria.

9

Giles had commandeered Briefing Room Eight, one of the smaller 'Brooms', for privacy. Bridge followed him inside, and took the seat he indicated for her.

Every Broom was a soundproofed, windowless box, and a baffled signal zone. No cellular, no wifi, no RFID or bluetooth. Even old-fashioned squawkbox walkie-talkies could barely penetrate the walls. The only outside connection was through a computer, housed in a separate secure server room, and accessed solely through a single wired mouse and keyboard placed at the top end of a four-seater conference table. Several wall monitors mirrored the computer's display, which currently showed a slow, gentle camera pan over verdant green fields. Bridge had come to hate that screensaver after several years of staring at it in various Brooms and departments, but as Giles sat down he made no move to log in to the computer and thereby remove it.

"I have a job for you," he said.

"I thought you said I wouldn't need to take notes."

"This isn't the briefing. First I need to know if you're willing to take it on."

Bridge's mind raced, trying to figure what analysis subject Giles might think she would potentially shy away from. She was the youngest member of the CTA, but there wasn't much she hadn't seen during the past seven years.

The Cyber Threat Analytics unit was Giles Finlay's concept,

created following the 7/7 London bombings. At the time he was a young, recently-promoted SIS ops controller, with an old school friend among those killed on the Russell Square tube-train explosion. Although the attack itself was on home soil, making it MI5's jurisdiction, Giles argued the security services had been left behind when it came to digital communications, especially terror co-ordination through private ad hoc networks and encrypted consumer channels. GCHQ did the best they could, and MI5 had stepped up their own 'real space' monitoring in the UK. But SIS' foreign knowledge and intel, if combined with the technical skills required to monitor and analyse digital comms, would place it in the best position to connect the dots between resident actors and their mentors abroad.

It had taken a year of persuasion, and no small amount of politics, but Giles was eventually authorised to create and recruit for the CTA. Ciaran had been his first hire, headhunted from his role as a technical analyst in another SIS department. Soon after, Giles had poached Monica from GCHQ and they'd operated as a two-person unit for a while until Bridge joined, fresh from Cambridge. She knew there had been other potential recruits along the way, both for Monica's position and her own, that Giles had rejected. But their identities were never disclosed, and if either of her colleagues knew, they weren't talking.

Within a few years, the CTA's score card had amassed enough gold stars according to its original remit, including direct prevention of at least four home-target terror attacks that Bridge knew of, to satisfy Whitehall and ensure its continued existence for the time being.

But Giles' timing turned out to be fortuitous. Digital communications rapidly became the global norm and intelligence channels were increasingly filled with 'OC', or Obscured Chatter; communications that were either encrypted, encoded, or both. Then came the Stuxnet worm that targeted Iran's nuclear centrifuges, the South Korean banks hack, the Refahiye pipeline explosion triggered by online attack, the cyber assault on government computers in Estonia, the Mirai botnet that took half the internet offline for almost twenty-four hours, and more and more every week. As the world was increasingly managed through computers, so those computers increasingly came under attack, and the same old actors came into play. The UK, the USA, Russia, China — instead of messing about with nuclear missiles, now they attacked one another with endless waves of network assault, while spies on the ground exploited the same technology on physical operations. The new cold war was digital, and every bit as dangerous. As Giles had argued to the Prime Minister, with the nuclear threat of Mutually Assured Destruction the end result was horrifying, but simple; complete global annihilation. A cyberapocalypse, on the other hand, was no less horrifying but much more complex. It left everyone alive to suffer, starve, and perish through the total collapse of society, government, and infrastructure. Was one really better than the other?

Thus, as digital warfare progressed, CTA's remit expanded accordingly. Now the unit also tracked cybersecurity developments, the latest breakthroughs in viruses, trojans, and other exploits, while also keeping a close eye on the 'black hat' international hacking community. Ciaran likened it to a game of whack-a-mole, except there were ten thousand moles, the mallet was operated via a remote control with sticking buttons and failing batteries, and the game never ended.

The CTA came across many items that had no real foreign component beyond communications, which were simply passed on to MI5. Others were foreign, but not international, and those were passed to the appropriate local agencies, with SIS maintaining an interest in case circumstances changed. But some items crossed borders, or threatened the UK, and those the CTA investigated itself. If a threat was purely online, they were authorised to mount their own counter-attacks where possible. If a problem spilled over into the real world, they could advise other SIS departments on the most effective deployment of officers, where to focus exploitation of local agents, and ultimately how best to take preventive action.

Not all of the cases concerned terrorists directly, but many of them used the cover of war and terror to hide their criminal enterprises. Money laundering and racketeering in the face of upheaval was common, and made up some items the CTA regularly passed on to other authorities. Undesirable arms sales were another regular feature, and an area where SIS often took a hands-on interest, sometimes to the extent of sending OITs to frustrate or redirect the vendor. The most disturbing case Bridge had seen was a sex slavery ring in Libya that used the chaos of the civil war following Qadaffi's death to abduct, hold, and exploit children as young as two. She could live without ever trawling through a sewer quite that foul again, but nevertheless it had been necessary. If that was what Giles had in store for her, so be it.

As a final thought, she wondered if he'd called this unusual meeting to suggest she move department. The CTA was his baby, and he naturally had a soft spot for it, but he also oversaw several other departments and active response groups.

"Try me," she said. How bad could it be?

Giles shifted in his seat. "I want you to infiltrate a startup. We suspect someone there is using foreign skillbase recruitment as a cover to bring radicals into the EU and naturalise them."

"That's Five's area," Bridge shrugged.

"Not this one. The startup is based in Zurich. You'd go in as a French native."

She was about to ask *What makes you think they'd hire me*

anyway, when she realised what Giles was truly proposing. Field work. A return to OIT. "Haven't you spoken to Dr Nayar yet?"

"Mahima briefed me immediately before I came to find you, and said the same as before. You're ready, you just don't know it."

"I told her to take me off the bloody list altogether."

"So she said. But, as I reminded you before, the final decision is mine."

Bridge looked away, trying to hide her annoyance.

"You're not the first officer to experience trauma, you know. Mahima, me, everyone here has seen it in plenty of officers. Some of our most valued OITs have been through what you're experiencing, but they came out the other side by easing back into the field with quiet jobs like this. It'll restore your confidence, have you going full speed before you know it."

"Why?"

"I beg your pardon?"

"Why are you so keen to get me back on OIT? I'm an analyst, Giles. Your man tapped me at uni because I know one end of PGP from the other, not to be Jane Bloody Bond."

Giles spread his hands. "Your overall Loch score was above average, and certainly better than anything Ciaran or Monica managed. Plus, Hard Man tells me you've kept up your CQC."

"In a gym, but I haven't sparred in months. Anyway, Dr Nayar advised I keep it up as complementary therapy."

"Bloody good advice it was, too. Look, I wouldn't have put you on OIT in the first place if I didn't think you had potential as a field asset. And this Zurich job is strictly no-contact, pure obbo. Get in, figure out if they're dodgy, then we pull you out."

Bridge's first instinct was to immediately say no, before she let herself think about it too much. But at the back of her mind, the woman who accepted the job offer from SIS to begin with — the woman who wanted to make a difference, to put her skills to good use, to feel like she'd done something positive with her life before she wound up as worm food — that woman was preaching reason, urging her to think positively and conquer her fears.

Giles was watching her intently. She said, "My entire thought process is written all over my face, isn't it?"

"On the contrary," he smiled, "you look like you're bored and thinking about what to have for dinner. Give yourself some credit, and sleep on it. Then come see me tomorrow morning."

10

"For heaven's sake, Bridge, how many times? Don't call me Izzy in front of the kids."

"You just called me Bridge."

"You're not their mother."

"Can you two stop it for one night? Look, our table's ready."

Bridge pursed her lips, clamping down a frustrated response. Then she noticed Izzy (Isabelle, whatever) was doing the same, so Bridge looked away as their waitress led Karen and Julia into the main room of the restaurant.

"Go in front of me, Stéphanie," Izzy said to her daughter. Stéphanie walked dutifully ahead of her mother, without a word. She was four years old now, but Bridge had often remarked on how remarkably self-composed she was, even as an infant. The current infant, Hugo, was rather different. Bridge made wide-eyed smiles at him as he struggled to escape Izzy's arms and clamber over her shoulder, and he gurgled back.

There were two high chairs waiting at the table, but Izzy turned to the waitress and said, "We won't need those."

"Your children are so young, madam," replied the waitress in a southeast European accent that Bridge identified as Slovenian. "Don't you think they would be more comfortable?"

"My daughter is perfectly capable of sitting in a chair, and my son will stay on my lap. Take these away and bring us a booster cushion."

Some nearby diners cast sideways glances at the fuss, but before Bridge could intervene, Karen spoke quietly to the waitress. "This is our last meal together for a few months, so quite frankly, we're going to spend a lot of money. Do as you're told."

"Not quite how I would have put it," said Bridge, sitting down.

Karen shrugged. "I'm in here three times a week with clients. They can bloody well shove it." She and Julia were more Izzy's friends than Bridge's, but she'd always had a soft spot for Karen. The eldest of the group by several years, Karen had worked her entire life in the City, and was now a 'wealth manager' for the sort of people she'd once sarcastically described as "too busy being rich to worry about their money, too busy being paranoid not to worry about it." Julia, meanwhile, had read English at the same university as Izzy, and worked her way up through the media to become a TV producer in Soho. She and Karen normally took it in turns to pick the restaurant for these get-togethers, with Izzy occasionally pitching in when she'd heard about somewhere new and fashionable.

Bridge was the baby of the group, four years her sister's junior, and if they'd asked her to suggest a restaurant, most of the good ones she knew were either places Karen or Julia had taken them to in the first place, or vegetarian. She couldn't really picture Karen licking her lips at a black bean and avocado wrap.

A waiter removed the high chairs, while the waitress returned with a booster cushion for Stéphanie, who thanked her, placed it on her seat, and climbed up on to it. Bridge smiled and nodded approvingly, and Stéphanie beamed back at her with pride.

"I pity her husband," laughed Julia, nodding at Steph. "She's going to be a right handful."

The young girl smiled back, "I'm going to marry a socialist."

Karen laughed and wagged a finger at Izzy. "Your Fred's got a lot to answer for. Why isn't he looking after the kids tonight, anyway?"

"Loads of admin to finish up before we go to the farm," said Izzy. "There's no internet or anything there."

"God, what a blessing," Julia laughed. "If I went off-grid for more than six hours, my PA wouldn't know how to tie her own shoelaces."

As if to prove her point, Julia's purse buzzed, making the table vibrate. She rolled her eyes and pulled her iPhone out, apologising. "See? You watch, I'll put it on do not disturb, and she'll be calling the police to say I've been kidnapped. Tell you what, Izz, you should rent your farm out with a big sign, '*No Mobile Signal*'. You'd make a fortune."

There were two things Karen and Julia didn't know about Bridge and her sister. First, Izzy's name was really Édith. Isabelle was her middle name, but for as long as Bridge could remember, she'd insisted everyone call her by it. She'd even considered legally changing her name to swap them round, but Bridge had talked her out of it. Édith was their late grandmother's name, and while Izzy's relationship with their *Mamie* had been strained — she was a strict old matriarch who tutted at every move the young Édith made, while letting '*petite Brigitte*' get away with murder — Bridge maintained she should carry it with a sense of lineage.

The second thing they didn't know was that Izzy's husband Fréderic hated Bridge. It was partly a simple clash of personalities. Fréderic was a dour and serious man, with no discernible sense of humour. He and Izzy had met while they were both doing charity aid work in East Africa, and over the years Fred had risen up through the ranks of do-gooders to his current position as a logistics manager for Médecins Sans Frontières. He was practically a Marxist.

And that was the other reason he disliked Bridge; because of her job. Or rather, the job everyone at the table thought she had.

As far as her friends and family were concerned, Brigitte Sharp was a junior civil servant for the British Government, currently working at the Department of Trade and Industry. Her job was intensely boring, with very average pay, and something she simply couldn't talk about. Not that most people were dying to discuss paperwork at the DTI anyway, but on the rare occasions someone asked, they'd understand when she made excuses and said she wasn't allowed to. It also gave her a reason to occasionally jet off somewhere, under the pretence of tagging along with a junior minister to a trade negotiation, or being forced to attend a dreadfully dull import/export dinner. Bridge worked hard to make her job sound so uninteresting that nobody would even contemplate asking her to talk about it.

In fact, she'd spent her day wrestling with whether or not to take the observation mission Giles had offered her in Zurich. She could see the sense in what he and Dr Nayar said. If she didn't go back into the field soon, she might never return at all. But was it what she wanted? She'd spent so much time over the past three years working her way through a process of recovery with an ultimate aim of making her ready for OIT again, she'd hardly stopped to wonder if she was sighting up the wrong target.

She enjoyed her work. She liked the CTA unit, and her colleagues, though Ciaran and Monica exasperated her from time to time. There was an old saying, "You can choose your friends, but you can't choose your family." Bridge had often wondered why it never ended, "…or your work colleagues." SIS was the only adult job she'd ever had, but she'd heard enough horror stories from friends to know it was the same in regular offices too, and that the occasional problems she had with other members of the CTA unit were relatively minor by comparison to some.

Her only longstanding issue was who truly ran the unit. Giles was in overall charge, but had other responsibilities besides the CTA. Officially they were all the same rank, but by default Giles gave his orders to Ciaran. That made sense to Bridge; Ciaran was the unit's founding member, was older than both she and Monica, and had worked at SIS longer than either of them. But Monica didn't like it. She regarded herself as more qualified than Ciaran and Bridge because of her prior experience in GCHQ, before she was headhunted for SIS. She had a point; her knowledge of electronic surveillance, digital countermeasures, and online security was deep and thorough. But as Giles often reminded them, this was a very different agency, and required a broader base of skills and resources. He'd brought Bridge into the unit because of her reputation as a hacker and zero-day aficionado, for example. And Ciaran was an excellent chatter analyst, able to dive into the gigabytes of surveillance data collected every week by GCHQ, along with his own bots that crawled chatrooms known to be frequented by suspected hostile actors, and surface with insight and meaning.

The three of them were pretty damned good together. Why mess with that? Why did Giles want to break that up, by making her the only OIT in the unit again? What on earth did he have in mind?

"Earth to Brigitte…come in, spacegirl, your time is up…"

Julia waved a hand in front of Bridge's face, breaking her train of thought. She smiled. "Sorry, Jules, I was out there for a minute. Thinking about work."

The wine arrived, something expensive that Karen had picked out. Julia handed Bridge a glass, laughing, "Well, we can't have that. Get some drink down your neck, girl." She pointed at the single women. "The trouble with you two is, you don't appreciate how good it feels to get away from the couch potato once you land one. Cheers!"

They all drank, and Bridge pretended not to care. True, she and Karen were both single. But Karen had a new pinstriped suitor every other month; they just never stuck. "They all look at the mirror more than at me," she once complained. Bridge had gently suggested she might have more luck dating men who didn't work in the City, but Karen looked at her as if she'd grown an extra head.

"Like Bridge is ever going to make me an aunt," said Izzy. "Can you imagine her in white?"

"Who says I need to get married to have kids? Anyway, you wore white."

"Bridge, I'd grown out of my all-black stage while you were still at uni. You, on the other hand…"

Karen laughed. "She's got you there, baby girl."

Bridge opened her mouth to protest, but checked herself before saying anything, and realised Izzy was right. She'd come straight from work, and was wearing black jeans tucked into her black leather boots, a black cotton shirt, a cardigan, and her usual black leather jacket slung over the back of her chair. She could muster an argument that the cardigan was technically dark grey, not black, but that would only make things worse.

"Honestly, I wonder sometimes if you don't work at the DTI at all," said Karen, and Bridge tensed. Like everyone in the Service, her cover was watertight, but she still had a certain paranoia that nobody really believed it. She watched everything she said, every opinion she held, ever mindful of giving herself away, of letting the side down. But to her relief, Karen continued, "Getup like that seems more like something Julia's lot would wear to the office."

Julia frowned. "Leave her alone, she looks fine."

"See?" laughed Karen. "Precisely my point, darling."

Bridge sighed. "I'm not public facing most of the time, you know that. You should feel sorry for the poor men, not me. They can't get away with anything except a suit, while nobody gives a toss what the women wear so long as we don't look like bag ladies."

"That's because we're invisible to them," said Julia with a scowl. "Guys like that, you could parade up and down the street naked and they'd look right through you."

"Papa sometimes comes out of the bathroom naked," said Stéphanie, "but Maman shouts at him."

Bridge and the others laughed, while Izzy blushed and scowled at the same time. "Yes, well, Maman has told him you're a little old for that sort of thing, now." She cleared her throat. "Can we please change the subject?"

The waitress took their order, and Bridge switched to orange juice. Karen rolled her eyes in disapproval, so Bridge said she needed a clear head for an important meeting in the morning. It wasn't entirely untrue; she just left out the details, as always.

And then they did change the subject, to the reason they were here in the first place. Izzy and her family were leaving tomorrow for their annual holiday back in France, at an old farmhouse owned by Fred's family in Côte-d'Or. Every year they spent the summer there, with no internet access, no cellular reception, barely any TV signal. Just a landline phone, in and out. To them, it was an idyllic paradise. To Bridge, it sounded like hell. All evening, her thoughts kept drifting back to Zurich. At least there, she would be connected — but she wouldn't be able to do anything with that connection. Once she was active OIT, all personal voice and data traffic would be heavily restricted, in some cases forbidden. If Izzy's farmhouse sounded like hell, how much worse to be surrounded by data but unable to do anything with it?

By the time dinner was over, Karen and Julia had demolished three bottles of wine between them. Karen insisted on paying, and was now debating with Julia whether they should get a cab to Julia's club, or find a grungy basement all-nighter and slum it. Bridge could have gone for late night karaoke, but didn't suggest it because she knew they'd just roll their eyes. Izzy had only had a glass more than Bridge because of the children, and was now busy wrangling them into position. Hugo was fast asleep, so Bridge took him for a moment while a waiter retrieved his stroller, and Izzy helped Stéphanie into her coat. When the stroller arrived, Bridge strapped Hugo into it with a kiss on his forehead, then gripped the handles while the waiter held the door open.

They emerged onto the street, still busy despite the late hour, and Bridge smiled a little at the noise. She had the same nostalgic affection for rural life as Izzy, but after the family had moved to London when they were children, Bridge had quickly discovered she was a city girl at heart — while Izzy spent most of her life yearning for a return to the country.

"Shit, my phone. Where's my phone?" Julia panicked, leaning drunkenly on Karen. She patted down her coat pockets and rummaged through her handbag. "Balls, balls, balls…"

Karen was in no fit state, and Izzy was dealing with a suddenly overtired and whining Stéphanie, so Bridge turned back to the restaurant. "You probably just left it on the table. I'll take a look." She gripped the door handle, about to pull it open, when Karen cried out.

"Thanks, babe — *oh!*"

Karen's purse clattered to the pavement, spilling its contents. For a moment Bridge thought she'd dropped it because she was drunk, but then saw her outstretched hand, pointing over Bridge's shoulder.

Izzy screamed, "Hugo!"

Bridge turned to see Hugo's stroller rolling down the sloping pavement, into the road.

Her limbs suddenly weighed a ton. Like a bad dream, everything happened so slowly, barely moving at all, and the cars were rushing by on the road, and little Hugo's stroller bumped and clattered over the uneven flagstones, and Bridge only just then saw the pedal, the little bright green brake pedal on one of the back wheels, the brake she'd forgotten to activate before letting go of the stroller, of little Hugo…

Izzy darted past her, faster than any human should move, and grabbed a handle on the stroller just as it left the pavement. The stroller jerked back, waking Hugo, and he started crying.

"You bloody idiot!" Izzy screamed. "What the hell were you doing?"

"I'm sorry, I…I forgot the brake."

"For heaven's sake, Bridge, this is why I can't trust you with anything. You can hardly take care of yourself, let alone anyone else!"

Stéphanie and Hugo were both crying, now. Karen tried to soothe Stéphanie, while Julia scrambled around on the pavement, sweeping everything back into her purse. She held up her phone and called out, "It's all right, it was in my purse. It's, um. It's all right."

"What the hell's that supposed to mean?" said Bridge, reddening with a mixture of frustration at Izzy and anger at herself. "I've done nothing but take care of myself since uni."

"Exactly," said Izzy, seizing on Bridge's choice of words. "All you've ever done is look out for yourself. Who was it looked after Mum when Dad died? Who was it dealt with her crying all night when you got arrested? Who sorted out the lawyers when Mum moved into the new flat? It wasn't you, was it?"

Julia moved between them and said, "Girls, what the hell are you babbling about?" Bridge looked at Karen, confused, then realised she and her sister had been shouting at one another in French. "Izzy, your daughter wants you," said Karen, ushering Stéphanie to her mother's side.

Izzy glared one final time at Bridge in silence, then turned away with her children in tow. "Don't worry, Steph, we're going home now. Karen, can you do the honours?"

"Yeah, that's sobered me right up, that has. Taxi!" Karen raised a hand, and within seconds a cab pulled to the side of the road. They always asked Karen to hail taxis, as she seemed to have a preternatural ability to summon them out of thin air. After the cab stopped, Karen helped Izzy and the children inside, then held the door open for Julia, who climbed in after them. "Night," she said, as the taxi pulled away, then turned to Bridge and shook her head like a disappointed schoolteacher. "She's just stressed, you know? One kid's hard enough, but can you imagine two?"

"Karen, you know even less about kids than I do. Besides, she's not stressed about them. I'm just an idiot."

The older woman put her arm around Bridge's shoulder and rubbed it affectionately. "One day, I swear. One day, we'll manage a night out without you two going at it." Karen hailed another cab and held the door open for her.

Bridge shook her head. "I'll walk."

"To Finchley? Are you mad?"

"It's only about five miles. I've done it before."

Karen sighed. "I'll bet you bloody have, as well. Just be careful, OK? We do all love you, you know." She gave Bridge a final hug and climbed into the cab.

Funny way of showing it sometimes, she thought as she walked north. Then again, sibling arguments like that probably didn't make it easy. And the night hadn't been a complete loss. She'd got to see her niece and nephew, who always made her smile, and it had all helped her make a decision about Zurich. She'd tell Giles in the morning.

11

"Giles, you can't send him in alone. He's just a doorkicker."

"He's not applying to work there, Bridge. All he has to do is get inside and plug in a USB stick."

"And get out again."

"Sure, if you like."

"But Adrian doesn't know a rack server from a stereo, let alone anything about POSIX threads. What if they question him? They're not going to let him just walk in there."

"He may not be an honours girl like you, but give the man some credit. We're briefing him on what to look for, which internal server to infect, everything you laid out in the advisory. And our local source has given us detailed location plans, including a secret infil method. Radović shouldn't need to talk to anyone on the way in or out."

"Assuming nothing's changed since we smuggled our source out of there."

"Then he'll have to improvise. Anyway, he's going in with Serbian cover, and we're false-flagging the whole op in case he gets blown. This is not Adrian's first rodeo, as our American friends would say."

"Send me in with him."

"There's no need, and besides, you're not yet OIT."

"So promote me. My scores from the Loch are good, and I know you've discussed it with Hard Man. He told me."

"Yes, because you've made it perfectly clear you want in the field."

"And this is an ideal job to start me on. Adrian can do what he does best, hitting the enemy and kicking doors. I'll just be there to make sure he kicks the right ones."

"Have you ever been to Syria?"

"You know damn well I haven't. But you said yourself, infil should be clandestine, no need for contact."

"Quoting a man's own words back at him is no way to endear oneself."

"We get one shot at this facility, one shot at these servers. As soon as Moscow realises we've targeted them, they'll pull out. Our only chance is to infect them before that happens."

"You'll need to be placed on the firearms list. And Hard Man will have to formally sign off on you. Don't make me regret this, Bridge."

"Je ne regrette rien, *Giles. You should know that."*

12

Thirty minutes into her workout, the kick bag almost smacked her in the face when she suddenly realised she'd forgotten to chat to Tenebrae_Z last night.

Fortunately, Bridge's instincts kicked in and she reacted in time. She swung back on her root leg, pivoted to deliver a roundhouse that sunk into the bag's padding, and followed up with two jabs and a body blow. Then she caught and steadied the bag with her hands, before wiping her face with a sweat towel.

How could she forget? Because of Izzy, and their stupid bloody argument. Bridge had spent the long walk home obsessing about her sister, her life, her job, and generally feeling sorry for herself. When she reached her flat it was gone one in the morning. She'd thrown her clothes on the floor, climbed into bed, and pulled the covers over her head without even bothering to set Radio 3 going on iPlayer. She did that most nights to help her sleep, but last night she hadn't needed it — the last thing she remembered was closing her eyes, swearing quietly at her sister, and clenching her jaw to stop herself crying.

Now she'd have to wait till this evening to find out what happened with Ten at his mysterious meeting, and how on earth he'd cracked the ASCII puzzle. They'd speculated on lots of things together, and one of Bridge's discoveries had been a strange pattern in the few postings she'd seen — the last characters in every image were always an asterisk followed by a sequence of numbers with the letters A and D inserted towards the end, like "*0 6 188 D16A". No matter the image, there were the numbers, always different but always with that A/D. Bridge and Ten had scratched their heads over it, trying to figure if it was some kind of artist signature, or an equivalent to a serial number. The sequence didn't match anything they could find. She'd even secretly run it through some SIS databases, but came up with nothing. She was dying to find out what it was really for, and now Ten could tell her.

Today, though, her mind had been on just one thing since waking; the Zurich field job. If anyone had asked during the long walk home last night, she'd have said she was absolutely not taking it, not after proving she couldn't be trusted with a child's stroller. But upon waking, she wondered if that was rash. So she'd come to the gym early, hoping a combat workout before the office might clear her mind.

Bridge hadn't been a physical child. She buried herself in books and music, voraciously reading her father's sci-fi collection several times over — to the point of exasperating her mother, who just wanted her *petite Brigitte* to spend time with other children, make friends, maybe try talking to boys like Édith (her mother refused to call her sister 'Isabelle') did so effortlessly. When they came to England, though, Bridge's self-sufficiency and contentment with her own company made the move an order of magnitude easier for her to cope with than for Izzy, who had to leave not just her friends, but a new boyfriend. As compensation, their parents paid for Izzy to take horse-riding lessons, dancing lessons, music lessons… Bridge saw this and exaggerated how completely devastated she was by their move to England, using it to bargain for her own computer. Her father justified it to her mother by insisting it would be educational.

It certainly was that, although in a strange way she was glad he hadn't lived to see her arrested for hacking the local government's website and defacing it with vegetarian propaganda.

Despite her disinterest in sports, she'd also taken up karate after coming to London. Her parents were delighted at her showing interest in a hobby that wasn't just physical, but disciplined. Her mother, in particular, had made for a strange sight in the audience at martial arts sparring events and exhibitions where Bridge competed, dressing for each occasion like it was Ascot, but shouting Gallic encouragement like she was ringside at a wrestling match.

The truth behind Bridge's interest in martial arts had been much less noble. Almost as soon as she arrived in England, the bullies at school found her out. Puberty had still been a year or two away, but the English girls didn't seem to appreciate a new pupil who'd rather spend her break periods reading the latest William Gibson novel, or listening to a new VNV Nation album, instead of gossiping and parading around for the boys. They called her 'Freaky Frog' and 'Spooky Slut', which Bridge found maddeningly ironic considering everyone else at the school seemed to be getting off with someone, while she walked home alone every night. They broke into her locker, stole her textbooks, hid her gym clothes, and waited for her after school with their hair tied back and fingernails sharpened.

She couldn't bring herself to tell her parents. What could they have done about it, anyway? If they made a fuss at school, the girls would simply renew their efforts. If she moved to a new school, everyone would know why, and it would just be a different group of kids that bullied her instead. And if they did nothing, the bullying would continue and she'd feel as useless as ever. No, the only way to stop it was to fight it. But Bridge had spent her entire life living in books, computers, and music. She didn't know how to fight back if she wanted to.

So she decided to learn, and she learned fast. By the end of the final term of her first year, nobody at school was bullying her any more.

But then she had another revelation; it turned out she really enjoyed martial arts. Sergeant Major Hardiman, or 'Hard Man' as he was better known, had commented on it while giving her top marks in her induction class for Close Quarters Combat. She shrugged it off, said it was a way of staying fit that didn't involve chasing a ball around a court. He never mentioned it again, but the look in his eye suggested he had some idea of the truth.

She didn't mind. CQC became her favourite subject at 'The Loch', the typically understated name for a training facility compound covering twenty square miles of Scottish highland. There, 'Hard Man' — an officially retired Royal Marine now running a distinctly unofficial facility — and his battalion of instructors taught non-military security service personnel the necessary skills to survive in the field. MI5, SIS, Special Branch, sometimes even the TSG and diplomatic corps. They sent their men and women to learn everything from firing standard issue pistols and close combat to advanced driving and surveillance. Everyone at the Loch attended those basic courses, but only certain students went a stage further to study what Hard Man and the other instructors referred to as "Nobby Bollocks" classes. Along with a small group of others, who she assumed were also intelligence or special forces officers of some kind, Bridge learned how to build improvised bombs with household cleaning products, how to resist interrogation, how to mix fast-acting poisons, and more. She absorbed it all like a sponge, and so long as Hard Man and the others kept teaching her, they could think whatever they liked about her motives. After a while, she even stopped asking who the hell Nobby Bollocks was. It was only when she returned to London, and Giles congratulated her on passing the 'Nasty Business' course, that she got the joke.

But then came Doorkicker, and reality. Bridge lost her partner, screwed up the mission, and nearly got herself killed. It was all a far cry from thirty minutes of controlled karate sparring at the Loch.

The gym was filling up. She grabbed her things and headed for the showers, nodding at the regulars as she went.

13

There was still no alarm at fifty metres, which surprised him.

He ran a hand through his sandy blond hair and considered the possibilities. He couldn't have heard an alarm anyway, as there was no audio feed. But he did have visual, and he'd expected to see something happen, for someone to make a call or issue a warning.

Could whoever designed the building security really have been so backward, so old-fashioned, that they didn't think it worth scanning for objects below a certain size? The city had a pigeon problem, it was true, but when it came to security it was always safer to have false positives than negatives. And if they weren't scanning for this kind of threat, it was all but guaranteed there was no automated defence system in place. Those were still considered bleeding edge experimental, and were extremely expensive. *Welcome to London*, he thought, *city of budget cuts, shortcuts, and half-finished jobs.*

Still, this was all better for him. Better for the plan. Alarm or not, if he could navigate the high winds well enough to get within fifty metres, he was confident he could reach the glass before a live officer had time to take action. The glass itself was strengthened, but he'd accounted for that. And once the glass was gone, the next stage would be out of his hands and the wind wouldn't be a problem any more.

The transceiver pods had passed his own rigorous tests under controlled circumstances. But out here, in a live field, there were a hundred different things that could interfere with their operation, block a crucial part of the signal, or randomly shield a particular bandwidth.

That hadn't happened. Even in Shoreditch, almost two miles away, signal throughput was over 85%.

At thirty metres he steered away from the towering glass edifice and smiled.

14

Bridge was still annoyed with herself for not logging on to chat with Tenebrae_Z last night, but felt better for a decent night's sleep and morning workout. Showered and fresh, she entered Vauxhall Cross ready to face Giles and, more importantly, a big decision for her own future.

She was an analyst, a hacker, made to sit in front of a computer and use her brain. Not a doorkicker like Adrian Radović or the hundreds of OITs like him SIS sent all over the world, to skulk in the shadows 'with gun and guile', as a senior ops director had once put it to her. Coming to terms with that would be a challenge, she knew. It was like she was admitting some kind of defeat. But this was one loss she was pretty sure she could live with.

She took a deliberately circuitous route to the CTA office, to ensure there was no chance she'd bump into Giles if he was in early. She even passed on her usual coffee from the floor kitchen, just in case.

Ciaran was at his desk, sifting through the overnights from GCHQ. "Morning, morning," he said, holding out his Captain Picard mug without looking away from his screen. "If you're making a coffee, I'll take one."

She hung up her coat and kicked her gym bag into the corner. "Not right now. I'm seeing Giles in ten."

Ciaran tore himself away from his monitor, peering out from behind it with a look of concern. "You make it sound like being called into the headmaster's office. Something up?"

Bridge shrugged and smiled. "Sort of, but it's OK. Don't worry, I'm not going anywhere."

Monica flung the door open and strode into the room, snorting impatiently. "Morning."

"Delays?" asked Ciaran, turning back to his screen as Monica threw her bag and coat under her desk.

"Didn't you see the news? They pulled some poor bastard out of the river. Turns out he lived at the end of my road, it took me fifteen minutes to walk a hundred yards thanks to the cops. I missed my train." Bridge winced in sympathy. Monica was a creature of punctual habit, and missing her usual morning train would sour her for the rest of the day.

She picked up the remote control and jabbed it at the office's wall-mounted TV. The remote practically lived on her desk anyway; nobody else wanted to delve into the mess they found there, so they just left it to Bridge to operate. The screen blinked into life, eternally tuned to BBC 24 hour news.

"Now, more on the body found floating in the Thames in the early hours of the morning. Police haven't yet released the man's identity, but gave us this statement:"

The feed cut to the banks of the Isle of Dogs, where a police Inspector spoke to reporters while officers and paramedics circled in the background. *"At oh-six-hundred this morning, we received an emergency call alerting us to the presence of a body in the water,"* said the Inspector. *"Upon investigation, we confirmed the body to be that of a fifty-year-old man, who was then pronounced dead at the scene."*

"Do you suspect foul play?" asked a reporter.

"At this time we're not prepared to speculate on the cause of death, but we would ask anyone who was in the area of Docklands either last night or this morning, and may have witnessed any

suspicious or abnormal activity, to come forward and speak to us in confidence."

"Have you identified the man? Did he have a criminal record?"

"We have made a preliminary identification, but until we confirm it we're not releasing that information at this time. We currently have no reason to believe the man was known to police."

The feed returned to the studio, and the newsreader moved on to the next story. Bridge muted the volume and turned to Monica. "He might say that, but if the cops were on your street, they must be pretty confident about that prelim ID."

Monica nodded. "Yeah, they had the house cordoned off and everything. No way they don't know exactly who he is."

"Did you?" asked Ciaran. "Know him, I mean."

Monica rolled her eyes. "It's Catford, not St Mary Mead. Why would I know some middle-aged bloke who lives at the end of the street? Anyway, we'll hear all about it later. They don't roll out that kind of police presence just for someone who threw himself off Blackfriars, do they?"

Bridge checked the clock in the corner of her computer screen and took a deep breath. Time to see Giles.

15

"I'm not going to Zurich."

Giles stroked his beard, releasing a fresh wave of hazelnut scent from his grooming oil. She wondered if he'd known all along that she'd turn it down.

"Furthermore, I'd like you to take me off the OIT waiting list, or spreadsheet, or whatever. I'm going to stay behind my desk. It's where I can do the most good."

Giles sighed. "Thank you for at least making a quick decision. I'll have to find someone else who can bluff their way through it, though God only knows where. But I'm absolutely not taking you off the list. Perhaps you just need more time."

"This isn't a question of time. I'm not up to it."

"So you say. Mahima disagrees, and so do I."

"You're not the ones who have to get out there and play spy, though, are you?"

Bridge didn't hear his reply, because his muted TV had caught her attention. The news was going over the drowned man story again, only now they'd chased down the dead man's house, and a reporter was standing in the street at Catford while the police searched it. Evidently the cops had decided to release the man's identity after all, and a passport photo filled half the screen. A middle-aged man, fairly regular-looking, with grey hair and a goatee beard. He had blue eyes that Bridge figured were probably attractive in real life, but in the over-lit passport photo made him look like a psychopath. An almost completely average man, the only really unusual feature being a necklace he wore. Well, more like a pendant —

"Bridge?"

An upside-down Celtic cross —

"Brigitte, are you listening to me?"

She ignored Giles, fumbling for the TV remote as the room lurched sideways and her stomach dropped into freefall. She found the remote and unmuted the news, never taking her eyes from the photo on the screen.

"*...Fifty-year-old computer programmer Declan O'Riordan, an Irish citizen who's been living in London for the past thirty years. Police haven't commented on the events of his death, except to say they're not ruling out foul play. We'll bring you more on this story as it develops. In other news...*"

"Definitely not a young Bowie," Bridge murmured, then jumped as Giles touched her shoulder. She hadn't noticed him get up to stand behind her.

"What's up?" he asked. "Did you know him?"

"Maybe? I think so. I'm not a hundred per cent..." Her mind raced, tracing back events, chat logs, connections, seeing if it all fit together. Computer programmer. Living in London for thirty years. The Celtic cross. Killed last night. After possibly meeting someone by the river?

"I need to go to that house."

Giles shook his head. "If that man was a friend of yours, I'm truly sorry. But this is a police matter, a domestic incident. I can ask someone at Five to keep an eye on it, if you like?"

Bridge snorted. "Oh sure, and of course they'd tell us straight away if they found anything. Shit, this is hard to explain."

"Try me," said Giles, returning to his seat and waiting patiently.

She took a deep breath, and began. She explained her history with Tenebrae_Z, their chats and hacks (leaving out the part about Telehouse for now), the ASCII art puzzle, his mysterious arrangement to meet whoever was sending the messages, Bridge's failure to check in with him the night before. The more she related the story, the more certain she became that this really was what it looked like.

"Wait," said Giles, "I'm confused. You said this was just a game, a puzzle?"

"No, we assumed it was. But we had no real idea, or at least, I didn't. He wouldn't tell me what else he found in the message he decoded, or how many he decoded."

Giles shook his head. "This is all very strange, Bridge. How can you be friends with someone for so long and not know what they look like?"

"It's the internet, Giles, do try and keep up. And is that really all you're taking away from this? What if the posts are some kind of criminal code? They're obviously worth killing for, whatever they are. You've got to let me in there."

"Easy, girl. Even if you're right, it's still a domestic case."

"Then we'll pass it on, like we've done hundreds of times in the past. But what if it isn't? I mean, the newsgroup's French. What if the source is, say, Tunisian?"

"I am not sending you to Tunisia on a hunch."

"So let me find out if I'm right. Give me authorisation to seize his computers, check his records."

"And if Mr O'Riordan turns out to be a random person, rather than your cyber friend?"

"That's why you should let me in there instead of going yourself," she said, smiling. "If I'm wrong, you don't get egg on your face."

"I'm not sure you fully understand the implications of our command structure," said Giles, dialling his desk phone.

"What are you doing?"

"Calling Andrea Thomson, across the river. If you think I'm letting you trample all over a domestic crime scene by yourself, you're less sane than I thought."

16

The expression on the Inspector's face was something Bridge had never quite seen before.

It seemed to be a mixture of suspicion and fear, and she couldn't really blame him. This was the same policeman who'd spoken on the news earlier, but now he looked much less self-assured. Here he was, overseeing what looked like a simple homicide case, when out of nowhere two strange women rocked up and demanded to be given access as a matter of national security. One was a fortysomething diminutive Scots terrier of a woman, all severe haircut, shoulderpads, and cheekbones to match. The other was younger, a full head taller and pale-faced, with a long black fringe and baggy black cardigan. The Inspector probably thought he'd stumbled into a comedy of errors — until Andrea and Bridge flashed their service IDs, at which point she was worried the poor man might have a cardiac.

"Should I be calling the bomb squad?" he asked warily.

"No," said Andrea. "At least, not yet."

"How comforting," said the Inspector. "Do try and give us some notice if that changes, won't you?"

Bridge and Andrea had slipped disposable forensic booties over their footwear — Bridge's block-heeled boots, Andrea's very sensible flats — so as not to leave any conflicting trace evidence at the scene. Now they both pulled on latex gloves, as the Inspector stood aside to let them pass and enter Declan O'Riordan's house.

She'd met Andrea Thomson twice before. The first time was at a COBRA briefing on Libya, where Giles had taken Bridge along as technical backup when the questions turned to whether Egypt's cyberwarfare division were taking an interest in Tripoli. They were, of course — every cyber warfare division, in every government around the world, takes an interest in every other government. But the Cyber Threat Analytics unit was still relatively new, and Giles wanted Bridge there to demonstrate how useful it could be. Andrea had sat across the table from Giles, part of Five's briefing team, as they discussed monitoring Libyan nationals in the UK. The Scot had taken copious notes, but said little, and at the time Bridge wondered if she was perhaps too timid to interrupt her male colleagues.

That notion was firmly put to rest the second time they met, at an inter-agency meeting with the Joint Intelligence Committee to address the government's options over Iran's nuclear programme. Bridge was there to explain Stuxnet, the mysterious worm creating havoc by infecting and destroying Iran's nuclear centrifuges. It was an open secret that Stuxnet had been built by Israel with American support, but Grosvenor House would admit nothing, despite backchannel assurances of discretion. The Oval Office might leak like a sieve these days, but the NSA remained tight-lipped as ever.

MI5, meanwhile, had been concerned with the possible leakage of information from Britain's own strategic nuclear commands to native British people suspected of being Iranian agents. And in contrast to the previous occasion, this time Andrea spent much of the meeting not only interrupting but actively contradicting Giles, C, Honourable Members of the committee, GCHQ representatives, and anyone else who stood between her and the extra resources Five was arguing for. Bridge noticed how Andrea's male colleagues were happy to sit back and let her go on the offensive, but couldn't decide if that was because they knew she'd get the job done, or simply to let her take all the heat if things went off the rails.

So it wasn't unexpected when Andrea greeted her by name outside Catford station. After all, Giles had called and asked her to accompany Bridge to the crime scene. When Andrea referenced both of their prior meetings, though, she was surprised. Andrea was more senior than she was, both in age and office, and Bridge hadn't realised she'd made an impression. "I'm surprised you remember," she said.

Andrea smiled. "What I remember is you patiently explaining to the Minister how, if we could get into Tripoli's servers, so could the Egyptians. I hear a lot of rubbish about 'golden keys' these days from people who should know better, and I've nicked some of what you said in there for my own meetings."

She wasn't sure how to respond to that. "I'm…flattered?"

"You should be. Now, let's go and see if Declan O'Riordan really was a terrorist."

Bridge was shocked. "Why would you think that? The news didn't say anything about terrorism."

"The first coppers who checked the house said it's packed to the rafters with computer paraphernalia. Naturally, they brought it to our attention." Now it was her turn to be confused. "I assumed that was why you were here?"

"Not exactly," she said, and explained how and why she believed the dead man was her friend Tenebrae_Z. In return, Andrea told her what they knew so far about Declan O'Riordan. He'd been born in Dublin, but moved to the UK when he was 22 after gaining a degree in the then-early field of computer science. He worked for various technology companies, then internet-related businesses, before becoming a freelance consultant thirteen years ago. He had no family here in England; his father was dead, his mother had returned to her childhood home in west Ireland, and his younger sister remained in Dublin. For more than twenty years he'd lived here in Catford, alone, in the terraced house now surrounded by police and forensic teams.

Bridge didn't want it to be him. As they entered the house she wanted this to be her imagination running away with itself, a case of mistaken identity, for Ten to turn up on chat this evening and regale her with an amusing story about how last night he met a computer geek, a hacker like them, who bought Ten a pint for solving the ASCII puzzle.

Per procedure, the house lights hadn't been activated, and the Scenes of Crime Officers had instead erected lamps to illuminate the rooms. The lamps threw hard, harsh shadows over anything not within their light field, making it difficult to tread carefully. The floor was almost completely covered with O'Riordan's belongings — books, newspapers, magazines, CDs, DVDs, bags, shoes, coats, candles, incense sticks, computer cables, portable hard drives, old computer games, new video games, even board games.

She turned to a SOCO and asked, "Was there a struggle? Is this all from a fight?"

"Not as far as we can tell, love." The man fixed her with a lopsided smile. "Some people are just messy bastards."

"Not what you expected?" asked Andrea.

Bridge stepped over a leather jacket on the floor, noting the Mission logo painted on the back, and peered into the lounge. "I'm not sure what I expected, to be honest. This gives my place a run for its money."

The lounge was the focus of the forensics team's efforts, and she could see why. It was packed with *stuff*, bookshelves overflowing (and not just with books), barely a flat surface visible under the piles of papers, magazines, and more books, walls covered in posters and cork boards…

One cork board was covered in photos, a combination of printouts and real photographs, of goths. She peered at it, and quickly realised she recognised some of them — other members of *uk.london.gothic-netizens*, either people she'd met herself at club nights, or who had posted JPEGs of themselves to the group. "Shit," she sighed, "it's him."

"What makes you so sure?" asked Andrea.

Bridge gestured around the room. "Everything."

The posters were all bands she knew Tenebrae_Z was into. The Mission, All About Eve, Faith and the Muse, Dream Disciples, and an old *Joshua Tree* era U2 poster. She'd never understood Ten's love of U2, but then she hadn't known he was Irish. Now she'd never know him at all, never chat with him again at two in the morning, never roll her eyes at his boyish pride in fitting a new exhaust to his latest sports car.

And it was all her fault. If she hadn't stayed subscribed to *france.misc.binaries-random*, if she hadn't noticed the ASCII posts, if she hadn't mentioned them to Ten, if she hadn't spent weeks musing with him on what they might mean…none of this would have happened, and Declan O'Riordan would still be alive, making bad jokes, fixing cars, and listening to all the wrong bands.

There was no way to make up for that. No way to turn back time, or undo the things she'd done. At that moment, she wanted nothing more than to be able to snap her fingers and make Ten live again. It was impossible. But finding whoever did this to him, and bringing them to justice? That was possible. That, she silently vowed to do, no matter how difficult it was or how long it took.

"One hundred per cent bachelor pad," said Andrea. "I expect he was a lonely soul."

That wasn't true, but trying to explain online friendships, and the goth lifestyle, would take more time than Bridge had patience for right now. Instead she turned to the desk, noting an empty space, and called to the SOCOs, "Where's his computer?"

"Which one? They're all bagged and in the van," replied a woman. "Weirdo like this, they're probably full of porn and guns. We'll get our nerds on it."

Perhaps sensing Bridge was about to say something impolitic, Andrea cut in, "No, I don't think so. We'll handle the computers. What about his phone?"

The forensic officer shrugged. "Nothing here, maybe it was on the body. Ask me, this is all a lot of trouble for a rando who got stabbed."

Bridge jerked up from the desk in surprise. "Stabbed? I thought he drowned?"

"Maybe I heard wrong," said the officer, shrugging again as she exited the room with a bag full of computer software boxes. "Best ask the Inspector."

"I'll go," said Andrea, "and I'll get whatever laptop was on that desk while I'm about it. You stay, see if you can find anything here that might tell us who he was meeting." Bridge was pretty sure his computer would hold that information, but something in Andrea's tone suggested she didn't trust her not to start punching people for their gallows humour. She was probably right.

It wasn't hard to see why Andrea would assume Ten, or rather 'Declan', was lonely. Despite his age, he lived like a student bachelor. The large flatscreen TV on the wall was hooked up to an expensive home theatre system, and one of every modern videogame console. His stereo could have come straight from a showroom, and was surrounded by racks of CDs piled three-deep or towering on top of the speakers. There was just enough space on the sofa for one person to sit, so long as that person didn't mind being surrounded by books, magazines, DVDs and videogames taking up the other seats, piled over the arms and back.

And the newspapers. God, the newspapers.

Bridge had a similar mini-tower of her own, old copies of *Private Eye* she kept around 'just in case', but Ten seemed to have bought and held on to almost every newspaper printed in the past year. The broadsheets she could understand, especially for a freelance consultant, but the tabloids baffled her. Ten had his foibles and the occasional odd opinion, but he'd never struck her as a *Sun* reader, let alone the *Mail*. There were a few copies of the *Daily Star* lying around, for heaven's sake, which didn't even have a crossword —

She stopped, stared at the piles of newspapers, realising why her mind had focused on that. They were all open to the crossword, but only a few were fully completed. Most had maybe half a dozen answers filled in. Here was the *Times*, June 18th. Four clues answered. Meanwhile, a copy of the *Mirror* from the same day had just two answers completed. Then there was the *Sun*, also June 18th…and the *Guardian*, June 18th…

Bridge found a second pile of newspapers, all different publications, and flicked through the pages. All from the same day, last month. She turned to another loose pile, thumbing through them. All from a single day, six weeks ago. All with part-finished crosswords. There was something here. Something she couldn't quite put her finger on.

"Hang on, isn't this you?"

Andrea re-entered the room. Under one arm she carried an evidence bag, inside which was a bulky Alienware laptop covered in stickers, and with her other arm pointed at a photograph printout on the cork board, pinned along with all the others.

"It can't be," said Bridge, looking over Andrea's shoulder. "We never met, and I don't post photos of myself to — *oh*."

Andrea raised an eyebrow. "I don't think this is a selfie."

The picture was taken from a distance, and Bridge could make out the tell-tale pixellation artefacts betraying excessive digital zoom. It was her, in everyday clothes, stepping out of a coffee shop in East Finchley. On her way to work.

She swore under her breath.

Andrea looked at her sideways. "You'll understand that I'm going to have to take this laptop. I can't let you have it, not after seeing this."

"Hang on, what mad conspiracy theory are you cooking up? Do you think I'd have gone to Giles, and got you involved, if there was something going on here?"

"Maybe not. But you know 'maybe' isn't good enough. Once we've taken a look around, we'll determine how to proceed, and if everything's kosher I'll read you and Giles in."

"Ten — sorry, Mr O'Riordan — was a serious hacker, remember. Does Five have anyone good enough to crack into that thing?"

Andrea stifled a laugh. "I'm going to assume that was sarcasm."

"Hey, I'm trying to help. Just…try '*ponty*' for the login password." She spelled it out, without explaining the joke. "It's my online handle. You never know."

"First thing I'll do when I get back to the office. Now, I think we've seen enough."

"Not yet," said Bridge, looking again at the newspapers. "There's something about these newspapers. This isn't obsessive everyday purchasing, but it's not random either. They're piled in groups, all from the same day, all with crosswords partially completed."

"Is there a pattern to the dates? Same day every week, or month?"

"No, the distribution seems random. But Ten was methodical, tenacious. There has to be some kind of purpose to it." She took sample pictures of the dates and crosswords on her work phone. "And we need to check with the pathologist, see if they found his phone. I think it was an HTC."

"Asked the Inspector when I went to grab the lappy. No phone or wallet on the body, and yes, he was definitely stabbed before going into the river, although they're not releasing that information yet. They're still assuming a mugging, to be honest. This," she gestured around at the forensic teams, "is all belt and braces."

"Mugging, my arse," Bridge snorted. "Whoever he went to meet last night killed him, and probably because he solved those ASCII art puzzles."

Andrea smiled. "Now who's wearing the tinfoil hat?"

"But nothing else makes sense. It has to be connected."

"Why? What's in those puzzles?"

"I don't know yet. Ten was going to tell me when he got back from the meeting. But whatever it is, somebody killed him over it."

Bridge shielded her eyes against the sudden bright sunlight as they exited the house. The SOCOs were finishing up, and the few reporters still hanging around stood on the other side of the street, recording to camera with the house as a backdrop. She and Andrea made their way to the back of the forensics van to remove their booties and gloves.

"I'll get our people looking over the laptop," said Andrea. "Meanwhile, see if you can figure out those puzzles. You might want to call on GCHQ. Maybe they can help."

"Monica in our unit used to be a Doughnut. If I can't crack it myself, I'll see what she suggests."

"Just try not to get yourself stabbed, OK? Unless you do turn out to be a filthy traitor, anyway. Then you can burn in hell for all I care." Andrea winked, and commandeered the nearest police car to take her back to Thames House.

Bridge took one last look at the house, then walked back to Catford station.

17

Whenever Henri Mourad came to Toulouse, it was raining. Practically in Spain, for heaven's sake, and yet here he was stepping off the train to the sound of a watery drumbeat on the station roof, and the smell of fresh rain on hot pavement. He'd neglected to bring an umbrella. Instead he turned up his collar, hunched his shoulders, and walked out of the station toward the old town.

After ten minutes he was thoroughly soaked, but found his destination; a small café on a narrow street in the 'pink city', the maze of old terracotta buildings at the heart of Toulouse. He entered, shook out his coat, and found a table against a wall. There were two other patrons, but neither of them was the man Henri had come here to meet. He ordered a beer and waited.

Two sips later the door opened, and Henri's contact poked his head inside. "*Viens, viens,*" he hissed, beckoning to Henri and wafting smoke from his cigarette inside the café in the process. One of the other customers coughed and glared at him, but he scowled back as if daring them to complain. "*Vite!*"

Henri sighed and gathered his coat. He left several Euros on the table, enough for the beer and a tip, and shrugged in apology to the waiter as he left. Outside, his contact hurried along ahead of him. "It's pissing down, Marcel," Henri said in French. "Can't we sit somewhere dry?"

Marcel scowled in reply, pulling on his cigarette. "Those men could have been listening. Out here, nobody can eavesdrop."

"No, because they're all sensible enough not to walk around in this weather." But Henri had to admit that, paranoid as he was, Marcel had a point. They were the only people on the street, and the noise of the rain would mask their voices from any long-range listening devices. Henri didn't expect anyone was listening — he travelled under a fake ID, and nobody had reason to think his leaving Paris was suspicious — but it paid to be careful. "So what do you have for me? What couldn't you tell me over the phone?"

Marcel walked alongside Henri, close enough to lower his voice but still be heard above the rain. It couldn't mask the smell of beer and sweat emanating from Marcel, though, and Henri wrinkled his nose as the man drew closer. "Three days ago, two men. Not local, they had Portuguese accents. Looking for someone to supply forged documents. French passports, ID."

"OK, passports means they're probably looking to leave the Schengen area. But they could be going in any direction, and there must be hundreds of people asking for those all the time."

"That's not all they were asking for. They also wanted a contact in Saint-Malo, someone who could get them an export officer."

That got Henri's attention. Saint-Malo's main shipping lanes led to the Channel Islands, and from there on to England's south coast. "So they're smugglers, and they intend to accompany the cargo. But it could be drugs, guns, whatever. I still don't see how this leads to what I'm looking for."

"That's because I haven't finished." Marcel lowered his voice further. "First, they killed the forger. Slit poor Benoît's throat," he said, dragging a finger across his neck for emphasis, "and they're probably halfway to Saint-Malo by now." Marcel took a final drag from his cigarette, blowing an angry jet of smoke as he tossed the butt into the gutter. "Bastards. There was no need to kill the old man." He paused to light another.

Henri pondered this. Why kill a forger, and judging from Marcel's reaction a well-liked one, unless the documentation you had him prepare was extremely sensitive and unusual? Fake EU passports were as common as the raindrops falling around them, available from every forger in every city. "What makes you so sure they're already on their way north?"

"Because there are a lot of people here who'd kill them in retaliation for Benoît, if they were found. That's the final thing; everyone in town went looking for them, and a couple of the lads found the shitty little guest house where they'd been staying. The landlady knew nothing. They paid in cash, kept quiet, and she assumed they were summer workers on their way to Provence or somewhere. The room had been emptied; there was nothing there. So the next day, the boys who'd been to the house passed everything on to the cops through back channels, to at least get something on the wires about these guys."

"Do you have descriptions of them?"

"Not really," Marcel shrugged. "They looked Portuguese."

"Oh, how helpful," said Henri sarcastically. "Still not seeing the point, here."

"So listen. The same boys who went to the guest house, they fell ill the next day. And then a couple of the cops did, too."

Henri perked up. "Have they checked it out?"

"Let's put it this way. All the other guests, the landlady, and all her neighbours were evacuated this morning. Now you can't get within a hundred metres of the place."

"Hazmats?"

"The works. They're not saying anything, but a little birdie tells me the Geiger counter was buzzing, if you know what I mean."

Henri did know what he meant. This was exactly what he'd been afraid of, ever since the chatter about *matériel chaud* began circulating. "Are you sure they were from Portugal?" he asked.

"Only we were thinking it would probably be another Mafia supply out of Italy, not from Portugal via Spain."

"It's possible, but if they came through Turin, why slog all the way over here? Plenty of forgers in Lyon for them to use up and spit out."

Henri paid Marcel his usual fee, then walked back to the station. As the train set off for Paris, the rain stopped and gave way to a beautiful Toulouse sunset, but he didn't notice it.

18

Bridge had never been any good at crosswords. Luckily, Tenebrae_Z had done most of the hard work.

After listening to her recount events at the house, and her confirmation that Declan O'Riordan and Tenebrae_Z were one and the same, Giles had given her the rest of the day off. She didn't know what he thought she'd do with that time, but Bridge had gone straight home and spent the rest of the day staring at the lines of ASCII art on her screen, trying to decipher their meaning.

She'd scoured the archives of *france.misc.binaries-random* as far back as she could, even peeking into private Usenet servers whose archives went back months further than regular public locations. Ten had said all the posts he'd found were no more than six months old, but he'd also found random pieces in other newsgroups. Who knew where else they might have been lurking, and for how long?

But she couldn't find anything older than six months either, and he hadn't told her in which other groups he'd found other examples, so it was a needle in a haystack. She'd turned instead to the five posts from *f.m.b-r*, going over them again and again. If only she had access to his computer, she could find his archive and see everything. But Andrea Thomson had been right. Not only was this so far still a purely domestic matter, but seeing a picture of Bridge on Ten's cork board had been a genuine shock to both of them. Now Andrea probably thought she was lying about not knowing Ten in person, and might even suspect Bridge was somehow connected to his murder. Under the same circumstances, Bridge wouldn't have let herself within typing distance of the Alienware either.

But knowing it wasn't true — that they'd never met, and she didn't know who Ten really was before today — made the photograph all the more unsettling. One consolation was that it had been just one among many pictures of *uk.london.gothic-netizens* members. It wasn't pinned out separately, or framed, or, God forbid, built into some kind of creepy stalker shrine. Another consolation came when Andrea confirmed that Ten's login password definitely wasn't '*ponty*'. They didn't know what it was yet, but they'd tried that without success, and Bridge had sighed with relief. It meant Andrea was taking her seriously, and was also further confirmation that Ten hadn't been some kind of weird obsessive.

Well, that wasn't true. He *had* been completely obsessed…just not with her.

She remembered the pictures she'd taken of the newspapers. Why collect newspapers, of all things? Ten was one of the most tech-savvy people she knew. But Declan O'Riordan was a middle-aged man, old enough to remember a time before home computers. The sheer weight of hardcopy stuff in his house was proof he was old-school enough to still enjoy owning physical things. Paper books, printed magazines, CDs, DVDs…and one of every newspaper he could find, but only from certain dates.

With the crosswords all partially completed.

Something stirred at the back of Bridge's mind. She took out her iPhone and swiped through the photos. She hadn't exactly been thorough, but from what she could see of the newspapers she'd photographed, there was enough here to support a theory. Several pictures showed not just the date, but the crosswords in question. She checked the June 18th papers, as those were the first where she'd made the date connection, and saw there were three pictures where the crossword was visible. She pinched to zoom, magnifying each of them as much as she could, and noted which clues had been answered.

They were all clustered around the same group. 14, 15, 16 across; 8, 9, 11 down.

As Bridge had come across each piece of ASCII art in the newsgroup, she'd made a text file copy and saved it, along with the date it was posted. She scrolled through the folder now, looking for a file around June 18th. And there it was, right on the dot.

She opened the file, and was confronted with a 78 x 78 grid of seemingly-random letters and numbers that, if you squinted, looked like a Volkswagen Beetle. Her eyes darted to the end, to the strange sequence of characters that made up the end of every image, in this case **0 6 188 D16A*.

The last five characters. *8D. 16A. 8 Down, 16 Across*?

That left four preceding, all numbers: *0 6 1 8*.

She could have kicked herself. A date, in American format: *06-18*. June 18th.

Bridge exhaled, only then realising she'd been holding her breath. She leaned back in her chair and clutched her head, trying to bring her racing mind under control. Ten had said the ASCII posts were a code, and here was the proof, or at least a part of it. He'd figured out the recurring characters were references to a date, and crossword puzzle clues. It was logical to assume they referred to a newspaper. But there was nothing to indicate which newspaper, so Ten had gone out and bought every single one. According to her copy of the newsgroup post, the June 18th ASCII art had gone live at 1500 GMT. Bridge smiled as she imagined Ten running around local newsagents, trying to find the last copies of every newspaper he could find. The locals must have thought he was mad.

Why not go online? All the newspapers put their crosswords up on their websites these days. And what had he found, anyway? The references made sense. She opened more text file copies she'd made of the Usenet posts and realised that yes, they all followed the same format. Only the spacing changed.

```
*0 51 5 21A 5 D (May 15th, 21 Across, 5 Down)

* 0 428 18D1 3 A (April 28th, 18 Down, 13 Across)

* 042 2 2 0D3 A (April 22nd, 20 Down, 3 Across)
```

But what did it mean? Even in just the three photos Bridge had of June 18th crosswords, the answers for '8 Down and 16 Across' were all very different.

The Times: 'Recalcitrant', 'Fallujah'.
The Guardian: 'Tankard', 'Epistemology'.
The Daily Express: 'Hughes', 'Europe'.

Bridge's stomach rumbled. It was 9 o'clock, and all she'd eaten since returning home that morning was a cereal bar. But she didn't want to turn away from this, and Ten, now. She'd done that the night before, and now Ten was dead.

She scolded herself. That wasn't fair, and deep down she knew it. If she hadn't gone to dinner with Izzy, what would or could she have done? Sit on the chat server all night, waiting for an alert that never came? The only way she could have helped was if she'd gone with Ten to that meeting, and that had been out of the question. He didn't give her any real details about the phone conversation.

The phone number. Ten had said he found it after decoding one of the ASCII pieces. But none of these crossword solutions were numbers. She quickly skimmed the text files she'd saved, but saw nothing resembling a string of digits that could be a phone number in them. Perhaps they were distributed somehow throughout the characters in the 78 x 78 grid? But then what would be the point of the crossword references, if the information was right there in the ASCII? It wouldn't need 'decoding' in the first place.

Bridge shook her head. This wasn't doing any good. "Valkyrie needs food, badly," she mumbled to herself, and put her monitor to sleep.

19

A halloumi burger, sweet potato fries, and processed orange juice probably didn't count as 'real food', but it beat mainlining coffee while devouring the half packet of chocolate biscuits in her cupboard, which was definitely what Bridge would have been doing if she hadn't left the flat.

The café had been here almost a year now. She hoped it would survive. East Finchley was hardly replete with veggie places, and it would be nice to have a local place where she could call herself a regular, although she did love the easy anonymity possible in London. The café was less than ten minutes' walk from her flat, and she came in every couple of weeks, but almost never saw the same patrons twice. Even the servers turned over every few months. In a city of almost ten million people, seeing the same faces on a regular basis took effort. She'd grown up in Lyon, which was the third biggest city in France. But with less than half a million people, it was a minnow compared to the shark that was London, and as a child she'd come to know many people, shopkeepers, and neighbours. If she'd been raised here in London, would she have had that same sense of recognising people every day? Probably not. But she had to wonder, was that so terrible? Mankind grew more urban every year, with ever-expanding cities swallowing the suburbs. Perhaps it wasn't such a bad thing to grow up with a certain self-sufficiency, not needing a sense of community to function.

Then again, Bridge knew analysts who would argue self-sufficiency was only a step away from alienation, and had a direct effect on the ease with which modern terrorism and right-wing populism had spread. Swings and roundabouts.

Thinking about terrorism brought her back to the codes. With Ten's solitary life, Bridge couldn't blame MI5 for suspecting he might be involved. She couldn't bring herself to believe that, though she could believe whoever killed him might have terrorist links. In the course of her work at SIS, she'd seen much more innocuous evidence that turned out to have militant roots. Then again, could it just be old-school espionage? The use of codes and newspaper crosswords put her in mind of old stories from the few remaining Cold War veterans at SIS, or tales of the Special Operations Executive during World War II. But that wasn't how espionage was done, these days. What kind of throwback would even consider using a cipher like that?

She swallowed the last of her burger, wiped her fingers on a paper napkin, and pulled out her personal phone.

A text from Izzy, with a short video of Hugo causing lunchtime havoc on the Eurostar that gave Bridge her first laugh of the day.

A calendar reminder for tomorrow, to visit the launderette.

An alert from her pedometer app noting she'd done over ten thousand steps today, thanks to her visit to Catford.

An email from Ten.

Her thumb hovered over the notification, ready to swipe but held back by her surprise. The email address was definitely him. It wasn't a mailing list notification, or a chat server alert, or a bloody Facebook birthday notice (not that she was FB friends with him anyway; she only kept it around because Izzy and her mother insisted on using it to message her).

No, this was an email from *Tenebrae_Z@top-emails.net*. Could she have been wrong? Was Declan O'Riordan someone else, after all? Was her friend still alive? But she remembered the photos of the *u.l.g-n* members, the picture of herself, how the posters were all Ten's favourite bands, and then she saw the subject line.

FAO Brigitte - Important

Her thumb had become stone, immovable. She lowered the iPhone, knowing the untouched screen would go to sleep in a few seconds. High in the restaurant ceiling the aircon vent vibrated, pumping out recycled cool air. Her fellow patrons, not many tonight, chattered and gossiped. The metallic clink of utensils and stainless steel cookware sounded from behind the counter, as orders were prepared. She focused on the sights and sounds around her, everywhere but the table, anywhere but her phone. Then Bridge exhaled.

Ten. And breathe, and count. Nine. And breathe, and count. Eight —

She lifted the phone and swiped her thumb.

FROM: Tenebrae_Z@top-emails.net

TO: ponty@top-emails.net

SUBJECT: FAO Brigitte - Important

Hi Brigitte,

Please don't be alarmed that I know your real name - I know most of ulgn's real IDs, it's not that hard when you have high access to routing servers and stuff. You could say it's part of my job...except it turns out, it's actually more like your job, isn't it?

I used your real name because I really, really need you to

read this. I�m setting this up just after you told me to be careful. I know I laughed, but in the back of my mind, I suppose I�m thinking it can�t hurt. And what could be more careful than a dead man�s trigger? So if I check in sometime in the next 24 hours, this email will never send, and you�ll never read this, and I�ll feel well daft for writing it.

But if you�re there now, well you know why. I�m going to take one last precaution, because if you�re right – and I suppose you�d know, wouldn�t you – then it�ll be worth it. I assume you can find out where I live easily enough. There�s a skull candlestick in the kitchen, and I�m going to leave my garage keys underneath. All I�ll say here is: Brockley Gate. TR7.

The game�s afoot, Ponty!

--

Tenebrae_Z

�We are the inheritors, the evidence of heaven�

She put her iPhone in her pocket, took one last swig of orange juice, and left the café.

20

How did he know?

A dozen questions cried out for attention in Bridge's mind, but that one kept surfacing, pushing the others aside, even though the others were more immediately pressing. OK, figuring out her real name probably wasn't that hard for someone of Ten's abilities. Obtain her IP somehow, drag through ISP records. And he'd used that info to find her address, which is how he'd taken a photo of her coming out of her usual coffee shop in the morning, before catching the tube. So then he must have — oh, God. Followed her to work? *That's more like your job, isn't it?* Had he watched her disappear through a secure gate at Vauxhall, and guessed what she did for a living?

It was all a bit creepy. Why not just ask her?

Simple: because she'd already lied to him, and everyone else, telling their online friends she worked in finance. Somehow, Ten had figured out she was lying, and decided to find out for himself. Bridge had always got the impression Ten worked in some sensitive areas — they didn't give any old BOFH a key to Telehouse, not any more — but he'd never been specific, and she'd never asked. Now she wondered if perhaps he'd ever consulted with SIS or GCHQ, if that was how he'd recognised that she lived in a world of lies and secrets familiar to him.

But the closer she got to London Bridge, speeding through tunnels on the Northern line, the more she doubted her actions.

An email, scheduled to be sent in the event of his death? It was like something out of Agatha Christie. Mind you, Mr O'Riordan had been an avid reader. The toppling bookshelves in his house were testament to that.

But it was the Faith and the Muse lyric in his sig that sealed it. Unlike normal people, Ten didn't have an email signature stored away to be sent with every message. Instead he typed his signature out, by hand, every time he emailed or posted to Usenet, allowing him to insert whatever quotation came to mind at that moment. And there always was one, right under the handle. Most of them went over Bridge's head, if she was honest. A few classical text quotes, occasionally some Shakespeare, sometimes a Yeats, Wilde, or Joyce (so obvious in hindsight), and the odd song lyric that she recognised. But just as often they were lines she wouldn't have known if they'd hit her over the head.

Except this one. She knew precisely one F&TM song, because Ten had once made her an MP3 playlist featuring his favourite bands. The ploy hadn't worked — she still couldn't stand The Mission, for example — but she remembered telling him she liked that particular F&TM song. And now its opening line was the signature quote in his 'dead man's trigger' email.

Who else would know? Who else could possibly know Ten's sig habits, and that Bridge would recognise a lyric from that one particular song, by that one particular band? Nobody. For the email to be fake required a level of coincidence that she simply wouldn't credit.

But if it really was Ten, why didn't he just tell her what he wanted to say? Why send her chasing down his garage keys, of all things? He wasn't a spy. And that was one thing Bridge knew for sure, as both she and Andrea Thomson had checked with their respective offices that very morning. He'd even made fun, with the 'cloak and dagger' reference. If this really was a practical joke or hoax of some kind, it had gone too far. But it couldn't be. Declan O'Riordan's corpse was currently laid out in a city morgue, awaiting autopsy.

No joke.

Perhaps he thought Bridge would appreciate this kind of thing, that she might actually enjoy it, having figured out what she did for a living. Or perhaps whatever he'd found when he decoded the ASCII messages was too sensitive to disclose in email. Ten, more than most, knew just how insecure most of the internet really was.

One other big question was more straightforward, and troubling. Why hadn't she called this in? What the hell was she doing out here on her own? As she changed to the overground at London Bridge, she considered several justifications. It was late; it might be nothing; Giles would be baffled by the email; she still didn't have anything concrete to show anyone, or prove anything.

But deep down she knew she hadn't called anyone, or asked for help, or advised the police she was on her way, for a simple reason. She had no jurisdiction. And Andrea would fight to take the case from her, citing its fully domestic nature, not to mention Bridge's relationship with the victim.

As she left Catford station and approached the house, Bridge wondered if maybe that wouldn't be such a bad idea. Night had fallen, and the earlier hue and cry of activity around the house had faded with the daylight. The only hint of anything amiss was the two uniformed police officers standing guard outside the door. But those officers stood between her and the only clue she had about what had happened to her friend.

"Evening, chaps," she said, displaying her ID as she walked up the front path. "I was here earlier, if you remember?"

The senior officer squinted, apparently struggling with that memory, but the younger officer smiled. "The spook girls," he said. "You and the short one."

Bridge returned the smile, suppressing the urge to wonder what Andrea Thomson would make of her new epithet. "Need to take another look inside, if you don't mind. SOCOs are all done, yeah?"

The younger officer nodded, and made to lift the crime scene tape across the front door, but the older officer stopped him. "Hold on," he said, "we weren't informed. Shouldn't we get notice from your boss?"

She'd anticipated this. Actually, she was a little disappointed in the younger officer for intending to let her in so easily. She tapped her ID card, still held loose in her hand. "Do you really think we announce this sort of thing over the radio? There is a reason we're called the *secret* service, you know."

The policeman shrugged. "Even so."

Bridge sighed theatrically. "All right, look. My boss is having dinner with the Home Office PUS tonight. And in about..." she checked her watch, "...ten minutes' time, the Secretary is going to ask him if the rumours about this case are true."

The younger officer looked confused. "What rumours?"

"Oh, you're not —" She stopped herself, then lowered her voice. "Look, you didn't hear it from me, but there's a suspected IS cell in Turkmenistan that we think might be connected to this Irish chap. You know he worked with computers, right?"

The senior officer looked sceptical. "SOCOs already took his computer."

"And we took it from SOCO, and I've spent all day trying to get some sense out of the bloody thing. Which is why I'm here, to make sure we didn't miss anything this morning." She checked her watch again, then looked expectantly at the policemen. "And I'm cutting it fine, if you know what I mean."

The moment hung in the air, then dropped as the senior officer lifted the tape. "All right," he said, "but I'd better accompany you."

Inside Bridge cursed, but outwardly she beamed a magnanimous smile. “Absolutely. Whatever you need to do.”

The electrics had been cleared as safe, and under the house bulbs rather than the hard light and shadow of SOCO lamps, Ten’s lounge looked much more mundane. It was still a terrible mess, but something about normal illumination made the scene almost banal. She had to remind herself she was standing in a room belonging to a man she’d known for more than a decade, but to whom she would never speak again.

The policeman following her hadn’t been part of the plan. She’d hoped to be left alone, to simply go into the kitchen, take the garage keys, and leave. Instead, she now had to play out a charade for the benefit of the officer, rifling through drawers and papers as if she was looking for something unknown. The back of her neck began to warm, and she hoped he wouldn’t notice the golf ball sized beads of sweat on her skin. A burst of static from the policeman’s radio made her jerk around as if someone had been shot.

“You all right, ma’am?”

“Yes, sorry…little bit jumpy. Like I said, terrorism. Never good.”

“No, ma’am.”

Bridge finished rifling through the stack of papers she’d occupied herself with and pouted, as if frustrated and considering another place to look. Then she shook her head and head walked past the officer into the kitchen, praying that Ten was the kind of person who kept books and papers in there alongside food-related items. Knowing there was a skull candlestick gave her some hope.

It turned out that not only was Declan O’Riordan the kind of person who kept books and papers in the kitchen, but he had also been the kind of person to keep bills, receipts, bank statements, and much more stuffed into kitchen drawers. She removed them all, placed them on the counter, then took her time leafing through while the officer paced around the room.

"Seems like a decent area, this," she said. "I need to find a new place. What do you know?"

The policeman shrugged. "Changed a lot since we moved here, back in the nineties. It was pretty rough, back then, but it was all me and the missus could afford. Now it's all slowly turning into cafés and crêches."

"Ah, hipster central?"

The policeman chuckled. "Used to be that if you came across a man covered in tattoos you kept your hand on your baton, know what I mean? These days…"

Bridge interrupted him, startled. "What was that?"

"What?"

"I don't know, did you hear it?" She fixed her gaze on the hallway. "I thought I heard… Oh, never mind. I'm hearing things. Maybe the place has mice."

But the line had worked, and now the policeman was also staring at the door into the hallway. Without looking away, he thumbed his radio. "You OK out there?"

The younger officer replied immediately. *"All fine. Something up?"*

"Stand by." The older officer walked into the hallway, cautious and alert — with, she noted, one hand firmly on his baton.

The moment he was out of sight she reached across the counter, lifted one edge of the skull candlestick, swiped the keys from underneath, lowered the skull, dropped the keys in her coat pocket, and replaced her hands on the bank envelopes she'd been sifting through. It took one and a half seconds, and she barely looked at the keys. If they weren't the right ones, she was out of luck. There was no way she'd be able to bluff her way back in a second time.

"All clear." The policeman returned to the kitchen, and winked at Bridge as he said into his radio, "The place has probably got mice."

She smiled as if embarrassed, then took three random bank statements from the pile in front of her and laid them on the counter. "I reckon this is what we missed," she said to the officer, taking out her personal phone, "I mean, who keeps bank statements in the kitchen?" She opened the camera app and took pictures, as if documenting the statements. "Some very interesting financial stuff on here. My boss is going to love me for this, thank you." She put her iPhone away, replaced the papers back in the drawers, and nodded to herself firmly.

"All done?" asked the policeman.

Bridge smiled as he ushered her out of the house. "All done."

21

They were the right keys.

Brockley Gate. TR7. That's all Ten had said, but it was enough. Out of context, to someone who didn't have the keys, or know Ten himself, it might appear meaningless. Brockley Gate was easy enough to find, a cul-de-sac of private lockups not far from his house. But the lockups weren't numbered in any way that resembled TR7, and when Bridge looked up the postcode, she discovered TR7 was for Truro in Cornwall. Anyone following that thread would be on a wild goose chase.

But the keys themselves had a homemade fob, a thin strip of paper folded once over the key ring and completely bound in sticky tape as a crude form of waterproofing. It was old, browning from light exposure and however many kinds of dirt, grease, and oil had been transferred from Ten's hands. Creased, crinkled to within an inch of its life, and curling at the edges. Underneath the layers of tape, the blue ballpoint ink of what Ten had written there seemingly decades ago was visible. Just two digits, *18*.

At this time of night, the lockup area was deserted. Bridge noticed the silent, dim red pulsing operation light of a CCTV camera mounted high on a corner wall, watching for thieves. But she was no thief; she had a key.

Lockup number 18 was one of the larger units, as wide as two of the nearby houses, with a double-width rollup door. She inserted Ten's key in the lock and turned it. With a solid metallic click, she felt it give and unlock. She pocketed the key, then lifted the door open with a grunt.

Inside it was completely dark. She had a flashlight on her iPhone, but didn't use it right away. To whoever was watching on the other end of that security camera, it would look pretty dodgy if she didn't appear to know where the light switch was. So she stepped inside, lowered the door behind her, and waited till it was completely closed, enveloping the lockup in complete darkness. Then she activated the flashlight, and found the light switch.

Bright halogen strips temporarily blinded her, but as her sight returned she knew she was in the right place. Tool racks lined the walls. Where the racks ended, metal shelves filled with parts and smaller tools filled the space. Next to the wall-mounted power point was a workbench covered in half-built parts, oily chamois leathers, an oil-stained portable stereo, stacks of CDs, an electric kettle and a coffee mug. The workbench was as untidy as anything in Ten's house. The tool racks and shelves, by contrast, were extremely neat and well arranged.

And in the centre of the unit, in differing states of repair, were four sports cars.

Bridge smiled to herself. Ten hadn't been bullshitting at all. They were real. The only problem now was that she knew very little about cars. Sure, she could drive. Advanced Driving and Pursuit was one of the many courses she'd undertaken at the Loch, though not her best, and once she got out of the driver's seat she stopped caring. To her, cars were nothing more than tools, a means of getting from A to B, and in London there were a multitude of ways to do that without the indignity of having to drive yourself.

So none of the cars were immediately recognisable to her, although she definitely remembered a couple from the days when Tenebrae_Z used to post occasional '*Adventures in Elbow Grease*' photo sets to *uk.london.gothic-netizens*, for the benefit of the half-dozen other members who *oohed* and *aahed* over them. Ten was always careful never to show anything that could give away his location, or include his own face in the photos — another reason why some had cast doubt on whether he was pulling their legs. But the more Bridge looked around the garage itself, the more she recognised it from the background of those pictures. She glanced over the manufacturer badges of each car. A green Austin-Healey, a white Lotus, a blue MG…

And there, a bright red Triumph TR7.

It was a funny-looking thing, a triangular wedge that was all hard angles and corners, none of the smooth curvature associated with modern sports cars. She'd seen it somewhere before, and not just in Ten's photos from the garage. A Bond film, maybe? She smiled and shook her head, wondering if that was why Ten had chosen to direct her to this car in particular. But direct her to it was all he'd done, and now she had to figure out why. She found the keys to the TR7 on a rack hanging above the work bench, opened the car door, and slipped inside.

The first thing she noticed was how small it felt. She couldn't imagine driving this thing for more than five minutes without needing to stop and stretch her legs. The thought made her realise that she had no idea how tall Ten was, no context for his own comfort in a vehicle like this. On the one hand, why buy a car too small for you to sit in comfortably? On the other hand, she knew enough about restoration geeks to guess Ten may never have intended to drive the car. She'd noticed on her initial walk around the exterior that it had no licence plate.

What was she looking for? She didn't know, but Ten must have thought it important enough to send her here, and specifically to this car.

Like most old cars, the interior was sparse. The driver's side had a small coin shelf, but all she found in there were two small screws. The gearbox was uncovered, affording a view down into the guts of the car, which made the lack of anything meaningful quite obvious. She turned round in the seat, wondering if there was something in the back — then laughed at herself when she came face to face with the rear window, and remembered that cars like this didn't have back seats. Probably didn't have much boot space, either. Not exactly designed for a family holiday; more for a day trip out to the country house, all goggles and driving gloves.

Gloves.

The glove compartment was locked, and she wondered who on earth would need to lock a glove compartment? But there was a second, smaller key on the TR7's ring that opened it.

Inside was an owner's manual, a logbook, and a Western Digital portable hard drive.

Chances were that nobody except Ten had touched the drive, but Bridge wasn't in the mood to take chances. She wasn't carrying latex gloves, but did have a pack of tissues in her coat pocket. She used one to pick up the drive, turned it over in her hands — two terabytes, she noted — and placed it in her inside pocket.

The train ride home seemed to take days.

22

"Sorry, but the number you have dialled is not in service. Please replace the handset and try again."

Bridge never understood the point of that last bit. Try what again, exactly? Dialling the same number, on the off-chance it might have come back into service in the last three seconds?

The number was the one Ten had called to speak with the man who'd been posting the ASCII art pieces, and arranged to meet twenty-four hours ago. The man Ten described as 'just a bloke', but who had presumably killed him. Far from ordinary. But when Bridge dialled it, the very polite pre-recorded woman's voice delivered nothing but disappointment.

To get the number, she'd had to decode the ASCII posts. To decode the ASCII posts, she'd had to figure out the encryption method. And to figure out the encryption method, she'd had to read through Tenebrae_Z's notes, on the cloned hard drive.

Bridge had returned home, found an old Thinkpad laptop, disabled all its networking capabilities just in case, dug a USB cable out of her desk drawer, and hooked up the WD hard drive from Ten's garage. To her surprise, the drive wasn't password-protected. It was a clone dump of his Alienware laptop, the whole shebang. She could have booted directly off it if she'd wanted to, but resisted that urge in case doing so might somehow lock her out.

She also resisted looking through the gigs and gigs of personal stuff. Andrea Thomson and her people at Five would undoubtedly comb through all of that, but Bridge wasn't sure she wanted to see it. The more she knew about Declan O'Riordan, the more her own image of Tenebrae_Z slipped away. She wanted to hold on to that image for a while longer.

Instead, she went straight for the desktop directory named '*ASCII posts*'. Inside were text-file copies of all the Usenet posts Ten had found, just like Bridge's own copies. But he'd found almost a dozen more files than she had, and more importantly, the folder also contained several files Ten had written himself. And one of them was called *Master_Decode.txt*.

It contained a list of fourteen entries, one for each ASCII post, labelled '*Date — clues — message*'.

```
Apr 28 - Thatcher/Wellington - ☺May 1/2100/Holland☺

May 15 - Pastime/Raccoon - ☺Cavendish-17-05-1230-urgent☺

Jun 18 - Recalcitrant/Fallujah - ☺June 20/2200/Gladstone☺
```

'Recalcitrant' and 'Fallujah'. Those were the answers from the *Times* crossword of June 18th. So that was the paper they were using. But how had Ten decoded all of these posts? How was this information hidden in ASCII art? And what on earth did the crossword answers have to do with it?

Bridge stared at the file, turning the questions over and over in her mind, letting her thoughts drift out of focus and waiting for the answers to surface.

Perhaps they used the *Times* out of a sense of tradition. Or perhaps because it was one of the few newspapers you could be sure to find in every major city of the world. Or, as she'd previously thought, perhaps the man posting the ASCII art was a genuine old-school spy from the days of the Cold War, and the *Times* was simply one of the few papers that had endured.

The dates and times meant the codes were probably rendezvous arrangements, but she had no idea what the other words and names could mean. Some were formatted strictly, some were more haphazard. More than one sender? They all used the same black-hole email address, but that didn't mean it was the same person using that email every time. Some messages read like instructions more than meeting appointments. They were all different character lengths, yet every ASCII art post was the same 78 x 78 grid. That was puzzling, though she also noted each post had a varying number of whitespace characters, owing to the arrangement of text into the 'pictures'. So it was possible they all had different character lengths, too, once you removed the blanks. Perhaps those message lengths related to the post length, somehow. A substitution code? But that would be too simple. If it was just ROT-13 or a similar sub cipher, Bridge and Ten would both have spotted it within minutes. Character appearance frequency alone would give it away. There had to be something more complex here.

Was it possible the posts were mostly a red herring, where the crossword reference was the only real information in each, and the remainder really was plain old ASCII art? *Ceci n'est pas une pipe*, and all that. But Ten said he'd found a phone number in one of the posts, and there it was, right in the decoded entry from two nights ago. How could you get that, and all these other messages, from two crossword puzzle answers? She thought of book lookups, where both messengers had a copy of the same edition of the same book, and looked up words in the book to render a message. But that would require much more than two words, and there were no number references in the crossword answers themselves. It all came back to these bloody crosswords, and how on earth you could combine them with the ASCII to decode a block of text...

Bridge groaned, then laughed, as the answer came to the surface.

Symmetric keys.

Modern cryptography contained a multitude of methods for encoding messages. The most common was public/private key pairing, where one half of the 'key' that would unlock a secret message was publicly known, because it was useless without the other half — the private half, which was kept secret. Millions of secure online connections and internet transactions around the world relied on public/private key pairing every day. But there was another kind, simpler though no less hard to break if the parties involved were careful. *Symmetric-key* encryption, in which the same key was used both to encode and decode a piece of data...or a message.

Without the key the message was garbage, impossible to decode using even the most powerful supercomputers in the world. But if you possessed the key, and knew which method had been used to encode it, the least powerful computer in the world could combine the two and decode it instantly. That was the weakness in symmetric keys; only one piece of information needed to leak for the data to become vulnerable. But the delivery method here was obscure, and the decoded messages filled with jargon. The sender must have been very confident the key wouldn't be discovered, and even if it was, the encoded messages would mean nothing.

They weren't entirely wrong. With the contents in front of her, courtesy of Ten's decoding efforts, Bridge still didn't really know what she was looking at.

A plethora of encryption algorithms was available to encoders, most of them based around calculations using enormous prime numbers. But then she remembered that only a few had one important thing in common; no matter what message you put in, you could ask the encoder to output an encrypted result of fixed length. One word, two words, a whole paragraph, it didn't matter. Whatever you put in, you'd get back a coded message of fifty characters, or a hundred, or two hundred, or whatever you asked for.

She smiled as all these pieces locked together in her mind, like a puzzle board. The ASCII art posts were encoded output, of a fixed length, with the exception of the final characters that referenced the crossword puzzle answers. Those solutions couldn't be matched to random output, meaning they had to be chosen, and that in turn meant they must be part of the encoding process. So, what if the original message *and* the two crossword answers were all entered into specialised software, using a fixed-length algorithm to output the final encrypted text…which was then posted to the internet, disguised as a piece of ASCII art. All the recipient had to do was copy and paste the ASCII text, remove any white space and line breaks, and feed it back through the software using the two crossword puzzle answers as the key. *Hey, presto*, and the original message would appear.

It had been hiding in plain sight all along. The whole thing, staring her right in the face. Bridge took some solace from the fact that even knowing all this, without identifying the encryption algorithm that had been used, she still couldn't have been expected to decode the messages when she and Ten were first looking at them.

But she could have had a bloody good go, and judging by the notes on his hard drive, that's exactly what Ten had done. Methodically working through all the newspapers, and all the fixed-length-output algorithms, no doubt producing mountains of garbled nonsense before he hit on the one that returned a message. A date, a time, followed by words, names…and, in one instance, a phone number.

Bridge called it, and heard the recorded message informing

her the number was out of service. That didn't surprise her. If Ten had stumbled upon some kind of criminal enterprise (and what else could it be, with this level of secrecy and subterfuge?) then the messengers would use disposable 'burner' phones, cheap Android models from China and Korea that criminals bought by the dozen, and used just once or twice before dumping them in the Thames. If they hadn't before now, realising their code had been broken by some random guy in London would have driven them to destroy their current phones.

Along with Declan O'Riordan.

She scanned the fourteen other messages. Most were the regular meeting schedules, or the shorter format which she presumed came from a second messenger. Three older messages also contained phone numbers, but like the most recent one, they were no longer in use. And then there were two messages that broke from the usual jargon:

Feb 10 – Existential/Libor – ☺Project codename EXPHORIA – source embedded☺

Mar 2 – Ballot/Trafalgar – ☺First handoff – success – delivery soon☺

Exphoria. It meant nothing to Bridge, but the message itself said it was a project codename, and the remainder of those messages made the hairs on her arms stand up.

Source embedded. First handoff. Delivery soon.

23

"How the hell do you know about Exphoria?"

Giles was already annoyed at Bridge for calling him out of his Friday breakfast meeting. When she then opened the conversation by asking what 'Exphoria' referred to, his reaction made her wonder if maybe this wasn't the best way to begin.

"Wait," she said, "let me back up. Declan O'Riordan sent me a scheduled email in the event of his death, and it led me to this." She placed the hard drive on his desk. "It's a cloned copy of the hard drive from his laptop. Five don't know about it..." Giles' eyes threatened to outgrow his glasses. Maybe this wasn't the best tack, either, but now Bridge was committed, and she walked him through everything. From the moment she received the email on her phone the night before, through obtaining the garage key, finding the hard drive in the glove compartment, searching through the files on the hard drive, figuring out the encryption method, and finding references to the 'Exphoria' project codename, embedded sources, and handoffs. Finally she said, "Whatever Exphoria is, I think there's a mole."

Giles wasn't often lost for words, and when he was, it was normally because of someone in Whitehall — frustration at a SPAD, PPS, sometimes senior mandarins or even ministers. But not this time. His mouth opened and closed in silence, then he narrowed his eyes at her while taking a long, steady breath.

At the back of her mind, she'd known her actions last night

were at best rash and unauthorised, and at worst simply illegal, but she had to get to the bottom of it all. The problem was that she didn't have the faintest idea what 'it' was until she read the decoded messages, and somehow she didn't think that would cut much slack with Giles. He had the look of a man about to do something necessary but unpleasant — like, say, sacking one of his best analysts.

Giles thought for another moment, then leaned over and jabbed a button on his desk phone.

"Hello, IT?"

"Giles Finlay, floor seven. I need a clean laptop, in my office, soonest."

"Five minutes, sir."

Giles turned back to Bridge. "When that machine arrives you're going to show me every file, every message, every code on this drive. Then you're going to recount every detail of your movements last night, including however the hell you convinced the police to let you snoop around the victim's home, until we're done."

"And then?"

"Then I'm going to decide whether or not to throw you on Five's mercy."

* * *

Ten minutes later, Giles had softened a little. Bridge guessed his main problem with her actions was simply that she hadn't told him; if she'd approached him first he might have told her to go ahead anyway, because then he would have felt in control. But he also could have completely shut her down, seeing as all she had to go on was a gut feeling and a frankly suspect email. She'd calculated it was better to ask forgiveness than permission — at least, so long as she came up with the goods. If it had turned out to be a wild goose chase after all, her current conversation would be very different.

"Just one question," said Giles, reading through the files. "Have you verified these decodes? Did your friend get them all correct?"

"First thing I did once I figured out the encryption method," she replied. "I had to try a few algorithms, but there are only so many that will do this kind of thing, and eventually I found it. All the messages checked out."

"What are the words and names, that stuff that isn't time or date? Code words for locations, perhaps?"

"Possibly, but why encode something twice? Either you trust your encryption or you don't."

"Silly Tommy maps," Giles murmured, lost in thought.

Bridge had no idea what that meant. "Excuse me?"

"Old SOE trick. Back in World War Two, saboteurs often needed maps, in order to know their targets. But if they were captured, the Germans would figure out our intel level, which could raise an alarm. So some SOE maps were only accurate as far as they needed to be; target locale, exfil path, that sort of thing. Everything else was slightly incorrect, enough that any captors would see it and assume our intel was poor."

She nodded, getting the slang. "And they'd say 'Silly Tommy, you know nothing.' When in fact we knew everything."

"Exactly," Giles smiled. "Encrypting twice isn't always redundant."

Bridge pulled up the master list of decoded messages. "Say we assume the other stuff is another code, then. But for what? They're real words, not encrypted garbage, so it must be a straight cipher of some kind. And look at the variety of them: Holland, Euterpe,

Cavendish, Gladstone, Temperance, Bunyan…do you think by any chance our mole is a classicist?"

Giles hummed. "Holland could simply mean the Netherlands. It's right next to France. And Cavendish — that could be connected to Terry Cavendish, in the Air Force. But the rest of it just sounds like a list of famous people. You've got Bunyan, and Gladstone. Is Disraeli in there, too?"

She scanned down the list. "No. Poor old Benny, never gets any respect. Even his statue's a poor job compared to Gladstone's…" she trailed off, her eyes widening. "Oh, bloody hell. Statues."

"I beg your pardon?"

"They're statues, here in London. Holland, in Holland Park. Cavendish, in the Square. Gladstone, down the far end of the Strand. Hang on," she said, walking round to Giles' computer and tapping in search terms. After half a minute, she clenched her first in triumph. "There you go. Euterpe is a muse, she's in St George's Gardens. Temperance sits on top of a fountain at Blackfriars. Get it? They're the rendezvous locations." She turned the laptop round so Giles could see.

"I should coco," he nodded, staring at his screen. "Now, show me the newsgroups where these were posted."

Still leaning over Giles' shoulder, Bridge navigated to Usenet. To her surprise, someone had posted another ASCII message sometime in the early hours of the morning. "Well, well, well." She smiled. "Do you have a copy of yesterday's *Times*?"

* * *

Five minutes later, Bridge returned to Giles' office with her HP laptop, and brought up the new ASCII post on her own screen.

Giles had found yesterday's *Times* under a small pile of document folders on his desk. "Good thing I hadn't chucked it in the recycling yet," he said. "But I should warn you, I only made it halfway through yesterday's puzzle before I was distracted." He turned to the crossword section, showing her the half-completed grid.

She checked the clue reference at the end of the post. "Ten across, four down."

"We're in luck, I did those already. Answers are *penultimate*, and *glockenspiel.* Is that really enough for you to decode the message?"

"One way to find out," said Bridge as she pasted the ASCII art into a script window she'd set up the previous night, using Ten's methods. First, the script stripped all the whitespace and linefeeds from the text, leaving a solid block of three thousand characters. Next it asked her for the key. She typed '*PenultimateGlockenspiel*' in response, and the decoding algorithm began to do its thing. Fifteen seconds later it had finished, and she read it aloud. *"Possible compromise - have returned - standby for next details."* She looked up at Giles, who was deep in thought. "They mean Ten. Shit, they think he was one of us. Please, we have to look into this. Has anyone come forward? Any witnesses, anything on CCTV to show who might have killed him?"

Giles leaned back in his chair, removed his glasses, and cleaned them with his handkerchief. "Not to my knowledge, but I don't believe the pathologist has conducted their examination, yet. Once they do, I'm sure they'll have a better idea of what happened."

"Well, is there at least some way I can be kept in the loop?"

"Seems to me you've done a pretty good job of getting inside so far, without my help."

Bridge sighed. "Surely you can understand why I was hesitant to come to you before I knew what I had."

"Deniability? You appear to have forgotten who we work for. I'd deny the sky is blue if necessary. Now, what are we going to tell Five about all of this?"

She hesitated. "I hadn't given that any thought."

"No, that much is clear."

Bridge resisted the urge to argue, even though she knew he was right, and after a moment's pause Giles reached a decision. "Here's how we play it. You called me as soon as you read the dead man's email, and I ordered you to proceed, following his instructions to locate the drive. We didn't inform Five, or the police at the house, for fear of leaks before we knew if there was anything solid. You then brought it to me this morning, and I'm going to hand it over to Andrea Thomson in about..." he checked his watch, "...forty-five minutes."

"What do we do in the meantime? Do you want me to clone our own copy before we hand it over the river?"

Giles shook his head. "Monica can do that. No, you have a rather more important meeting to attend. I'm going to read you in on Exphoria."

24

While Monica made a second clone of Declan O'Riordan's hard drive, Giles left Bridge alone inside Broom Eleven, a tiny two-person cupboard, for ten minutes. Then he returned and led her downstairs to Broom Three, one of Vauxhall's larger briefing rooms. Two people were waiting for them inside, and a third looked out from a wall-mounted screen.

Giles indicated the older person of the two in the room, a white-haired and straight-backed man in the greyest of grey suits. "Brigitte, this is Devon Chisholme, SEO at the MoD." She nodded at the civil servant as Giles turned to the second person, a large middle-aged woman she recognised. "And you know Emily Dunston, our head of Paris bureau." Dunston had been H/PAR since before Bridge had entered the Service, and grew up in the Cold War era, giving her what could charitably be called an 'old school' approach to espionage. She especially disdained computers and data analytics, as Bridge had found the first time she tried to discuss the topic, and relations between them had been cool ever since. Now Dunston gestured at the man on the video screen, who smiled. He was slim, handsome, with dark skin and alert brown eyes. Something of the Berber about him, thought Bridge.

"This is Henri Mourad," said Dunston, confirming her hunch. "One of my men in Paris."

"*Enchanté*," he waved at Bridge.

"Algerian," she replied, recognising his accent. "Native?"

Henri shook his head. "Only my dad," he said with a surprisingly strong south coast twang, and smiled again. "Born in sunny Brighton."

"And this is Brigitte Sharp, one of my CTA officers," Giles said, indicating her to the room. "She found the material that indicates a leak in Exphoria."

Chisholme raised an eyebrow. "Indicates? We're not certain?"

Giles sat down across the table from Chisholme and Dunston. Bridge took the hint and sat next to him, still a little confused as to what exactly was going on. "The probability is high," said Giles, "and that's why we're here. I'm proposing a mole hunt."

"You mean a fishing expedition," said Dunston, peering down at her notes with disdain. "'*Source embedded*'? '*Handoff*'? This is paper-thin, Giles."

"I'd say someone merely knowing the project codename justifies a certain amount of digging, Ems," said Giles, and Bridge resisted a smile at his needling. He knew as well as she did that Dunston hated that diminutive, especially in formal circumstances.

Chisholme nodded in agreement. "The fact these messages appear to have come from France is very unsettling."

Bridge cleared her throat. Giles hadn't said if he expected her to speak at this meeting, or if she was supposed to be quiet and listen. But then, she'd never been very good at that. "That's not confirmed," she said to Chisholme. "The posts were made to a French-language newsgroup, but they decode to English, and anyone can post to that group from anywhere. I could do it right now."

The civil servant frowned. "What about that tracing thing, where you work out someone's location on the internet?"

Bridge didn't need to see Giles' expression to know he was praying she wouldn't patronise Chisholme for his obvious ignorance of the internet. In fact, she was relieved the civil servant wasn't actively dismissive, or accusing her of being a "jumped-up computer game expert," both of which had happened before in dealings with the MoD. "The sender obscured their internet address, and posted with a false email," she explained, "which means no, we can't back-trace them. Unfortunately, these methods are widespread among hackers, and even security personnel. All of our own traffic does the same thing, for example."

Dunston sighed. "So not only could these posts have been made from anywhere, they could have been made by anyone."

"That's correct." Bridge decided to go out on a limb, guessing this was part of Giles' game plan. "And that's why we need a mole hunt. We can monitor these posts till we're blue in the face, but right now we have no way to connect them to a source."

"Exactly so," Giles nodded, and Bridge relaxed. Now she knew why she was here.

Chisholme pushed again. "But you've worked out how to decode the messages, yes? So why not sit back and read their conversations?"

"Because there may not be any more," said Dunston. "Since Ms Sharp's friend interrupted what we presume was a handoff, we must also assume they, whoever 'they' are, know their code is compromised."

"I thought this man wasn't connected to the security services."

"He wasn't," said Bridge. "But I think Ms Dunston's point is that his killer didn't know that."

"We can continue monitoring that group," said Giles. "But even if more messages are sent, they may not lead us anywhere. We need to gather physical evidence."

Henri Mourad, the Paris officer on the video link, spoke up. "Which needs a physical investigation. So you want me to start questioning people?"

Giles held up a hand before Dunston could respond. "Let's not get ahead of ourselves. The first thing we need to do is read both of you in on Exphoria." He pulled the room's keyboard towards him, and looked to Chisholme. "I'll bring up the slides. Devon, would you be so kind as to walk us through it?"

The civil servant took a pair of reading glasses from his breast pocket and propped them on his nose, while Giles logged in and called up a document. A crude project logo filled the screen: the Union Jack and Tricolour flags side by side in the background, with the word *EXPHORIA* superimposed in bold black letters.

Chisholme opened the files in front of him and read from them. "Exphoria is a joint UK-France defence project to design the next generation of control software for unmanned combat aerial vehicles." On the screen, Giles brought up a photograph, and Bridge noticed Henri Mourad look down from the video link, presumably seeing the same images on a second secure screen at his office. "Or, as everyone calls them nowadays, 'drones.'"

Bridge had thought the photo was of a stealth bomber, all strange angles and swept wings, but then realised there was no cockpit or viewport. This was itself a drone, an attack craft designed to be controlled by a remote pilot in a command headquarters halfway around the world, with limited software for autonomous flight and targeting.

"This is just one potential model, using the same anti-radar design principles as a stealth bomber. There are several prototypes in development for the hardware, but whatever the final design, it will use Exphoria software technology."

"Is the hardware a joint operation, too? Like a drone version of the Eurofighter?"

Chisholme bristled at Bridge's interruption, but nodded. "Something like that, although we do rather hope to keep more of a lid on the finances this time around. Giles?"

The screen changed from a still image to a video. It showed a more traditional-looking drone flying over a mostly empty airfield. The letters *X-4* were stencilled on the drone's fuselage. As they watched, the drone made some high-speed manoeuvres, then resumed a direct flight path. A barrage of small missiles flew toward it from below. The drone deftly avoided them all, and fired its own payload while taking evasive action. The camera quickly panned down to the grey airstrip below, where a dozen blue cars were all tightly parked, surrounding a single red car in the middle. The missile bullseyed the red car, while above it the unharmed drone cruised on.

"Impressive," said Bridge. "Targeting error correction isn't easy. Full marks to the pilot, too."

Chisholme half-smiled. "On the contrary, all the pilot did was feed in target parameters and activate lift-off. The evasive manoeuvres, and the ultimate firing decision, were made entirely by the UAV. The corrective targeting you mentioned is also a core part of the Exphoria system. We believe this kind of actively engaged drone will become standard in the next decade of warfare." The image changed again, this time to a large steel building. It was wide and low, isolated and incongruous within a sunlit pastoral environment, surrounded by grassy fields and hills. The building had no windows. "The software is being developed by a joint team here, just outside Agenbeux in northern France, under cover of a company called *Guichetech* who make software for retail outlets. Supermarket tills, entry kiosk cash registers, that sort of thing. It's in the Champagne region. Ms Dunston and her French counterparts selected it as the best compromise of security and access."

A map appeared on the video screen, and Bridge saw the facility wasn't too far from where her sister was staying. Their childhood had been spent in the Rhône-Alpes region, and Izzy's farmhouse was in Côte-d'Or, just a couple of hours' drive north of their home town. Keep on north for another few hours and you'd be in Agenbeux.

Dunston broke her train of thought. "It's also suitable because the presence of British people doesn't raise too many eyebrows in such a tourist-heavy area."

The slideshow moved through several images, showing the exterior of the building, the security fence surrounding the grounds perimeter, and the topography of the region.

"How many people work there?" asked Henri, on the video link.

"Total staff is one hundred and twenty-eight," said Chisholme. "Just over eighty French, the remainder British — though that includes the site manager, who's from our office. All thoroughly vetted by both us and *la Défense*."

Bridge guessed that last bit was included because the MoD was offended by the suggestion of a mole slipping through that vetting process, and was laying groundwork that would enable them to shift blame onto *le Ministère de la Défense* if necessary. The *entente cordiale* had its limits.

Henri Mourad whistled quietly. "That's a lot of people to sift through. Is there a deadline on this?"

"That's rather the kicker," said Dunston. "As you saw from the demonstration video, Exphoria is at an advanced stage, and nearing completion. Phase one of the programme will be feature-complete in a little more than two weeks."

Bridge whistled. "That's not a kicker, that's an own goal. So our first job has to be narrowing down the candidates, filtering out people we can eliminate entirely. I can start on that as soon as I have access to personnel files."

"You'll have access to everything we have, including our copies of the French vetting files, but I'm afraid that's all," said Giles.

"We can't be certain the mole isn't at *la Défense* itself, so we're not informing them of this operation."

Henri looked worried. "They won't like that."

"And I don't much like a mole going undetected, so today, nobody's happy." Giles shut down the slideshow for emphasis; there would be no argument.

"That just leaves one rather important question," said Chisholme. "Who are they working for? Any theories?"

"Plenty," said Giles, "but no hard evidence to point fingers with yet. And we can't rule out that this could be ISIS or someone similar."

"Isn't it a bit sophisticated for them?" asked Dunston.

"It would be an escalation, but not beyond their reach," said Bridge. She couldn't decide if the thought of Ten being killed by terrorists was better or worse than falling victim to common spies. "ISIS are surprisingly tech-savvy. The CTA comes across them fairly regularly in the course of our monitoring."

Chisholme closed his files, tucked them away in his briefcase, and stood. "This is the point where I bid you good day," he said. "Emily, Giles, keep me up to date but leave out the gory details. Don't need to know, don't want to know."

"Naturally," said Giles, holding the door open for the civil servant. "Preliminary report as soon as." Giles closed the door behind Chisholme, then turned back and clapped his hands. "Let's get down to the business end. Henri, you're in Paris, correct? How long would it take you to drive to Agenbeux?"

"Not too long," said Henri, looking at a map off-screen. "I'd say two or three hours, depending on traffic." He looked back at the main screen. "I'm still on the *matériel chaud* op, boss, but I can hand it off if you want me to switch to this. What's my cover? You don't want me to go in and declare as SIS, right? Will anyone at the location be read in to the hunt?"

"No, stay where you are," replied Dunston. "I assume Giles was asking in case of emergency."

"Exactly so," said Giles, smiling. "I just want to know how quickly you can get there if Bridge needs you."

25

If anyone had asked the clerk to describe the man who came to pick up package delivery #48 that day, he would have shrugged and pointed to the CCTV camera in the corner of the front office.

But if anyone had analysed the footage from that camera, they would be disappointed.

The man was white, of average height and slim build. He wore a large white baseball cap and aviator-style sunglasses that obscured much of his face, while a sandy blond beard obscured the rest. Apart from the cap, his clothes were wholly unremarkable — black t-shirt, slim blue jeans, black Chelsea boots. He wore a black messenger bag over his shoulder. The only thing that separated him from London's army of young male baristas, barmen, and buzzfeeders was the lack of visible tattoos on his skin.

It didn't matter. Nobody would request the footage from that day.

The man had exited King's Cross, noting once again how much it had changed since his last time in England. He crossed the square and entered the parcel-holding office. The office was a destination for deliveries from Amazon, eBay, and the like, for people who were not at home during the day. Instead of doing the missed-parcel dance, the recipients could set this holding office, which was always open during work hours, as the delivery destination. For a small fee the office would hold on to the package for a couple of days, until the customer had time to collect it before catching their train home.

The man with the sandy beard wasn't catching a train home.

The clerk checked his ID, typed his name into the system, and located the package. The man paid the fee with cash, then the clerk fetched the package and handed it over the counter. The man took it, thanked the clerk, and left. It was a decent-sized package, maybe half a metre on all sides, but light.

If anyone checked the name to which the delivery had been addressed, they would find it was as false as the name registered to the pay-as-you-go Oyster card he'd used for today's travel. And if they checked the name used for the Amazon account that placed the order, they would find it belonged to a sixty-two-year-old man from Surrey who barely used his computer. Everything about the transaction was false, just like the other names, identities, and travel cards the man had used more than a dozen times over the past two months, at other addresses and pickup locations around London and the Southeast.

With the package under his arm, he caught a cab at the nearby rank and gave the driver an address in Shoreditch.

If anyone had stolen the package — well, if anyone had tried to steal the package, the man would have shot them with the unregistered and untraceable automatic pistol concealed in his messenger bag. But if by some miracle they escaped, and looked inside the package, all they would find was a toy; a modern gadget that anyone, anywhere, could simply buy. It was a small, black, polycarbonate quadcopter.

Otherwise known as a 'drone'.

26

"Mange ton cul, connard! Dégage avec tes putains de moutons!"

Bridge checked her rear-view mirror. The car was still there, two behind. She couldn't make out the driver's features, couldn't tell whether the figure behind the wheel was a man or woman. But they'd been following her for the past fifteen minutes, and now both she and her shadow were stuck in a stationary queue of vehicles while a languid French farmer led his sheep across the road. Not for the first time that day, Bridge wondered what the hell she was doing here.

But Giles hadn't given her much choice. When he'd dropped the bombshell that he intended to send her to Agenbeux to conduct the mole hunt, Bridge had frozen. For the next ten minutes she listened in silence, only occasionally nodding her head, as Giles and Dunston discussed her cover as a 'workplace satisfaction inspector' from London, the parameters of the hunt, and Henri Mourad's support role. She was to relay all findings to Henri in the first instance, and let him dig into anything that looked unusual, to keep her one step removed from any suspicious activity.

It occurred to her that Giles had put the groundwork of this together in the ten minutes she'd spent sitting alone in Broom Eleven, after looking over the laptop clone with her. While she'd been wondering if she was about to be fired, Giles had been preparing Chisholme, Dunston, and Mourad for the Exphoria read-in. Now he was planning the op more or less on the fly, making fast decisions about mission procedure and protocol. As frustrating as she sometimes found him, Bridge admired his ability to do that. She liked structure, plans, and logical systems. She'd never seen improvisation as one of her core skills.

As they wound down the initial brief, Giles turned to her and said, "Everything OK? All on board?" But something in Bridge's facial expression must have made him finally realise she hadn't spoken for some time. He turned to Dunston and Henri and said, "Thanks for your attention, chaps. Let's leave it there for now, and I'll be in touch later today." He cut the video link with Paris, and Dunston left the room with barely a nod.

Bridge and Giles were alone, in silence. She got up and paced around the room, struggling to put her anger into words. "Are you serious?" she said at last, hands shaking.

"You're the best woman for the job, no doubt."

"I told you I don't want to go OIT again. I turned down the Zurich post."

Giles counted off on his fingers as he spoke. "One, you've already been back in the field. Last night you bluffed your way past two policemen, stole an item from under their nose, followed the lead, and located an asset. All of your own volition, I might add."

Bridge threw up her hands. "That wasn't 'the field', it was Catford."

"Don't interrupt. Two, as I said, you are unquestionably the best woman for this job. You have the required technical knowledge, the people skills to ferret the mole out — as you so ably demonstrated with Robert Carter — and the advantage of native-language proficiency both to conduct these interviews and investigate locally. Perhaps most important of all, you've effectively been watching this mole longer than anyone else here. You just didn't know it before today."

"But it was Ten who figured out the code, not me. And look

what happened to him. We were just contemplating that ISIS might be behind this, for heaven's sake. These people are serious."

"So am I when I tell you not to interrupt, but that doesn't seem to stop you," said Giles. She opened her mouth to reply, then thought better of it. "Even if ISIS is pulling the strings, there's no indication they're on the ground. They'll be directing remotely from very far away." He paused, and frowned. "But most importantly of all, and now I really am serious — you've thrown a big old nasty cat among the pigeons, and it's your job to wrestle it back into the bag so we can chuck it in the river. Either do as you're told and conduct this hunt, or pack up your desk and leave."

Bridge stopped pacing and stared at Giles, speechless.

"I'd be sorry to lose you. You're a superb analyst and, I maintain, potentially a great hard asset as well. But this is crunch time, Bridge. You consistently ignore my advice, and your doctor's, you're reluctant to put your full capabilities at the Service's disposal, and now you're threatening to disobey orders." He gave her a lopsided, sympathetic smile. "For God's sake, you're half-French, not half-American."

She dropped into a chair at the far end of the briefing table, and stared down at the polished wood grain. SIS was the only job she'd had since university. They'd made their approach during her second year at Cambridge, she'd been vetted and examined before her degree was confirmed, and within weeks she was cleared to begin work at Vauxhall. But that wasn't what really bothered her. Bridge was naturally self-effacing, but even she knew her skills would allow her to find a new job with ease. She and Ciaran often joked that if they had any sense, they'd be writing algorithms for City trading firms and earning five times what SIS paid them. And did she really imagine herself still here in thirty years, managing her own team of analysts? Probably not.

No, the real problem was the debt and guilt she felt over Ten's death. Dr Nayar would tell her she wasn't responsible, that it wasn't her fault, that guilt was an irrational response to an emotional situation. But that didn't make it any less real, and this could be Bridge's only chance to find out who was responsible.

As if reading her mind, Giles said, "I'll make sure Five liaise with the Met on Mr O'Riordan's murder here at home, and give it priority. If it's truly connected, that elevates his case to national-security status in any case. And it's entirely possible the killer is still here in London. After all, nobody's been killed in Agenbeux."

"Yet."

"It's France, not Fallujah. You're in more danger crossing Oxford Street than you will be over there."

But if that was true, why had someone in a midnight-blue Audi begun following her after she collected her car at the airport?

She'd flown in to Paris Charles de Gaulle and, instead of connecting to a local flight to Champagne, had used her cover ID to hire a car and drive out to the region instead. For the purposes of her time here in France she was an HR inspector for the civil service, supposedly assessing workplace morale on behalf of Whitehall to compile a report. Her passport was issued to 'Bridget Short', ostensibly to minimise the time needed to acclimatise herself to the false name, though when she'd collected it from OpPrep she suspected someone was also enjoying their little joke.

Bridge could have arranged the car before leaving London, but that risked the possibility that the mole might somehow get wind of it, discover which car was destined to be hers for the next couple of weeks, and bug it. She could have had Henri Mourad arrange a clean car for her, and meet her with it at the airport. But if anyone knew Henri was SIS, and saw him not only meeting with her but handing over a car, that would only raise more suspicion.

All this was completely paranoid, she knew. But that was the job.

So she'd picked out a small blue Fiat and driven straight down to Agenbeux. She'd been to this region of France only once before, as a child, on holiday with her parents. She and Izzy had been bored senseless, especially by the landscape, so flat and empty compared to the Alpine-heavy lands around Lyon. That was a long time ago, but not much had changed; although, as she drove into the region, Bridge was happy to realise she'd forgotten how forested it was in places around the river.

It was while taking in the scenery that she noticed the Audi following her. She couldn't recall exactly where it had joined the road — if it had fallen in behind her somewhere between here and the airport, or joined the N4 when she did. Regardless, the driver was staying firmly two cars behind her. Even when she put on a spurt of acceleration and overtook some slower cars, the Audi kept pace. Finally, she turned off the highway onto smaller country roads, but not at the turn she should have taken for Agenbeux. Instead, she deliberately exited several kilometres in advance.

The Audi followed.

Bridge gripped the wheel to stop her hands trembling, and swore under her breath. She'd been OIT again for a little under forty-eight hours and already she was potentially blown, gaining a tail before she'd begun the assignment proper. She tried to lose it; a turn here, a turn there, another, and another. Her driving wasn't completely random, because she didn't want to risk being pulled over by any police. But after a short while she'd lost her bearings, and wasn't entirely sure where she was going. The built-in GPS kept squawking at her to turn around, take this turn or that road, but she muted the volume and ignored it.

And then she nearly rear-ended the car in front, as it suddenly halted for a flock of sheep.

"Mange ton cul, connard! Dégage avec tes putains de moutons!"

she shouted out of the window, but the farmer studiously ignored her and continued to move his livestock slowly across the road. Bridge felt pinpricks of sweat building on her skin, despite the air conditioning. She glanced in the rear-view mirror. The Audi was still there. Where else? Like her, it was stuck in this traffic queue. For a crazy moment she considered abandoning the car, just getting out and walking to the next village, to call Henri and ask him to put her on the next flight home. Or she could take the car south, to Côte-d'Or, to throw herself on her sister's mercy and go AWOL for the summer. She wasn't cut out for this. No matter what Dr Nayar said, or Giles thought, she wasn't ready.

And yet. Ten's death, and her dinner with Izzy last week, had made Bridge realise how few friends she really had. If she gave up now, Ten's killer might never be punished, perhaps never found. And that would hurt her more than Doorkicker ever could.

The sheep were thinning out at last. She sounded her horn, but the car in front didn't budge. She checked her rear-view mirror and saw the other drivers inching forward, preparing to move. The Audi was pulling out a little, as if to overtake the other cars, and — draw level with her, maybe? There were two sheep still yet to cross, but they were lagging behind the main flock by quite a way. Enough to fit a small car, like a Fiat.

Bridge floored the accelerator and pulled away, out from behind the first car in the queue, one wheel churning up the grass verge, and sped through the gap between the sheep. The farmer shouted and swore at her, his arms flailing with angry disbelief. One straggler sheep panicked, and ran into the road. She spun the wheel to avoid it, bringing the Fiat back onto the tarmac, narrowly missing the rear end of another sheep halfway across. She yanked the steering wheel back into the turn to maintain control. The wheels skidded under her for a second, leaving their mark on the road. Then they made purchase and she was away as fast as she dared, speeding through a junction, back toward the highway.

In her mirror she saw the other cars following, now the sheep were out of the way. The car that had been in front of her was stalled, and the others driving round it. The blue Audi turned off at the next junction, heading deeper into the countryside.

It hadn't been following her.

She pulled over to the side of the road and, when she was finally able to prise her fingers from the steering wheel, turned off the engine. Her rapid, ragged breath was like a roar in the quiet of the countryside.

27

The windscreen exploded, showering her with fragments of glass.

The jeep had no rear-view mirror. Bridge wiped sweat from her eyes with her sleeve, glanced over her shoulder, and saw another vehicle following her across the desert. One man driving, two shooting.

The jeep had been under a camouflaged gazebo, guarded by a single armed sentry. His companions were presumably away finding out what the hell was making the ground shake, but the sentry himself wasn't on high alert. Bridge almost felt bad for shooting him in the back of the head while he blew smoke rings from an acrid Russian cigarette.

Almost.

It started first time and she stood on the accelerator, kicking up a dust cloud twice the vehicle's size as it sped away. At the last minute, figuring it couldn't make things any worse, she yanked the wheel hard right and smashed head first into the comsat dish — the site's only uplink, according to the mission data. The mission plan said to leave it operational, to spread the infection if the server was ever put online, but with the server room now a pile of rubble it seemed almost churlish not to destroy it, too.

She tried not to think about Adrian, lying underneath all that rubble, and to focus instead on the route ahead of her. That was proving difficult. Sure, he'd screwed up, but so had Bridge. If she'd been more assertive, had been able to persuade him that she knew what she was doing…but then she didn't, did she? Her first OIT, and when the bullets began to fly she'd frozen up. Now the Russians knew this location, a repurposed bolthole from the Iraq war, was compromised. Screw their legends, it didn't matter now if Moscow thought she and Adrian were Serbian, British, or even Chinese. The whole op was a bust, and instead of infecting the target server, she'd had no choice but to blow it up.

She'd escaped, and driven like a madwoman through the desert night, because there was no sense in both operatives being killed. But the more she thought about the mission's complete failure, the more she wondered if Giles would disagree with that assessment.

Out here in the silence of the desert, the jeep's engine was a cacophony of white noise, drowning out all other sounds. But somewhere in the roar Bridge detected a high-pitched keening, something like…a siren? A motor, spinning up? The sound faltered, broke, and then she recognised her own voice, screaming into the wind. Tears filled her eyes. Whether they were born of the stinging sand grit blown into her face or genuine self-loathing, she neither knew nor cared.

Until the Russians shot out her windscreen from behind.

"Over there!" Adrian leaned across her, pointing to a collection of shanty houses and temporary structures up ahead, sheltered behind hills rising to the north.

Adrian?

Bridge stared at the empty seat, knew he couldn't really have been there only a moment before. But she didn't argue. She turned hard, wrestling with the jeep's bad joke of a suspension as it threatened to tip over and roll the vehicle. More shots flew past, each with a tiny supersonic crack as it whistled close to her head, but none hit.

The settlement was abandoned, but now that she was among it, the structures didn't seem so temporary. Some were made from breezeblock, and several had second floors held up by metal scaffold.

Bridge wondered how big the area was, whether she could lose her pursuers in here somewhere. The jeep created an enormous dust cloud behind her as she turned through the settlement's makeshift streets, and she hoped it would be enough to make the Russians take a wrong turn, or give up the chase.

As if in answer, bullets slammed into the jeep's rear. She yanked hard on the wheel to avoid a stone wall rising out of the ground ahead, twin-paddling the brake and accelerator to drift through the corner. The vehicle's back end clipped the wall, grinding the tailgate in a frenzy of sparks and groaning metal, but then she was out of it, speeding away. Behind her, the Russians took the corner more slowly, avoiding collision but losing ground.

Perfect.

"Grenade, now!" she shouted, holding out a hand.

Then remembered, again, that Adrian wasn't there. Bridge fumbled in her jacket pocket, fingers closing around the last of his ICE grenades. She gripped it, pulled the pin with her teeth, and dropped the grenade out of the driver's side. The Russians shot at her again, but she ducked down into her seat, counting off.

Three. Two. One.

The grenade exploded under the back half of the pursuing jeep, blowing out the rear tyres and killing one Russian soldier instantly. A second later the fuel tank caught and erupted, tossing the others like rag dolls into a breezeblock wall. The wall collapsed, burying the burning wreckage.

Bridge glanced over her shoulder. No survivors.

Then she hit a low hill, and the jeep sailed ten feet into the air before crashing down into the scrub outside the settlement.

"Watch out, BB! Bloody women drivers," Adrian laughed from the passenger seat, wincing in pain as the jeep bounced and rattled through the scrub. He'd christened her 'BB' the moment he discovered she was a French woman named Brigitte. She'd asked

him not to. He did it anyway.

"Don't call me that," she grunted, turning to face him. But he still wasn't there. Of course he wasn't. He never had been. Adrian was dead, lying in the server room rubble, lost forever.

Her eyes stung with tears. She cried out, unleashing pent-up adrenaline in a wordless scream that was lost to the empty landscape, drowned under the waves of wind and engine noise.

She wiped her eyes with a filthy sleeve and clung hard to the wheel.

28

If anyone had asked for her first impressions, Bridge would have said security at the Guichetech facility could be tighter.

It wasn't terrible, exactly. The grounds were surrounded by a security fence topped with razor wire, with only a single gate, and being in this relatively flat, featureless region of the country afforded the location good all-round visibility. It would be almost impossible to sneak up on the facility without being seen. At the gate her car was swept for bugs, and upon entering the lobby of the facility itself, she and her briefcase were put through a scanning setup similar to airport security. But like that security, Bridge knew it was mostly theatre. Someone determined enough, sneaky enough, could get a weapon through if it was disguised and placed well enough. Then there was the social engineering aspect, which didn't just apply to hacks and stolen passwords. She wondered if the security guards here were paid well enough to resist bribes.

Getting something into the facility wasn't their prime concern, though. They were much more worried about people taking things out. According to the operational procedure files Giles had let her access, random searches, scans, and bag checks were conducted every night, and on some evenings the entire workforce was subjected to them before leaving. Bridge would have preferred everyone being searched every single day, but with almost a hundred and thirty staff that would be extremely inconvenient, and seriously affect morale.

Yesterday, before leaving Vauxhall, she'd asked Monica to monitor the newsgroups, in case any new messages were posted while Bridge was in theatre. After the last message spoke of '*possible compromise*' they couldn't be sure the ASCII code would ever be used again. But if there really was a mole, the approaching end of the Exphoria programme would almost certainly mean one or more meetings and handoffs had to be arranged somehow.

However, Monica had a mountain of her own work to attend to — "Sorry, North Korea's trying to plant one-click spyware on cabinet-member laptops again, let me hand you to Lisa," — and so she'd briefed Lisa Hebden, a former 'Doughnut' colleague of Monica's at GCHQ, the government's electronic surveillance centre. Everyone called it the 'Doughnut' because of the building's flying-saucer shape, which always made Bridge wonder why they didn't just call it the 'Flying Saucer' and be done with it. Perhaps it was a generational thing. Back when GCHQ was built, the idea of adults being entertained by sci-fi sounded ridiculous. How times had changed…but not nicknames.

Bridge had first met Lisa on her only trip to Telehouse, and a couple of times since at joint briefings. Her primary impression was of a woman who didn't talk much, and didn't like being told what to do. At first Bridge had taken against that, but after some reflection realised her own colleagues could just as easily say the same about herself. Besides, Monica knew and trusted Lisa. So Bridge sent her the files, and briefed her via video link. Lisa was sceptical of the whole operation, but would keep an eye on things while Bridge was otherwise occupied.

And as she was given *le grand tour* around the Guichetech/ Exphoria offices, Bridge could see she really would have her hands full for a while. The site manager, the MoD civil servant spoken of in London, had welcomed her to the facility before immediately excusing himself from showing her around. His name was James

Montgomery and he oversaw day-to-day operations, assigned tasks to department managers, supervised staff hiring and firing (although with a project like this, unproductive members were more likely to be shunted somewhere unimportant than outright fired, for security reasons) and reported back to Chisholme's department in Whitehall. Bridge knew from his file that Montgomery was an officious man, a former SPAD to the Secretary of Defence, with an especially good reputation for his paperwork. And no doubt, there was plenty of that paperwork to go round here. But she also got the impression most of his colleagues were more than happy for him to work somewhere else, where they wouldn't have to deal with him.

It fell to Montgomery's deputy, François Voclaine, to show Bridge around. He complained under his breath in French that he had much more important things to do than be tour guide to a jumped-up secretary, but nevertheless gave an insincere smile and ushered her through the offices in merely adequate English. She would have understood him better in French, but neglected to tell him that just yet, preferring instead to let him stumble his way through the tour while muttering and grumbling uninhibited to himself.

Security inside the offices was more impressive, and modern, than outside. Every room and department was sealed off by windowless soundproof security doors, and entered with keycards that were renewed weekly. Most offices contained no more than half a dozen people, while the largest space housed just twenty coders, and Bridge noticed there were even some single-person rooms.

"Why are these men working alone?" Bridge asked her guide. All the single-office occupants were indeed men.

Voclaine shrugged in reply. "They make work better alone," he said. "Many are the elite code writers, who do not have need to be

part of a group. Some of the men are not pleasant. Some are both."
Antisocial hackers were nothing new to Bridge, but she nodded firmly, as if digesting this information for the first time.

In the multi-occupant offices, everyone's workspace was arranged to prevent staff from being able to peek at each other's screens. From what she saw, it would be extremely difficult to see what your next-door neighbour was working on without them, and everyone else around you, knowing it.

"How flexible are your working practices?" Bridge asked. "Can staff work where they prefer?" She knew the answer, but it was the sort of thing an HR inspector would ask.

"No," said Voclaine, full of contempt, "everyone is to stay at their desk, and using only their computer. For the security, so these files do not have need to be moved."

So there was no 'hot desking', where staff might carry their own files with them on a thumb drive and plug in to whichever computer was available. That was good for security, and as they went from office to office, Bridge guessed the working files didn't live on individual computers. The coders appeared to be operating dumb terminals, linked to a server where the actual data was held. That, too, was good. It would always be easier to secure half a dozen servers and backups, in a controlled and fixed location, than a hundred laptops moving around a building.

But if data security was this tight, it meant the mole must be clever indeed. To extract and copy files from a secure server, without leaving a trace, took more than plugging in a USB drive and hitting control-C. At some point Bridge would have to take a look at the server logs herself, just to check. But Exphoria operating procedure, which she'd read, dictated the logs be on a constant analyse-and-verify pattern, where unusual behaviour would be automatically flagged up by the server itself, and also double-checked by a rota of human analysts from the coding team once a week. To evade that kind of scrutiny took skill, deep knowledge of a system, and above all a devious mind. The sort of mind that might also come up with the idea of using ASCII art to send encrypted messages.

For the sake of completeness, Voclaine walked Bridge around the entire facility, including the bathrooms and maintenance crew areas. There were ten maintenance and janitorial staff, all French, and by necessity they had access to every room in the building. But what they didn't have was any kind of system-login access, and like everyone else on Exphoria, they'd been thoroughly vetted. Bridge couldn't count them out entirely, but it was unlikely any of them would be the mole.

No, the most likely candidates were the coders and their project leads, and that was where Bridge intended to focus. She'd already done some preparatory filtering, and if she had to interview every remaining name on the list in order to find the mole, she was prepared to do just that.

First, though, the tour was finished. Voclaine showed Bridge to her desk for the duration of her stay, in a small room to herself, off the managerial section and near Montgomery and Voclaine's shared office. It was spartan, with just a couple of chairs, desk, and bookshelf. But like every other room in the building, it had privacy blinds on the windows, so Bridge could work unseen.

"Monsieur Montgomery and I are both very busy," said Voclaine, frowning. "If you have need of someone to help you, call the secretary. Also, she can translate, when you make to interview the French staff."

"Je vous remercie Monsieur, mais ça ne sera pas nécessaire," Bridge smiled. *"Je parle et comprends assez bien le français. Et maintenant, je souhaiterais parler à Monsieur Montgomery, s'il vous plaît."*

Voclaine sputtered in disbelief. "I'll ask him to see you if he's free," he replied in French, and stormed out of the room. Embarrassing one of the most senior staff on the project could prove unwise, but Bridge hadn't been able to resist pricking his bubble. Besides, it wasn't necessarily all bad. If Voclaine was the leak, throwing him off-guard might force him to make a mistake.

She arranged what few possessions she had on the desk and shelves, then opened her laptop, a cheap Dell. It was a mission prop, almost empty except for deathly dull HR management files, a spreadsheet of the facility staff, and vetting files. But there was also a secret encrypted partition, hidden from the main file system and password-protected, where Bridge could take her real mission notes before switching back to the regular, boring files when she was done.

She'd just finished logging in to that boring section when Montgomery knocked on the open door. "I'd advise you to keep this closed at all times," he said. "Security protocol, you know."

Bridge smiled. "Monsieur Voclaine failed to close it on his way out, and I was expecting you. I'll make sure it's closed in future, though. Please, sit."

"I can't possibly do the interview now. Frightfully busy, as I'm sure you're aware. Can we schedule for tomorrow?"

"This isn't the interview." Bridge closed the Dell and clasped her hands on the desk, her smile unwavering. "I've been considering how I'm to go about my task here. And as the site manager has ultimate authority, I'd like to run my intentions by you before I begin."

The gentle flattery worked. Montgomery sat in the chair on the other side of the desk, and Bridge was reminded of the Carter sting earlier that week and half a lifetime ago. "I understand," said Montgomery. "Do go on."

"The first thing I have to say is —" Bridge paused, and made a show of turning in her seat to look up at the ceiling corners. She turned back to Montgomery, lowering her voice. "Are we, um," she spun a finger in the air, to indicate the room, "are we being watched? I noticed the outside was covered in cameras."

Montgomery dismissed her concerns with a wave. "Not in here. Exterior, absolutely. Every location and angle is covered several times over. Do you smoke?"

"Yes," said Bridge, to keep the conversation going. In truth, she hadn't touched a cigarette in four years, but maybe she was about to start again?

"Well, even the smoking compound is festooned with cameras. But inside the building there are no such monitoring facilities, for purposes of security. It's not unusual in operations like this. I don't know how much you know about the work we're doing here, Ms Short, but if it were to get out…well, we wouldn't want that. So, no cameras inside. Why do you ask?"

"Oh, don't worry, James — may I call you James? Please, call me Bridget — I'm cleared on Exphoria. In fact, I'm told you're going to come in on-time, on-budget, and with remarkably little staff turnover."

Montgomery straightened his back a little, and leaned back in the chair. "Just doing my job," he said. "One takes pride in one's work."

Bridge smiled. "Well, it hasn't gone unnoticed in Whitehall. Part of the reason they sent me out here is to get an assessment from the staff, so we can learn from your managerial process and hopefully implement it in other areas to increase productivity. A happy staff is an efficient staff, after all." She lowered her voice again and continued, "A little birdy tells me there may even be a new post in it. The department's changing so much these days, new posts being created all the time… There are people at the FCO keeping an eye on you, James." And that, she thought to herself, was completely true.

Montgomery flushed a little and made a fist. "I knew it."

"Knew what?" Bridge had created the entire pep speech out of thin air, so whatever Montgomery knew, it would be quite a coincidence.

"The celebration party in London," he said, lost in thought. "A big shindig next month for Exphoria's launch, with the Secretary and Joint Chiefs and lord knows who else. I'll be there, naturally, as the project site manager. But I knew there had to be more to it. I wonder if it'll be black tie..."

Launch drinks weren't unusual, although Bridge didn't know the specifics of this one. But she did recognise vanity when she saw it, and it was fast becoming apparent that James Montgomery had a surfeit of it. Briefly, she wondered if she'd be able to find low-cut blouses and short business skirts in Agenbeux — today she was in a dark trouser suit, with a simple polo neck and ankle boots — but then thought again. She'd known plenty of company men in her clubbing days, buttoned-down careerists who were absolutely proper Monday to Friday, but come the weekend could be found haunting dark, smoky corners of basement clubs, clad in PVC and fishnet. And many of them liked nothing better than a woman in a power suit and heeled boots; whip optional. If that was really James Montgomery's style, it certainly didn't hurt that Bridge stood several inches taller than he did. Regardless, he could turn out to be very useful.

"I'll start the interviews tomorrow morning," she said, "and begin with the junior project leads. I'll have to talk to you and Monsieur Voclaine as well, of course, but that's just a formality. If I email you a schedule tonight, could you forward it to the appropriate managers? Then I'll just go and fetch people myself."

"Oh, you won't be able to do that. Your lanyard is only cleared for level *B-Limité*, which will get you in and out of the main door, and the common areas. Bathrooms, the kitchen, lunch table area, that sort of thing. We've also added the necessary access to this office, but that's all. If you want to go anywhere else, you'll need to ask my secretary to escort you. And you can email her the list, as well — just CC me and François. I'll get you added to the internal directory, so you can call people when you're ready to see them." He stood, preparing to leave. "Anyway, good luck. And thanks for the tip, it's good to know Whitehall is pleased with how it's all going here. We're a little isolated, to be honest."

Bridge smiled. "Well, just remember that you didn't hear it from me."

Montgomery paused at the door. "Where are you staying? Did they put you up somewhere?"

"Little guest house on the edge of town. I gather Agenbeux isn't exactly teeming with hotels."

"Well, do keep me apprised, Ms Short. And if there's anything you need to know about how the facility is run, I'm the man to ask."

Bridge waited till he was out of sight before rolling her eyes.

29

Naturally, she approached it like a programmer.

She'd spent the weekend in the CTA unit office, going through the preliminary Agenbeux staff files to eliminate personnel who scored as low-risk on the standard metrics. Identifying a mole was more of an art than a science, to be sure, and an HR file could only say so much. If nothing came up from her questioning of the people remaining, still a daunting fifty-three members of staff, she'd go back to the people she initially eliminated and take a closer look. But, at this early stage, it seemed safe to give them a pass for now.

One section where nobody got a pass was the project facility's upper management, from coding directors through studio managers, and all the way up to Voclaine and Montgomery themselves. No matter what their files said, no matter how they measured up on the metrics, everyone with direct report underlings was to be questioned and examined.

The method of questioning was equally formulaic. Big spreadsheet, methodical set of questions, checkboxes and custom drop-downs for answers, metrics to flag and score responses, the works. If anyone asked, Bridge would shrug and say a nice young man in the civil service had made it for her, and she just filled in the blanks. They'd believe that without a second thought. The French-English split on the project was roughly 65/35 per cent, but the male-female ratio stood at 90/10. And many of those ten per cent were maintenance staff, not coders.

Bridge lowered the window blinds around the room, took a deep breath, and closed her eyes.

Ten. And breathe, and count. Nine. And breathe, and count. Eight…

When she reached zero she opened her eyes, exhaled hard, and began calling the interviewees. They filed in, inevitably annoyed at the interruption to their work by this busybody from London, and reluctantly answered her busybody questions.

Are your working hours shorter than you expected, longer than you expected, or about what you expected?

"Longer."

"Shorter, but less so than I expected. I thought the French had really short hours?"

"Longer than what they told me, but I knew they underestimated. They always do."

"I don't really notice, once I get stuck into the code."

"Longer, because it takes too much time to get through the entrance security."

"Longer. That's why I smoke."

Does the work here fulfil your professional desires?

"Yes."

"Absolutely. This is the future, man."

"Not really, but it's a step up toward management."

"I wish I could tell people about it."

"It might, if people would stop wasting my time with stupid questions."

Do you feel your opinion and viewpoint are considered valuable to the direction of the project?

"God, no. I just do what I'm told."

"I'm a project lead. They'd struggle to achieve their aims without me."

"Sometimes. Mainly when they happen to be the same as my manager's."

"We're just the workers. Nobody listens to us."

"No, but they should. I've found some possible implementation flaws, but my project lead won't escalate."

Given the chance to move to another role here, what would you choose and why?

"I'd be a project lead. We do all the work while they take all the credit."

"No, I think I'm most useful where I am."

"I might move to Target Balancing. I'm really interested in that procedure."

"I'd run the place. And a damn sight better, let me tell you."

Do you think you're paid well enough?

(A trick question: answering 'yes' would immediately raise Bridge's suspicions. Nobody did.)

Are you under any undue stress?

"What do you think?"

"Yeah, it's stressful. That's what we signed up for, what we're paid for."

"Define 'undue.'"

"People round here are cry-babies, they can't handle a bit of pressure."

"No, it's fine."

"Every bloody day."

Do you feel comfortable addressing issues with your direct superior?

"Why shouldn't I? We're all on the same side, aren't we?"

"I can barely talk to him about what I had for lunch."

"No idea, I haven't had any issues to discuss."

How difficult is it to conceal your work here from family and friends?

"I just don't talk about work at all."

"I have to be careful how much I drink, you know?"

"I wish I didn't have to. I mean, couldn't I at least tell my girlfriend?"

"We're doing important work, but all my friends think I make the stupid tills for Leclerc."

"Not difficult at all. It's 'top secret' for a reason, right?"

* * *

By the second day Bridge had become rather efficient at getting people in and out of the process, but she calculated she'd still need the rest of the week to interview everyone on the initial suspect list. Every night she forwarded her notes to Henri Mourad in Paris, marking people she thought particularly nervous or noteworthy, and he ran double-checks on them. But so far, nobody had thrown up any hard evidence beyond Bridge's instincts.

The evening after meeting Montgomery, the site manager, Bridge had stopped at a *tabac* on her way back to the guest house and bought cigarettes. She'd lied to him on instinct; she was trained to keep every line of conversation open, never shut down an enquiry, because it could lead to vital information. So when he'd asked if she smoked, she unconsciously assumed he did too, and was hoping to cash in on smoker's camaraderie. France was a long way behind the UK, but smoking rates were decreasing here like everywhere else. In fact, he'd only asked because of her enquiry about the CCTV. Montgomery didn't smoke, and judging by his skin and fingertips, had probably never smoked in his life.

His deputy François Voclaine, on the other hand, was a perpetual inhabitant of the smoking compound. It was a bare yard ringed by a steel fence bolted on to the side of the building, accessible only from inside and invisible from the road. Bridge visited the compound two or three times a day, enough to keep up the pretence and eavesdrop on office gossip, but not so much that she felt in danger of becoming a real smoker again. Almost every time she did, though, Voclaine was there.

The first time she encountered him was mid-morning on Thursday, when she went out for a quick smoke after conducting interviews with some senior coders. She'd started lower down the ranks to get herself in form and up to speed before tackling the more likely suspects on the project teams, and it had worked. After the first half-dozen interviews she'd eased into it, asking each question with enough confidence that she could focus more on the subject's emotional reaction than the mere words of their answer. Today had continued well, and she was confident about working through some of the senior project leads in the afternoon.

Voclaine stood alone, wearing his trademark scowl. He saw her light up and called over, "Hey, Miss Short. Come here and share a fag with an old warhorse, I want to know how you're settling in." He spoke in rapid French; vernacular, colloquial and thick with what Bridge guessed was a Normandy accent. She wondered if he was still stinging from her sudden French outburst yesterday, and trying to catch her out.

"I'm fine," she replied in French, walking over to his corner, "just never been to this region before. I'm a Saint-Étienne girl."

Voclaine snorted. "With a name like Short?"

Bridge shrugged. "English father."

Voclaine made a disapproving noise, but said nothing. There had been no time, and seemingly no real need, to construct an elaborate biography or 'legend' for the HR inspector Bridget Short. The legend was fully backstopped, if anyone cared to look, but they'd left the personal history similar enough to Bridge's own bio that she wouldn't have to learn an entire fake life.

"So why do you work in London? Why not serve the Republic?"

"Father, again. He was a civil servant, got me a job in the department." That was one detail created especially for the cover, as an easy explanation.

Voclaine took a drag on his cigarette, and narrowed his eyes at Bridge. It occurred to her that he'd reversed their natural roles entirely, and with ease. Suddenly she was the one being interrogated by a suspicious questioner. "And why the hell does London think we need you here? What does an 'HR inspector' do?"

Every instinct in her body wanted to scowl back and reply with as much contempt as the question had been asked. She'd had a lifetime of barely competent middle-aged men questioning her skills and attitude, her *bona fides*, her basic right to do her job and hold the position she did. Giles was an exception, and that was one reason she'd never looked for a position outside the CTA unit. Twenty-first century or not, the vast majority of the higher ranks in the Service were still filled by men, and most of them retained a distinctly twentieth-century attitude toward women, dividing them into either *Secretary* or *Mata Hari* as they saw fit. Anyone who sat at a computer most of the day must, therefore, be a secretary and act accordingly. Bridge had clashed with more than one senior officer over that.

But here, today, she wasn't herself. Today she was Bridget Short, and Ms Short needed to make the people who worked at Agenbeux like her. The fastest way to do that, especially in a male-dominated environment like this, was to acquiesce and play to their egos.

"Productivity here is very high, and you've managed to retain nearly all the staff you've taken on," she smiled. "That's very unusual for Government projects in England. So I'm here to find out what you and Mr Montgomery are doing to make Agenbeux such a success. I know it's not very exciting, but at least I get to come back to France and claim it on expenses." She didn't quite wink, but her expression was close enough.

Voclaine scowled, crushed his cigarette butt under his heel, and lit another in silence. The moment stretched, and Bridge wondered what she'd said wrong. Had she misjudged him? Her mind raced, playing back the workplace tour alongside the last two minutes of this conversation, searching for a mistake. Her neck grew warm, and the pleasant French summer had little to do with it. Finally, he spoke. "We're under budget and on time, Miss Short. But you want to spend our money on fine food and expensive wine?"

Bridge was taken aback. She'd thought Voclaine to be a blue-collar labour man, a worker at heart, who'd take any opportunity to stick one to his bosses. And yet, he was worrying about budget and expenses. "That's, that's not really what I meant, Mr Voclaine, and besides, my expenses are being paid for by Whitehall. I really don't think…"

She trailed off as a smirk spread across Voclaine's face, slowly becoming a smile, then an outright grin. She'd been had.

"I was joking," he laughed, and dropped a heavy arm around her shoulder. "Ah, the look on your face. Now, I think perhaps we've both jumped to conclusions that we shouldn't, eh? So you can make it up to me by using those lovely expenses to buy dinner tonight. Email me the address where you're staying, and I'll pick you up at eight."

Bridge sighed and smiled, letting Voclaine have his moment of victory. But then she slipped out from under his arm, flicked her cigarette through the bars of the steel fence, and turned to go back inside the building. "I have my own car, thank you," she said, holding up her lanyard to the contactless security reader. The door clicked open in response. "Email me a good restaurant in town, and I'll meet you there at eight-thirty."

30

"Behave yourself, François," she laughed, removing his hand from her knee.

Voclaine had been seated at the table when Bridge arrived, and two glasses through what she hoped was only his first bottle of wine. She was fifteen minutes late, but for two very good reasons. First, and most obvious, she was a woman in France. No reasonable person would expect her to be punctual.

Second, and more important, Henri Mourad had forwarded the Exphoria server log dumps. Bridge requested them before she left London, but it had taken Emily Dunston several days to authorise and compile them, and when she returned to the guest house that evening they were finally waiting for her. She'd originally planned to leave early, and follow Voclaine from his house to the restaurant to make sure he didn't do anything weird. But that was a mere shot in the dark. By contrast, even a cursory skim over the logs before having dinner with the second most-senior person at the facility would surely be beneficial.

But it made her late, so she dressed rather more casually than she'd first intended. She threw on a skirt and vest, pulled on a pair of tights and wedge heels, and hoped a wrap around her shoulders would suffice as a minor nod to elegance. Head-to-toe black, but unlike in England, she didn't expect anyone here to comment. They'd just assume she was Parisian. And as it turned out, any worries she had about being underdressed vanished when she entered the restaurant, and saw Voclaine was still wearing his office clothes.

"Ah, you've dressed to apologise. Very good, and I accept." He smiled, nodding at the chair opposite. Bridge wondered how long it had been since he took a woman to dinner, if he regarded this as dressing up. "Now drink." He poured her a glass of wine from a local vineyard.

"You're from further north, aren't you?" she asked after they toasted. "Do you work in this region often?"

Voclaine shrugged. "A few times. I go wherever they send me. Same as you, I expect."

"True, although I don't get to come to France as often as I'd like."

"Oh? Where do you normally go?"

The look in Voclaine's eye confirmed to Bridge that this was definitely his first bottle. As in the smoking compound, he'd turned the tables. His questions were no more innocent chit-chat than her own, and combined with what she'd seen in the logs, she was now certain this dinner wasn't a coincidence born of an awkward misunderstanding. He'd planned it from the start.

"I can't say," she smiled, taking a sip of wine. "Same as you, I expect?"

Voclaine laughed, recognising Bridge's own turnaround, and finished his glass. "Then I think we both need more wine," he said, refilling their glasses.

They ordered food; a plate of meat and potatoes for Voclaine, a salad and cheese selection for Bridge. The waiter huffed at the very word *"végétarienne"*, but had the grace to confirm she could get a salad without chicken, if for some strange reason that was truly what she wanted.

Voclaine fixed her with a look of disbelief as the waiter retreated. "You grew up in France, but you don't eat meat?"

"Funny, but I don't remember them crying *'Liberté, égalité, fraternité, carnivoré'* at the gates of the Bastille," said Bridge. Voclaine grunted in disagreement. She decided to change tack and play to his vanity. "Tell me, what did you do before…well, this sort of thing? I've been in the civil service since I left university, which is kind of dull. I expect you've had a much more interesting life than me."

He shrugged. "I started in computers, in the '90s, when France was still at the cutting edge of software. I made computer games, if you can believe that. Physics engines, inverse kinematics…' He paused and smiled sympathetically, trying to explain the jargon. "They're like building blocks in a piece of software that make the objects you see on screen behave the way you expect them to. Very low-level stuff, essential to the product, you see," he added, just in case a mere woman wouldn't realise that.

Bridge held her tongue. Unlike her real self, Bridget Short was not a coder, and had no reason to know what Voclaine was talking about. Ms Short probably didn't play video games, and certainly hadn't made *Unreal Tournament* mods in her spare time at uni. On the other hand, an HR inspector would have enough cultural familiarity to make assumptions. Such as how this explained Voclaine's idiosyncratic social skills.

"It sounds very glamorous," said Bridge, leaning forward. "Why did you leave?"

Voclaine shrugged. "I was too good. I kept being promoted, and before I knew what was happening, I woke up one day and realised I'd been a manager for the past five years."

"Surely that's a good thing? More responsibility, better pay…"

"…And no time to actually write code. The higher up the chain you go, the less chance you'll get to do the thing you took the job for in the first place. I had to make a choice. Either I could effectively demote myself, return to the coding ranks, and be happy but earning a fraction of what I'd built myself up to. But that wasn't really an option, because by then I'd somehow got saddled with a wife and son along the way. There's no way I could have supported them on a coder's salary."

"What was the second option?"

"Say fuck it and become a real manager, in an industry that pays real wages." Voclaine raised his wine glass and winked. "The games industry is shit now, anyway. I still have old friends there, and they all wish they could escape."

Bridge smiled, relieved at the mention of a wife and child. It might not stop him getting fresh, but it would reduce the chance of him trying anything serious. "Escape like you did," she said. "And I bet your family is much happier for it."

Their food arrived. As the waiter slid plates onto the table, Voclaine smiled back. "I wouldn't know. I send them a cheque every month, call my son at university every two weeks, and that's enough contact for me. I'm a free spirit." That was when he placed his hand on her knee, and while he tried to laugh it off as drunken high spirits after she removed it, Bridge suspected Voclaine was nowhere near as drunk as he made out. Did he simply want to use the wine as an excuse? Or was he hoping Bridge would drop her guard, too, and let something slip?

She poked at her salad, thinking about Voclaine as a coder, and what she'd seen in the server logs before leaving the guest house. According to the logs, Voclaine frequently *checked out* assorted code branches of the Exphoria project — in other words, transferred the data to his terminal, effectively telling the rest of the team that he was working on it. Some of these sessions lasted half a day or more. That in itself rang alarm bells in Bridge's mind, but stranger still was Voclaine's habit of also making *commits*, or changes to the code. He really was working on it, and as far as she could tell, none of the other coders were flagging up errors or reverting his work.

It was always possible someone else was using Voclaine's login and terminal to work on the code incognito, and that had been Bridge's first thought. But it would be difficult, and now that she knew Voclaine was a coder himself, the question was why anyone would bother. The only plausible reason would be sabotage; if you were writing flaws and errors into the code, naturally you wouldn't do it from your own login. And the lack of CCTV cameras in the facility, perversely for security purposes, meant anyone could use Voclaine's terminal and remain unseen. But they'd have to get into an office he shared with Montgomery, know his login, and stay there for hours at a time undetected. That seemed impossible, and it left just one conclusion: that Voclaine's code was good, and he was using Exphoria as an opportunity to show he still had skills, despite years of getting fat on a manager's wage.

It was also the only thing that made sense. The notion that Voclaine, or anyone, could sabotage a project like this by writing bad code was ridiculous. Coders were always reluctant to tell their boss if his commits were bad, for obvious reasons. But on a project like this, with so much money at stake, and so many highly-skilled people reviewing every line? It was inconceivable that seventy-plus coders, reviewers, and testers would all lack the balls to point out bad code just because it was written by a senior manager.

So Voclaine's actions were highly unusual, but hardly treason. Perhaps not even espionage. The logs confirmed what she'd been told, that there was no sign of unverified data extraction or copying. Whatever his reasons for working on the code, they didn't seem to involve copying them onto external storage.

For the second time tonight, Bridge was frustrated that her cover wasn't suited to asking the kind of technical questions she so desperately needed answers to. She wished they could have sent her in as a tester, or better still a coder. But she knew why they hadn't. Nobody would trust a last-minute addition to the engineering team, and as soon as she started to ask those kinds of questions people would become yet more suspicious. The mole might even directly suspect she was SIS or French DGSI. At least this way, her being a government employee was built into the cover, and allowed her to talk to anyone she liked without raising suspicion. In the long run, that kind of access was probably more useful than being able to ask geeky questions.

Plus, now that Voclaine had opened up about his past as a games programmer, Bridge could simply ask questions under a pretence of ignorance. But she let the matter drop for now, not wanting to push too hard. Instead she laughed at Voclaine's bad jokes, told him girlish anecdotes about flat-sharing in London, and lied that she had absolutely every intention of marrying an eligible French bachelor one day, *bien sûr.*

It was exhausting, and as she drove back to the guest house — having bundled Voclaine in a taxi, politely but firmly declining his offer to share a ride while removing his wandering hand from her waist — Bridge considered herself lucky for not having to go through that crap in her everyday life. How regular women managed it without wanting to kill someone, she'd never know. But it had been worth it; she'd learned more about François Voclaine in two hours of dinner than she ever could from thirty minutes of fake HR questions.

And now he was her prime suspect.

31

The next day was Friday, and Bridge interviewed the last of the senior supervisors on her candidate list before entering their answers into the spreadsheet at the end of the day. Then she logged into the secure partition of her laptop and entered everyone's final, weighted score into a separate spreadsheet, which used her own formula to rank them all by likelihood of being the mole, and/or source of a leak. It didn't yet include entries for Voclaine, Montgomery, or the other twenty management staff at Agenbeux. She'd deliberately left them till last, to give herself time to get into the role, and find out as much as she could about them before their interviews. Like Voclaine himself. But while he was now suspect number one, she couldn't ignore the possibility that she might simply have misjudged him. The previous weekend, while she'd been ploughing through the personnel files in advance, she would have placed good odds on the mole being someone at a middling-to-low level, dissatisfied and easy to bribe or blackmail. She was no longer quite as convinced of that, but it remained the most likely scenario.

It was also fair to assume the mole was smart, and may already suspect her real purpose here at the facility. Whoever it was, they wouldn't want to draw attention to themselves. So anyone whose answers to her questions were completely negative and dissatisfied would find themselves ranked at the bottom of her list. And likewise with anyone who appeared to be too happy, too eager to say everything was fine and dandy — though she couldn't completely discount the few people that applied to, just in case the mole wasn't so smart after all.

But mostly, Bridge was interested in those staff who fell squarely in the middle of her ranking. People whose answers were unremarkable and average, who seemed happy enough with their role at 'Guichetech' but admitted that yes, they could be happier, because that was human nature.

As expected, that covered the majority of people she'd spoken to so far at Agenbeux. But what the numbers couldn't take into account was Bridge's own reading of the staff. How each person behaved when answering, what it said about their personality type, and whether they just felt 'off'. So much of that relied on instinct and gut feeling, and fortunately, Bridge's gut had settled down a lot during the week. Giles had been right as usual, and despite her earlier paranoia she soon realised this job wasn't dangerous. As the days passed she settled into the role, and actually started to relish the challenge of sniffing out a liar every day. She was even looking forward to interviewing the managers.

She'd also found she enjoyed being back in France more than expected. The food, the weather, the people...simply hearing the language of her childhood everywhere helped her relax. She knew herself well enough to guess that after a couple more weeks she'd go stir-crazy, but for the time being she understood why Izzy enjoyed coming back here every year. And now that the weekend was here, with her sister's farmhouse only a couple of hours' drive away, Bridge intended to take advantage and pay her an impromptu visit so she could see Stéphanie and Hugo. Fréderic would be there too, but he'd just have to sit and suffer.

A loud rapping on the office door startled Bridge from her thoughts. "*Moment*," she said, logging out of the encrypted partition and closing the Dell. She raised the door blind to see

Montgomery, smiling on the other side of the glass. She let him in, then walked around the room raising the window blinds.

"Not many left here last thing on a Friday," said Montgomery. "Mostly us *rosbifs*, naturally. But even we have our limits, eh? So how's it all going? You'll be sending in a good report, I hope?"

"I'm sure you know I can't discuss that, James. Besides, I have a lot of number-crunching to do. The Department does love its numbers. But I can say it's certainly promising. I think we can all learn a few things from the way you and François are running things, here."

Montgomery snorted. "Yes, I heard you had a lovely time last night."

She paused midway through packing her briefcase. "I'm sorry?"

"Surely," he said, smug and secure in his victory, "you didn't think you could have dinner with a man like Voclaine and expect him to be discreet about it."

Bridge was having real trouble figuring James Montgomery out. She'd hoped he would join her for drinks, so she could try to loosen his lips. As site manager, he doubtless knew much more about what went on here than he'd ever say officially, and might have seen things that seemed perfectly innocent to him, but to Bridge would be a sign of something unusual or noteworthy.

But contrary to her first assumption, Montgomery didn't seem remotely interested in her, and failed to respond to the smiles and gentle flirting with which she'd laced their brief conversations. It was possible he simply didn't fancy her, of course. Izzy had always been the more glamorous sister, with men falling at her feet even as she was oblivious to them, while Bridge needed to make an effort. But when she did, it normally paid off. Being a young goth had given her an independent and self-assured side that made her perfectly happy to be the first mover, and in her experience it was an unusual Englishman who didn't at least flirt back when a tall Frenchwoman flung herself at him.

In his own way, though, James Montgomery was indeed unusual. His egotism seemed reserved purely for his work and status within the MoD, in contrast to Voclaine's easy willingness to use his position as a licence to grope. Bridge had even begun to wonder if Montgomery was secretly gay, despite his wife and children back in England. Yet now he was talking like a jealous lover.

"We just had dinner," she shrugged. "We didn't discuss my work here, and besides, François had a little too much wine, so I put him in a cab and sent him home. If he says anything more than that happened, he's mistaken."

"He didn't say anything specific, but he certainly didn't deny anything, either."

"Typical. I assure you, nothing happened. Besides, what's the problem?"

Montgomery stepped into the room, and closed the door behind him. Bridge had just slid the Dell inside her briefcase, and her hand was still inside it. It closed around the hard cylinder of a small can of pepper spray she kept there.

"The problem, Ms Short, is that you should not be socialising with upper management while you are also conducting a survey of workplace morale. It could influence your results, and your report, and therefore reflect badly on us all." Bridge relaxed, and removed her hand from the briefcase. This wasn't jealousy. This was Montgomery showing his desperation to be recognised in the corridors of power, for Whitehall to acknowledge his work here at Agenbeux. She'd planted the seed of that idea in his mind for convenience, just to get him on her side, but now it was growing. She almost felt sorry for him. He was going to be confused as hell when he returned to London. "Besides," he continued, "Voclaine is a natural curmudgeon. He's good at his job, but he's made no secret of the fact that he thinks he deserves my position, and should be in charge of Exphoria. You must bear that in mind when considering anything he says." He paused, and a sudden thought came to him. "Did he tell you his wife left him?"

"Yes, he was quite open about that."

"Did he tell you why?"

Bridge shook her head, so Montgomery pursed his lips and made a slapping motion with his hand. She nodded, understanding, and found it easy to believe. Voclaine hadn't threatened her in any way, but he'd shown more than once that he was, to put it politely, a tactile man. "I see," she said, "no, he didn't mention that. But he also said nothing out of order about this facility, or about you. In fact, I don't think your name came up at all." She'd meant it to sound reassuring, but regretted it the moment the words passed her lips, and she saw Montgomery's disappointed expression.

"Oh. Well, well, that's good. But I insist you don't do it again, with Voclaine or anyone else for that matter. If you do, I shall have no choice but to inform the MoD and have you removed."

Bridge was taken aback by Montgomery's sudden hostility. "That really won't be necessary. Besides, I'm not entirely sure that's your call to make."

"I am in charge of a multi-million euro project facility, Ms Short. You are an HR functionary. I strongly doubt the PUS would prioritise your concerns over mine."

If only you knew how wrong you are, thought Bridge, but said, "I suppose you're right. Please accept my apologies, Mr Montgomery. I assure you it won't happen again."

He straightened a little at being formally addressed, and opened the door for her. "Very good. Now, do you have anything nice planned for the weekend? I can recommend some excellent local restaurants."

They left the office together and walked through the quiet, empty corridors toward the exit. "I thought I'd take a drive around and see some of the area while I'm here," said Bridge. "This is vineyard country, isn't it? Have you visited any?"

"Oh, yes," Montgomery smiled, grateful for the chance to show off his superior local knowledge. "I can thoroughly recommend the *Fortalbis*, about ten miles north-east. It's a sublime grape, and the sampling is excellent. The owners are descended from Italians, but they're lovely people all the same."

Bridge sighed inwardly at Montgomery's offhand racism. Some things, the English just couldn't leave behind. "Thank you," she said, "I'll be sure to look it up."

They'd reached the security barriers. Bridge placed her briefcase on the scanner belt and emptied her pockets, making a mental note to research the vineyard. She had no intention of visiting, but James Montgomery didn't need to know that.

32

At first he assumed it was nothing more than an amusing coincidence. *Kids today*, he thought, and then shook his head at the ease with which the phrase popped into his mind. Steve Wicker had only recently turned thirty himself, and here he was decrying unruly youth.

There had been just two similar incidents, but it was enough to nag away at him. Was it a common prank? The latest in amateur black hat 'lulz'? He'd seen nothing to suggest it was, and a cursory scan of the GCHQ monitoring archives also came up empty. When he got to the point of asking colleagues during screen breaks if they'd seen anything similar, he realised that no matter his conscious thought process, subconsciously he was treating it as more than just a coincidence or prank. Especially when two of those colleagues recalled seeing something similar in the past few weeks.

Like Steve, they'd thought it was probably nothing more than 'script kiddies' having a laugh, spending someone else's money on toys they could never afford themselves. But four instances was more than a coincidence.

It took him three days to track down the rest, not least because half of the incidents hadn't yet been logged. Those victims only found out when Steve called their local police department to check for reports, and they followed up to confirm.

He presented it to his boss Patel, who said, "Are you sure this isn't just the latest hacker craze? For the lulz, like?"

"That's what I thought at first," said Steve. "But if so we'd expect to see it all around the country, maybe all over the world, right? Not just London and the Southeast."

"How did you find this? When did you take over identity theft collation?"

"I didn't. This was blind luck, because of the retail fraud angle. I found two incidents that matched, asked around, and some digging turned up the other..." he checked his notes, "fourteen. Sixteen cases total, over the past four months. Assuming we've found them all."

"Are the cards from a public dump of a known breach? Pastebin, Textdump, something like that?"

Steve shook his head. "Either it's a private list, or the victims are being targeted individually. They're all completely nondescript people. No records, no priors, and no flags in our own system."

Patel spread his hands, trying to get a handle on the situation. "So someone targets innocent people. Steals their identities and credit cards. Uses that information to make precisely one online purchase, which is delivered to a third-party pickup address and collected the next day. After which the stolen identity is discarded, and never used again."

Steve nodded. "That's about the size of it."

"But you think this isn't sixteen similar cases, all following instructions from a 4Chan thread. You think it's one person's MO, doing the same thing sixteen times."

"Well, that's my suspicion. But I don't have any hard evidence, yet. Hopefully CCTV footage from the pickup locations will give me something. I'd like to request that from the locations, but it'll have to go through Five."

"Go for it. If you get any pushback from them, CC me in. I'll wave my big stick around if I have to."

"Thank you, sir." Steve gathered up his presentation notes and stood.

Patel gazed into the distance and snorted in frustration. "Drones, of all things?"

"Drones, sir. Sixteen of the best consumer-grade quadcopters money can buy." Steve closed the door behind him, attempting to mentally draft his request to MI5 in a way that wouldn't make him a paranoid laughing stock.

33

Fréderic was up a ladder, hammering away at the main building's gutters, when Bridge pulled up in the Fiat. *La Ferme Baudin* was an old, squat, stone building of modest size, but surrounded by a large yard for vehicles, and beyond that were acres of land that, after centuries of crop tilling, now grew wild. An old wood lined one edge of the property, away from the road by which Bridge had approached.

Now Fred paused mid-swing and peered down at the car, to see who was inside. Bridge took her time, hoping that Izzy would come out to greet her instead, but she could only sit here for so long before it became weird. Fred climbed down the ladder, hammer still in hand, and walked towards the car. Then a door banged open, as Stéphanie ran out to see who had come to visit them, zooming past her father. Fred called to her, but she ignored him, and made a beeline for the car.

Bridge opened the door and stepped out, waving and smiling. "*Salut*, Steph."

Steph gasped and cried, "Auntie Bridge!" Then the girl crashed into Bridge's legs and wrapped her arms around them.

She staggered back, laughing. "Calm down, Steph, it's only been a couple of weeks."

"Stéphanie, behave yourself," said Fred. Steph immediately let go of Bridge and stepped back, looking contrite. "What are you doing here, Brigitte? Has something happened?"

Bridge shook her head. "I'm on a work trip up north, and I have the weekend free. I thought I'd pop in and say hello." She reached inside the car and retrieved a small paper bag, holding it up for Steph to see. "I brought *macarons*."

"Isabelle is out shopping," Fred scowled. "You should have called ahead."

Lying to Voclaine, Montgomery, and everyone else at Agenbeux was something Bridge had worried about constantly before she arrived. She'd expected to be a ball of nerves, to hesitate and stammer over aspects of her cover bio. And while the legend OpPrep had put together helped, being so close to her real background, she'd nevertheless surprised herself at the ease with which she'd spun her tale to the Exphoria staff.

But lying to her family sadly came more easily; she'd been doing it her entire working life. The truth was that she daren't call ahead in case she was being watched or monitored. A call from the guest house would leave a record, using her cover mobile would immediately blow her cover, and using her real mobile would raise questions about mission security. After all, she hadn't told anyone in Vauxhall she was coming here, or that Izzy's place was so relatively close.

So instead, she continued lying. "I wanted it to be a surprise. The work trip was kind of last-minute, so Izzy doesn't know I'm here."

Fred grunted, and took Steph's hand. "I suppose you'd better come in, then. I'll make coffee while you wait."

Bridge followed them inside, ducking her head under the low overhead beams, and rested her bag against the kitchen table. She had always been terrible at small talk, but refused to sit in hostile silence, for Steph's sake more than Fred's. So while he prepared the coffee, she asked, "Fixing the roof?"

"Every year. Old houses need care and attention."

"This is your family's place, isn't it? How far back?"

"Four generations of my fathers. And I'll pass it on to Hugo."

"Stéphanie's older," said Bridge, noting the absence of women in this pattern of inheritance.

"Hugo is my son."

"Hugo will let me stay here as long as I want," said Steph. "He does whatever I tell him to."

Bridge smiled at her. "Oh, I bet he does."

"Can I have a coffee too, Papa?"

"No," Fred grunted. "Not until after lunch."

"But Auntie Bridge is having one."

"Brigitte is our guest," Fred said, passing her the coffee. At least he had the grace not to say, "*your mother's guest*".

Steph watched Bridge intently while she sipped the coffee, as if she could somehow drink it vicariously. Then she said, "Is it true you're a corporate lapdog?" Bridge almost spat coffee over the kitchen table. She didn't need to ask where the girl had heard that phrase.

Fred shrugged. "It's a fair question. What's the British government doing in France, anyway?"

"You know I'm not allowed to discuss it," said Bridge, wiping her lips with a napkin. "It's just a trade visit; the usual. And no," she said to Steph, "I don't work for corporations, I work for the government. Which means that, really, I work for ordinary people like you and me."

Fred snorted, but before he could inevitably disagree, they heard the sound of a car pulling into the yard. Steph jumped down off her chair and ran to the door, calling out, "Maman! Maman!"

Bridge followed, waving at Izzy as she approached the car. "Anything I can carry?"

Izzy stopped mid-exit from the car, confused. "What the hell are you doing here?"

"Lovely to see you, too, *ma soeur*. I'm on a work trip up north; thought I'd drive down and surprise you."

"Maman, Maman," Steph tugged at her mother's leg. "Auntie Bridge brought *macarons*."

Bridge shrugged, and Izzy rolled her eyes. "Well, maybe you can have one — *one* — after your lunch. Now help take the shopping in while I get your brother." Hugo was fast asleep in the back. As Izzy removed him from the child seat, Bridge opened the boot and picked out a small bag for Steph to carry into the house, taking a larger one herself. Her niece walked side by side with her, carrying the bag with a pride normally reserved for diplomatic gifts at state functions.

Lunch was a simple affair of bread, cheese, and a light wine. Bridge didn't allow herself to drink too much despite her sister's protestations, and was momentarily horrified when Izzy poured a small glass for Stéphanie. But it was relaxed and cheery, and as the tension in her shoulders eased, Bridge realised how rigid she'd been for the past few days without noticing. Even Fréderic begrudged her a smile or two.

After lunch, Steph took Bridge by the hand and marched her out through the yard, collecting a football along the way. Bridge was somewhat surprised that the miniature lady she'd had dinner with less than a fortnight ago now wanted to kick a ball around a field, but didn't argue, and Steph ran rings around her. Bridge was working out a little in the guest house room, and taking an occasional run around the streets of Agenbeux, so keeping up with her niece wasn't a problem. But her ball skills were non-existent, much to Steph's delight. After five minutes she accused Bridge of letting her win, and a laugh from the direction of the house revealed that Izzy was watching them from the yard, with Hugo sleeping on her shoulder.

Over the years Bridge had often been envious of Izzy, for various reasons. Her beauty, her sophistication, the ease with which she moved through life. But now there was something different, a longing for a way of life she knew, deep down, she would never have. Calm, content, bucolic; these were not words Bridge ever expected to feature in her story. She walked a very different path to her sister, one Izzy didn't even know existed. It was undeniably stressful, and the sudden temptation to surrender and move to a farm in the middle of nowhere, popping out children while cooking for a gruff French husband, was strong. But it also struck Bridge as an undeniably *English* fantasy, and that part of her — the aspects of her father's character she'd so easily inherited — was the very same part that ensured it remained a fantasy. Six months living like this and she'd be bored shitless.

After the football they returned inside to nap, read, and prepare for dinner. Bridge put all thoughts of work out of her mind, until later that evening after Fréderic had taken Hugo to bed. She'd found a battered old copy of Moebius' *Le Garage Hermétique*, in the original black and white, which she'd only previously read in translation. Engrossed in Major Grubert's travails, she lost track of time and only realised it was dark when a cough from the doorway made her look up. Steph was standing there, with Fred behind her, looking stern.

Izzy, who'd been reading a magazine on the couch, looked over at them. "What's up?"

"Auntie, why does your computer say 'Bridget Short'? That's not your name."

Bridge inwardly cursed her niece's insatiable curiosity. She'd brought the Dell laptop with her as a matter of habitual security. Leaving it behind in the Agenbeux guest house was out of the question. If anything happened to it, Giles would roast her alive. She didn't intend to actually use it here, especially with the lack of internet access at the farm. But Steph must have opened the lid, and been confronted with the login screen for Bridge's cover identity.

"Stéphanie, those are Auntie Bridge's private things," said Izzy. "You mustn't touch them unless invited to."

"I wanted to play a game," said Steph, downcast.

Bridge smiled sympathetically, grateful Izzy had unwittingly given her a few seconds to think. "It doesn't have any games on it, I'm afraid. It's a work computer. And that's why it has that name, it's a silly joke by the people I work with."

Fred looked sceptical. "What kind of joke is that?"

"If you hadn't noticed, Fred, I'm quite tall."

Izzy snorted. "Not very funny, if you ask me."

"Well, that's the civil service IT department for you," Bridge shrugged. "Stitch me back together again, know what I mean?" She took a swig of wine, hoping to put an end to the line of conversation, but she could see Fred didn't believe a word of it.

He looked at Izzy and said, *"Glaubst du wirklich diesen Mist?"*

Izzy looked annoyed, though whether it was because of what Fred said, or because he'd lapsed into German, Bridge couldn't tell. It was a favourite trick of his. Bridge's German was poor, and Fred knew it, so he did this when he didn't want her to understand his conversations with Izzy. Izzy shot back, *"Nennen sie meine Schwester nicht eine Lügnerin. Und sprich gefälligst französisch."*

Bridge caught the gist of that, and realised she didn't care if Fred believed her, so long as Izzy did. But there was now tension in the air, and Steph looked from one parent to the other, confused. "I know," said Bridge, smiling at her niece, "how about we all play a game together? Do you have any cards in this big old house, maybe?"

Steph clapped her hands together. "No, *les Petits Chevaux*! Please can we, Papa?"

"You're supposed to be getting ready for bed," Fred grumbled.

"Oh, don't be a grouch," said Izzy, "let's have one game. We're on holiday, remember?"

Fred returned to the kitchen, saying nothing. Steph skipped to a cupboard, and flung open the door to reveal half a dozen battered and worn board games that looked as old as the farm itself. She reached in and carefully removed one from halfway down the pile, steadying the games above it with her other hand as she pulled it out.

It was a game of pure chance, a French version of Ludo, that Bridge had never seen before. She'd always been more of a strategy game player, from furrowing her brow at her father over a chess board as a child, to complex real-time computer wargames as a student. Since joining SIS she'd lost her taste for those and turned instead to European social board games, mostly German, that simulated things like 18th-century Caribbean trading or railway building in Central Europe. Not that she had much opportunity to play these days. So, despite the absurd simplicity of this game, Bridge found herself having fun just because Steph was, delighting in watching her niece go through the seven stages of grief in five seconds flat when one of her pieces was captured, or in celebrating like a lottery winner every time she rolled a six.

"One game" turned into two, because Izzy won and Steph looked like she was about to explode. Bridge won the second, quite by chance, so both she and Izzy breathed a sigh of relief when Steph won the third. While her niece was celebrating, Bridge gave Izzy a look and tipped her head toward the stairs. Izzy smiled, evidently thinking the same thing, and made a big show of looking at the clock. "All right, miss champion," she said, "you beat us fair and square. Now let's get you to bed."

Steph protested, as expected, but Fred picked her up and carried her to her room. He might be an insufferable prick around the dinner table, but he loved his kids, and Bridge began to understand why her sister might be happy enough with him. Wondering if the subject might come up in conversation, she reached for her wine glass — and came face to face with Izzy, frowning at her.

"Why are you really here, Bridge?"

"I told you, I wanted to see you and the kids."

"I just saw you two weeks ago, and now we're in a different country, for heaven's sake. When was the last time you came to France?"

Bridge puffed her cheeks, thinking back. "A while, I guess… oh, I visited Mum last year. Or was that the year before?"

"It was three years ago," Izzy sighed. "You need to sort yourself out. I don't know why you're such a workaholic, you know? It's not like you have a mega-exciting job, you shouldn't give it the best years of your life."

"Oh, come on, let's not start this again."

"Start what? I'm just saying you need to get out more. Put yourself out there, before you get left on the shelf."

Bridge sighed. "That's Mum talking, isn't it? I'm not like you, Izz. I'm not looking for a husband."

"Good thing too, because you're not going to find one if you still insist on hanging round the goth crowd."

"Says the woman who introduced me to them. Just because you don't go clubbing any more, doesn't mean the rest of the world has to stop."

"There you go. 'Clubbing', for heaven's sake. You're thirty years old."

"Twenty-nine," Bridge protested. "I can't believe you forgot how old I am."

"Whatever, the point is you're too old for that shit. Don't they have apps on your computer for finding men, these days? Get someone to do your make-up, put a nice photo online. You're pretty fit, you just need to sort out your hair and wear something…" she flustered, reaching for a word, "something more attractive. Look at Karen, she was Miss Ubergoth. Then she grew up, and now she looks miles better."

Izzy had met Karen on the London darkwave scene while at uni. Karen had graduated a few years before, but was still a stereotypical big hair/white face/big dress girl with a habit of getting completely shitfaced, dancing like a whirling dervish, then drunkenly swearing everyone to secrecy about her straight-laced City job. Every weekend, without fail, until one day she just wasn't there. Izzy had told Bridge the story many times, how she eventually went round to Karen's flat to find she'd given half her wardrobe to charity, destroyed the other half, and spent the previous two weeks getting through several crates of wine and as many boxes of tissues. A mohawked mutual friend called Big Darren was to blame, and while he soon found himself *gotha non grata*, the damage was done. Karen joined a gym, found a tailor, and let her roots grow out. After six months she could have walked straight past the old crowd without being recognised by all but her closest friends, and that was how she wanted it.

A year later Izzy had followed in Karen's footsteps, but Bridge had no intention of suffering the same fate. She didn't club or drink as often these days, and she certainly didn't date like she used to, but she'd always had a sort of faith that the universe would figure something out. Staring into her wine now, she wondered if she'd subconsciously been waiting for Tenebrae_Z to make some kind of move, maybe ask to meet in person or simply find her and sweep her off her feet.

"Oh God, Bridge, I'm sorry," said Izzy.

Bridge was momentarily confused. Sorry for what? But when she looked up from her wine glass, she couldn't seem to put her sister in focus, and realised she was crying.

Izzy put down her wine and wrapped her arms around Bridge, whispering soothing noises. She took her glass, set it down, and held her tight. Bridge was transported back to childhood, to her mother's hugs after a grazed knee or climbing accident. All the tension washed out of her body, and without at all meaning to, she fell asleep.

34

"AuntieBridgeAuntieBridgeAuntieBridge!"

Just in case shouting at full volume down her ear didn't work, Stéphanie also jumped on top of Bridge, squeezing the breath out of her and making her wince. But the girl got her wish, and Bridge was now awake. She mumbled an approximation of "Good morning," wondering why Izzy had allowed Steph into her bedroom, then recognised the coffee table, wine glasses, and fireplace. She was still on the sofa, fully clothed, under a blanket presumably laid over her by her sister.

Bridge checked the time. Not yet 0800, but Steph was wide awake. Izzy shouted from the kitchen, "Leave your Auntie Bridge alone, Steph. She's an ogre in the morning."

Stéphanie fixed Bridge with a sceptical look. "You don't look like an ogre."

Bridge jerked upward and roared, looming over the girl with her hands. Steph shrieked, a mixture of shock and laughter, then leapt off the couch and skipped into the kitchen. "Maman's making cakes," she called back to Bridge. "I'm going to help."

"You do that," Bridge whispered, and swung her legs off the sofa. To her surprise, she felt better than she'd expected. The wine bottle on the table was empty, but she was pretty sure it had still been half-full last time she looked at it. Izzy must have finished the rest herself, which only made her early rising more annoying.

After a quick shower, Bridge followed the warm, sugary scent emanating from the kitchen to find Izzy and Steph taking cake-filled trays out of the oven. Hugo slept in a carry-cot on the counter.

"Cups, coffee, all in those cupboards," said Izzy, directing Bridge with a nod of her head as she manoeuvred a hot tray onto a cooling rack.

"What's all this for?" Bridge asked. It wasn't either Steph or Hugo's birthday, but she couldn't swear to Fred's date of birth. "Are you having a party?"

"No," said Steph, as if it was the most obvious thing in the world. "Maman sells cakes at the patisseries in town. They put them in their window, and everyone says they're quite delicious."

Bridge busied herself taking milk out of the fridge, so Steph couldn't see her trying not to laugh at the girl's pomposity. It was quite sweet, really. When Bridge turned back, Steph was holding up a paper bag with the words *Délices de la Ferme Baudin, Côte-d'Or* printed in a faux-handwritten typeface.

"See? Now everyone knows Baudin Farm makes the best cakes." She noticed the carton in Bridge's hand, and grimaced. "Ugh, are you putting milk in your coffee? That's so English."

This time Bridge didn't bother suppressing her laughter as she poured the milk. Even as a child in Lyon she'd always hated black coffee, but she didn't have the energy to contradict Steph and get into the inevitable conversation that would follow.

"Don't be rude, Stéphanie," said Izzy, and held out a filled bag to her daughter. "Now give these to Auntie Bridge." Steph took the bag and formally presented it, complete with a curtsey. "Knowing you, you've eaten nothing but salad leaves and walnuts since you got here," Izzy continued. "Get something filling down your neck for once."

"Vegetarian, not vegan," Bridge sighed. "I've been eating just fine."

Fred walked into the kitchen and nodded at the bag of cakes, now in Bridge's hand. "Is she paying for those?"

"Don't be silly, Fred, she's our guest."

"I didn't invite her."

Bridge placed the bag back on the table. "No, he's right. If this is your business, I'll pay. Let me get my purse."

"Brigitte Joséphine Sharp, you pick up that bag right now and you bloody well keep it." Izzy turned to glower at Fred. "We do not make family pay for food. Make yourself useful; go and chop some wood." Fred returned the glare, but backed out of the room. A moment later, the door to the yard slammed shut.

"Why didn't Papa invite you?" Steph asked.

Bridge couldn't think of an answer that wouldn't cause another argument. "I should head back," she said. "Thanks for putting me up. I'm only in Agenbeux for another week, so I won't see you again till you're back in London."

"Well, that won't be till school starts, so have fun till then. And for God's sake remember what I said, OK?" Izzy gestured at Bridge's hair and face. "Just do…something."

Bridge kissed Izzy on the cheeks, and Stéphanie on the head, then retrieved her bag. Outside in the yard, Fred was chopping wood with a heavy axe, swinging it over and down on logs balanced atop a squat block. He paused when he saw Bridge emerge and said, "You should call, next time."

"So you don't mind if there is a next time?" Bridge replied, surprised.

Fred planted the axe in the block and walked over, lowering his voice. "As long as you two are related, I don't seem to have much choice. But remember: Hugo, Stéphanie, and I are Isabelle's family now. It's my job to take care of them, and put their welfare first."

"Are you saying I'm bad for my sister's welfare? Are you worried she might remember how to have fun?"

"You're a child," Fred shouted, and wagged a gloved finger at Bridge. "Building a family is not about fun. It's about loyalty, and commitment. I'd die for my wife and children, you understand? But you, you have no commitments, no responsibilities; nothing. I don't want Stéphanie to think she can live her life like you."

Bridge turned away and climbed into the Fiat hire car. "On the bright side, Fréderic, at least I'm not bitter. You should try it some time." She fired up the engine and drove away before he could respond.

35

GROUP: france.misc.binaries-random

FROM: zero@null

SUBJECT: new art

```
                                             !A^"
           %                              */sA#H/
      !.oLhy+-                            -syhyhyh+
      $:s5vnhFs-                       *.+yhesYY1sy/
    `.-o@sylAh##+-                 ^.-/s##kyyyyys5ss.
     .y+Vo£y#c0yhd!!o:-  =x0._.\ x-of][hhyssg8sd0+o.$
     -sd0sxy?XPCghoslV7osyo@-Ø6B8yhx)h%yomcwo@yhso+o-
     -o/+shDdstzd0sh42ug=mdhyAHep0mdsqrRqV+/X+sssd0+/^
    r-HKiqyh4so@+oHwW2mdL9lz5gMmMjIc*Au1U1r+/8coxRns/.
    $/x+nsYhkL7KO!3xhyhmzafahyhvnh4yg8yyhhso+!sCgsTFN9b
    !-//oD2y3IUxQs5sUulax$hxhA#Hyscdo7ys5xh3haPX0KsoGZeWe
    ./AD+oysosCgszOJNHbGc5UcKKRGqJ9lP39scV2DJA55m5iBNEs:^
   I:o++osyXPs-Ø+o@7B$Ui7OhM?djt9G8s36d0so@dpøsyhYGAExLbFuv
  !./ssD2yhso+x/+osqc65aYq9fB@d[h]y6Npzc0hYRKGoAR8FdXHhQis/-
  $-shFdhyso@+xH+O0o+osYdQIsHSmpc1xZAMJByylWcpoo1su6b6K2yhy5bZ[f
 ^.:+shhs-txxSDu1ju692o@s##kyqLw8oe4K4laspy!3x]Ffys?syhmd[h]Wrw3s
  -:+s_o+O0ouE6Ez/=:/++d56sq3L0gghsWMMso@xEthYUjF6IMnxqF1NRe5o/-!
 '.b7adxiqzTS3ss+oCgyso/+o36sOPI7co+5yXPh3sEu2Xx2RXD2yhuwIY4e9HV41
  `:oswbmsjcdzb+/:+sYF$x/+os6B8@od+hmhs+X:/omTh5i3Wbt1PZIWtv5e7v:-$
!.//+s3O0-Øo@oy+/  :X+yh+zXSeRhmd+/oyo/;  ZK2oOyxh3]b[so+UmOuxLDGVqCe
 ^-/+o@5ysosdpøo+4    B+/:/+oD2o@+xHo+X   +shyhYd34owqXWi /mwmoypJuvU-`
 *-:AX\+-ØFVcBzo-Ø+  +!WN//FpofY+++sO0oWVqwj36yys++o@+o+/::/+ooyvlunvs:'
 rmqW1pCHUZ   vEMgWn++X/A:/otvWB2+/jT6NaIzT3RlfC6 /oso^x^+O03W429HhXMrys/.$
  '-:/+xH+/.  /af5Ekwm/ e:+ovdrido++rmpmyo@-Øsso//+sahrlqpghqxsyhd0MBy35so:!
 A-peo0bO0/:-  6tsBc/   -jwiw$kaosz+ +/+s6B8esasho@ssciuzm++osyA#HdEc5ICldkxd
 ^.:+-ØsnOjs6:    j86Ts .amrz0iqhrh*  /+O0o36gvjyp  o@sgWbqjvzeshXBKBOhbhpeny
  o-+osD2o^x^/:-  pLKd8$ -XyMNXddho/  opghqx7fcmv ipkgxARK6YATUVq6Wf9Ey]Ffys!
   mIeA5-Ø+/:-   -nxBoS.!:dm$dASGDmm x^ohndVgcys +o+xwqcheydly4n2fpiarkxHi8X4
    S-+sO0orq6Ln  /oHd:   hMXS0FHE!d  oopDm2lwpme5nq1KWfHlsXqynOwyhsy[#]hddhy
      /xnzdpø+/-   :PY+di !hmOVhazec -Øshybschlegxhjbywlo##ysO0oEEgDNhdxh3!8x
       T-/++oso:  -:  o/::/oy++ddhyso@ycpZemdu92GDdpeVUhhyo@o+xBtdw7(y%XPAgDy
        $D:/jTlPeH4e  x60Dy58Sm:Sdy2yXPhddRu6T1LBdhjhysO0oxnz++ +og3xu5H4Y?6M
          B-os+/+!WN/:  zFKOHB8o48LTjRg786q9RHCX8I9RiMbG6m2 P45OAsyyf][yXPyVh
           6/o@so/+xH/  C  emV3U8Cgh##dUqjioDMdIzO0omwmAX\  ntCGJTSnZyO0Scjs1
           8-:ofRxJ2XY/    -?$+osyhmdOaDekS:dA#Hydpø+8:/   o+O0soD2Uz24U8BMjr
            !1:oys+4uWxOT  D&uzxKKJoZCeSd%(huifjVo/+o@xnz ØEz0rN2OxD4+n/+o@sy
              ]kgycw+N!N/:    ;/sy)h%!3xatCHwsm8hfo* x  ZcplCbhVD5oo  9AEtS(s
              4:/og8yo+/:   yuxGgTU9Nd[#]hhyysCgyho+o@/+-Øox95NtNxnz  +B7vHJP
             $.kl+syhyomqcZ2Q+oyf][hrVoH2jMzlxo+ss/fT4UyLRCbDzEeayl*071415D9A
```

36

"It was posted yesterday, how the bloody hell could you miss it?"

If Bridge hadn't been wearing headphones, she might not have heard Lisa Hebden's barely audible sigh in response. But she was calling GCHQ from her room in the guest house, on secure VOIP via the Dell's encrypted partition, and so was trying to keep all noise to a minimum.

That became an order of magnitude more difficult when Lisa admitted she hadn't seen the new ASCII post yet. It had been sent early on Sunday, while Bridge was still driving back from Izzy's farm, and when she arrived at the guest house she hadn't thought to check the newsgroups herself. After all, Lisa was supposed to have that covered back in England.

"I'm sorry, Ms Sharp, but I wasn't here yesterday, and when I got in this morning I prioritised my own work. Your newsgroup check just hadn't made it to the top of my pile, yet."

"You didn't brief anyone to watch over the weekend?"

"GCHQ business takes priority."

Bridge's hands trembled. She and Ten had a running joke that her get-rich-quick scheme was to invent a machine that allowed you to strangle people over the internet. Right now she would happily use that machine, and was glad the call was audio-only so Lisa couldn't see the anger in Bridge's face. On the other hand, maybe then she wouldn't be so bloody relaxed about the whole thing. "Leave it with me," Bridge said after a deep breath. "Giles Finlay will be in touch."

She ended the call, immediately switched to Giles' profile, and hit the button for his mobile. He answered after one ring.

"Yes. Line?"

"Secure. Giles, it's Bridge. We may have a problem."

"You've been blown?"

"No, my position's good. I spent most of today talking to senior staff, making progress. But there's been a new coded post, and GCHQ missed it."

"How?"

"Didn't prioritise. To be honest, I don't think they ever took it seriously. But listen, the post was made twenty-six hours ago."

She heard Giles curse at the other end of the line. "What day was the paper? I've still got Friday's *Times* at the office."

"No need. They put the answers on the website the day after, and I already decoded it. It's for a meet this evening, in fifteen minutes' time."

"Shit. What does it say?"

"Just today's date, location, and time: Myddelton, 2130."

"Twenty-one? Half nine, you're sure?"

"Yeah, it's —" Bridge realised what Giles was asking, and sighed at her oversight. "Oh, I'm on Paris time. So you've actually got an hour and a quarter."

"Brilliant. Now what on Earth is 'Myddelton'?"

Bridge smiled. "Oh, that's an easy one. Hugh Myddelton, there's a statue of him on Islington Green."

"Are you sure? No chance it could be something else?"

"Trust me, he's the only Myddelton with a statue."

"Then leave it with me." She heard the scratch of his pen as he made a note. "Bloody good work, Bridge. And I'll put a rocket up GCHQ's arse in the morning."

"Anything I can do right now? We have no idea what the target looks like."

"No, but there's no way you can chase that down inside the next hour. Relax and get some sleep. Tomorrow, try to find out if anyone from the project left town at the weekend, and I'll update you on tonight's events."

She ended the call and removed her headphones, wishing she was back in London. She knew Islington well; what she hadn't told Giles was that she'd spent many a night drinking at the feet of Hugh Myddelton's statue with her friends, after leaving the local goth club and waiting for the tube to resume morning service. If there was reconnaissance to be done, she could be valuable. But it was impossible. There was no way to get back to London in time, and even if she could, doing so would completely blow her cover here.

Besides, whoever was meeting in London tonight, it wouldn't be the mole themselves. They were still in Agenbeux, right under Bridge's nose and laughing up their sleeve.

She opened the interview spreadsheet and began reading it over, to refamiliarise herself with everyone she'd spoken to so far. Tomorrow and Tuesday she was scheduled to finish the project leads, then on Wednesday she'd do Voclaine, Montgomery, and their secretary. After that, it was all down to her own instincts and judgement.

She made some coffee, set Radio 3's online feed playing on her iPhone, and settled in for the evening.

37

Andrea Thomson kissed Giles when he joined her at the window table of the pub, which was something of a surprise. "Just pretend we're together, I think I've got them," she said quietly in response to Giles' raised eyebrow. "Corner of the bar, having a quiet wee argument. Get yourself a drink, see what you can hear." She raised her own glass, barely touched, indicating she didn't need another herself.

Giles had phoned Andrea the moment his call with Bridge ended, and asked if she could help him with a surveil and potential shadow. She wasn't impressed. "I've just finished eating, Joan's putting the boy to bed, and we're halfway through the last *Downton* box set. Can't one of your own help?"

"There's potential for arrest, and you know how bad that looks on the Service. Besides, this is almost certainly linked to…the other matter." Giles was hesitant to say too much on an insecure line, but knew she'd understand. "And there's nobody I trust more for a shadow in London."

Andrea sighed. "Yeah, yeah, butter me up. But I'm telling Joan it's you who owes her dinner for this one."

"Promise," he said, and gave her the details as he left the flat. Even with that head start Andrea had beaten him to it, texting him as he exited the turnstiles at Angel to say she was in a pub, across the road from Islington Green and the statue of Hugh Myddelton. Giles kept an eye on the roads as he walked, just in case, but there was almost nobody around, and certainly not two shifty people having a shifty meeting.

That wasn't entirely surprising. After Bridge had decoded the posted messages, Giles ordered Monica to collate and scan all the CCTV they could find for the known meeting locations and times. It had taken her most of the past week, and at first they'd been hopeful. With more security cameras per capita than anywhere else in the world, London was the most surveilled city in history. But many of the city's statues were in parks, with limited camera coverage, if any. Much of the footage Monica had been able to find was from nearby streets and businesses, with only limited views of the locations they wanted. And when there was coverage, the places and times of day lent themselves to crowds of tourists, drinkers, or lunching office workers, making it hard to isolate a particular face. There was also no guarantee the people they were looking for were in those crowds; some footage showed nothing — empty spaces devoid of people — meaning either those meetings had failed to take place, or the people holding them knew exactly how to stay out of sight of the cameras. The whole thing had been an exercise in frustration, and a grudging respect for the culprits.

But now, inside this pub, Andrea may have found those same culprits. After greeting her, Giles dropped his jacket on the seat and walked to the bar, standing a couple of stools down from the men. There was quite an age difference between them. The older man was of average height but thick build, a combination of muscle and weight that spoke of a man still capable of intimidation, but relying too much on past glories. His face was thick and fleshy, with eyes set among deep lines of hard experience that ran all the way to his thinning silver hair.

The other man was younger, tall and slim. He kept in shape, but unlike his acquaintance, didn't hold himself with the air of a man trained to fight. He wore a cream coloured woollen cap which, judging by the stray curls escaping at various places, struggled to hold a mass of hair in place. The hair was the same sandy blond colour as his beard.

The men stopped their quiet, urgent discussion when Giles reached the bar. He ordered a beer and made a show of checking his phone, hoping they'd resume, but instead they chatted much more amiably, with the younger man asking the other how France had been on his last trip. Giles resisted smiling as he put away his phone and carried his beer back to the table. To anyone else, chatting about a recent trip to France would mean nothing; just innocently passing the time of day. But in the context of Exphoria, it spoke volumes. He sat next to Andrea and asked, "How did you spot those two in here?"

"They weren't in here at first. I got to the location in time to see them crossing the road together, away from the park and heading for the pub. Nobody else looked likely, so I figured I'd give it a chance. And there's been no-one around since." Giles noticed that she'd chosen a table window, affording a view of the green space across the road, to keep watch.

"Bloody good work," he said, sitting down. "If these really are our guys, it sounds like the older man was recently in France, so could be the mole's contact. I wonder who the other chap is?"

"He looks like a computer type. Maybe he's the mastermind, and the bruiser's just a merc."

"Certainly possible. Idealism is the province of the young."

"Speak for yourself, gobshite," Andrea laughed. She took out her iPhone and switched to the camera, casually holding it up with one hand. "Lean in. Pretend I'm showing you a photo album. Smile, for God's sake."

Giles did as ordered, and saw that Andrea was pointing the camera in the general direction of the two men at the bar, who had resumed their argument, although in a calmer fashion than before. He smiled, said, "Oh yeah, that's great," in the most vacuous tone he could muster, and pointed at the screen. His finger touched the on-screen shutter button, snapping a photo. They continued the charade for a while, taking subtle photos where it would seem natural, even taking a selfie at one point to maintain the illusion.

"Pity these things don't come with boom mics," said Andrea. "You should get your tech boys on that. They all like to think they're Q."

"And here I thought you people could hack someone's phone mic from across the room," said Giles. "Or do you have to call in GCHQ for that?"

"Cheeky bugger."

"Yes, well, don't look now." The older, thickset man was gathering his coat, preparing to leave. He checked his watch, said something to the younger man, then headed out of the door. Giles took a sip of his beer and said, "Quick, call me."

Andrea still had her iPhone out. She dialled Giles' number, while pretending she was still looking at photos.

Giles answered his buzzing phone and conducted one side of an imaginary 'work emergency' conversation for the benefit of anyone within earshot, particularly the younger man at the bar. He didn't seem to be paying Giles and Andrea any attention, but neither would anyone trained in surveillance.

Giles ended the fake call, said, "Sorry, love. Emergency, I've got to go in," and kissed Andrea goodbye.

38

The thickset man had left less than a minute before. Giles stepped onto the street, still carrying his Samsung phone, and pretended to make a call while scanning the street for his quarry.

The first surprise came when the man set off walking west, towards King's Cross, instead of making a beeline for Angel tube station as Giles had expected. He was going at a fair clip, too. Keeping his phone pressed to his ear, Giles turned in the same direction and followed.

Monday nights were quiet around this area, but the weather was good, and the street became busier as they drew closer to King's Cross. Giles crossed the road several times, sped up and slowed down to put more or fewer people between him and the target, and occasionally made fake calls on his mobile, all in an attempt to blend in with the crowd and look like any other Londoner on the street, in case the target was looking for a shadow. It was routine, the result of years of training and OIT work before he moved up the Service ladder, and he did it almost automatically. But was it really necessary? Not only was Giles pretty sure the thickset man hadn't made him, but the man didn't seem to care. He wasn't changing direction, didn't stop to check for a tail, and at no point did Giles see him look from side to side, let alone behind him. None of the usual tradecraft one would expect from a trained espionage officer.

Had they got it wrong? Was this an innocent man who just

happened to look like he'd stepped off an FSB production line in Moscow? Then again, even on a pleasant night like this, why would an innocent man spend fifteen minutes walking from Islington to King's Cross, rather than catch a bus or train?

The second surprise came when the man continued walking straight past King's Cross. Giles had assumed he'd catch a train or bus from here.

And then he vanished from sight.

Giles had been waiting to cross the junction under the clock tower, where the crowds and corner walls made visibility poor. He knew he'd lose sight of the target for a moment, but expected to see the man ahead of him when he crossed the road, on the pavement. Instead, he was nowhere to be seen. Giles scanned the other side of the road, but quickly discounted it. To cross the road here without causing a fuss or being seen was impossible. And there hadn't been enough time for the thickset man to walk up to the hotel, above the road. So where was he?

Giles saw the street entrance marked *Underground* ten feet away, and groaned at his oversight. So obvious he'd almost missed it. He ducked in, quickly scanning the entrance hall, but still there was no sign of the man. He jogged down the ramp to the ticket hall, passing by the entrance to St Pancras International…

Then stopped, turned, jogged back up the ramp. According to their conversation, the man had come from France. Was he now heading back on the Eurostar?

Giles rushed through the secondary entrance into the main station. He glanced up at the first floor, but that seemed unlikely. Who stopped in at St Pancras for a bite to eat last thing on a Monday night? He kept walking, checking, hoping he hadn't lost his target.

And then Giles saw him, walking through passport control,

the last man catching the last train to Paris. It left in two minutes, and the thickset man had timed his journey perfectly. All Giles' doubts now disappeared. This man knew exactly what he was doing. He probably carried nothing incriminating, nothing that would look remotely suspicious if he were arrested. Now he was heading back to France, no doubt under a false ID, leaving Giles faced with a dilemma. He couldn't board the train himself, as the only ID he carried was his driver's licence. He hadn't thought he'd need anything more official when he left home this evening. In theory, he could make some calls and ensure the border guards would let him through, but that might take too long.

Or, he could stop the train altogether. Ironically, that would be easier than trying to board. He could go through those same channels, order the train stopped, and commandeer the police to help him escort the man off. An even simpler solution would be to set off the fire alarm, immediately shutting down all train movement in and out of the station. But what then? What good would come of detaining the man who, Giles was now certain, acted as contact and go-between for the Exphoria mole? If this was one of Giles' operations, he'd go dark as soon as the contact was arrested. No, arresting the thickset man now would achieve nothing. They needed to know who he was, and exactly what he was doing, before making a move.

There was a third option. Giles watched the train pull away, then approached the border security office and asked to speak to the officer in charge. Next he dialled a number from memory, a number never stored in contact address books, and apologised to the man who answered for calling at an unsociable hour.

Three minutes later, the senior border security officer arrived, talking on his own phone. He made affirmative noises, then ended the call and nodded to Giles. "Mr Finlay," he said, "apparently

I'm to let you look over all the passports we scanned for the last departed train. Any chance you could tell me why?"

Giles smiled sympathetically. "Sorry. National security, and all that. Please lead the way."

39

At least Andrea's target didn't leave the country.

The young man with the sandy blond beard waited almost ten minutes after his friend had left, and Giles had followed him on the pretext of a phone call, to finish his drink. Then he abruptly walked out, perhaps hoping he would catch anyone following — like Andrea, seemingly absorbed in her phone with Giles gone — off-guard.

But Andrea wasn't caught off-guard, and certainly wasn't absorbed in her iPhone. If anyone had looked at her screen they would see a vacuous match-three game, something she'd first downloaded on her personal phone for her son Alex to play when he needed a distraction. She'd put a copy on her work phone specifically for use cases like this; in public, when she needed to look like her mind was elsewhere. She pretended to play, while her attention was on everything but the game she held in her hands. Her high score was a little under two thousand. Alex's was over a million.

So as the young man approached the bottom of his glass, Andrea was ready. Giles' joke about her being able to break into someone's phone from across the room wasn't entirely a joke. She couldn't quite do that, but with the right gadget she could have cloned the young man's mobile. Not from across the room, though. She'd have to get close, and that would almost certainly mean flirting with him. And while she'd learned over the years to feel less weird about doing that with men, and could now make a seemingly-real attempt, the bigger problem was that she and Giles had acted as if they were an item. If she played the 'lonely businesswoman' angle now, the young man would assume she was cheating, and that would make it almost impossible for her to subsequently tail him in the street. Besides, while cloning his mobile would give access to his GPS, that would only provide his location. It couldn't give the context of what he was doing at those locations, which Andrea felt was sometimes more important.

But all this was moot, because she didn't have a cloner unit. What she did have was a reversible jacket, which she turned inside-out when the young man stepped outside, and slipped on as she followed him thirty seconds later.

Of course, all of this assumed Giles was on the level. She was still annoyed at him for letting Brigitte Sharp run around Brockley like an amateur detective, and she didn't believe for a second that SIS hadn't scanned everything they could on Mr O'Riordan's cloned hard drive before forwarding it to her office. On the other hand, they did forward it, and Giles had been open about why he needed help this evening. As she turned to follow the young man, who was now walking east at a fast pace, she made a mental note to have a word with Patel at GCHQ in the morning and remind them who they worked for.

Like Giles, Andrea had expected her target to go straight into the Tube. Was he heading to another meet? Perhaps, but inside the pub she hadn't once seen him check his watch, suggesting he wasn't on a schedule. And if these two were indeed stealing secrets from a classified MoD project, they wouldn't leave their timing to chance.

So perhaps he was done for the day. He might live around here, though she doubted it. Arranging a meet close to your home, even a temporary one, was the last thing a professional would do.

Then again, if Andrea found out her rendezvous code had been compromised by a random hacker, she also wouldn't dream of using that code again, not even with the hacker dead. But these people had. So either they weren't so professional, or they were so arrogant they assumed killing O'Riordan had removed the threat. And to be fair, it almost had. Without Bridge's connection to the victim they might never have found the link to Exphoria, and they certainly wouldn't have known about this meeting.

The young man walked east, through Hoxton and into Shoreditch. He didn't act like a professional, and she didn't think she'd been blown, but nevertheless she almost lost him a couple of times. After about fifteen minutes, they turned left at Old Street station. As Andrea took the corner, his grey jacket was nowhere to be seen. She kept walking, scanning intently, and soon saw him on the other side of the road with the jacket slung over his shoulder, exposing a bright blue t-shirt. Simple but effective.

Ten minutes later, weaving through the streets of Shoreditch itself, she lost sight of his cream-coloured woollen cap in a crowd. Andrea's height was a disadvantage in crowd situations, and the daylight was fading, which didn't help. So this time she paused, pretending to look at something on her iPhone, while scanning bodies and legs instead. She found him, resumed following, and when the crowds parted saw that he'd removed the woollen cap to free his thick, tousled sandy hair.

All of these changes could be explained. None of them definitively marked him as a professional. Once again, Andrea wondered if they really were following the right people. This was reinforced when the young man reached his destination, an anonymous door set back into the corner of an anonymous building. He used a contactless keycard to enter, and Andrea briefly caught a glimpse of a standard small business lobby — steel, glass, and trendy bare brick. No receptionist; just an elevator.

She couldn't follow him inside. Even if she'd been able to open the door, stepping into that lobby would blow everything. But as she watched from the other side of the street, and the young man waited in the lobby, she noticed glass panes running the height of the building that showed the elevator's progress. Andrea watched it descend from the second floor to ground level where the young man stepped inside without a care. Then she watched the elevator rise without stopping to the third floor, top of the building.

She couldn't risk going over to look at the door for company names; the buildings around here may have been positively Victorian, but there was no question several high-tech security cameras would be watching the main door and lobby, feeding the images to every company inside. Instead she noted the address, and continued walking east until there was no chance at all that the young man could see her from his third-floor window. Then she turned south, and as the Gherkin came into view her iPhone vibrated.

`GJB when safe - G`

Andrea veered right, toward Liverpool Street station.

40

Lights reflected off the wide, dark water, giving the Thames a glamour and appeal that Giles had never really thought it deserved. By day, it was still just a dirty old river.

He saw Andrea approaching from the north end of the Golden Jubilee Bridge long before she reached him. He'd texted after leaving the St Pancras security office, without knowing where she might be, and had only arrived here ten minutes ago himself. "You didn't go far, then."

"Bloody far enough," said Andrea, leaning on the railing. "Hipster boy walked all the way to Shoreditch, and went into an office building. I'll check on it in the morning, but with the location and everything else, my money's on a tech startup."

Giles paused, considering this. "My target walked to St Pancras and hopped on the last Eurostar before I could stop him. He certainly moves like a professional, but I can't be entirely sure if he made me or not. He didn't seem to take any specifically evasive manoeuvres."

"Same here. Hipster took off his coat, and then his hat, which threw me a couple of times. But it could have just been an innocent guy, taking off layers on a warm evening."

"You mean like you just happened to be wearing a reversible jacket?"

Andrea looked down at her inside-out jacket, then back up at Giles, and laughed as she reached the same conclusion. "It's exactly what we'd want from our own people, isn't it? To make closing-door getaways and costume changes look like innocent actions. Yeah, this pair are professionals, all right."

Giles pulled out his phone and unlocked it. "Here's further proof, if we needed it." He swiped to a photograph of an open passport and pinched to zoom in on the picture ID, recognisable as the burly man. "I got this at Eurostar border control. Marko Novak, an import-export businessman from Croatia. I'll have the ID checked out, but if it's not a legend I'll eat my hat."

"At least we have a picture." Andrea checked her watch. "There's still plenty of time to get someone in position to follow him after he arrives in Paris."

"I have a man taking care of it. Now, what about this startup? Do you think we can break in?"

Andrea rolled her eyes. "I swear, you lot think you're *Mission: Impossible*. How about you let me check them out first, and maybe I'll make an appointment to look around, like a civilised person? You're not the only ones who go undercover, you know."

"If Bridge wasn't away, I'd send her in with you. Might take a nerd to figure out what they're up to."

"We don't know for sure that they are. At this stage, all we have is assumptions and coincidences."

"No smoke without fire."

Andrea sighed. "And you're not the one who has to submit eighteen reports to the Home Office if we're wrong. Christ, even if we're right." A train leaving Charing Cross rumbled past, and she shouted to be heard above the noise. "Just let me know whatever your man in Paris finds out about Novak."

She walked away, leaving Giles alone on the bridge.

41

From one and a half metres, she could see everything. And that was just with her work phone.

Giles had told her to get some sleep, but Bridge had known that wasn't going to happen. Her argument with Fred had put her in a bad mood since Sunday. Not just because of his comments about her lack of responsibilities, which in light of her current mission she found risible, although she could never tell him why. It was more because, without even knowing it, he was right. Her life — both real and cover story — was no model for a clever young girl like Stéphanie, who at the rate she was going would probably grow up to run the EU or something. Then the discovery of the new ASCII post, and Lisa Hebden's incompetence, had set Bridge raging all over again. It was going to be a long night.

First, she went back over the spreadsheet. She'd picked out half a dozen potential candidates for the mole before going to Côte-d'Or, letting them stew at the back of her mind over the weekend. Now she looked at them again, discounted one, and forwarded the remaining five names and positions to Henri Mourad in Paris, for him to dig into tomorrow morning. She wondered if he'd raise an eyebrow at her sending email at this time of night.

Then she cast an eye over who she still had to interview, and saw James Montgomery's name there at the bottom of the list. She'd missed him all day earlier, but there was something at the back of her mind, scratching to get out like an insistent cat, something she'd told herself to remember…

Oh, shit. The vineyard.

Fortalbis, Montgomery had called it. Bridge exited the secure partition and searched the name online. The first three hits were all the same place, *Champagne Fortalbis*. She clicked through and read the About pages. She was relieved to see it had been open at the weekend, and there was no need to book for a tour. She noted the route as an easy, uninteresting drive. One where she could say she used GPS and wasn't really paying attention, so had no significant memory of any landmarks. Next she crammed the vineyard's history, noting the parts a tour guide might highlight; its age and provenance, how the variety originated, that the vineyard was still owned and managed by the same Italian immigrant family who first planted it almost three hundred years ago.

Finally she checked the photo gallery, memorising features and *terroir* so she could bluff her way through a conversation. Then she went back to the secure partition to conduct an image search, looking for photos taken and posted by tourists that she could download to her phone, passing them off as her own. It might not fool someone who knew the *Fortalbis* intimately, but who ever looked closely at other people's holiday photos anyway? In fact, she could probably just take photos of her laptop screen rather than bothering to download them. She magnified one of the search result images, a samples table of the vineyard's bottles, to fill the screen. Then she picked up her phone and snapped a test shot. Both the screen and camera were hi-res enough that all he she had to do was crop, and it would look like she'd taken the photo herself. If she zoomed in close enough she could even just about read the sample labels…

Thirty seconds later Bridge was leaning out of the guest room window, inhaling a cigarette.

The Exphoria logs showed no indication of unauthorised data extraction from the server, and nobody's terminal had been used to copy any code. There was one incident where a junior clerk had tried to copy a USB stick full of MP3s *onto* his terminal. But the junior, terminal, and USB stick were all immediately quarantined and investigated, and nothing else was found. He really had just been stupid enough to bring pirated music into work.

There was nothing else. The logs were clean, the security was intact and verified. If the mole was copying data somehow, they had to be an elite hacker in possession of world-class black hat software that could not only break into highly-secure servers, locate the data, de-encrypt it, and copy it to a second location, but do all that without anyone, or any part of the system at any time, noticing it was happening.

Or they could be taking photos of code on a terminal.

Bridge swore under her breath, coughed as she inhaled the very end of her cigarette, and lit another. It sounded crazy, so low-tech and old-school it couldn't possibly be true. But then, this whole affair was at odds with itself. Passing coded messages online by pairing them with clues inside newspaper crosswords, transferring data by physically meeting a contact, and now stealing bleeding-edge computer code by snapping pictures of a screen.

And yet, was it really that low-tech? This wasn't a cat burglar sneaking in at midnight with a microscopic camera hidden inside a matchbox and only enough space for ten pictures. If she was right, the mole was using a modern phone camera to take dozens, hundreds, potentially thousands of very high-resolution images, sharp enough that someone else could read them back and type them into another computer. Hell, you could probably automate it, hand it off to an OCR program and let it transcribe the lot. Although, if Bridge were in charge she wouldn't do that. Recent

OCR was much improved from the days of getting schoolboy laughs from trying to read words like 'flick' and 'burn' from bad photocopies, but it still wasn't perfect. And for something as error-sensitive as code, she'd want someone familiar with the language doing the typing. That meant a coder, stashed away somewhere, touch-typing what they read on pictures from a phone.

That was how she found the maximum distance: standing one and a half metres from the Dell, with a terminal window open, she could take a photo of the screen that — when zoomed in sufficiently — made every line of her bash session legible. And that was with the cheap HTC phone they'd given her to use while she was undercover. With a better model she could probably stand two, maybe three metres away and get the same results.

It still sounded absurd. She was loath to float the idea to Giles, let alone Dunston, who would probably laugh her out of the room. But the more she thought about it, the more she realised it made a perverse kind of sense. The lack of data breach, the meetings in London…if they were passing USB sticks, they could be filled with photos as easily as code. And by doing physical handovers they were bypassing the cloud completely, which was entirely sensible. Despite whatever public assurances the tech companies rattled off, it was an open secret in the intelligence community that every agency in the world was monitoring cloud activity.

The mole probably also had auto-upload switched off, or could be using a phone with no SIM, completely disconnected from the cellular network. And the lack of CCTV at Guichetech meant that, so long as they took photos while no-one else was physically present, they would be unseen.

Bridge thought of her daily trips through facility security. All handheld electronics were scanned separately, like at an airport, and every day random employees were chosen to be searched more thoroughly. The mole would have to get through that somehow. Security didn't open and scan everyone's phone or tablet as they went through the scanners; they were just looking for explosives, contraband, drugs. Still, it would be pretty risky to carry photos like that through on any device. And a USB stick by itself would surely stand out. But if Bridge was right, the mole had already managed to avoid security, and other watchful eyes, many times. So how on earth could she find and track this, to prove her theory?

She took a drag, felt nauseous, and realised this cigarette was now down to the filter too. She tossed it into the night, disgusted with herself, and leaned out to look around at the rest of the guest house. Hers was the only light on this side of the house. If she wasn't careful, she'd gain the reputation of Crazy Englishwoman Who Stays Up All Night sooner than she liked.

She resolved to call Giles in the morning. With any luck, he'd had a breakthrough in London.

42

"Ah! Excusez-moi, monsieur." Henri Mourad apologised for bumping into the thickset man, but even as he spoke he knew it wasn't the man in the photograph.

Henri ignored the man's obvious disgust at being touched by an Algerian, and resumed his frustrated scanning of the crowd disembarking the Eurostar. He'd rushed to Gare du Nord after a call from Emily Dunston and Giles Finlay in London. He'd worked for her long enough, and taken enough calls from her, to know immediately that Emily was annoyed at Giles about something. Henri wasn't sure what, until she made a sarcastic remark about 'new information', and the way she said it made him realise it was new to her, as well. Giles had a reputation in SIS for running his own *petites féodalités*, doing things off the books until he thought there was something worth recording, and ensuring his officers' first loyalty was to him, not their department. It was exactly the kind of behaviour that infuriated Emily, because it was exactly how she also liked to run the Paris bureau. Like matching magnetic poles, their similarities pushed them apart.

Henri was annoyed, too, but for a different reason. He'd not long returned from Saint-Malo, where he'd spent the weekend putting out feelers and working on potential agents, posing as a smuggler looking to prevent a Portuguese gang from muscling in on his patch. He used the story of Benoît, the slaughtered forger, to gain sympathy. Not that the underworld of Saint-Malo cared what happened in Toulouse, per se, but the unnecessary slaughter of a native French crook by foreigners was an affront to anyone's national pride. Henri didn't want to use the *T* word, not yet, in case it brought the wrong kind of attention. But he made it clear that the men he was looking for were more than just regular criminal smugglers, and bad for business if they could be traced back here to Saint-Malo.

Eventually, two people came out of the woodwork and ventured into the bar where he made it known he could be found. It was a sailor's bar, the type of hard-drinking establishment that had been dying out in France for decades, and was now an endangered species everywhere but places like this.

On Sunday he got his first bite when a local fence came to offer his services. Henri could tell immediately this man would screw over anyone for a payday, but in his experience that was a double-edged sword. Such a man wouldn't hesitate to feed you intel, even if it meant dropping his own mother in it, but he was also prone to telling you what you wanted to hear, regardless of the truth. Nevertheless, Henri encouraged the fence, and dropped hints about the unusual nature of the package the Portuguese men would be looking to move. He'd hoped to return to Paris that evening, but one source wasn't enough, especially one so potentially unreliable. So he stayed an extra day, gambling that a working day like Monday would help to spread the word further.

It did, and Henri was rewarded Monday afternoon when a tall, wide woman in a high-vis jacket lowered herself onto the bar stool next to his and introduced herself as 'GL'. She was a dockside supervisor, and claimed to have 'green routes' into the UK via the Channel Islands. If GL was to be believed, not much departed Saint-Malo without her knowing about it. She was surprisingly forthright, and no less direct about what she expected to be paid for her services, although she did offer Henri a "Tunis discount" on account of their shared skin colour. He wasn't about to correct her; thinking he was a fellow countryman could only increase the chances she might tell him something useful, despite it costing him an arm and a leg. Maybe just an arm, after the discount.

Henri had caught the next TGV back to Paris, hoping his weekday absence hadn't ruffled too many feathers. Not for the first time he thought about the days before budget cuts, when he could have stationed a junior officer in Saint-Malo to focus on the task, rather than splitting his own time and attention. He was just old enough to remember those days, when he'd been a junior officer in Marseille. Nowadays they didn't even have a permanent office in Marseille, or Toulouse, or anywhere else besides Paris. The Service maintained apartments in all the major cities, but they remained empty and unmanned, waiting for the occasions a visiting officer needed somewhere secure and pre-swept to stay.

His iPhone vibrated as the TGV pulled into Gare Montparnasse, and Emily had opened a conference call with Giles. She explained that Giles had lost a target in London (Henri could easily picture her satisfied expression at that part) and the man was now expected in Paris, arriving on the last Eurostar of the day. Giles forwarded a photograph of the target's passport, the photo showing a thickset Croatian man, and explained they simply wanted Henri to follow the man from Gare du Nord and report where he went. Henri sighed inwardly, knowing it could mean an all-nighter, maybe even a trip back out of Paris. But it was easy enough.

Or it would have been, if the man was anywhere to be seen at Gare du Nord.

Henri swore under his breath. Monsieur Closet Racist had been one of the last passengers off the Eurostar, and from a distance he fit the target's description. But it hadn't been him, and Henri was confident he hadn't missed anyone else. He watched the rest of the passengers leave the platform, then showed his ID to the guard and walked the length of the train, hoping Novak was dallying. But the target's reserved seat was empty. Perhaps he'd expected them to be waiting in Paris, and so had disembarked at an earlier station. Or perhaps he'd got off at Calais and caught a night ferry straight back to England on a new passport. Either way, he wasn't here.

The train guard nodded at the seat. "The cleaners haven't been through yet. You could swab the table for DNA."

Henri scowled in frustration. "You should lay off the *Tatort*," he said. "We'd be lucky to get a fingerprint off that, let alone DNA. No, he's given us the slip. And we have no idea where he'll turn up next."

43

"Morning, Ms Short. I completely missed you yesterday. Did you have a good weekend?" Montgomery closed the door behind him and lowered the blind without being asked.

Bridge looked up from her screen, smiled, and gestured for him to take a seat. "Yes, thank you, James. Oh, and thanks for recommending the *Fortalbis* vineyard, too."

"You visited?"

"I did, and it was great fun. You were right, the family are lovely people."

"Funny," said Montgomery, sitting down, "I didn't see you there." Bridge's fingers froze above her keyboard. "I mean, it's such a small place," he continued. "I don't know how we didn't bump into one another."

The room's air conditioning was state of the art, but Bridge felt much too warm. "What day did you visit?" She asked.

"Saturday, of course."

"Ah, well, that explains it. I was dog tired on Saturday, spent the day going over my notes from last week and then lazing around the guest house watching bad TV. I drove up on Sunday, instead."

"Well, then. That explains it, as you say," said Montgomery, smiling. "I'm glad you enjoyed it."

The back of Bridge's neck cooled. She could have kicked herself for almost being caught in a simple lie — why not just say she hadn't gone, after all? — but it was too late now, and she'd got away with it. She changed the subject. "Actually, I'm glad you looked in. You were originally scheduled as my first interview tomorrow, but circumstances have changed, and I need to talk to you now."

"Changed? In what way?"

Bridge had thought that line might intrigue his need for validation, and this time her gamble paid off. A man like James Montgomery couldn't stand the idea that there was a plan he didn't know about. She made a show of looking around the room, checking the blinds were all down, then leaned over the table and whispered, "I've had authorisation from London. I'm going to tell you why I'm really here."

In fact, she was going to do nothing of the sort.

Earlier that morning she'd called Giles, who related the events of the night before in London and Paris, and forwarded Marko Novak's passport image. Bridge didn't recognise it, and was sorry the men had both got away, but was relieved the meet appeared to have been real. The ASCII code hadn't been a red herring, and Giles said they'd found the same passport was used to enter the UK on several trips that coincided with past rendezvous dates in the coded messages. She thought of Ten, and how she wished she could tell him he'd been right. But so had she, of course — she'd told him to be careful, and one way or another, he hadn't been.

Bridge pushed the thought to the back of her mind. She couldn't allow herself to feel guilty or mawkish.

She'd explained her photograph theory to Giles. He agreed it was feasible, and would explain the lack of obvious system penetration, but remained sceptical. "How can you prove it?" he asked. "If you hang around too much, people will get suspicious, and nobody's going to stand there taking photos while you watch. Short of rigging up your own CCTV all around the building, I'm not sure how you can catch someone in the act."

"But we don't need to," she said. "If they're smart, and everything so far suggests they are, they're not putting the photos anywhere online. Which means the handoffs must be to deliver the photos, maybe on a thumb drive, and if so then they have to physically get it out of the building. There's absolutely no legitimate reason for taking photos like this. If we can find them on someone's phone, we've got them."

"Might they have transferred them to a computer?"

"No personal computers allowed into the building. Phones, tablets, and music players; that's all."

"So what are you suggesting? Black bag job on everyone you've flagged, lift their devices?"

Black bag jobs were thefts and burglaries, carried out in cases where obtaining a search warrant was either impossible or undesirable, to obtain evidence. Authorised, yes, but also illegal, and rare enough that the idea hadn't occurred to Bridge. "Could we really do that?"

"Of course we could," said Giles. "But in the short time we have, it would make a terrible fuss. What are security checks like at the facility?"

"That's what I was going to suggest. The problem is, whoever's doing this is already getting through security on a regular basis. I think we should take a more direct approach, but I need your buy-in. Probably H/PAR too, come to think of it."

She described her plan, and Giles agreed to cajole Emily Dunston, so while he was busy doing that she'd called Henri Mourad. "Henri, it's Bridge. Can you prioritise those five names I sent over last night?"

"I literally just stepped through the door," he said, stifling a yawn, "and I've got a to-do list that'll keep me busy all week."

"Sorry, but I need you to stop and dig these up by this afternoon if possible. We can't question Novak, so in the meantime this is our best lead. I need to know if any of those people are high risk;

susceptible to blackmail, communist family, money problems, anything at all."

"Yeah, thanks and all, but I know how to do my job," he said, but Bridge didn't apologise. She was convinced she was onto something, and she wanted to chase it down as fast as possible.

Giles had called back ten minutes later. The bad news: as Bridge had feared, Emily Dunston was enough of a technophobe to insist her scepticism about the photograph theory be placed on the record, in the strongest possible terms. The good news: that same old-school attitude meant that off the record, she prioritised the instincts of an OIT above trifling details like proof. H/PAR was on board.

And that had brought Bridge to this moment at Guichetech, about to tell an expectant James Montgomery something that would blow his mind — and put her at risk.

"I'm not really an HR inspector," she said.

Montgomery's eyes widened. "What are you saying?"

"I'm not authorised to tell you everything, but here's the situation: the MoD is concerned about security here at Agenbeux. Exphoria is a very expensive project, after all. The future of aerial independence rests on your shoulders." She saw him tense, and said, "Nobody is questioning the project's success. You're doing a fine job. The demonstration I saw was very impressive."

"Demonstration?"

It was possible none of the people working here had seen the results of their work in action. But surely the site manager must know? "The airfield. With the blue and red cars."

"Oh, the targeting compensation test. Yes, that went off without a hitch. I gather Sir Terence was very pleased."

The name 'Sir Terence' rang a bell somewhere, but Bridge ignored it for now. "I wouldn't know. Those sorts of conversations are above my head, so to speak."

The flattery worked, and Montgomery relaxed. "So what's the concern over security? I admit, it's not really my area of expertise. Voclaine is more hands-on with that sort of thing."

That was interesting, but it didn't change the plan. "Well, I'm afraid you can't tell him anything. In fact, we think the French factor here may be the root of the problem, if you catch my drift. But we can't be sure. After all, if we could, then I wouldn't need to be here."

"Why are you telling me now? How can I help?" Montgomery was sitting more upright now, excited at the notion of doing something clandestine.

"I'm glad you asked. First, we'll pretend you're having your interview with me right now. I've asked everyone so far not to discuss what we talked about, and you can use the same excuse. But I'm not going to interview you. I'm going to outline a plan, and I need your help to put it into action."

A plan within a plan within a plan, she thought to herself. Could she trust James Montgomery? She had no choice. She couldn't do this without authority, and with Voclaine still sitting at the top of her suspect list, that authority had to be absolute. Montgomery was an egotistical bore, but he had his uses, and Bridge intended to make the most of them.

44

At lunchtime she drove to a small café in Agenbeux, and settled in a corner table with the Dell laptop. Not so long ago she might have been frowned at, but even rural France was slowly dragging itself into the modern age, and several other young people had laptops and tablets out on their tables. Being one of the only places in town with free wifi probably had something to do with that, and Bridge connected after ordering a sandwich and coffee. But that was a feint, her natural paranoia kicking in, just in case someone checked the base station logs to see if she really had connected. Sure enough, there would be her laptop, innocently surfing the web.

Meanwhile, she logged into the secure partition, tethered it to her cell signal, and used an encrypted connection to check her real email. Henri Mourad had come through after all, running checks on the shortlist. There was only time to gather their security background checks and any related records; no real digging. But it was enough to make a start.

First there was a junior programmer. Bridge looked up the entry in the spreadsheet, and recalled the woman's interview. Standard answers, but she was fidgety and nervous. She'd spent most of the session tugging at the hem of her pullover, like a nervous tic, and spilled water in her haste to leave the room when the interview was over. But her background check was fine, and she had no police record or note of interest from security. She seemed clean.

Next, a QA tester: a tall, rangy Bosnian guy that she remembered well. Orphaned, turned up in Strasbourg, adopted at six years old. His questionable origins were a black mark, but he'd spent his entire life since then in France. Good educational records, very respectable adoptive family. Bridge had mainly marked him because of his combative attitude in the interview, a real resentment of the interruption to his work and to all her questions. But again, his check was overall clean.

Two senior coders, one of them a project lead. She couldn't put her finger on why, but there was something about the woman, a British programmer a couple of years younger than herself, that made Bridge uncomfortable. The woman had been friendly, relaxed, answering the questions with an ease and thoughtfulness that should have made the interview fly by. Instead, Bridge somehow found the experience tense and exhausting. But the only black mark on the woman's background was her connection to a Polish 8-bit demoscene group while she was a student, and according to Bridge's own colleagues at SIS she'd ceased communication with them upon graduation.

The man was simpler to figure out. He was a Scot who'd charmed his way through the whole interview, giving Bridge exactly the kind of answers befitting an experienced but still ambitious thirtysomething programmer, never once hesitating or thinking too hard, always smiling except when that would have been inappropriate. Bridge had long been a sucker for a Scots accent, but this was something else, a natural charisma she found fundamentally untrustworthy. His background check was even cleaner than the woman's, though, with zero worrisome history or connections. If he wasn't the mole, Bridge had half a mind to recommend Giles run an approach when he returned to Britain. A man with his charm could be an excellent spy.

Then, finally, there was François Voclaine. Most of the

background check told her things he'd volunteered at dinner the other night. Some of the other details didn't paint a flattering picture of the man, but then security background checks weren't designed to make people look good. She noticed there was nothing about domestic violence, however. Had security missed that? Were there no official records, no hospital visits or complaints, and the French DGSI officer who did the check didn't dig that deep? Or was it possible Montgomery was merely repeating gossip he'd heard? Rumours like that travelled fast.

Bridge was surprised to realise she was disappointed. She'd added Voclaine to the list before his formal interview, just because her gut told her there was something off about him. But now it appeared she might be wrong. This initial check contained nothing to suggest he might be inclined to leak secrets. He was a drinker, a curmudgeon, a wannabe womaniser — she was amused to note his apparent lack of actual lovers — but he had no debt, no ties to foreign states, and the closest he'd come to the Middle East was a holiday in Slovenia two years ago. Hardly the stuff of double agents.

So as she stood with Montgomery that evening, watching the security feed from a dark room behind one-way glass, she had no idea what to expect. It was a long shot, no doubt. But Montgomery had agreed to his part, and to keep Bridge unseen and anonymous. All she could do now was wait.

On regular weekdays, searches and scans were random. Most people left the building through standard barriers, using their lanyard for access. But Jules, the head security guard, would pick out every sixth or eighth or ninth person for a check, and those people would put their belongings through the scanner, while Jules ran a wand over their outstretched bodies, airport-style.

Today, it wasn't random. Jules picked out a few people of his own, to obfuscate the real targets, but he also had a list from

Montgomery, a list with five names on it, and he was under instructions to pick all five of them for searches.

The first was the tall QA tester, the Bosnian. He placed his bag on the scanner belt, emptied keys, loose change, and a Samsung phone from his pockets, then waited for Jules to run the handheld metal detector over him. The wand remained silent. In the hidden, darkened partition nearby, Bridge and Montgomery watched the feed from the bag scanner. A half-eaten chocolate bar, three sci-fi paperbacks, two packs of cigarettes, a bottle of water, and a metal tub of mints. No electronic devices beside the phone. "Ask him to unlock it," said Bridge.

"Why?"

"Humour me. Tell him you're looking for unauthorised apps."

Montgomery shrugged and left the room, the bright light of the corridor outside piercing the inner gloom. She watched him approach the tester, who took his Samsung, ran a finger over the unlock pattern, and handed it over without protest. Montgomery made a show of swiping through the app screens, but Bridge had already moved on. Either he knew his phone contained nothing incriminating, or the Bosnian wasn't their man.

Montgomery returned to the monitoring room. "It would help me very much if you told me what you were looking for, you know."

"I wish I could, James, but I know you understand that I can't. It's like porn; I'll know it when I see it." Despite the dark of the room, Bridge saw him blush from the corner of her eye.

After two truly random checks, the next person on her list to be pulled aside was Voclaine. He sighed and huffed his way through the ritual of putting his bag on the scanner belt, emptying his keys and iPhone from his pockets, and so on. His wand sweep was clean. But, watching his belongings go through the scanner, Bridge saw that the phone he removed from his pocket wasn't the only device he carried. There was another inside his backpack, stuffed inside padding by the looks of it, but visible on the scan.

"Bring him in," said Bridge.

Montgomery hesitated. "François? You can't think he's a security risk."

"Let's find out, shall we? Just like we discussed."

Once again he stepped outside, but this time asked Voclaine to enter the security interview room. Voclaine looked at Montgomery like he'd gone mad, and protested loudly. Several other staff were leaving at the same time, and Bridge didn't need audio to tell they were all wondering what the hell was going on. Just like Voclaine. She wondered for a moment if Jules and the other security guards would have to wrestle the Frenchman into the room, but eventually he relented and stormed in. Montgomery followed, closing the door behind them, and now they were both on the other side of the one-way glass from Bridge.

Bridge silently thanked whoever designed this facility with the foresight to install a private monitoring and interview room. Behind the mirror, Voclaine had no way to see or identify her, but she could see and hear everything on the other side. As if to demonstrate, he sat down and said in English, "Who is behind that glass? Police? DGSE? What in the hell is it all about?"

Montgomery didn't reply. He'd agreed to keep Bridge's role in this incognito, so she could continue with her work at the facility if necessary, and Voclaine would have no idea who had accused him. Instead, he hoisted the Frenchman's backpack onto the table and unzipped it. "Why do you have two phones, François?"

"What does it matter to you?"

Montgomery sighed. "You know the security protocols around this facility as well as me. The moment you set foot on this land, you give up any right to privacy. Now, answer the question…or would you rather I just have you carted off to Château d'If?"

"Château d'If? What in the hell are you talking of?"

Bridge wondered that herself. The legendary prison island itself hadn't been used for over a century, so the French had recently repurposed the name for their Guantanamo Bay equivalent, a permanent holding pen for suspected terrorists with no rights, no trials, no lawyers. If Montgomery knew about the new Château d'If at all, it suggested he was better connected in the MoD than Bridge had realised.

Or maybe he was just joking. It was hard to tell, with Montgomery.

Inside the room, he upended the backpack and spilled Voclaine's possessions on the table. Pens, notepads, his wallet, two magazines (one about videogames, one celebrity gossip), an empty water bottle, and a bundled scarf. The phone was nowhere to be seen — until Montgomery picked up the scarf and a second iPhone tumbled out, clattering onto the hard surface.

He had his back to her through the glass, but the room also had cameras feeding visual through to the monitoring room, and from those she saw Montgomery hit the power button, only to be confronted by a lock screen. The phone wallpaper was a middle-aged woman on a small boat, presumably Voclaine's ex-wife. Montgomery held it up in triumph, but Voclaine merely shrugged. "It's my old phone. I use it for to call my son and ex-wife. When we split apart I took a new number, and I don't want her to know."

"Nonsense. Why bring it to a secure workplace? Why hide it inside a scarf, of all things?" Bridge had guessed that Montgomery would enjoy this small taste of power, and she was right. He was practically grinning.

"If I tried to hide it, I'd make it a better job than that," said Voclaine. "I had this phone with me each day since the project began, but before it's never been a problem."

"Well, it's a problem now. I'd like you to unlock it, so I can see what's on it."

Voclaine shook his head. "I've told you, it's all personal. There's nothing for you on there to need to see," he said, directing this last to the mirror.

Montgomery noticed. "Don't look at her, look at me. What are you being so secretive about? Are you working for someone? Is it the Russians?" Bridge could hardly believe what she was seeing. Montgomery had gone power mad within a matter of seconds, and now he was talking about the Russians? What the hell was he playing at?

Voclaine suppressed a laugh. "You're out of your mind, James."

But Montgomery couldn't back down now. He thrust the iPhone under Voclaine's nose and almost screamed, "I order you to open this phone!"

Voclaine took the phone, dropped it on the floor, and crushed it under his heel. Then he smiled and said, "Would you call that open?"

Montgomery froze, unsure how to proceed, and looked to the mirror for assurance. But Bridge was equally uncertain. On the face of it, Voclaine had just given himself up. Why destroy the phone, unless it contained incriminating secrets? Thinking back to their dinner conversation, it was possible those secrets were personal. Family stuff, photos, text chats with his ex-wife and son. But then, as Montgomery had asked, why bring it to the office at all? Voclaine had told Bridge he spoke to his family only rarely.

Voclaine was glaring defiantly, not at Montgomery, but at her — or rather, the mirror. "I will say not another word without my legal representative with me. Whoever you are behind the glass, it's big trouble for you."

"On, on, on the contrary, François," Montgomery stammered, as Bridge knocked on the glass to summon him out of the room, "you're the, the one in trouble. Oh, yes." He exited the room, leaving Voclaine alone.

Bridge watched the Frenchman glare at the mirror, still and calm. He focused on a point just above and behind her shoulder, as if expecting a taller man to be standing here, but it seemed like his eyes were locked to hers in a test of will. He hadn't once raised his voice or lost his cool in there. If only the same could be said for his interrogator, who now stumbled wide-eyed into the monitoring room.

"I don't know what exactly you were looking for, Ms Short, but I'd say we've found it. What now?"

What now? At that moment she wanted to kick Montgomery's arse for his tinpot Hitler act, an act that may well have cost them a vital piece of evidence. And as a result, she *still* couldn't be a hundred per cent sure. Someone in tech would have to try and recover the data from Voclaine's destroyed iPhone to get anything solid, and meanwhile Bridge would have to remain here at Guichetech to maintain her cover. But still, it was a break of sorts, and those were rare enough in this line of work.

"Leave him here for now," she said, dialling London. "Now please step outside while I make a phone call."

45

Montgomery drove fast that night. Twice he doubled back on himself, worried someone might be following him, before starting up the tree-lined road to the car park at the top of the hill.

"Another fine night, Comrade," said the Russian, waiting for him as always.

He ignored the greeting. "You won't think so in a moment."

The Russian's wide shoulders sagged. "You did not bring me a card." A statement, not a question.

"I couldn't. I think someone's onto us. London sent a woman…"

"What?" The Russian turned on him, faster than he thought a man that size could move. "What woman?"

"She's supposed to be an HR inspector. But it's just a cover."

The Russian wrapped his big hands around Montgomery's jacket lapels and pulled him close. He recoiled from the sour stench of booze and cheap German cigarettes on the thickset man's breath, which seemed to grow stronger every time they met. "You should have told me this before."

"She, she only arrived last week. And I only found out she's undercover today."

"How? Who is she?" The Russian let go of his jacket.

Montgomery leaned back against the side of his car, in the hope it would make his head stop spinning. It didn't. "She wasn't specific. She's MoD, sent to investigate a security issue. She was very concerned about everyone's phones." He groaned in realisation. "Oh, of course. that explains why she lied to me about where she was last weekend..."

"Lied? Did you follow her?"

"No, no. She said she'd visited a vineyard, but I know she couldn't have, because there was a truck accident that closed the main road all day. Not something you'd easily forget. Maybe she went back to London for the weekend."

"Why did the woman tell you she is undercover?"

"I suppose she thinks she can trust me. Perhaps I'm a better liar than you give me credit for."

"London," the Russian considered, then barked a cruel laugh. "Five and Six working together. Yes."

Montgomery's eyes widened. "I'm sorry, what? Do you mean MI5 and MI6? Jesus Christ."

The Russian smiled, a lopsided and sad smile, and reached inside his coat. Montgomery caught a glint of grey steel in the moonlight, the semi-fist of the Russian's hand as he drew it back out, and knew he was done for. He imagined himself jumping back into his car, slamming the door closed, ducking down behind it while bullets slammed into the metal. The engine would start with a growl and he'd reverse at high speed, throwing up gravel and dust, speeding out into the trees. He'd drive all night, through to Paris, crash into the barriers outside the British embassy and demand protection, throwing himself on a diplomat's mercy. He'd be sent home, interrogated, tried for treason, imprisoned for life. But he'd be alive.

It was absurd. The Russian would shoot him before he reached the car, bundle his body into the boot, drive him to the Marne, and dump his body in the river. He would die here, in this godforsaken car park, and his body would never be found.

As Montgomery thought through these events, the pistol cleared the Russian's coat. He closed his eyes and waited for the impact, wondering how it would feel to be shot, or if he'd feel anything at all. Would that be better, or worse?

"Stupid amateur," said the Russian, and Montgomery heard the sound of the trigger pulling closed.

Followed by that cruel laughter again.

He cautiously opened one eye and realised he hadn't been shot. The gun wasn't loaded. The Russian turned it around and held it by the barrel, butt-first, for him to take. Montgomery was too surprised to argue, but as soon as his hand closed around the cold and surprisingly heavy metal, he regretted it. "I've never fired a gun in my life," he said.

"And unless you find someone to give you bullets, you will not. But as you have demonstrated so well, to fire a weapon is not always necessary for it to be effective. If you need to scare a British woman…" Montgomery stared down at the gun as the Russian's heavy hands sank into his shoulders. He assumed the gesture was supposed to be reassuring, but their sheer weight distracted him. They, and the whole world, were an impossible weight. "Now to business," said the Russian. "Your debt is almost repaid…but not yet. You must finish taking the photographs."

"You can't be serious. I told you, Short is here to look for exactly this sort of thing. I mean, I steered her towards Voclaine, instead, and I even tried to blow her cover, but she didn't seem to care. She's still there; she hasn't packed up and gone home yet."

The Russian shrugged, and lit one of his cheap German cigarettes. "So she is a mole hunter, and you have given her a…" he pondered over the correct word, "a 'patsy' to take the fall. That is good. Now she thinks you are an ally, not a suspect. Has she altered the security protocol?"

Smoke from the cigarette drifted across Montgomery's face, and he forced himself to swallow a cough. "No, not at all."

"Then proceed as before."

"But how can I? How am I going to take pictures of Voclaine's terminal when he's locked up?"

The Russian looked amused. "This is what you give us? Pictures of another man's computer?"

"He takes ten smoke breaks a day. How else do you think I have chance to take the photos? But that's all gone, now."

"Then photograph your own computer, instead."

"But I'm not a geek. How, how can I justify looking at code I know nothing about?"

The Russian leaned in and held his cigarette close to Montgomery's face. The Englishman coughed, to cover up tears from the smoke. "You will think of something," he said. "Only one more week and you can return home to England and celebrate, yes? Do not worry about the woman. I will take care of her if it is necessary."

Starlight glinted off the Russian's teeth as he grinned. Unbidden, an image of just what 'taking care' of Ms Short might mean flashed in Montgomery's mind. He tried to suppress it, not least because he had a terrible premonition that he might see it first-hand before he was ever allowed to return to England. But it haunted him all the way during the drive back to his apartment on the edge of town, and as he lay awake praying for sleep, the thought hung in the blind void, refusing to fade.

46

They told her she'd been in the hospital for two weeks. Or was it three?

Bridge couldn't remember. They told her a lot of things she had difficulty remembering afterwards, as her mind slowly pieced itself back together. Like how Dr Nayar had started visiting before she left the secure ward. Bridge didn't remember that. The first time she remembered seeing the doctor was at her flat, after they discharged her and put her on leave. She remembered thinking Dr Nayar was polite not to comment on the state of her flat, which grew ever more unkempt with each visit, because Bridge was going stir-crazy cooped up in there.

Eventually, after six weeks that seemed like a year, Giles gave in to her begging and allowed her to return to her desk. But nothing more; her OIT status was rescinded, her duties strictly office-bound, and every moment of every day she felt the eyes of everyone in the building on her, chipping away at her fragile façade of control.

There she is. The one who got Adrian Radović killed. The one who cracked under pressure, who tried to run before she could walk, who wasn't ready for the big time, wasn't ready for theatre.

Ciaran was very supportive. Monica said nothing either way. That was fine.

Dr Nayar said she was mistaken, that everyone in the Service understood the perils and challenges of going OIT. That nobody blamed her for Adrian's death, she'd done all she could. But she hadn't, had she? She'd frozen at the first sign of real trouble. Adrian was dead because she hesitated, as sure as if she'd fired the bullet herself. Of course Dr Nayar would say she wasn't to blame — it was literally her job to make Bridge feel better so she could get back to work, back to her desk.

Sometimes, her desk was part of the problem. Every so often, on hot days, her chair became the seat of a stolen jeep roaring across the desert, with soldiers chasing her and Adrian at her side, laughing over the sound of wind whistling through the bullet holes in his head. The first time it happened, she cried out so loud that Ciaran spilt coffee over his keyboard. Monica sighed and shook her head. Over time those days became less frequent, and Bridge learned to live with them, or at least make no outward sign anything was amiss.

Server rooms took longer. The first time she tried to walk between two racks the thick spaghetti of network cables seemed to flex, trying to trip her, while the racks loomed and bowed inward, ready to crush her under tons of sweltering metal. Ciaran found her crouched on the floor, covering her head with her hands, sobbing. She still hated going in them.

But all of that was behind her now, wasn't it?

She'd returned from Guichetech, after waiting for the local police to pick up François Voclaine. She'd called Giles, who'd put her on to Emily Dunston, who'd authorised Voclaine's arrest and made arrangements for him to be taken into custody. In the morning, Henri Mourad would come and transport him to Paris for questioning. Bridge remained incognito the whole time, watching from behind the one-way mirror as Montgomery dealt with the police.

"Why do you need to remain hidden," Montgomery had asked, "if you've got your man?"

"Because I'm still not a hundred per cent sure Voclaine is who we're after," she said. "But if he is, imagine I leave now, immediately after his arrest. Do you think anyone here will still believe I'm an HR inspector? Or that whoever he's working for won't become suspicious and ask awkward questions?" She could tell Montgomery didn't like it. No doubt her presence here was causing disruption, and the final stages of any project like this were the worst time for any kind of turmoil. But to his credit, he didn't object further.

She picked up a microwaveable dinner on the way back to the guest house, eating it in hurried bites between relating events to Giles at the other end of a secure VOIP call. He was pleased, and like her, hoped she'd struck gold. He reminded her that this, her first return to OIT, had been entirely safe and risk-free, and she was forced to concede that yes, he knew what he was doing and he'd been right all along. Well done, Giles, well done.

But after she ended the call, and tossed her dinner packaging in the recycling, Bridge couldn't relax. She opened the Dell and re-examined the spreadsheet yet again, not entirely sure what she was looking for this time, but determined to find it all the same.

47

Twice a week, James Montgomery wished he had bigger feet.

He was a size 9, quintessentially average for a man of his height, and nothing in his life had ever made him question them. But now, he realised with grim humour, they were an essential part of what spies called 'tradecraft', the methods and techniques by which they schemed and deceived.

He still didn't think of himself as a mole. Not *technically*. But Bridget Short's arrival, and Voclaine's arrest, had brought things into sharp focus. He could no longer escape the fact that his actions here at Agenbeux were, at the very least, treason of a kind. And hadn't they always been? Not just here, but before, when he was first approached.

London, three years ago, and Montgomery had enjoyed a recent promotion within the department. Enjoyed it so much that when a friendly banker, drinking at the Old Crown one evening, had begun chatting and buying him drinks, he thought nothing of it. Why shouldn't people buy him drinks? He was a very successful and important man. People thought politicians ran the country, but those who saw behind the curtain knew better. It was the civil servants who did the real work; they who negotiated deals, who made good on ministerial promises, who conducted reviews and assembled reports on what was feasible within the labyrinthine corridors of Whitehall. The banker knew that — bankers ran more of the country than civil servants, after all — and therefore knew

Montgomery was a good friend to have, someone in a position to pull strings behind the scenes and make things happen.

Someone in a position to influence the allocation of a defence contract worth billions of pounds.

Nobody in the department knew the company was Russian. It was a shell within a shell within a shell, a tangled maze of holding companies and 'brass plaque' conglomerates registered in sterling-friendly tax havens. These shadow companies had no premises beyond the same offshore address as a thousand others, no named directors or stakeholders, and unseen paperwork kept well away from prying legal eyes. But if you knew how, and could follow it back far enough, eventually you would find that Joint Allied Star Defence was owned by a syndicate of Russian oligarchs, many of whom had ties to the mafiya and FSB, one of the KGB's successor agencies. Meanwhile, the other successor, the SVR, was the real employer of Montgomery's new drinking friend. He discovered this the next morning when, waking in a Soho hotel room, he struggled through his hangover to understand why images of himself in places he didn't recall were flashing before his eyes. Then he recognised the shape of a television, and the telltale transition flicker of a PowerPoint slideshow, and became nauseous. He remembered nothing of the previous night past his fourth gin and tonic, not even the bored-looking woman with him in the photos, but he was suddenly sober enough to know drunkenness would be a poor defence.

The Russians understood the value of both stick and carrot. Yes, they threatened to send his wife and employers the photos. But they also opened a Zurich bank account in his name, and wired money into it at regular intervals. And all he had to do was persuade his colleagues that the new equipment contract should be awarded to Joint Allied Star Defence. He didn't have to leak any secrets, so it's not like he was betraying anything. Not *technically*.

But the Russians and Montgomery alike overestimated his power and influence. He mounted a good argument, but the contract was ultimately awarded to a different supplier. All the money Joint Allied Star Defence had spent on Montgomery, routed through byzantine layers of corporate obfuscation, had gone to waste. For weeks, he expected to suffer a terrible accident at any moment. The pinprick of a hypodermic needle as he crossed London Bridge, or the unusual aftertaste of a drink at the Black Horse, or a sudden hand at his back on the platform at Embankment. The Russians would not forget.

And yet, they did. Montgomery's contact, whom he only ever knew as 'the banker', stopped calling. After a couple of weeks he looked for the banker, worried that this lack of contact would prevent him from being able to explain what happened, how he'd done everything he could to ensure Joint Allied got that contract. He didn't want to die because the Russians thought he was lazy.

But weeks turned into months, and still the banker was nowhere to be seen. Nobody contacted him. Nobody tried to assassinate him. Nobody sent the photos to his wife. Montgomery began to relax, and his life returned to normal. He might have thought the whole thing was a fever dream, if not for the Swiss account, and the payments still being made into it. He'd always been cautious with the money — being compromised in the first place through a lack of discretion had taught him a valuable lesson, so he restricted his spending to treats for his wife and family, nice meals out, a new car that was only slightly too expensive. He didn't want to draw attention to himself through extravagance. But for some reason, the Russians were still paying him. Perhaps it was connected to the banker's sudden disappearance. Perhaps they'd just forgotten about him. Whatever the reason, within a couple of years Montgomery could have paid off his mortgage, except that he couldn't begin to justify why he had enough money to do so. By now there was too much to simply explain away as an inheritance or windfall.

And then, not long after he was chosen to run the Exphoria facility at Agenbeux, they found him again. He asked the new contact, the Russian he met every few days here in France, what happened to the banker. He was told it was none of his business, and he should only be concerned with the matter of his debt to Russia, for his previous failure. That debt was not yet repaid, as the Russian regularly reminded him.

But the payments kept arriving in Zurich, and Montgomery finally concluded that it was a mistake. The Russians thought they'd stopped paying him, but they hadn't. He briefly considered telling his new contact, but only briefly. After all, if they hadn't noticed yet, why should they now? It was, he considered, worth the risk.

And it really was quite a risk. Every day, he waited until Voclaine took his first post-lunch smoke break of the afternoon. In the morning, the Frenchman's breaks were fairly short. Even a man like Voclaine knew he shouldn't really spend all day outside, smoking. But come the afternoon, and especially if he'd had drinks with lunch, Voclaine adopted a more relaxed routine of fifteen minutes or more at a time in the compound. And every time he went out, he invariably left some part of the Exphoria code on his monitor. All Montgomery had to do was cross their office, double-check the blinds were drawn — sometimes the secretary raised them in the morning, despite his pleas for her to stop — and take pictures of the screen using the mini-tablet he kept in the office drawer, paging up and down to capture as much as he could of whatever Voclaine was working on that day. He allowed himself no more than five minutes, just to be sure he'd finish before there was any chance of Voclaine returning. It was normally enough to capture fifty screens or more of code.

He had no idea if it was useful. The programming side of things was completely beyond him. But the Russian seemed happy enough with what he delivered them.

That was where his feet came in. Every day, he brought a new Toshiba SD card into the office, from a batch the Russian had given him. Before taking the pictures, he inserted the card into the mini-tablet, and ensured the camera was set to save photos directly to the card, not the internal memory, which contained nothing more than his family photos and Chris Rea albums. After taking the pictures, he ejected the SD card and slid it into his pocket. The mini-tablet, which had its wifi permanently switched off and possessed no cellular capability, was replaced in his drawer. It never left the building, so never drew suspicion from the security guards, or the likes of Bridget Short, for being a 'second device'.

The only remaining conundrum was how to get the SD card out of the building. That was where his feet came into it. At around five in the afternoon, an hour before his normal leaving time, Montgomery visited the bathroom and installed himself in a cubicle. There, he carefully and quietly removed one shoe and sock, usually his left, and placed the memory card inside the sock before sliding his foot back inside. It fit under the arch of his foot, and it was just a little too big for comfort. If he'd been just one shoe size bigger, he'd barely be aware of it.

But he was aware of it, every evening as he left the building. Although the staff complained that security at the facility was like going through an airport, it wasn't really that bad. For one thing, staff weren't required to remove their shoes, and the detector wands weren't powerful enough to 'see' the SD card tucked under Montgomery's foot. If someone suspected, the shoes themselves were perfectly ordinary Oxfords. No secret compartment in a pivoting heel, no hidden piano wire in the laces. An inspector would have to insist Montgomery remove not just his shoes, but his socks as well, to find the card.

Today, though, was different. For one thing, Voclaine wasn't here. Montgomery knew Voclaine's login password, and could access his computer easily. But he didn't have the first idea of how then to 'check out' the Exphoria code, or which part of it to look at. He could hardly ask one of the staff to show him, and even if he could, what if someone noticed that a computer belonging to a man who was no longer in the building was still looking at code?

He'd considered asking Ms Short to show him, while claiming to be curious at what Voclaine was doing with that second iPhone. She'd returned to the office that morning as if nothing had happened, and he overheard her asking a couple of the project leads if they knew where Voclaine was, to build the pretence that she didn't know. Now she was maintaining the illusion by interviewing his secretary. But would she believe Montgomery's curiosity? Surely she knew he wasn't a computer expert. So he sat alone in his office, frustrated and worried. He had the whole office to himself, but he couldn't do a damn thing with it.

And yet, he had to. The Russian had made that clear, and while Montgomery had already expected to die two years ago, he had no desire to hasten the event now. As he exited his office, mini-tablet in hand, he was assaulted by a sudden memory. Hard steel, the Russian's pistol, pressing against his body while the scent of cheap German cigarettes and vodka-soured breath flooded his nostrils. He almost retched, stumbling into the eastern corridor and steadying himself on a wall as two French junior programmers walked past, consumed by their conversation. Montgomery's French was good, and he knew they were talking about something technical, but he didn't have the specialised vocabulary to follow exactly what they were saying. It didn't matter. They barely registered his presence as they turned ahead of him, down another corridor and toward the office of a project lead.

He wondered where they'd come from. Perhaps one might have left their screen on, with code still visible?

Montgomery's lanyard gave him access to the whole facility, and he was in and out of enough staff rooms and offices on legitimate grounds that nobody would question him using it to access an office now. All he had to do was find the unattended screen of a random coder, someone like Voclaine who was casual — one might say *laissez-faire* — about the requirement to lock all screens when leaving a desk, click around, and take photos. He could do it. It would be fine. He was the boss, wasn't he?

The third office he looked into, a two-desk setup, was empty. Only one desk looked in use, but the glow of the screen illuminated the empty chair in the dim lighting. Montgomery touched his lanyard to the entry lock and stepped inside. Definitely nobody here, and judging by the mess, whoever used the occupied desk had become used to working alone. But when he stood before the monitor, Montgomery's heart sank. It was locked, fixed on a password login screen. The username, 'Derek Angler', meant nothing to him. Evidently one of the British staff, but not one he'd come across personally, so he had no hope of guessing the password. He wondered if Derek could be persuaded to give him access, somehow. Perhaps a simple bribe would suffice? Could it be that easy?

"Can I help you?" Derek Angler entered the room, carrying a small plastic tray of pasta salad and a plastic fork. Montgomery flinched, startled, and muttered something about mandatory computer breaks. Derek gestured at the food in his hand. "It took me ten minutes to retrieve this from the back of the fridge, it'll be fine. Besides, I'm on a crunch at the moment. Sorry, who are you? Are you from HR?"

"I, I'm James Montgomery. The site manager."

Derek shrugged. "Oh, right. Excuse me," he said as he squeezed past Montgomery to sit in his desk chair. "So what's the problem?"

"Oh, there's, there's no problem. Just checking up on all the Brits here, you know? Have to stick together, all strangers in a strange land. *Haha*."

Derek shovelled a fork of pasta into his mouth. "I've been living here for three years. Not that much of a stranger, *n'est-ce pas*?"

"Ah, yes, well. Enjoy your lunch." Montgomery backed toward the door, collided with the closed glass, fumbled for the door button, and finally staggered out into the corridor.

He returned to his office, and found his secretary back at her desk, while Bridget Short's office was empty. She must have gone for a smoke break. He entered, and saw her computer was still logged in.

48

Bridge had been fifteen when she was first arrested for hacking. The police asked her why she did it, and she replied, "For the truth."

Bridge had always thought of the truth as a mountain peak, a hard and solid thing that stood proud and unchanging. To reach it, you might have to negotiate tricky paths, shifting scree, falling boulders. But if you were persistent enough, determined enough, you could eventually reach the summit and the truth would be revealed. It was a philosophy she was already inclined towards, that became fully crystallised by her father's death.

She was fourteen when he died, and undergoing a particularly morbid period where she spent most of each day contemplating her own mortality. After several years raiding her sister's music collection and removing all colour from her wardrobe, her teenage years had begun the process of backcombing her hair, covering herself in silver jewellery, and experimenting with stark black, white, and red makeup. The year before, at the moment her mother served an evening dinner of pork, Bridge declared her conversion to vegetarianism and accused them all of dietary murder. Her plate ended up on the floor. She ended up in her room.

At her father's funeral, she did the bare minimum required of her: turn up, be present, accept people's condolences. She said little, and at the small reception afterwards spent most of the time either locked in a bathroom stall, or standing outside smoking. It was the first time her mother had seen her smoke, but to Bridge's surprise, she didn't object. What if she had, anyway? What was there to say, what was there to do? In a matter of centuries — the blink of an eye, in cosmic terms — everything Bridge was, everything she'd done and was yet to achieve, would be dust. Nobody would know she'd ever existed. So what was the point? Why bother doing anything?

Because there was one constant, one thing that gave existence in this cold universe a singular purpose. Truth.

Even through grieving for her father, and troubles at school, Bridge's affinity for mathematics and computers never wavered. They'd always been good subjects for her, but now she had an epiphany that mathematics was the true language of the universe. Numbers couldn't lie, couldn't deceive, couldn't be incorrect.

Numbers couldn't die.

Later, looking back, she understood that it had ultimately saved her from depression. She spent the summer holiday after her father's death locked in her room, her computer in constant activity, obsessed with code. Not just computer code, but DNA sequencing, astrophysics, quantum mechanics, chemical formulae: the codes of existence, of life itself. Cold, implacable, unassailable Truth.

Later that year she was arrested for the first time. A vegetarian message board she frequented linked to an exposé revealing a chain of abattoirs that followed inhumane and unhygienic practices. But instead of being penalised for it, the company continued to enjoy local subsidies, because the owner was related to a local councillor. All of the message board posters decried the scandal. Many of them bemoaned that the slaughterhouses' true conditions would never make the national news, because if they did then surely everyone who saw it would realise the error of their ways and go veggie. Some of them voiced a desire to shut down the abattoirs. One outlined a plan to sneak into a facility, steal chunks of raw meat waiting to be processed, and throw them at the councillor during a public meeting. But none of them actually did anything.

Bridge did.

It wasn't much — there was only so much a fifteen-year-old ensconced in her bedroom with a computer could do, no matter how determined — but it was something she knew none of the other board members were capable of. She found the website of the corrupt councillor, hacked into the disappointingly insecure server, and defaced the home page. An admission of guilt, a statement of his wrongdoings, screengrabs from the leaked surveillance footage that had exposed the abattoirs, and a hand-drawn diagram showing his relationship to the owner. Finally, she used GIMP to alter his welcoming photo. She painted devil horns over his head, added crudely-drawn blood leaking from his blank eyes and plastic smile, and superimposed a pile of cattle carcasses spilling out of his shirt.

When the police marched her out of her house into a waiting car, Bridge wasn't afraid or nervous. What she felt was something she'd never truly known before — the thrill that came from complete certainty, of knowing that she had absolutely, undeniably, done the right thing. She had told the truth.

The police wouldn't say how they caught her, but she knew immediately it was, ultimately, her own hubris. She'd been unable to resist bragging on the message board. Either someone from the police was monitoring the board, or another member had ratted her out. It didn't matter, because she had no intention of denying it. She was proud of what she'd done. She'd scaled the mountain and shouted from its summit.

They let her off with a fine, because of her youth and her family's standing in the community. Her mother cried that even in death, her father was still protecting Bridge from consequences. Their relationship, hardly stellar to begin with, had never been the same after that.

Later in life, Bridge would cringe at some of her actions during those complex years. But that thrill of certainty propelled her through, and saved her from herself. By her nineteenth birthday she'd known two people who'd committed suicide, three more who'd attempted it, and she suspected at least another two of having tried, but would never admit it. Whereas Bridge, despite what many assumed, never contemplated taking her own life. What was the sense in it, when any moment unwilling death could come calling? Bridge's unshakeable, inarguable, immovable belief in the value of truth was the closest thing she had to a religion.

Ironically, much of her work at SIS consisted of telling lies upon lies. But they were merely a means to an end, only to deceive the unworthy, and the truth itself never wavered. The problem was that, like quantum waves, truth could exist in a state of uncertainty before it collapsed into the real. And the truth here at Agenbeux was bifurcated, existing in two equally likely states until Bridge could climb the last stretch, crest the peak, and define reality by its observation.

Either Voclaine was the mole…or he wasn't. How certain could Bridge be?

That was the simple, but enormous, question that had nagged her the night before, sending her back to the spreadsheet to search for truth in numbers. She'd almost fallen asleep at her desk, with the secure partition still open, but managed to stay awake long enough to log out and crawl into bed. She slept quickly, before she even had a chance to set Radio 3 playing. And when she woke five minutes before her alarm, as always, the question was still there — as if it had merely paused while she slept, waiting for Bridge to regain consciousness so it could resume its endless loop.

If Voclaine wasn't the mole, who was?

She tried to maintain a semblance of normality when she arrived at the facility that morning, but couldn't shake the feeling everyone was staring at her, watching her. Surely Montgomery hadn't told them. That would be outrageous. She tested the waters by chatting to some project leads over first coffee, pretending she wanted to speak with Voclaine this morning, and did they happen to know where he was? They were amazed she hadn't heard that Voclaine hadn't been seen since he was marched into a room during security checks the previous evening. Nobody knew why, or where he was now. Bridge faked amazement while sighing with relief inside, and returned to her office to conduct her scheduled morning interview with Montgomery's secretary.

But she remained distracted throughout, unable to really focus on the secretary's answers. At one point she asked if Bridge was OK, as she looked unwell. She said she was fine, but she couldn't stop replaying the Voclaine interview in her mind, looking for something she'd missed. Some piece of truth she'd been unable to see the first time around, because she was overwhelmed by excitement and confusion that Voclaine could be the mole, as she'd suspected.

Voclaine fitted the profile. The mole had to be smart. Cunning, quiet, secretive — and the Frenchman was all those things. But the mole would also know how to deflect suspicion. How not to draw attention to himself by, say, destroying his private phone the moment someone discovered it. Was it possible Voclaine threw himself on his sword because he was guilty...but not of being a mole? Maybe he was embezzling. Maybe that 'family phone' was actually full of porn. Or maybe he was just paranoid.

The golden rule of tracing leaks was simple and eternal. *Cui bono?* Whose life was now made easier, if Bridge thought she had her man?

There was only one candidate.

But it was absurd, wasn't it? Montgomery was the most senior British civil servant at the facility, literally trusted with overseeing the entire software operation. If he was dodgy, wouldn't the MoD know? Wouldn't SIS, and Giles, know? Besides, he had no expertise. Montgomery's file credited him with experience at managing teams and projects, but there was no indication he knew the first thing about computer programming. Voclaine would know what to look for, where to find it, and understand what he was looking at. Whereas Montgomery, unless he was leading a double life as a hardcore coder, didn't know one end of a Unix linefeed from the other. Then again, would that matter? If Bridge's hunch was right, the mole wouldn't need to know what he was looking at. All he had to do was take photos of the screen.

A horrible thought crashed into her mind. Were there two moles?

Exphoria was an important project; something any number of hostile states would love to get their hands on if they knew it existed. The notion that it could have been infiltrated by more than one foreign actor was plausible, if unlikely. But the two most senior managers at the entire facility? That would be incredible.

And yet, and yet. She remembered watching through the glass, as Montgomery lost his composure while questioning Voclaine. As if he had something to prove. He'd said something, something that bothered her at the time but she'd put it out of her mind…

"Don't look at her, look at me." Of all the things he could have said to call Voclaine's attention away from the mirror, all the ways he could have phrased it, he said that. Don't look at *her*. Had he been trying to give Bridge away? Trying to signal to Voclaine that it was she who watched from behind the mirror, she who was behind the whole thing? He hadn't named Bridge, but it wouldn't take a spy to figure out that the new arrival from London asking

lots of questions was the *her* in question. Had he hoped to blow her cover, so she'd be forced to return to England?

It was the final straw that broke the back of her focus. She wouldn't get any more work done today. The secretary had nothing to hide, and her only remaining scheduled interviews were with Voclaine and Montgomery. Pointless. What could she do instead?

The answer came as simply as the question. She stepped out for a smoke break, almost expecting to see Voclaine loitering in his usual corner of the compound, puffing away on a cigarette. Despite everything, she found herself missing his sarcastic, cynical asides. When she returned inside, as she approached her office, something wasn't right. The door was open. But she was sure, absolutely sure, that she'd closed it behind her when she left for the compound. Hadn't she?

Montgomery stood at her desk, tapping on her laptop keyboard. He looked up as she entered, flustered.

"Can I help you, James?" Bridge asked.

"Ah, there you are. I was just, just wondering what your schedule was for today. If you still needed to talk to me. With Voclaine gone, you know." He moved to click something with the trackpad, but from this angle she couldn't see the screen.

"Please don't do that."

"Oh, I was closing your calendar. Sorry, sorry. I'll leave you to it."

Bridge stood aside to let him through the door. After he passed, she said, "James?"

He stopped, looked back. "Yes?"

"There's a copy of my schedule in your email."

He paused, then said, "Really? Ah, François must have dealt with that. I didn't realise. Well, very good. Carry on." He walked into his office, closing the door behind him.

Bridge checked the Dell. She hadn't logged out when she left the room, which was foolish, but there was nothing in the unrestricted partition that would give her away. If anyone thought to check the disk volume, they might wonder what the separate partition, small and unrelated to the OS, was for. But she doubted Montgomery would know where to find the partition map, much less wonder at its composition. She couldn't risk logging into it here at Guichetech, in case someone noticed it on the network, but made a mental note to check it as soon as she was outside the facility with a signal. And that, she now knew, would be very soon.

She spent the next twenty minutes with nonsense work, tidying up spreadsheets and pretending to think. But her mind had been made up since returning to find Montgomery standing at her laptop. She closed the lid, gathered her things, and knocked on his door.

"*Entrez,*" he called from inside. Bridge opened the door to find Montgomery alone, lost in thought. "Oh, um, Ms Short. How are things?"

"Mostly fine, but…I'm afraid I'm rather unwell this morning."

Montgomery seemed to palpably relax at the news, and adopted a sympathetic expression. "Oh, I'm sorry to hear that. Anything serious?"

"Stomach pains," she said meaningfully, hoping that would curtail any further questions. "I think maybe I should go back to the guest house and lie down for an hour or two, if that's OK?"

"Ah," said Montgomery, understanding. "Well, um, why not take the afternoon off, if you need it? After all," he half-smiled, "you have your man. You're just here for show, now, aren't you?"

"Yes, that's right. Just for show. Thank you, James." She smiled, and left to go and break into his apartment.

49

The Russian had put him in an impossible position.

He had no realistic way of obtaining more code, whether by taking photographs or any other method. He couldn't very well come clean to the MoD, or security services, and hope they'd be lenient. He knew they wouldn't, and they might throw him to the French authorities, who would almost certainly be worse. And he couldn't stay here. Sooner or later Bridget Short would realise that Voclaine wasn't the mole, and her attention would return to other suspects. Meanwhile, Montgomery had been foolish enough to make himself look suspicious when he tried to get into her laptop that morning. He was due to return to England in less than a week, after the final deadline. But did he really think he could string both the Russian and Ms Short along for all that time?

A knock at the door broke his train of thought. His heart sank when Ms Short entered. Surely she was here to accuse him, and that would be the end of it. But to his surprise, she merely complained of 'stomach pains', and asked to go home for a while. She didn't need to be more specific. Montgomery suggested she not only return to her guest house, but that she stay there and recuperate for the rest of the day. He couldn't believe his luck, but such a sudden proximity to catastrophe cemented the only realistic option open to him.

He had to run.

The Swiss account was still there, but for how long? The Russians didn't seem to realise it, but he was certain they would when they discovered he'd abandoned them, and so a plan formulated in his mind. He would drive to the bank in Switzerland, switch the money to a fresh account at a different bank, withdraw a large amount in cash, use some of it to buy a new car under a fake name, and keep the remainder hidden inside the vehicle while he found a place to live incognito.

He would take the gun the Russian had given Montgomery, in case anyone tried to stop him. He'd tossed it on his bedside table as soon as he returned home that night, but as the Russian had said, even unloaded it could be a useful bluff. And surely there were places in Switzerland, of all countries, where he could buy ammunition.

Finally, he would drive his existing hire car off a cliff, to fake his own death.

He thought of his family, then, and realised he was more saddened by the thought of never seeing his children again than his wife. Perhaps because he knew she'd be fine. If he was assumed to be dead, she could live off his life insurance and pension. She might even find a new husband, though he didn't like to think so. He wondered how much his children would grieve for him. They were still in high school, not yet blunted by the harsh winds of adulthood.

He waited until lunchtime, then took the mini-tablet from his desk drawer and placed it in his bag. He shouldn't take it out of the facility at all, but with Ms Short gone, nobody was checking for second devices at security. Besides, the tablet contained perhaps the last pictures of his family he would ever see, and its SD card held several hundred photos he hadn't yet given to the Russian. They might be useful as a bargaining chip if they hunted him down. Which they would surely do.

Perhaps he could sell the photos to the Chinese.

Montgomery shouldered the bag, took a deep breath, and headed back to his apartment.

50

"Thanks for joining me," said Andrea Thomson as the black cab drove slowly through East London. "Figured it couldn't hurt to have someone with me who knows what they're looking for."

"You mean a geek," said Steve Wicker.

Andrea smiled in return. "If you like."

"I thought Lisa Hebden was liaising with you and Six on this one?"

"Not any more."

Andrea had spent ten minutes on an early call with Hebden, and her boss Sundar Patel at GCHQ, explaining that they almost missed this very lead because they didn't follow SIS' instructions. Andrea stopped short of delivering the bollocking herself, leaving that to Patel, but made her feelings known. Then she asked to borrow Steve Wicker, one of the surveillance service's youngest and brightest, for a recce.

She'd worked with Steve several times before, turning to him when she needed something non-specialised from the surveillance division, and as the car rolled towards Shoreditch high street she reflected on how much he and Brigitte Sharp had in common, now that she thought about it. Both began as self-taught hackers running afoul of the law, and both seemed to operate on a combination of equal parts instinct and logic that marked them out from their colleagues in the computer divisions.

Andrea realised with surprise that the main difference between them was to be found in her own reactions. In Brigitte she found those qualities maddening, but in Steve she found them reassuring. No doubt Joan would have a field day with that, but gender aside, perhaps the difference in their ambitions was also a factor. Despite her protests, Brigitte obviously wanted to be a field officer. By contrast, Steve was never happier than when sitting behind a keyboard. He was only with Andrea now because, when she'd looked into the Shoreditch offices to which she'd followed the young man from the pub two nights ago, her guess had been proven right. The third floor did indeed belong to a tech startup, a relatively new outfit called 'SignalAir'. They were something to do with wifi technology, a subject way over her head, so she wanted someone there as a bullshit sniffer. And while the security service still employed some technical specialists, these days the best and brightest geeks were generally found at GCHQ.

"When did you call them?" Steve asked.

"Yesterday afternoon. Said I was from 'Hackney Modern Business Bureau', that we advocate on behalf of local businesses, and we're always recruiting for new members."

"Is that real?"

"The bureau? Oh, yes," said Andrea. "But only as a shell company with a PO box address, and some planted online puff pieces, thanks to some of your lot. It comes in handy from time to time." She produced a business card from her handbag: *Andrea Thomas, Outreach Manager, Hackney Modern Business Bureau.*

Steve smiled. "Do I get a card?"

"No," said Andrea, replacing it in her bag, "you're just the boffin. If he asks, tell him I pulled you out of the IT department so you could talk shop."

"Not far from the truth, then."

"Exactly the point. The closer you stay to the truth, the easier it is to lie your socks off without giving anything away."

"So the cover is that we're approaching now because they're a new business?"

"Incorporated four months ago. I told him we normally wait three months before contacting firms, just to make sure they're going to stick around."

"Him? Male secretary?"

"Not sure they have one. Startups are often just two guys doing everything themselves, right? The chap I spoke to was Nigel Marsh, one of the directors."

"And he agreed to see you right away. Does that strike you as odd? Is it possible he knows it was you that followed him?"

"Not a chance. We didn't speak directly in the pub, he didn't see me tailing him, and yesterday I was just a voice on the phone. But a visit from a local business org is an opportunity for him to look legit, so I'm not surprised he jumped at it."

"Or maybe he really is legit. You said you don't have anything conclusive. It could all be coincidence and mistaken identity."

Andrea nodded. "Sure, it could. But Giles Finlay and I both got the same vibe. There's more to this than meets the eye."

The cab dropped them off near the startup's corner entrance. While Andrea paid, Steve quickly looked around the street, glancing up at building corners, lamp posts, above road signs. "Plenty of cameras," he said. "Anything dodgy going on here, not much chance we'd miss it."

Andrea leaned past him and pressed the top button of an intercom buzzer next to the entrance keycard reader. "It's inside I'm worried about, not the street."

"Hello, SignalAir."

"Oh, hi there. It's Andrea Thomas, from the Bureau. I spoke to Nigel yesterday."

"Sure, sure. Third floor, yeah?"

The door made a buzzing noise, accompanied by the sound of

heavy locks disengaging. Andrea pushed it open and they entered the lobby. Just as before, it was cold and spartan. No desk, no receptionist, not even a sofa. A single dragon plant stood in the corner, next to the fire escape stair entrance, simultaneously in need of water and yet threatening to outgrow its pot.

The elevator was steel and glass, like the lobby. It arrived unbidden, sent by whomever had answered the intercom. They stepped inside, and Steve pushed the button for the top floor. "What's on the first two floors?" he asked.

Andrea shrugged. "More tech businesses, but they're older and unconnected, as far as I can tell."

The doors opened onto a spartan corridor of whitewashed brick and harsh lighting, with two doors; the fire escape stairs, and a code-locked entrance to SignalAir, complete with company logo 'plaque' made from an inkjet printout. The door opened, and the young bearded man Andrea had followed two nights before greeted them with a smile, extending his hand.

"Hi, I'm Nigel."

As they shook hands, Andrea looked for any trace that the young man might recognise her, but saw nothing. "Andrea Thomas, and this is my colleague Steve. He's the technical one," she smiled.

"Right on, brother," said Nigel. "Come in, come in."

The office was open plan, with whitewashed brick surfaces, a concrete floor, wall-mounted wiring, and exposed ducting in the rafters. The bare minimum necessary to make a functioning office, thought Andrea, which was typical of tech startups. The business itself seemed to follow a similar ethos, with five desks arranged in a quarter of the room, and only two that looked to be in use. The wall next to the door was lined with shelves, empty except for a few binders. Against another wall were several filing and storage cabinets. One was open, revealing stationery. A third wall was an ad hoc kitchenette area, with a kettle, small fridge, sink, and enough crockery for three people. The final wall held windows looking south, towards the City, in front of which was a standing workbench covered in computer chips, circuit boards, and antennae. Andrea had no idea what they were, and made a note to ask Steve later. There was nobody else in the office. "Is it just you here, Mr Marsh…?"

"Nigel, yeah? There are three of us here normally, but Andy's on holiday and Charlie's in Reading for a meeting. We hot desk, so none of us need to be here in the building, yeah? Just me holding the fort today. Tea?"

It had been a long time since the kitchenette area had been cleaned properly, and Andrea was sorely tempted to decline. But that would seem unusual, and she didn't want any of this to strike young Nigel as odd. So she said, "Yes, thanks. Milk, no sugar."

"Same," said Steve, and looked around at the workbench and shelves. "So what are you working on here, Nigel? Something to do with eight-oh-two-eleven, is that right?" *802.11* was the technical term for the set of standards defining wifi signals. Steve used it casually, without explanation.

Nigel didn't miss a beat. "Sure, sure," he said, pouring the kettle, "but we're not working with the alliance. It's kind of a parallel protocol, yeah? Like, we're theorising range extension through quantum state information in the bandwidth. It's amazing, as if you're stretching the wavelength out for more effective penetration, yeah?" He moved his hands apart, like pulling taut an invisible string, to demonstrate.

Steve seemed sceptical. "That sounds ambitious. How far along are you?"

Nigel laughed. "Early days, brother, early days. But it takes real disruption to stand out now, yeah? Andy's the physicist, the science man. Charlie's the coder. It's him you want to speak to if you're all about the hacking. I'm just an entrepreneur, but I know the jargon and I get the mindset."

Andrea nodded, understanding. "You're the man who sweet-talks the investors and lets the others be creative while you take care of the business side."

"Sure, sure, and this is such an amazing place to do it. So… vibrant." He said it with reverence, and if there was any lingering doubt in Andrea's mind that Nigel Marsh was an archetypal class tourist, it was dispelled when he handed Steve his tea and said, "Where you from, brother?"

"Croydon," Steve replied.

"Sure, sure, but I mean where are you *from*, yeah? What's your *homeland*?"

"My mum and dad were both from Kingston," said Steve, with only the hint of a sigh. "But they met after they came to London."

"Right on," Nigel smiled. "What an amazing world, yeah?"

Andrea would have happily punched Nigel right in his smug, bearded hipster face herself, but Steve was remarkably sanguine about the whole thing, and for now they had to play along.

Play along with what, though? There was something off about Nigel, and not just his class tourism. But SignalAir's lack of substance, or tangible products, meant nothing. There were plenty of tech companies, some of them pulling down millions in investments, with no more staff or equipment than an anonymous, archetypal 'new Shoreditch' office like this. As they made small talk, and she gave Nigel her fake business card in preparation to leave, she realised there was nothing here she could put her finger on, nothing to make her any more suspicious of him than she already was. Nothing except an unease deep inside that said: *something is wrong.*

In the cab heading back, Steve laughed off the 'homeland' conversation as nothing he hadn't heard before, and, inevitably, from rich white kids. "Bet you anything he spent six months backpacking around Asia," said Steve, "and now he thinks that was enough to erase all his racial privilege. I mean, he probably lived in a yurt for a whole month, so he might as well have grown up working on a plantation, yeah?"

Andrea laughed at Steve's imitation. "I'm just impressed you managed to hold on to your tea. So what's your take? Racism aside, does he seem on the level to you? I'm no techie, but that stuff about quantum waves sounds like sci-fi."

"Yeah, but..." Steve shrugged. "I mean, I once knew a bloke who managed to encode tiny bits of data into DNS traffic, so I'd never say it's impossible. But what Marsh is proposing would be a massive breakthrough in physics. They'd be legends, potential Nobel winners."

"Hmmm. That kind of fame doesn't exactly sit well with covert ops. Could they maybe sell the tech to foreign actors? Would it have any application in guerrilla tactics, maybe drones?"

"I guess long-range ad hoc control, without the need for extenders or satellites, would be something." Then he jerked, as if startled. "Hang on. Why drones?"

Andrea grimaced in apology. "Can't say; sorry. Would it make a difference?"

"It might be nothing." Steve pulled out his Nexus and started typing. "But let me check with Patel."

51

Bridge went straight back to the guest house from Guichetech. She wanted to ensure anyone following would see her do as she'd said, but she also knew she'd need items from her go-bag to break into Montgomery's flat.

In the room, she opened the Dell and signed into the secure partition, to check he hadn't tampered with anything while he was messing around in her fake calendar. God, what an arrogant prick. It would have been bad enough before, when he thought she was an HR inspector, but to start messing around now that he knew she was here undercover —

FROM: Mourad, Henri

TO: Dunston, Emily / Finlay, Giles / Sharp, Brigitte

SUBJECT: Where□s Thumper?

Bridge froze, her finger hovering above the trackpad button as she re-read the subject line. 'Thumper' was the code name they'd assigned to Voclaine after his arrest. What the hell? She clicked through.

Arrived Agenbeux local police 1015. No sign of Thumper, officers clueless - no idea who he was, said he was never there. Unable to locate senior officer, refused help.

Please advise if further action needed, but I have MC to follow up (see H/PAR).

Bridge guessed 'MC' stood for *Matériel Chaud*, the codename of the case he was pursuing before Mourad got roped in as Bridge's backup. She didn't know what the case was, much less where it might take him. But the important part of the email was right there in the subject line. Where was François Voclaine? She'd watched the local police come and pick him up from Guichetech herself. Someone from that station had taken Emily Dunston's call, agreed to come and arrest Voclaine at the facility, and sent officers to do so. But now they were denying it had ever happened. How? Did Voclaine bribe them all to let him escape?

The walls of the room slid sideways, skewing off-axis as Bridge fought to stay calm. Had she second-guessed herself one too many times, and got it all wrong? Perhaps it really was as simple as it looked, and Voclaine was the mole. He had backing from a hostile actor, and they'd somehow been alerted to his arrest. Perhaps the local police had been in their pocket all along, paid off and ready to protect Voclaine if necessary. She was angry at herself for not following through, for staying incognito and trusting the local authorities. If she'd gone with him to the police station, stayed with him till Mourad arrived, maybe questioned him herself... She could have gone with them to Paris, left behind this bloody place and been home in time for the weekend...

No, surely she was overreacting. This was a simple administrative error, and she'd find Voclaine stewing at a different police station, in the next town over. And if that turned out to be the case, she'd kick herself if she wasted this opportunity to check up on Montgomery. It was still possible he was the mole, and Voclaine was innocent, at least of espionage. The truth remained suspended in a superstate, waiting to collapse and become reality.

All it would take was one last scramble to clear the mountain summit.

She typed a quick reply —

`worrying, but hopefully simple admin error? will investigate`

— And logged out, turning to her rolling suitcase. She flipped it on its front, with the steel tubes that encased the telescopic handle uppermost, and took a 10 cent euro coin from her purse. At the base of each tube was a horizontal depression in the metal, an innocuous moulding artefact. Bridge fitted the edge of the coin into the depression in the left-hand tube, and turned it anticlockwise. It was stiff, but it turned, and half a dozen revolutions later the hidden bolt came free, allowing the base of the steel tube to slide down and reveal a small, hollow space. Crammed inside was a Ziploc bag, which she removed and opened. Packed into the bag were a length of high-tensile monofilament, a solid-state micro camera, a tiny wireless audio bug and receiver, an LED flashlight the size of two matchsticks, five hundred US dollars, and a set of lockpicks. Bridge hadn't expected to use any of these items, or to need the emergency Ziploc at all, while here in Agenbeux. But it was standard issue in OIT luggage, and now she was glad of it.

Her clothes were a different matter. As the job was supposed to be observation only, OpPrep hadn't kitted her out with any serious gear, so she'd have to make do with what she'd brought of her own casual clothes. She'd worn most of them to Izzy's farm, but hadn't yet put them through a wash, so she rifled through the pile and pulled out a few things. Two minutes later she was wearing black jeans and a plain black t-shirt. She found a pair of clean socks, pulled her own casual walking boots over them, and finished with her leather jacket, dropping the emergency Ziploc in one of the pockets. She only really needed the lockpicks, but as they were probably the most incriminating thing in the bag, she might as well take the whole thing.

She wished she had some kind of hat, but didn't, so donned sunglasses instead. Then she caught sight of herself in the mirror by the door, and suppressed a laugh. All she needed was big hair, some purple lipstick, and she'd look eighteen again. Except when she was eighteen, the only break-ins she did were virtual ones on computer servers. Now she was about to do it for real. She took an elasticated hair band from the dresser and scraped her hair back into a ponytail as she exited the room.

Montgomery's apartment was on the other side of town. Agenbeux was small enough that she could have walked, but it would take at least twenty minutes, and the midday heat would tire her before she got there. Taking her car was a risk. If anyone really was following her, they'd know she wasn't having a 'lie down' after all. But being followed like that would mean the game was up anyway. Better to try and fail than do nothing and let it all collapse around her.

Nobody appeared to be watching her as she left the guest house, and she didn't notice anyone tailing her car across town. By the time she arrived at Montgomery's apartment, she was confident it was merely her usual paranoia that was warming the back of her neck. The address led her to a row of three-storey townhouses, so she parked around the corner and took the driving gloves from the dashboard compartment, shoving them in her pocket.

His apartment was on the top floor. The upper floors of each house had balconies, and below the top floor these were roofed with tiles. Climbing up them to break in through a window wouldn't be all that difficult, but doing so without being seen or heard would. Instead, she gambled that a town like Agenbeux didn't expect crime, and walked right up the steps to the front door. Sure enough, the main house door wasn't locked, although the lack of security cameras was an unexpected bonus. There was a hallway, no lobby, and no elevator either. Just a stairway, leading up through the house. She took the steps quickly but quietly, not wanting to attract attention, but doing her best to look like she belonged here. Then she remembered it was lunchtime, and relaxed. Most of the residents were probably at work, and those who were here would be busy eating.

At the top of the stairs was a single door. The apartment took up the whole floor, like a penthouse suite. Very nice, thought Bridge, and wondered if the project accountants back in London knew what Montgomery's expenses were paying for. She pulled on the driving gloves, took the Ziploc from her pocket, and removed the lockpick tools. With a final glance over her shoulder, and keeping an ear out for any sudden noise on the stairwell, she set to work.

She'd been surprised, during the first Breaking & Entering class at the Loch, how easy lock-picking was. She'd always imagined it to be a precise, delicate skill, like the old myths of safecrackers with stethoscopes carefully listening for falling tumblers. In fact, with most modern locks it was more of a brute force act; a simple matter of keeping rotational pressure on the plug with a torsion wrench, then shoving a pick inside and lifting the pins until it opened. Advanced classes for more secure and industrial mechanisms would take longer, but by the end of the first morning Bridge and her classmates had mastered the basic skills well enough that they could now open, the instructor gleefully informed them, eighty per cent of all domestic locks.

Montgomery's apartment was no exception. She felt the plug turn a fraction of a millimetre with each pin release, then rotate completely with a satisfying click. Picking the lock had taken less than fifteen seconds, and now all she had to worry about was a burglar alarm. But this was an old town, and old-fashioned with it. The kind of place where her mother would insist people still left their front doors unlocked and were never burgled. Bridge seriously doubted that, but regardless, it wasn't the sort of place where rented apartments had pre-installed alarms. She slipped inside, closing the door behind her, and found herself in a hallway that opened out on the lounge. When she saw the state of the place, though, she was shocked.

The second law of thermodynamics states that the universe tends towards entropy; that order is more difficult to maintain than chaos, and such chaos is sometimes irreversible. Bridge had once demonstrated the second law to Izzy by dropping a tea cup on the floor, and asking her sister to imagine how much more energy it would now take to reassemble the pieces, let alone make an entirely new cup, compared to the ease with which it had fallen. Izzy just sighed, and handed her a dustpan and brush. But, sibling mockery or not, Bridge regarded the second law as an important universal constant. She often used it to make a joke of people's reactions to her desk, or apartment, or the contents of her handbag. If the universe was heading inexorably toward entropy and chaos anyway, Bridge was just doing her bit to help it along.

In a similar fashion, she'd assumed a single middle-aged man, living alone away from home for months, would tend towards that same entropic state and follow a kind of 'second law of manhood'. But, whether he was a spy or not, James Montgomery was definitely some kind of lawbreaker. His apartment was spotless, cleaned to within an inch of its life, and squared away like an army barracks. If she didn't know better from his record, Bridge would have assumed he served in the military. She ran a gloved finger over the surface of an occasional table, and it came up clean. Even the space behind the TV was immaculate. Did he have a cleaner who came round and did the place? If so, the longer Bridge spent here, the greater the risk of her being discovered. But surely a cleaner was too much of a potential security risk for Montgomery to employ. Bridge began to think she'd misjudged him.

Until she saw the gun on the bedside table.

It was an MP-443 Grach, standard-issue Russian military. Bridge was no firearms expert, but the Grach, and its predecessor the Makarov, were among the first weapons that intelligence officers were trained to identify. She was actually surprised it wasn't a Makarov. Officially the Grach had replaced them years ago, but Makarovs had been in service in the USSR and former Eastern Bloc for so long that many soldiers still carried them out of habit, and the European black market was awash with them. Buying one was as easy as clicking a link on a darknet website and collecting it from whichever dive bar the local criminals patronised.

Bridge found it hard to imagine Montgomery entering any kind of dive bar, but the very presence of the gun on his bedside table implied there was a secret side to him. And unlike Makarovs, buying a black-market Grach was neither easy nor cheap. What else did this officious little man hide from the world, she wondered? But, much as it raised serious questions about his character — and was surely enough to justify interrogating him — the Grach was, so to speak, no smoking gun. It didn't prove he was the mole.

She was about to replace the pistol on the bedside table when she heard the front door unlock.

The bedroom door was open behind her, and in a smaller apartment she might have had a clear line of sight to the front door. But here, she couldn't see who was entering, and they couldn't see her. Had she been wrong about the cleaner? She quickly concocted a cover story: she was Montgomery's French mistress, she'd spent the night here, she'd slept in all morning, and now she was just leaving, *merci beaucoup et au revoir*. So long as the cleaner didn't somehow recognise Bridge, she should be able to get away fast and worry about the consequences later.

But it wasn't the cleaner.

Pressed against the wall, craning her neck to see through the door, allowed her to see a sliver of mirror in the interior hallway. Reflected in it was the unmistakeable figure of Montgomery. What the hell was he doing back here at lunchtime? He usually went to a café in Agenbeux. Bridge had never heard him, or anyone else, suggest he ever returned home for lunch. And yet, here he was.

She instinctively thumbed the safety catch on the Grach, not taking her eyes from the mirror. Montgomery had moved out of sight, into the kitchen. She heard the sounds of him opening cupboards, rifling through drawers, looking for something. Bridge moved to the door, still watching the mirror. Montgomery's kitchen search was keeping him occupied. Good. If she was quick she could sneak out and, missing gun notwithstanding, he'd be none the wiser. She contemplated tossing the gun on the bed, but a man as neat as Montgomery would know it was out of place, and she didn't have time to return it to the bedside table. Better to take it with her, let him think he'd been burgled, or mislaid the weapon. She could return later for a better look around.

It was a nice theory, while it lasted.

She made it through the interior hallway, into the lounge. Montgomery's briefcase lay open on the couch, suggesting he'd returned to find something he'd forgotten to take to the office. She was almost out, just passing the very clean occasional table, when she heard footsteps behind her and Montgomery call out, "*Qui va là?*" Bridge continued to the door, not turning to look back. If he was asking, that meant he didn't recognise her, and if she could get out quickly, he'd never know it was her.

Another nice theory that didn't last.

She knew she wasn't going to make a clean exfil in the split second before it struck, as she struggled to identify an odd sound. She was already ducking on instinct, but while her perception was working at double speed, her own movements were merely normal, and it was only immediately after impact that she realised the sound had been an almost imperceptible *whistling*.

The cup glanced off the back of her head, smashing to pieces as it hit the floor. She stumbled, more from shock than pain, as her mind struggled to catch up with events. Montgomery had… thrown a cup at her? There it was, in a hundred entropy-fuelled pieces on the floor. She put out a hand to stop herself from colliding with the front door, and the impact pushed the Grach's hard steel into her palm. Behind her she heard Montgomery gasp, followed by a sound she could now identify with ease. Footsteps, fast and hard on the wooden floor. He was running towards her.

Bridge turned, letting herself fall back against the front door so she could brace herself, and raised the gun. "Stop," she said, but he didn't. Montgomery had picked up his briefcase, and was swinging it above his head like a mallet. His face was a strange, twisted mixture of surprise and fury, and Bridge had no doubt in her mind that he would beat her to death if he could. She had no choice, but she needed him alive to interrogate. She aimed for his knee and pulled the trigger…

The firing pin clicked. Twice. The gun wasn't loaded, and Montgomery had known all along.

He caught her with a downward swing of the briefcase, striking her head and one shoulder. It was only a briefcase, but it was surprisingly heavy. Combined with Montgomery's desperation, plus her own surprise at the gun's failure to fire, it made a blow strong enough that she fell to the floor, the gun escaping from her fingers. The case burst open on impact, spilling its contents, and as Bridge fell with them, she couldn't help identifying what she saw; three briefing folders, two notepads, three ballpoint pens, a roll of English mints, a mini-tablet, a micro-USB cable and power brick, and two hardback novels.

Montgomery stood over her in the narrow hallway and shouted, "I knew it!" She wasn't sure what he'd known, but there'd be time to ask later. Right now she was more concerned with regaining control of the situation, if she'd ever had it to start with. From this position on the floor there were limited options to attack a standing opponent, but Bridge knew them well enough, and decided that in the narrow confines of the hallway, simplicity would carry the day.

She kicked out, bracing her shoulder against the door for extra leverage as she slammed the sole of her boot against his shin. It didn't crack, but it made him yelp and stagger back, giving Bridge enough time to scramble to her knees and deliver a rising punch to his kidneys. It was minimal power compared to what she could do while standing, but she was gambling that Montgomery wasn't a practised fighter, and not used to taking body blows. Sure enough, he doubled over in pain, giving Bridge time to get to her feet. She moved around, standing tall and imposing behind him. "That's enough, James," she said between breaths, "you're coming with me." She reached out a hand for his shoulder.

"No!" he roared and, still doubled over, rushed at her. His head and shoulders slammed into her chest, driving them both back into the lounge. Bridge stumbled, bracing herself for impact with the floor, but instead hit the back of the couch and fell backwards over it. She rolled with it, landing on the floor. Montgomery, holding a hand over his kidneys, limped round the back of the couch and reached for a wooden fruit bowl on the coffee table. While Bridge regained her feet he picked it up and tipped it, apples and oranges falling to the floor around him.

They seemed on equal terms. Both winded, both standing, with only the coffee table between them. But Bridge knew she had the advantage, and not only because of her height. Nevertheless, she had to finish this as fast as she could. The less damage she did to Montgomery, the easier it would be to persuade him she'd only used minimal, necessary force, and to confess his crimes. He swung his arm back, confirming in her mind that he lacked CQC training; to an experienced fighter, any backswing was a telegram to your opponent, telling them what you were about to do. She waited for Montgomery to commit to his forward swing, then immediately took a step forwards to bring herself inside the length of his arm. She half-turned, pivoting to face the swinging arm, and raised a forearm to block the overswing as the attack missed its target. Meanwhile, Bridge's free arm swung up and back, elbow first, travelling with the full momentum of her turning body. Montgomery's nose broke on impact.

He staggered back, moaning, and dropped the fruit bowl so he could nurse his useless, bleeding nose. The bowl clattered harmlessly to the floor, but Montgomery stepped blindly onto one of the fallen apples and twisted his ankle. He lost his balance as his leg buckled under him. He fell backwards, cracking his head on the corner of the occasional table with a hard, sickening crunch.

Bridge stood over him, ready for his counterattack. He stared up at her in silence. She stared back, and finally realised no counterattack was coming — not now, and not ever again.

James Montgomery was dead.

In the Good column: she could now take as long as she wanted to search his apartment, and find more evidence to incriminate him. In the Bad column: MI6 could no longer interrogate him to find out who he was delivering information to.

Good: if Montgomery really was the mole, his spying days were over.

Bad: if he wasn't the mole, Bridge's spying days were over. Possibly also her days as a free woman.

Good: …she was struggling to think of any other silver linings, if she was honest.

Bad: plenty more in that column, though. Where to start?

First, she wondered if she should hide the body. But Montgomery's sudden disappearance would raise as many questions as the discovery of his corpse. Plus — and here was one for the Good column — she'd worn gloves the whole time. Her prints weren't on the Grach pistol. There was nothing to directly tie her to the scene during the inevitable police investigation.

Next, she considered using his landline to call Giles. She'd left her phone at the guest house, and while Mourad was closer, the only number she knew by heart was Vauxhall. But that would absolutely tie her to the scene, and not through fingerprints but simple deduction. Nobody would believe that Montgomery, if he was a spy, had made a sudden phone call to the very people he was betraying, at the exact same time he was apparently fighting for his life. Whitehall was pretty good at spin, but even the powers that be would struggle to explain that away. No, phone calls would have to wait. The most important thing Bridge could do right now was gather more evidence.

As she chased down these cascading, branching possibilities of action, her unconscious mind replayed the fight on a constant loop, a natural side effect of the residual adrenaline still pumping through her body. Every moment, every detail, held in a moment of clarity. The sensation and surprise when the cup hit her, the impact of her boot on Montgomery's shin vibrating through her body, her world turning upside-down as she fell back over the couch, the sensation of Montgomery's briefcase on her already-bruising face, the apples and oranges falling from the bowl…

Other things had fallen, too. She walked to the entrance hallway, where Montgomery had hit her with the briefcase, spilling its contents on the floor. There was one item in there, something odd, that she'd glimpsed during that moment of pain.

A mini-tablet.

Its screen had cracked when it hit the wooden floor, but when she thumbed the power button the device lit up, still working. And it was another 'second device', the very thing for which she'd called out Voclaine, that Montgomery had neglected to mention. More worrying was the unmistakeable small glass dot on the rear. It had a camera.

She slid the tablet inside her hoodie, and wondered again about Voclaine. Every revelation made him look more innocent. But if so, where was he? Why escape from police custody? Why break his own second device, the presumably incriminating iPhone, rather than let security inspect it?

Lost in thought, Bridge almost missed the sound of footsteps outside the front door. Two sets, at least. There was mumbling in French, then a key in the lock —

She backed towards the lounge, too slowly. The door opened to reveal an elderly landlord, keyring in hand, staring at her in confusion. Behind him stood a curiously familiar *gendarme*. It took Bridge a moment to recognise him from the passport photo Giles had sent her.

Marko Novak.

52

Henri Mourad eventually admitted to 'GL' that he wasn't Tunisian, hoping it would stop her making half-drunken passes at him whenever they met. Instead she seemed to find the idea of sleeping with an Algerian *très exotique*, and persisted in her efforts. On the bright side, she didn't withdraw the discount, and Henri suspected he might need it as she led him through a noisy, crowded sailors' bar. At the back of the room an older man with a pale, rough face sipped a glass of dark beer.

GL addressed him only as "Old Philippe", and while he wouldn't elaborate further, GL vouched for him as a long-time friend. Old Philippe had retired from the sea years before, following a mild stroke, and now worked out his years on the docks, supplementing his retirement fund with a well-earned reputation for discreet handling of 'green routes'. Not so discreet that he wouldn't accept a higher payment to spill the beans, mind, and after a furtive exchange of euros he did just that.

"Two of them; Spanish-looking," he said. "They had a package they wanted routing to England, and I sorted passage for it via Guernsey."

"When was this?"

"Last night? Maybe the night before." Old Philippe shrugged, and swigged his beer.

Henri cursed. One way or another he'd missed the package, and probably the men too. "Where's the boat now? Could it still be in Guernsey?"

"Portsmouth by now. It might sit there for a while, though."

"And the men? They were carrying forged passports; did they travel with the package?"

"They were in no fit state to go anywhere," said the old man with a cold, dry laugh. "One looked like he was going to pass out right where you're standing. Green as grass, he was."

"What was wrong with him?"

Philippe raised an eyebrow at GL. "Does your toyboy think I'm a doctor?" GL snorted with laughter.

Henri remembered something Marcel had said during their last meeting. "You're the contact they were directed to from Toulouse, aren't you? They were looking for someone who could help them smuggle an item from this port."

"I have friends everywhere."

Henri doubted that. "Could they still be here in Saint-Malo? Did they ask about hospitals, or where to get help without attracting attention?"

"The only thing they asked about was handling procedures for the package."

GL nudged Henri. "This is why I think it's your men. Go on, Philippe."

"I was about to, if you'd let me speak, woman," said Philippe, taking another swig of beer. "They insisted it not be opened, which is normal enough. But they also wanted to make sure it wouldn't be scanned, at any time, and that costs extra."

"You mean scanned with X-rays?"

"X-rays, microwaves, they even wanted assurances it wouldn't get sniffed by dogs. I don't know what's in that package, but if it's just drugs I'll eat my gloves."

"And yet you agreed to ship it anyway."

Old Philippe shrugged. "Money is money."

Henri balled his fists in frustration. "And they're probably already halfway back to Portugal. Dammit."

Philippe reached into his jacket and pulled out a piece of paper. "Get over yourself and pay me another hundred euros," he said.

The paper was folded; impossible to see what it contained. "What's that?" Henri asked.

"I wasn't born yesterday, boy. I made a copy of their initial manifest. All the way from...well. That would be telling."

Henri looked to GL. She shrugged and said, "It's your money. How badly do you want this?"

He sighed, knowing she was right, and that he had little choice. He gave Philippe the extra cash in exchange for the photocopy, unfolded the paper, and scanned the form. It was unfamiliar, and he knew almost nothing about shipping conventions or lingo, but he didn't need to in order to find what the old sailor had teased him with.

At first he was surprised, then confused, and finally deeply concerned. These emotions must have run over his face in quick succession, because GL whispered in his ear, "Come on, babe, you're a gangster like I'm a Barbie doll. What is this, DGSI?"

Henri kissed her on the cheek, excused himself, and ran outside to call Emily Dunston.

53

For the second time in ten minutes, Bridge was caught by surprise. Had the landlord heard the fight, and called the police? What were the odds that the responding *gendarme* would be Novak, of all people? Or was this no coincidence?

Novak stepped inside, never taking his eyes off Bridge as he bent to retrieve the Grach pistol from the hallway floor. Behind him, the wide-eyed landlord backed away down the stairs. Novak held the pistol by his side, pointed down at the floor, and pulled the trigger. Once, twice, three times.

He already knew it wasn't loaded. He expected it to be empty. And that could only mean one thing: that Novak knew James Montgomery, and knew he kept an unloaded Grach in his apartment. Bridge's mind began speculating wildly based on that conclusion: Novak may have given Montgomery the gun; this all but confirmed Novak as the mole's French contact; Novak's position as a *gendarme* gave him a licence to move and go almost wherever he wished; how many other Agenbeux police officers might be involved in this? And, and, and… But the facts as they stood were simple.

Montgomery was dead. Novak was here. And Bridge had been caught red-handed.

She scrambled back, ducking around the corner of the lounge, and listened to Novak's steady footsteps approaching down the hallway.

"What is your name, miss? Why are you in Mr Montgomery's apartment?"

His accent was so good, it took her a moment to realise he was speaking English. He knew damn well who she was.

With the sun overhead, the strongest light came from the landing outside the apartment, throwing a long shadow in front of Novak. Bridge watched it carefully, edging closer to the corner where she still stood with her back pressed against the wall, its shadow hiding her own.

Before Novak could round the corner, Bridge pivoted on the ball of her foot, swinging her other leg up and around with her full bodyweight behind it. She was tall, but Novak was taller, and her boot struck him on the shoulder. He flinched, surprised by the blow, and grabbed for Bridge's foot. She'd expected that, and retracted her leg immediately, but before she could plant it on the ground Novak followed through and barged into her, leading with the same shoulder. She staggered back, and he swung at her with the empty Grach, the pistol butt missing her face by millimetres.

He took one more step, then stopped when he saw Montgomery's body on the floor.

Bridge saw her opening and kicked out, landing a blow square in Novak's kidneys. He crumpled to the ground, dropping the useless Grach. She moved in for another strike, but he recovered quickly. With a single smooth action he pulled and extended his baton, swinging it at her knee. Bridge's leg buckled as it hit, and she dropped to the ground. Suddenly Novak was on her, holding her down with one hand, the other lashing out with the baton. She raised her arms, taking the stinging blows on her forearms instead of her face.

"So he was right about you," said Novak, tossing the baton aside, and now Bridge noticed a slight accent. St Petersburg? She couldn't be sure, and this wasn't the time to wonder. His breath was a sour mixture of alcohol and German cigarettes, and as he closed his thick hands around her neck, she couldn't help noticing how smooth and uncalloused his hands were, more like an office worker than a stereotypical Russian thug. It all reminded her of an old boyfriend at uni, and not one she particularly wanted to remember.

She tried to break his grip, or roll him off her body, but it was no use. He was too strong, and too heavy, to prise off easily. He squeezed, slowly but firmly. Bridge flailed her arms around, reaching for something, anything, to use as a weapon. Her fingers touched something hard, solid. Darkness blurred the edges of her vision, all of the focus on Novak's smiling, gloating face. She walked the solid thing toward her by her fingertips, closed her hand around it, swung it up and around at Novak's head without a second thought, because there was no time for thought.

The wooden fruit bowl hit the side of Novak's head with a satisfyingly deep crack.

It stunned him enough for Bridge to push him off and roll out from under him. Gasping for breath, she pulled herself to her feet and staggered toward the hallway. She tried to call out to the landlord, but all she could manage was a hoarse croak. Surely he must have heard the commotion. Would he just assume it was the police going about their business, or would he come to check? If he did, would Novak kill him, too?

Strong, bulky arms closed around her from behind, swung and tossed her back into the apartment. She tried to find her footing, failed, and fell into the kitchen. She pulled herself to her feet, catching a glance out of the window. She expected to see *gendarmerie* cars, maybe a patrol van, in the street outside, and Novak's colleagues rushing into the building. But there was nothing.

The window exploded behind her. Novak had drawn his sidearm, a SIG Sauer SP2022, and this gun was definitely loaded. But he was unsteady on his feet, still reeling from the blow to his head, throwing his aim off. He took another step toward Bridge, steadying himself, ready to fire. She grabbed the nearest thing on the countertop, an aerosol spray cleaner, and clamped hard on the nozzle. He winced and coughed as the spray covered his face, shooting blind again. This time he barely missed Bridge's head, sending a bullet into the wall two inches from her head.

She closed on him, still spraying the aerosol, grabbing for the gun with her other hand. Novak screwed his eyes tight against the cleaner spray, and Bridge saw tears streaming down his face, but he held onto the pistol with a grim, determined strength. He squeezed the trigger again, shattering a line of splashback tiles above the counter.

The spray was running out. Bridge adjusted the aerosol can and drove it into Novak's face base first, then bit into his hand. He cried out and finally dropped the pistol. Bridge braced herself on the counter and kicked him in the chest. He rolled with the blow, and she crouched to retrieve the gun.

As her hand closed around it, Novak grabbed and swung a cooking pan from the stove, slamming it into her shoulder. She staggered back, firing at him as he continued forward. The bullet hit him in the thigh, and he cried out. But his momentum carried him through, falling into her before she could brace herself, and now Bridge fell back, expecting to slam into the wall, but there was no wall, only the empty hole of the shattered window, nothing to stop her from tumbling backwards, out and down…

To land on the tiled roof of the balcony below. She groaned with pain and rolled onto her front, looking up and down the street as she ran through options in her mind. She could turn back, kill Novak, and then escape back down the stairs. But the Russian had proven a hard opponent, and what if the landlord saw her leaving, after all this noise and destruction? Worse, what if the rest of the street came out to see what the noise was? At this moment the road was empty, but lunchtime or not, that surely couldn't last. Someone must have called the police. Every moment she spent here was another moment she risked arrest and, no doubt, a fatal 'accident' in custody.

Or she could run from this position. She was now outside, Novak had a bullet in his leg, and she had his gun. More worryingly, Novak somehow knew who she was. If the police weren't already searching for her, the murder of a *gendarme* would put every other policeman from here to Lyon on the lookout for Bridget Short. Not that she intended to keep that name, compromised as it now was. There was a clean passport, under a new ID, in the lining of her case back at the guest house. She didn't have time to change her appearance, but a new name would give her a short head start over Novak and the police. She probed her knee with her fingers, relieved to find it was only bruised, not broken, from Novak's baton.

Her mind made up, Bridge scrambled over the edge of the roof to land on the balcony below, then climbed over the parapet and dropped the final three metres to the street. The landing sent a shockwave up her legs, and as she limped to her car, Bridge sighed, knowing she wouldn't be able to rest for several hours at least. The guest house would be a short pitstop to collect clothes, the emergency passport, and her phone. Then she'd have to hit the road before the police figured out where she was staying, and call Mourad in Paris to be ready for her.

She climbed into the Fiat, fumbled with the keys, and started the engine. Before the car was fully in gear she stomped on the accelerator, burning tyre marks on the road as she screeched away. Turning the corner, she glanced in the rear-view mirror and saw Novak limp into the street from Montgomery's building, shouting at her to stop.

Instead, she accelerated.

54

The police were waiting for her.

It was mid afternoon, broad daylight, and the local *gendarmes* evidently weren't used to being discreet. Two marked vans were parked right on her street, while two uniformed officers stood guard outside the guest house. Presumably that meant the remaining officers were inside, searching her room. Watching through sunglasses from her car parked far down the other side of the street, Bridge's stomach dropped. Had she left the suitcase's hidden compartment exposed? Was the Ziploc still on her dresser, half-empty? No, that was here, in her pocket. But the Dell laptop and HTC phone were both inside, along with her emergency passport. She had to assume they were all now compromised. Everything in that room was lost to her.

Alone and outgunned, surrounded by the enemy, lost in the desert…

Bridge suppressed the thought. While there were similarities to Doorkicker, this was not the same situation. Yes, she'd completely screwed the mission. Yes, the mole and main witness was dead. Yes, she was now blown, and on the run. But this time, she didn't just speak the language; she looked and sounded native. And the $500 in her pocket could be exchanged for euros, with which she could buy a whole new wardrobe and hairstyle.

How much did they know? That was the real question. Nobody in the DGSE or DGSI had been informed of Bridge's mission. If the police discovered she was SIS, they'd call her a spy. If she could make them listen, and let her call London, she could prove who she was… but that assumed Giles would back her up. Sending an officer undercover into foreign territory, without declaring them to the host country, was a textbook definition of espionage. Would SIS hang her out to dry, to protect Britain's relations with France? One last option: she could go to Paris, and find Mourad. But if the police suspected her real purpose they might have him under surveillance, just waiting for her to make contact.

There was one other big difference between this and Doorkicker. She had a bolt hole.

Bridge started the car and drove casually down the street, turning off onto a side road before she reached the guest house. She gasped as a *gendarme* stepped out into the middle of the road, signalling for her to stop. But it wasn't Novak, and with half a dozen more officers within shouting distance, ignoring him was too big a risk. She slowed to a stop, pulling the band from her hair but leaving the sunglasses on. She lowered the window, looked out, and shrugged. *"Qui se passe, officier?"*

"An English woman is missing," replied the *gendarme* in French. "Can I see your ID, please?" He held out a hand, expectantly.

Bridge shrugged, and spoke in perfect French. "Sorry, I don't like to carry my *carte* in case I lose it. My name's Édith Baudin. What's going on?" She regretted using her sister's name the moment she said it, but with no other working alias to hand, it was the first thing Bridge thought of.

"Not even your driver's licence? You're supposed to carry ID at all time."

"I know, but it's bad enough I keep leaving my phone everywhere. I can't go to a café without putting it on the table and walking out by accident, you know? And replacement ID cards aren't cheap."

"Where have you come from?"

"Just now? I had lunch in Saint Dizier. I'm on my way home."

"And where's that?"

Her sister's name was one thing, but Bridge wasn't about to give Izzy's address as well. "Chalons-en-Champagne," she lied. "We just bought a place on the river."

The *gendarme* raised an eyebrow at her hand on the steering wheel. "We? You're not wearing a wedding ring."

"I lost it, gardening." Bridge gave him a lopsided smile. "I told you, I'm hopeless."

The young officer hesitated, then sighed and waved her on. "All right, move along. But you should start carrying your card. Put it on a string around your neck."

"Oh, that's a really good idea. I'll get my husband to make one." Bridge was two streets away before she realised she was still wearing a fake smile, like a rictus grin that made her facial muscles hurt. She massaged her jaw, nodding to herself that she was doing the right thing. *"An English woman is missing,"* he'd said. Careful code, so as not to panic the locals. But whether or not they knew her real identity, they were looking for her. And considering the number of *gendarmes* at the guest house, they probably considered her dangerous. She took a wide circle around several streets, circling back round to drive south, rather than north as she'd told the police.

She regretted losing the computer more than the phone, but she'd sent Henri Mourad an update the night before; a full data dump of her work so far, so he could pass it all back to London. Unfortunately, she hadn't mentioned her suspicion of Montgomery, because yesterday it had been nothing more than a hunch.

Once again, she wondered about Marko Novak's timing. He hadn't seemed at all surprised to find her in Montgomery's apartment, and making the landlord open the door, rather than knock, suggested he wanted to surprise whoever was inside. The only thing that had seemed to catch him unawares was Montgomery being dead. Then there were the words he spoke as he tried to strangle her. "He was right about you." That suggested Montgomery had talked about her, and it was now a safe bet he'd told Novak about her mole hunting. But had he also guessed she'd come to suspect him rather than Voclaine, or was at least working her way towards it? That would explain why he attacked her with such force, because there was no chance of mistaken identity. Montgomery had known exactly who he was fighting in that apartment.

As she drove along the N4, a theory formed. Could the apartment have been bugged? If so, Marko would have known something was wrong as soon as she and Montgomery began fighting. If it was also wired for vision he would have known even sooner, possibly from the moment Bridge broke into the apartment. And that could explain why he expected to see her, but was surprised at Montgomery's body. If Novak headed for the apartment as soon as he saw her enter, then he would have been in transit when Montgomery returned home, fought with Bridge, and died, which all happened in the space of a few minutes. He hadn't known Montgomery was there until he saw the body.

If Bridge was right, that meant the Russian was spying on his own mole. Not too surprising, but she wondered whether he trusted his fellow *gendarmes* more than that. Were they all in it together, coordinating the leak between them? Was he simply bribing them to look the other way? Or were they blissfully unaware one of their own was betraying not just the British, but their own country as well?

It was all too risky. If just one other *gendarme* was working with Novak, all it would take was a word to the wrong person and she'd find herself staring down the barrel of another SP2022. Agenbeux wasn't safe for her any more, and as for trying to get into Paris unseen; she might as well shoot herself now.

She turned the Fiat south onto the N67 and began the long drive towards Côte-d'Or.

55

"It was originally shipped from Hong Kong. And it could already be in Portsmouth."

Two short sentences that had sent Emily Dunston into overdrive, a flurry of phone calls and emails that culminated with Andrea Thomson sitting next to her in the back seat of a car as it raced to Portsmouth. While both women were veterans of their respective departments, their paths had rarely crossed. But Andrea had received a call from Giles Finlay — at home, of course — asking if she could accompany a colleague of his to Portsmouth for the night. A smuggling concern of urgent priority, he said, but couldn't elaborate on the phone. Eight minutes later, a blacked-out car quietly pulled up outside her flat and Andrea climbed in to find Emily Dunston waiting for her.

"Thank you for coming, Ms Thomson. Technically I could just invoke the Terror Act, but I have a sense this will go easier if someone with domestic authority can pull a few strings."

"Giles said it's connected to smuggling. That's not really my area…?"

"Doesn't need to be. Let me worry about the details. Giles may act like he's everyone's friend, but he doesn't trust people lightly. That's why he recommended you."

It took a moment for Andrea to realise this was a compliment. "You'll still have to give me more to go on. I'll help if I can, but I'm not willing to throw Five's authority around without some kind of brief."

Emily exhaled loudly through her nose. Finally she said, "No paperwork. Not yet. Strictly verbal only. Will that do?" Andrea nodded, and Emily continued. "We've been tracking an amount of what we call *matériel chaud* through Europe. It appears to have sailed from Hong Kong, over the Indian Ocean, up through Suez, to make landfall at Sines in Portugal. From there it travelled through Spain and into France, making its way to Saint-Malo. It shipped from Saint-Malo one or two nights ago, heading for Portsmouth by way of Guernsey."

"Easy entry into the islands, no questions asked. And that puts it firmly inside UK territory, so getting it onto the mainland becomes easier."

"Precisely. We assume that's also why it came onshore at Portugal, rather than somewhere closer like Italy, southern France, or directly to the UK. To be blunt, it's much easier to get the Portuguese to look the other way. Fortunately for us, the men entrusted with the package have been as subtle as a brick through a window. Our sources flagged them early when they crossed the Pyrenees, and we've been chasing them ever since."

"I haven't touched French since high school, but doesn't *matériel chaud* mean, well, hot stuff? Is this an arms shipment?"

Emily snorted. "In a manner of speaking. We believe the package contains radioactive material, possibly caesium-137 or similar. We haven't been able to determine where it's bound for, or to what end. But now that we know it was sent from Hong Kong..."

"...You suspect Chinese involvement. I know we're hardly best buddies with Beijing, but that seems a little extreme?"

"It could be a rogue actor, rather than state. Or it could be fully deniable by design. Or it could simply be a money maker. Certain groups will pay through the nose for this stuff."

"And by certain groups, you mean terrorists. ISIS, and the like."

"They'd have a field day. Just ten grams of caesium can contaminate a square mile of land. More, if the weather's right."

"And how much *matériel chaud* have you been tracking?"

Emily lowered her voice. "About fifty grams."

As the car sped south on the motorway, Andrea wondered if this week could get any stranger.

56

Izzy didn't believe a word of it, and said so.

Bridge had arrived in the early evening, after a deliberately careful drive. Her instinct had been to race down to Côte-d'Or, to escape Novak and his *gendarme* flunkies as soon as possible. But driving like a maniac risked attracting police attention, and with her name and description on every *gendarme*'s dashboard, that could only spell trouble. So instead she drove carefully, always five kilometres per hour below the speed limit, always staying on boring, anonymising highways as far as possible, and always erring on the side of cautious driving once she had to come off the highways onto local roads.

Halfway down the N67 she'd remembered Montgomery's mini tablet, tucked inside her hoodie. It had taken several blows during the fight with Novak, and the already-cracked screen was now a spiderweb of shattered glass. When she pressed the power button, the black glass defiantly refused to show anything other than her own cracked reflection. She wanted to pull over and scream at her own incompetence, but instead tossed it on the passenger seat, gripped the steering wheel, stared straight ahead and continued to drive. If she was lucky — *if* — then she might be able to hook something up to the data port and somehow extract data. It was a long shot, and she'd need specific equipment to attempt it, but it was enough to keep a tiny drop of hope alive in her stomach.

Only a drop, though. She'd blown the most important part

of the mission by killing Montgomery. The more she thought about it, the more certain she was that he was indeed the mole. Assuming he was the only one, his death meant no more leaks from Exphoria. But it also meant no SIS interrogation, no opportunity to find out why he did it, who was paying him, who wanted these secrets. Marko Novak may have been his handler, but he was just muscle. A point man, not a mastermind. So who did he work for? Was he FSB, on 'official unofficial' business for Moscow? The FSB had grown in leaps and bounds since Putin's second presidency, and Bridge's whole life would have been different if not for Russia's march into Syria. It didn't seem far-fetched to imagine military espionage was also on the agenda. But with Montgomery dead, imagine was all SIS could do. Even if Bridge could somehow capture Novak, the chances of making him talk were slim. Everything about the man spoke of experience, a veteran spy who would rot in a cell before giving up his agency. And that assumed they could nab him at all. While Bridge could testify that he tried to kill her, he'd also caught her red-handed, burgling the apartment of a man she'd killed. All he had to say was that he tried to apprehend her, defending himself when she resisted arrest, and then it was his word against hers.

She'd been rash, moving forward with only half a plan and no contingency, like a novice. She'd wanted to find the mole so badly, and was so concerned she'd wrongly accused Voclaine, that she barged in to Montgomery's place without stopping to think what might happen if things didn't go to plan. She'd never imagined it could go so wrong that she now found herself on the run with nothing but the clothes on her back, a Ziploc of spy tools, and a tablet computer that was both potentially incriminating and also possibly broken beyond repair. She should call London, but first she wanted to make sure she knew what she was doing. She needed some time to think, to figure out the best way of fixing the terrible mess she'd made. Once she had a plan, she could call from Izzy's place.

But to do that required privacy, if she was to maintain her employment cover story, and that same story was wearing increasingly thin on her sister.

"You seriously expect me to believe your office politics are so bad that you can't stay there, but you also can't go home, and couldn't grab a change of clothes from your hotel? Who the hell do you think you're talking to, Bridge? I may not be some jet-setting PA, but I'm not stupid."

"It's really complicated, Izz. Can you just bear with me for a couple of days? Please?"

"You know Mum thinks you're a criminal? That this civil service stuff is all rubbish, because they wouldn't keep paying for you to fly all over the place, and that you're actually smuggling drugs for the mafia?"

"Don't be ridiculous. Bloody hell, she's never said anything to me."

"Because you never talk to her, do you? I swear…"

"Auntie Bridge!" Stéphanie ran across the courtyard and hugged Bridge's legs, before looking up at both women. "Why weren't you talking in English?"

Bridge winced. Once again, they'd argued in French without realising. "We forget sometimes," said Izzy, taking Steph's hand, "just like how Daddy sometimes talks French."

They walked back to the farmhouse. "But Daddy *is* French."

"And so are Maman and Auntie Bridge, darling. We were born here."

Steph's mouth dropped open in surprise. "What, here? At the farm?"

Bridge smiled despite herself as Izzy and Steph's voices faded inside the house. She took the broken mini tablet from the car and made to follow them. Fréderic stood inside the doorway, scowling as she approached, and nodded at the tablet. "No internet here," he said. "You can't get online with that."

"Can't anyway," said Bridge, showing him the shattered screen. "Won't even switch on. I just don't want to leave it in the car." As she turned it over in her hand, though, she saw something she hadn't previously noticed. An SD slot, with a card still lodged inside. She tried to prise it out with her fingernails, but the slot was crimped, bent from all the damage the tablet had sustained. She looked to Fred. "Do you have a pair of tweezers?"

He led her into the kitchen, and proceeded to rummage through several drawers before producing a battered old pair of flat-nose pliers. Not quite what Bridge had in mind, but they'd suffice. She pushed them into the slot, slow but firm to get as deep as she could, then carefully prised them open. If the tablet had been made from better material she might have had difficulty, but the metal was thin enough to give under pressure, and the slot widened. She reset the pliers, leaving just a sliver of a gap, and this time pushed them in to gently clamp the nose around the SD card itself. With a cautious pull the card came free. It had suffered a dent, but the golden contacts were intact.

"And why is this so important?" asked Fred, who'd been watching over her shoulder.

"It belonged to my boss," said Bridge, which wasn't entirely a lie. "He asked me to see if I could retrieve any data from it. I thought I might have to try and cable up the SSD..."

"...But now you think this card contains what you need?"

"Maybe. I'll have to wait till I can get near a laptop to find out, though."

Fred smiled, which in itself took Bridge by surprise. She couldn't remember the last time she'd seen him smile at anything other than his children. "Wait there," he said, and put a finger to his lips as he ducked out of the room.

He returned with a courier bag, which he placed on the kitchen table and unbuckled the flap to pull out a small HP laptop. "Don't tell your sister," he said as he leant over Bridge and typed his login password. "Do you need cables?"

Bridge peered inside the bag and saw a nest of power and connectivity cables inside, but the laptop had its own SD card slot. "No, this should be fine," she said, and took a deep breath, ready to insert the card. She looked at Fred, sceptical of this sudden change of heart. "Why?"

"Because you're obviously in trouble, and whatever it is, I want it dealt with quickly so you can go back to work and leave us alone."

Bridge rolled her eyes. "Be still, my beating heart." She pushed the card into the laptop slot, dreading any one of a dozen sounds that would tell her it was broken. But it clicked into place, and after a few nervous seconds appeared as a drive in the disk explorer. Her pulse quickened. This could be it, the proof she needed.

But the drive was empty. "Shit," Bridge said, balling her fists in frustration. "Shit shit shit *shit*."

"Is it all lost? You can't repair the drive?"

"There's nothing to repair," Bridge sighed. "The card's — wait, hang on." She'd been about to say 'empty', but her eyes had instinctively gone to the drive information summary on screen, and something there didn't make sense. The HP said the drive had 61.5GB free. But it was a 64GB card. Even with a bloated directory tree, it should have at least 63GB remaining.

It was possible the reading was a by-product of damage to the card, and it was simply feeding incorrect information to the laptop. But there was another possibility; that the card contained data, potentially two and a half gigabytes' worth, and it was the directory itself that was damaged or corrupt. Bridge fired up a shell prompt and started typing. She was more comfortable in Unix than DOS — it had been a long time since she'd operated a Windows machine, instead of just hacking into an MS server — but this, of all things, was worth a try. If she was right, and she could recover data from the card, it might vindicate everything she'd done.

"What the hell is this? We said we were leaving the computers at home."

Bridge turned to see Izzy in the doorway, arms folded, glaring at Fred. He shrugged. "I have to get the Senegal pitch finished by the end of the month. I'm not doing anything in front of Stéphanie, don't worry."

"Not doing what?" said Steph, appearing behind her mother in the doorway. She gasped as she saw the laptop. "A computer? I want to play a game!"

"No, Stéphanie," said Izzy, crossing the room. "Daddy and Auntie Bridge are just about to put it away, isn't that right?" She took hold of the screen, trying to close the computer.

But Bridge gripped it and held it open, meeting her sister's gaze. "I'm sorry, Izz, but this is really, really important. It could save my job."

"Screw your job," Izzy shouted. "If it's so bloody great, why aren't you still there instead of squatting here? My family is supposed to be on holiday, and we have rules about our holidays, and you're ruining all of — Jesus, have you started weightlifting or something?" She gave up trying to close the lid against Bridge's resistance and stormed out of the room, leading Steph away by the hand.

"Isabelle," called Fred, following her. He stopped at the door, turned, and said, "Just hurry up."

Bridge nodded in silence, mentally crossing her fingers as she continued typing.

57

The cold air was recycled and stale, belched out by noisy climate control units. Bridge wouldn't have minded if this was a day raid, and they were escaping the searing heat that had threatened to overwhelm her every day since she arrived. But at night the desert froze, and they'd just spent two hours driving through it, with Bridge huddled under layers of blanket and a keffiyeh *woven around her head.*

She said nothing, maintaining mission silence, but she didn't need to. Ahead of her in the stone corridor, Adrian turned and grinned. "Never bloody happy, are you, BB? Can't live with the heat, can't live with the cold. It's a wonder you made it out of here alive..." He looked down at the dark patch spreading over his chest, looked back at Bridge with unusual sympathy, said, "You'd better go —"

She was in the jeep, rattling over rocks and sand while bullets zinged by her ears. The headlamps were barely strong enough to show ten feet in front of her. "How do you know where you're going?" Adrian shouted from the passenger side. "You can't see a thing." Daylight flipped like a light switch, noon sun high and hot, foiling Bridge's sight with heat shimmer, exposed for all to see. Night again, flip, and a bullet from the pursuing jeep ripped through Adrian's shoulder —

The Russian guard demanded to know what they were doing here, who authorised their presence, what papers did they have? Adrian played the self-righteous alpha male card, puffing himself up and gambling the guard wouldn't argue with an alleged order from an alleged senior officer. His Russian was excellent. Bridge's wasn't, but she had enough to interject with technical bluff that would lend veracity.

The guard said OK, but he'd need to go and check. That was fine. Bridge knew they only needed three minutes, tops, inside the server room. Adrian knew that, too, but he still killed the Russian, stabbing the guard in the back with his dagger as he turned away. Up and through the lungs, preventing any cry of pain. All that escaped from the young soldier was wheezing air and blood.

Bridge stared down at the man's body, and he stared up at her, and blood bubbled up from his mouth as he smiled and said in Adrian's voice, "First one's always the worst —"

She was so close now, the ruins of the village behind her, if she could just keep the damn jeep upright and rolling for another twenty clicks she'd be home, and she thought of Adrian's body lying in the ruins of the Russian base, and then she remembered there wouldn't be a body because of the grenades, but there was something on the passenger seat, underneath a desert blanket, and when she pulled it back with one hand and glanced down, not wanting to take her eyes off the dirt track she was now following, it was Adrian's head that looked back up at her, and he laughed, "Silly girl, didn't you notice how quiet I'd been? As if I could have lived through that —"

She said it wasn't necessary to kill the guard; they could have been in and out before he came back. Adrian argued the kill had bought them time, because now they wouldn't raise an alarm until they found his body, and to make his point he dragged the Russian's corpse behind one of the server racks. Bridge was still in mild shock. Her first live kill, and she'd been trained to expect some disorientation, but she had no doubt that Adrian had made a mistake.

"What if they expected him back right away? What if there are hidden surveillance cameras here, and someone just watched you kill him? This was never part of the plan."

"Neither was getting stopped by someone guarding the bloody computers," said Adrian, red-faced from hauling the body by himself, "so we improvise. Anyway, this is a cave. You can see for yourself there's no cameras here."

"No, I can't. Have you even seen the latest stuff? The Chinese are making wifi cameras the size of a pound coin, these days. Christ, you can buy them on Amazon. I bet the Russians get first dibs."

"There are no bloody cameras," Adrian shouted. "Fuck's sake, I knew you weren't ready for this. You're panicking."

"I'm not panicking," she shouted back, "but now I might only have half the time I need to locate the right server."

"Then you'd better hurry up and get looking, hadn't you?" he said, just as another guard ran into the room and she'd never been so sorry to be proven right —

Driving through the desert, alone, swallowing back tears —

Adrian's hand at his stomach, blood spreading through his manicured fingers —

The jeep sputtering to a halt, fuel gauge bottomed out —

Adrian pulling his ICE grenades, shouting at her to hurry —

And the icy dark of the desert night, closing around her as an Allied patrol drove by.

58

"*Bonsoir*," he said to the young *gendarme* sitting in the hallway, before pressing a chloroform-soaked cloth to the policeman's face.

Marko Novak — an alias, but it sufficed for this mission — made no apologies for being an old-fashioned kind of spy. As long as he could remember, he had wanted to follow in his late father's footsteps and become a KGB officer. But then the USSR collapsed while he was a young man, and Marko had to settle for a place in the FSB, the crippled successor to the mighty security agency. Old KGB spooks who were recruited to train the new FSB officers would joke that if the KGB stood for intelligence, the FSB stood for halfwits. Novak was just old enough to share their fond memories of that lost time, a simpler time, when the enemy was known and the mission was clear. He had been an outstanding FSB officer. But there was no place for a man like him, so out of step with his own time, in Yeltsin's 'New Russia'. After yet another round of cutbacks he quit.

Ironically, if he had waited just a few more years for Putin, Novak had no doubt he would be running a bureau by now. But in that time he had come to enjoy the freelance life.

Besides, it was all so complicated these days. Everything was so political, sometimes it was hard to know in whose interests you were working. That was why Novak liked to keep his own operations as simple as possible. He'd built a good reputation as an old-fashioned freelancer, someone who didn't rely on fancy computer tricks and technology that might fail in the middle of a job. He tracked and found people by old-fashioned means, and eliminated them in ways that had been tried and tested for decades by legendary spies from both sides of the Cold War. Most importantly, he never gave up.

One client had likened Novak to a bulldog, which he knew was meant as a compliment, but made him uncomfortable because of the image's association with the English. The old days may have gone, but as far as Novak was concerned the English remained lapdogs of the true Enemy; the hated USA.

And now this English woman, this obvious agent of MI6 sent to find the Exphoria mole, had killed Montgomery, Novak's own resource. Such action demanded retribution, a message to London that this was not acceptable. More than that, he was unsure how much Bridget Short knew about the operation. The man Novak had stabbed and thrown in the Thames had no ties to the British government, no intelligence work under his belt that the Russian had been able to find. He had intended to search the man's house to make sure, but the police beat him to making an identification, leaving Novak frustrated until his client assured him the man's interference was nothing more than bad luck.

Ms Short, on the other hand, appeared after he'd been followed to the Eurostar. Did MI6 not know there was a mole on the project until then? Or had their previous mole hunts simply proved futile? The alias 'Bridget Short' was unknown to him, as was the tall, dark-haired woman he'd fought at Montgomery's apartment. But she was fast, strong, a good fighter. Perhaps she was a specialist, someone the English sent to identify and kill moles when other means had failed. The thought excited him, and he remembered his hands around her throat, her ragged gasps as he held her down. A good memory.

After she escaped, Novak dressed Montgomery's apartment a little, to hide his involvement and give the police a wild goose chase to conduct. Then he returned to his rented apartment near the river, taking the empty Grach pistol with him. After tending to the bullet in his leg, which left him limping but able enough to walk, he loaded the gun and pocketed a spare magazine. Then he stuffed the *gendarme* uniform into a suitcase with some soiled clothes, and drove to a secluded spot by the riverside where he burned them all and kicked the ashes into the river.

When that was done, he drove to the guest house where Ms Short was staying. His police scanner told him the local *gendarmerie* was all over it, and he didn't expect Short herself to return there any time soon. No doubt the police would confiscate any electronics, and Novak would have to try and retrieve those at a later point for his client. But first, he must find and eliminate Ms Short.

She might return directly to England by diplomatic transport, and if so there was nothing Novak could do about it. But a sweep of Montgomery's apartment after she escaped, plus a review of the footage he'd missed while he was on his way there, suggested that she might have uncovered Montgomery as a mole — without truly knowing what he was leaking. She hadn't found the bag of blank SD cards Novak supplied, and the footage showed she tried to avoid Montgomery when he arrived home unexpectedly, rather than confronting him directly. So she might remain in Agenbeux, to find out more about what Montgomery had been doing. She might try to find Novak, now she could recognise him. That only made it more important that he find her first, instead.

It was dark when the *gendarmerie* left the guest house. He took a case from the boot of his car, booked a cash room under an alias, and went straight upstairs. He noted the sole *gendarme* outside what must be Bridget Short's room, sitting on a chair, looking tired and bored. Novak entered his own room, prepared a chloroform pad, made sure he had lock pick and camera with him, then rendered the guard unconscious. The door behind him was unlocked, and the *gendarme* would sleep for thirty minutes at the dosage Novak had delivered, giving him plenty of time to search the room undisturbed. He dragged the young officer inside, laid him out on the floor, and closed the door.

The police had turned the place upside down and, as he expected, taken anything that looked electronic. That didn't bother Novak. There were other ways. The bathroom contained just toiletries, nothing identifying or useful without a DNA test, and that would tell him little he didn't already know. The bed had been stripped and searched. They'd even removed the bedknobs, in case Ms Short had hidden something inside the frame. If she had, the police had taken it, as they were now empty. Nothing else about the bed indicated a hiding place, so they'd tipped her suitcase over the mattress. But again, it all seemed very normal and innocent, with nothing that would tip off a normal investigator that she was a spy.

Novak turned over the suitcase, noting tell-tale marks around one of the ridges at the base of the handle tubing. He took a one euro coin and placed it edgeways into the slot, turned it, and found a hidden compartment — empty, but evidently something the *gendarmes* had missed. Did this mean they didn't know she was a spy? That would explain why they also hadn't checked the inner lining. Novak took a small knife from his pocket and slashed the lining, revealing the deep red of an English passport taped to the inside of the suitcase's outer shell. He opened it to the photo page. The picture was of Bridget Short, or 'Catherine Pritchard' as she was called here, but with shorter hair and less makeup. An emergency backup, then, designed for getting out of trouble and out of town in a hurry. If the police hadn't been here, she'd presumably have returned for this passport and used it to flee to England.

Novak allowed himself a grim smile, as this supported his notion that she was still in France. Her handlers had known that if the Bridget Short identity was compromised, she'd need an emergency passport to return home. But without it, she was stranded.

Novak could find nothing else in the clothes or suitcase, and the rest of the small room was also devoid of clues. A few clothes hung in the wardrobe, but after cutting them all open he found nothing hidden in the lining. Nor was there anything in the heels of her shoes, which he broke off one by one. Only detritus remained on the desk and in its drawers. The waste paper basket had been upended, presumably by the *gendarmerie*, and its contents left on the floor; two empty Marlboro cigarette packets, a banana skin, a plastic salad container from the local *marché*, a paper bag from a local farmhouse containing two stale cakes.

Novak crouched to poke through the trash, found nothing, stood, hesitated, crouched again.

Délices de la Ferme Baudin, Côte-d'Or.

Côte-d'Or was far from local. It was two hours' drive away. He remembered something Montgomery had said, that Ms Short lied about visiting a vineyard. He thought she might have returned to London that weekend. But what if she actually spent it at a farmhouse in Côte-d'Or? A farmhouse she didn't want Montgomery to know about?

Novak emptied the bag of its stale cakes, folded it, and placed it in his pocket. He stepped over the unconscious *gendarme*, who was murmuring and sweating in his sleep, and entered his own room. There, he returned his tools to their pockets in his case, removed all trace of himself from every surface, and left the guest house to drive south.

59

Andrea Thomson cursed and kicked the side of a cargo container. The metallic clang rang out across the dockside tarmac.

The cargo ship carrying the *matériel chaud* had docked the night before, and its cargo finished unloading several hours ago. The dock kept a record of each container's location within the port, among the rows and rows of multicoloured stacked metal boxes, but some had already been placed on trucks and driven away. So there was no way to know if the smuggled material was still at the port, or on its way. Even if it was still here, the chances of it being part of the ship's registered cargo were essentially zero. Everyone along the chain would have been paid handsomely to look the other way and wave the mysterious package through. Emily Dunston believed it would likely be buried inside a random legitimate container.

Andrea had demanded every container from the ship still at Portsmouth be detained until port security opened each one and ran a Geiger counter over it. She'd also insisted that every container leaving the port be scanned for radiation, but the port manager had put his foot down over that.

"We process more than a thousand import containers through this port every day," he said, "and we conduct random scans of departing containers at all times. We can add radiation scans to that procedure, and increase the frequency by maybe thirty per cent, maximum. But any more than that would cause an impossible bottleneck. It'd make French fuel strikes look like a day at the beach."

"I don't care," protested Andrea. "This is a matter of national security."

"And this is an international port with some of the strictest security measures in Europe," said the manager. "I'm sorry, but even you lot don't have unlimited authority here. Technically, this whole area is answerable to the Crown, not Parliament."

Andrea wasn't convinced that was true, but arguing the point would only waste more time. The manager turned on his heel and left, with an I'll-see-what-I-can-do shrug.

Emily Dunston scowled. "Never mind the Crown, this is a right royal balls-up. I should have pushed for more resources. Now you lot are stuck with chasing a radioactive box around the country, and we can't tell you where it is or who has it."

As the *clang* from Andrea's kick faded, she sighed. "It's got to be London, hasn't it? You don't ship a box of nuclear waste halfway round the world, smuggle it up through Europe and over the Channel just to unleash it on Skegness."

Dunston looked amused. "Surprisingly London-centric for a Scot."

"Call it realism. Comes with the job."

"That it does. And you're right, if this is to be weaponised, we have to assume London is the target. But there's still a chance it could be on its way to a buyer, who might then ship it on somewhere else."

Andrea snorted. "Chance'd be a fine thing. At least then it'd be someone else's problem." They walked back to the car. "But something tells me we won't be that lucky."

60

The data recovery process on the SD card had been running all night — she'd had enough foresight to plug the laptop in before she went to sleep — and was eighty per cent finished at six-thirty in the morning, when Bridge was woken by Izzy and Steph making cakes again. In the bathroom, visions of Syria drifted behind the mirror as she cleaned her teeth with Izzy's brush. The sight of Adrian's blood, his nightmarish head in the jeep's passenger seat…it was just dream logic, they weren't real memories, they meant nothing. And yet.

She took a scalding hot shower to distract herself, and move the thoughts to a dark corner of her mind. Dr Nayar would frown at that, but she didn't have time to process this stuff right now. If past experience was anything to go by, they'd stop bothering her in a few hours. As she entered the kitchen they were already little more than phantoms, tenacious but insubstantial.

"Are you coming with us to the patisseries, Auntie Bridge?"

Steph's question pulled Bridge from her thoughts, but before she could respond, Izzy cut in.

"Actually, sweetheart, I think this morning it'll just be Maman and Auntie Bridge by ourselves. We need to talk about grown-up stuff."

Steph was devastated. Bridge thought she might burst into tears at any moment. "But I'm four. I can talk about grown-up things."

Bridge didn't know what her sister was up to, but playing along was the surest way to earn some brownie points. She smiled sympathetically at her niece. "We'll talk about more grown-up things with you when we get back," she said, "but Maman and I have to talk about things for sisters. When you and Hugo are older, you'll talk about brother and sister things."

"But! But!"

"Auntie Bridge is right, Stéphanie," said Izzy, packing the last of the cakes into their paper bags. "We'll bring you back some pastries, OK? Then we can all have brunch together. You like brunch, don't you?"

The look on Steph's face suggested at that moment she didn't like anything at all, not even breathing or existing. She slid off the stool without a word, head hung and shoulders slumped, every step out of the kitchen a leaden thump on the floor. Bridge pulled a face and turned to Izzy, but her sister shook her head and rolled her eyes. "Ten minutes with Fred and she'll have forgotten this entire conversation. Come on, let's go."

They drove for several minutes in a silence that Bridge didn't want to break, not knowing exactly why Izzy wanted to get her alone, and her sister didn't appear to be in a hurry either. Then Izzy finally spoke, and Bridge realised it wasn't nonchalance. Her sister was anxious, steeling herself to ask a difficult question.

"Why are you really here, Bridge? What the hell is going on with you?"

"I —"

"And please don't give me that rubbish about office politics. Credit me with some intelligence."

Bridge was torn. She'd always hated lying to Izzy about her work, but the rules were clear. She spoke slowly. "I'm not sure what I can say that'll satisfy you."

Izzy yanked the steering wheel and pulled the car to the side of the road, stepping on the brakes to bring them to a halt. "Satisfy?

To hell with satisfy, tell me the bloody truth. First you just happen to be working two hours up the road from where I'm on holiday..."

"I swear, that is pure coincidence."

"Shut up. And then you turn up again less than a week later, dressed like a bloody burglar, with no luggage or even a toothbrush — and don't think I hadn't noticed the bruises on your arms, by the way — and you want to, what, lie low for a few days? So either you're some kind of international art thief, or some bastard work boyfriend is knocking you around, or maybe both, or whatever. Tell me, for heaven's sake!" Izzy was shaking, breathing hard, and Bridge realised her sister was more anxious about this conversation than she was. A memory slid into the front of her mind. They were teenagers, and Izzy had begun stepping out with grown men, guys in their twenties who seemed impossibly mature to young Bridge. She remembered Izzy in tears, pulling down the hem of her sleeve, thinking Bridge hadn't seen the bruises. Perhaps hoping more than thinking.

As tears welled up in Izzy's eyes, another memory leapt unbidden into Bridge's mind: the night their mother shouted herself hoarse, swearing at the same young man when he rolled up drunk after Izzy broke up with him. Izzy had sat at the top of the stairs, quietly crying, while Bridge peered out from behind her bedroom door.

Neither of them had ever spoken about it. And now, Bridge realised, Izzy was worried she'd got herself into the same situation, but like her sister before her she couldn't face talking about it. She leaned over to stroke Izzy's hair, and smiled in sympathy. "It's not that, Izz, honestly it's not. You know me, if some bloke tried that I'd kickbox his arse until he only wished Mum was throwing plates at him."

Izzy snorted with laughter through her tears, remembering that same night. "You promise me, OK? You promise you'd tell me?"

"I promise. It's not that."

"Then what, Bridge? What's going on?"

She'd backed herself into a corner by not lying. But she couldn't bring herself to lie about that, especially not to Izzy. She was so tired of lying. "I work for —" She choked on the words, cleared her throat, tried again. "I work for the government."

"I know you do," said Izzy.

"No, you don't. I'm not at the DTI. I'm not a junior civil servant. I work at..." She struggled to say it. It felt absurd, now more than ever, to say out loud: *I'm a spy*. How could anyone say it with a straight face? It was impossible. She tried to imagine how Giles might phrase it, using political language to disclose the minimum amount of necessary truth, but not a shred more. "I'm a technical analyst," she said slowly. "You know I've always been the big nerd, right? And now I monitor computer hackers all over the world."

"You monitor hackers all over the world. For the British Government."

"Really, I just sit at a desk in front of a computer all day. It's dead boring."

"But you're supposed to keep it a secret, and tell everyone you're a secretary."

"Well, not really a secretary...?"

"And now you're working here in France."

"It's just a one-off, honestly."

"Bridge, are you a *spy*?"

She tried to reply, hesitated, tried again, got as far as "Um," tried another tack but only made it to "Well," and then gave up.

Izzy rescued her. "That's why you had a different name on your laptop, wasn't it? IT department joke, my arse. Oh my God, are you on the run? We should call the police."

"No," Bridge shouted, and regretted it immediately. She lowered her voice. “I just need somewhere to crash for a couple of days while I figure out my next move. I can’t trust the police.”

“What the hell do you mean, you can’t trust the police? They’re the police. That’s who you call.”

Bridge shrugged. “Not me. Officially, they don’t know I’m here. And they might be involved.”

“Involved in what?” Izzy was leaning forward, now, wide-eyed and excited, and Bridge knew she’d said too much.

“I really can’t say. This isn’t a movie, Izz. My chewing gum doesn’t explode, my watch doesn’t shoot poison darts, I haven’t got jets in my boots; none of that. I’m just a computer nerd, same as always.”

Izzy snorted, and put the car into gear. “Computer nerds don’t get into fights and go on the run,” she said as she pulled back onto the road. “But don’t worry, *ma soeur*, your secret’s safe with me.” Bridge wondered about that. Besides, the way this mission had gone, she was far from confident she had a job to return to in London anyway. Maybe that was for the best. “Oh, *shit*,” said Izzy, “do you know how to fire a gun? Have you got one?”

A horrible image flashed into Bridge’s mind, of Stéphanie finding the SIG Sauer SP2022 in her car back at the farm. But the car was locked, and the gun was hidden in the glove compartment. Nobody would stumble across it. There was no need to worry.

Worrying about Novak, though, was a different matter. Bridge declined to talk about guns, and Izzy appeared satisfied with the rest of Bridge’s explanation, so that was that. They went around the town, stopping off at patisseries to deliver a box here, a bag there. But Bridge, though she smiled and gave pleasantries, was preoccupied the whole time. She peered round every corner, looked down every narrow street, watched every passing car, alert for signs of danger. Izzy either didn’t notice, or was polite enough not to comment out loud, and Bridge was grateful for that. She didn't relish the prospect of telling her sister about the big Russian spy who tried to kill her yesterday, and would certainly finish the job given the chance.

But anonymity was her best advantage. True, she'd given the *gendarme* her sister's married name, but 'Baudin' was hardly rare. She'd also lied and told him she lived north of Agenbeux. Finally, the *gendarme* hadn't recognised her, or questioned her as if she was a suspect. The chances were slim that he'd remember her, let alone mention her to Novak. And yet… Much as she tried to convince herself nobody would find her here, the possibility nagged at her, floating at the back of her mind, refusing to sink below the surface.

They reached the final patisserie a little before eight. As usual, Bridge hung behind Izzy, casually glancing around, checking they weren't being watched or followed. She smiled and said '*bonjour*' to the owner, who asked where *petite Stéphanie* was. Izzy said she was under the weather, but had still helped make the cakes that morning, and pointed out one particular batch with iced topping that Steph baked all by herself. The owner hoped the girl would feel better soon, cooed appreciatively at the cakes, and asked for a stash of Izzy's printed paper bags. She only had a couple in hand, so she turned back to Bridge and said, "Can you get me a half dozen more bags from the car? They're on the back seat."

"Sure," said Bridge, taking the keys and stepping out onto the street. She quickly scanned the area, a habit she'd internalised over the course of the morning, but saw nothing. The bags were where Izzy had said, in the car. Bridge removed a stack, locked the car, and returned to the shop. She'd brought too many, so Izzy counted off six, then handed the rest back to Bridge while the owner paid her.

As they drove away, Bridge said, "It can't earn you much, doing this. After what you must spend on ingredients and fuel, are you even turning a profit?"

Izzy shrugged. "A bit, but that's not the point. Steph loves doing it, and I think it's good for her to understand how the world works. That's why she normally comes with me to the shops, to see the money changing hands; a bit of haggling, you know."

"Izz, she's four years old."

"Exactly. What were we doing at four? Climbing trees, poking worms with sticks and getting bloody knees."

Bridge frowned. "What's wrong with that?"

"Look, I know you think I spoil her, and I'm not stupid. She can be a right little *madame* at times. But I just want better for her. I want her to be smarter than us, to learn her way around the world a bit faster." Bridge didn't reply. Izzy glanced over, to see Bridge staring at the spare paper bags in her lap. "Bridge, are you listening?"

Bridge exhaled through her nose in frustration, then whispered, "For fuck's sake."

"Excuse me?"

"Not you. Me, my life, my fuck-ups." Bridge spoke slowly, carefully. "Izz, I think it would be a good idea for the four of you to go on a family road trip. Maybe drive down to see Mum." Bridge spoke slowly, carefully, not taking her eyes from the paper bags in her lap.

"What are you talking about? Bridge, what's wrong?"

Bridge realised that what she'd been feeling all morning wasn't just anxiety that Novak might track her down and try to kill her. It was that he'd come, and she wouldn't be ready. That she would freeze up, instinctively try to escape, try to run away and hide all over again. It had never been much of a workable option, but now it was impossible. Now she'd put her sister's family in danger, just by coming here. *Délices de la Ferme Baudin, Côte-d'Or*, the printed label on every bag. Just like the one she'd brought back from her first visit. The one she'd left in the guest house.

A wave of emotion passed over Bridge, exhaustion mixed with the terror of knowing her family was in danger. And not only was it her fault, but only she could put it right. She was sick and tired of running away.

She turned to Izzy. "When we get back, I need you to get everyone together and pack the car while I scout your land."

"Scout? What does that mean? Scouting for what?"

"Vantage points."

61

The good thing about these backward rural areas was how few questions people asked. Everyone wanted to talk, to pass the time of morning, but nobody was rude enough to ask what you were up to. Marko Novak looked like a man who had slept in his car at the side of the road, and not without reason. But when he asked how to find the Baudin Farm, people would either say they didn't know, or give him vague directions, and then proceed to talk about the weather, how the mayor was making a mess of things, the state of the roads, anything but ask why he was looking for the farm.

It wasn't hard to find, in the end. He arrived a little before eight, to find a tall, thin man chopping wood in the courtyard. Novak drove into the yard, parked, and exited the car. "Good morning," he called out in perfect English. "Do I have the right place? I'm looking for my colleague, Bridget."

The man had paused chopping as Novak drove up, and now he shrugged. "Colleague? Where from?" His English was heavily accented. Presumably this man was the Baudin in the farm's name.

Whatever Novak said now, it would be a gamble; a combination of guesswork and years of experience at letting other people do the work. Tell people just enough to sound convincing, act as if you naturally expect them to understand what you're talking about, and they will fill in the blanks for you without realising it. Whether or not this man believed Novak to be a threat would determine the course of the next twenty seconds, and both their lives. It would decide whether Novak needed to draw the Grach tucked under his shoulder. "Up at Agenbeux," he said, and winked. "Rather hush-hush, you know?"

The man looked sceptical. "I'm sorry, but there's no person here called Bridget," he said, returning to his wood. "I can't help you."

Novak weighed his options. The man was obviously lying, but now he faced a tricky decision. If Bridget Short was in the house he would need to get inside quietly, or risk her making a pre-emptive strike. But if she was somewhere outside, on the farmland, he had to conduct a search without alerting her. The man's wood axe was no threat against Novak's gun, but would he remain quiet? It was a chance Novak would have to take. He reached inside his jacket, fingers closing around the butt of the pistol.

The farmhouse door burst open. A young girl ran out, shouting, "Auntie Bridge, Auntie Br — *oh*. Who are you?"

Marko Novak smiled. *"Au contraire,"* he said to the man, and drew his gun. "I think you can help me a great deal."

62

The first thing Bridge noticed was an absence; the lack of noise, of Stéphanie running out to greet them and shouting their names. The first thing Izzy noticed was an object out of place; the wood axe, lying carelessly on the ground. Fréderic was strict about leaving it safely embedded in the chopping block when not in use, but there it was, seemingly discarded. Around it were scattered loose logs, some chopped, some still whole.

"Izzy, stay in the car and wait for me."

"What's going on, Bridge? What the hell is going on?"

"Hopefully nothing. But stay in the car." Izzy killed the engine, and Bridge stepped out into the yard. No Stéphanie, no Fréderic, no sound except the distant call of blackbirds from the trees at the edge of the estate.

She opened the front door slowly, making as little noise as possible. Her natural urge was to call out, to shout "Hello," and see if anyone responded. But her professional paranoia was at the forefront of her mind, and she said nothing. In the kitchen, she quietly picked up the keys to her Fiat and slipped them in her pocket. She glanced down at Fred's HP laptop and saw it had finally completed the data recovery. But now wasn't the time to go browsing photos. She gently closed the lid, slid a kitchen knife out of the block, and moved toward the lounge.

Fred and Steph were facing her, their back to the fireplace, sitting on wooden chairs from the dining area. Their arms were pulled behind them, tied to the chair backs. They were gagged, with scarves stretched across their mouths and tied behind their heads, and both were wide-eyed with fear and frustration.

Behind them stood Marko Novak, in plain clothes, pointing a Grach at the back of Steph's head.

"The game's up, Marko," Bridge lied. "Exphoria is safe, and SIS is onto you. My colleagues are picking up your contact in London right now, and the DGSE is going to hunt you down like a dog." She was surprised at how calm she sounded. Was it because the danger was now to her own family? Or had she simply had enough of running away, tired of always playing defence?

To her surprise, Novak laughed. "The DGSE couldn't find their arse with four arms," he said in perfect English. "And you, Ms Short — am I to suppose you lured me here deliberately? Using your own family as bait would be a most unorthodox tactic."

She noticed he'd used her name, just as she'd used his. This was now a battle of wits, to see who could persuade the other that they had the upper hand, that resistance was futile. But Novak had called her 'Short', which boosted Bridge's confidence. "That was a mistake," she said. "I didn't think you'd be stupid enough to actually follow me. I thought you'd be licking your wounds in Zurich, after the pasting I gave you at the guest house. How's the leg?"

Novak grunted in acknowledgement, then smiled. "I realise now that I was wrong about you. I thought you were a specialist, but it seems you're just another MI6 *durak*. And so —"

Whatever Novak wanted to say next would be forever lost, as he was interrupted by a sudden loud gasp from a window behind him. He turned, startled, and Bridge just had enough time to make out Izzy through the glass before Novak raised his pistol and fired.

Bridge and Stéphanie screamed in unison, though for different reasons. Reacting instinctively, Bridge threw the kitchen knife at Novak. It wasn't designed to be a weapon, much less thrown, and missed him by more than a metre, clattering off the brick chimney breast behind him. That didn't matter, because at the same time as throwing the knife, Bridge broke into a run and charged at Novak. He was caught off guard, first by Izzy's gasp and then the knife, and Bridge was able to close the gap, throwing her entire body weight at him before he could fire again.

They fell back against the fireplace. Novak's head hit the chimney and he spasmed, dropping the gun. Bridge followed up with two quick punches to his head, then picked up the knife and cut through the zip tie securing Fred's wrists to the chair. He reached for his gag, but shouted a muffled cry before he could remove it, his eyes wide. Bridge ducked, and Novak's boot glanced off the side of her head. It hurt, but not enough to stop her. She turned, and wrapped her arm around his leg before he could raise it again. Even with two arms she couldn't have pulled Novak to the ground, but she wasn't trying to. Instead Bridge used his leg as leverage to pull herself up, headbutting him in the crotch and throwing him off balance. He fell, and Bridge turned to see Fred cutting through Steph's bonds.

"Go, go," she shouted, knowing they didn't need her encouragement, but feeling bound to give it anyway. She heard Izzy call from the direction of the hallway, and the knowledge that Novak had missed — that her sister hadn't been shot by a man Bridge should have finished off herself the day before — filled her with relief. Here, now and at last, she could make sure the threat was neutralised.

Novak had other ideas. Bridge glimpsed a dark line, tracing an arc through the air, a split second before the fireplace poker struck her on the back of the head. The world spun, then drained of colour as the floor rushed to greet her. Her reflexes saved her, throwing an arm in front of her face as she fell so her elbow smashed against the floor instead of her mouth.

"Bliyad," she heard Novak mutter, and it gave her some small sense of satisfaction to know she was getting under his skin. The Fiat car keys dug into her stomach from the hoodie pocket, and she wished she'd grabbed the gun from the car instead of bringing a knife. The rational part of her brain knew she hadn't because she didn't want to waste time reaching Novak; that if he'd heard her enter the house and then leave again, he might have killed Fred and Steph before she could get to them. She'd done the right thing, and handled it correctly — so how come he was winning? How come Novak was about to kill her stone dead, if she'd done the right thing? Why hadn't she been able to even the odds?

And then she remembered the other thing in her pocket.

Novak was bending to retrieve his gun. Bridge summoned a burst of energy, pushed herself to her feet, and charged. She slammed into him and they fell together through the French windows, shattering glass that rained around them as they tumbled down the low steps, onto the waiting gravel that crunched under their weight.

Now, while he was dazed. Bridge fought through the cotton wool in her own head to pull out the emergency Ziploc bag, and find the loop of monofilament wire. Only a metre long, but that was enough to wrap around Marko Novak's throat and pull tight.

He gasped, clutching at the line as it closed around his neck, with Bridge's weight pinning him down. Hard Man had warned them at the Loch that strangling a man was a slow process. It wasn't like the movies, where people collapsed after ten seconds. Death took a minute or more to arrive, and the instinctive will to live made it an exhausting business for both participants. Bridge was ready for that; she'd use her own last breath if necessary, to make sure Novak couldn't endanger her family any more. But she wasn't ready for him to grab a terracotta pot from the foot of the steps and slam it into her face.

It shattered on impact. Bridge fell sideways, losing her grip, and the monofilament slackened. Novak pushed himself up, throwing her off. As she lay on the ground, wiping blood from her eyes, he kicked her in the head, then twice in the stomach. But the kicking stopped, and Bridge looked up to see him returning inside. She was confused. Why stop? Why didn't he keep kicking until she couldn't take it any more? Then she remembered what was in the lounge.

His gun.

She scrambled to her feet and ran, half-blind in one eye as blood flowed from a gash in her forehead. She was a sitting duck out here, and relied on Izzy having enough sense to take Fred and Steph out of the house. Bridge hadn't seen where they went, but hoped they'd run into the yard. She wanted to keep Novak as far away from them as possible.

She ducked back inside the house through the utility room door, picking up an iron foot scraper on the way, and continued on to the hallway. While she didn't know the layout of the farmhouse very well, she guessed Novak didn't know it at all. She picked one end of the hallway and waited behind a corner. Footsteps came from the direction of the lounge, and Bridge steeled herself. Novak appeared in the hallway, near the stairs. She drew a foot back, ready to kick the wall and get him to come towards her. She gripped the foot scraper, ready to swing it.

At least, that was the plan until Hugo cried out from upstairs.

Fred must have put him down for a morning nap before Novak got here, because when she dared to look round the doorway, Novak was smiling and making his way to the stairs. He hadn't known there was another potential hostage.

Bridge had to make a decision. If she attacked Novak now, in the hallway, he'd have time to shoot before she could reach him. The first bullet might not be fatal, but he'd already demonstrated his willingness to kill her, and would doubtless finish the job before leaving. Nevertheless, Bridge was clearly his principal target, so with her dead he might leave her family alone.

Or she could wait, follow him upstairs, and take him unawares. But every step of the bare wooden stairs creaked like a rusty old door, and even if Novak didn't hear her climbing after him, she'd have to take him out dangerously close to Hugo. The worst of both worlds.

Bridge decided an attack now would at least give her the element of surprise. She raised the iron boot scraper and rounded the doorway, breaking into a run —

"Get off those stairs, you coward, and face me."

A man's shout, hoarse and delirious, and Bridge was shocked to realise it was in French. Not Novak, but Fréderic. He advanced from the other end of the hallway, hefting the wood axe from the yard at the Russian.

She shouted, "Fred, get out," but it was too late. Novak raised his pistol and fired. Fred groaned and crumpled to the ground, falling like a dead weight.

Novak had heard her, and turned to fire at Bridge too. She ducked back behind the doorway, crying out as splintered pieces of architrave blasted through the air like shrapnel.

Fred was on the floor, dead or dying. If she couldn't help him fast, the distinction wouldn't matter. But she was literally outgunned. If she tried to reach him now, Novak would shoot her before she got within five metres.

Only one option remained. She ran through the kitchen and back out of the main hallway, into the yard. She'd expected to find Izzy and Steph out here, perhaps hiding behind a car, but they were nowhere to be seen. A movement at the edge of her vision caught her eye, and she turned to see her sister and niece running into the estate woodland. Good. If they stayed there Novak wouldn't find them, and they wouldn't have to see Fred.

Bridge fumbled with the keys in her pocket, pressing the blipper twice before the Fiat finally unlocked. She leapt inside, turned the key in the ignition —

Nothing. She tried again. Not a whimper or groan.

Novak emerged from the doorway, laughing as he saw her behind the wheel. He raised his pistol and shouted, "You didn't think I'd leave a perfectly good car just sitting there, did you?" He fired twice, hitting the bonnet and the windscreen. Bridge ducked, pressing her face into the passenger seat as glass exploded around her. She reached out blindly, fumbled with the glove compartment latch, and reached inside. The car had been locked, so Novak must have forced the bonnet open to remove the starter motor. He hadn't been inside. It should still be there.

It was. Bridge felt the loaded weight of the SP2022, and the unnerving sense of comfort that came from knowing the odds were now even. She pushed open the passenger door. The window immediately shattered as Novak fired at it, followed by another two bullets slamming into the metal of the door. But Bridge had expected that Novak would assume she was trying to flee the car, using the door as cover, and so would focus on that area. Instead she sat bolt upright inside the car, raised her pistol, and shot twice at Novak through the empty windscreen.

He crumpled like a sack of potatoes.

Bridge staggered out of the car, and saw Izzy and Steph running back across the field toward her. She motioned at them to stay away, then turned back to the house.

Fred lay where he'd been shot, shivering in a pool of his own blood, clutching his abdomen. He was alive, barely, but his skin was ten shades whiter than healthy. Bridge tried to pull him up, but he was too heavy even for her. "Fred," she shouted, "Fred! Can you hear me?" He looked at her for the first time, his eyes focusing into a glare filled with blind hatred. Good. Anger would keep him alive longer than fear. "I need you to stand for me," she said, helping him into an upright sitting position. "Put your arm over my shoulder, OK?"

He said nothing, but grunted and seethed through gritted teeth as he pushed himself up. Bridge dropped one of his arms across her shoulder and took the weight on her legs. He reached out for purchase, smearing bloody handprints on the wall, and after a couple of false starts he was as upright as he was ever going to be. Bridge began a slow limping walk back through the utility room, out into the yard. Fred grunted in pain with every step.

Izzy yelped in horror at the sight of him, and Stéphanie started crying again. Bridge couldn't blame either of them, but she needed Izzy's car, and shouted at her to open the passenger door. Izzy ran to the Renault, holding the door open while Bridge pushed and folded Fred inside. She removed her hoodie, balled it up, and pressed it against his stomach. "Hold this tight," she said to him. He nodded weakly, placing his hands across it, then coughed as his head lolled back.

Izzy was trying to reach Fred, to comfort him, but it was just wasting time. Bridge pushed her sister away, closed the door, then gripped her by the shoulders. "Hey, hey. Look at me. You and Steph need to go inside, call the *gendarmes*, and tell them what happened."

"But I don't — I mean, what about —?"

"It doesn't matter. I don't care. Tell them everything you know, everything you saw. Tell them it was me who killed the Russian, me who made this whole mess, and if they want me they can find me at the hospital." It was true; she didn't care. She got in the car, fired up the engine, then lowered the window when Izzy tapped on it.

"The hospital is on the north edge of town. Turn right out of the driveway, and there's a sign at the first junction."

Bridge placed her hand over Izzy's, resting on the window. "He'll be OK," she said.

"He'd better, or I'll kill you myself," said Izzy, and Bridge knew she meant it.

"Maman, Maman, he's not dead," said Stéphanie, tugging at Izzy's arm.

"I know, darling," Izzy said, "but he has to go to the hospital."

"No, the other man. Look!"

Time slowed as Bridge turned to where Novak lay on the ground. Except now he wasn't on the ground. He was pushing himself up, staggering to his feet, raising the Grach.

Bridge stood on the accelerator, leaned hard on the wheel, and jammed the car into gear. The Renault surged forward in an arc and broke Novak's knees as he flew onto the bonnet, slammed against the windscreen, then fell off the side.

Bridge opened the door and stepped out. Novak squirmed on the ground, his mouth howling a silent scream of pain. His pistol lay nearby. She picked it up.

"Izzy, take Stéphanie."

Izzy understood. She pulled her daughter toward her, burying Steph's face in her dress.

A single shot rang out across the farmland, scattering blackbirds.

63

The Renault itself was innocuous and unremarkable, but the deep dent in the bonnet, along with Bridge's driving, was anything but. As she sped down country roads, Bridge saw several drivers reach for their phones.

Let them. Let them call the police. The cops would be on her soon enough anyway, with all the red lights she was running. The Renault was the diametric opposite of a performance getaway car, but it was small and nippy enough to weave through crowded junctions and cut across traffic islands with abandon. If Hard Man could see her now, it was equal odds whether he'd praise her daring, or bollock her carelessness. Driving may not have been Bridge's best class at the Loch, but she'd never been this motivated before. Motivated to save the life of a man who disliked her intensely, but meant everything to the only people she had left to care about.

Blood soaked into the passenger seat, and Bridge wondered if Izzy's insurance would pay for this kind of thing. Did 'acts of God' cover international espionage? Would "front seat, footwell carpet, and door lining irrevocably soaked with human blood" make the car a write-off?

It would definitely write off her hoodie, which was now soaked through with blood as she held it pressed against Adrian's stomach whenever she didn't have to change gear, or spin the wheel with both hands. His own limp hands rested on the jacket, but as soon as she let go there was no pressure. She squinted ahead, trying to see beyond the dim headlamps in the desert night, looking for a landmark.

Not the desert. French roads. France, not Syria.

A road sign pointed to the local hospital, left across a traffic island. She took the direct route, skipping the island itself, and cut in front of a courier van taking the same turn. The van driver blasted his horn and slammed on the brakes. Bridge sped away, flicked the car back into high gear, and thrust out her hand to press her hoodie against Fred's wound. Her fingers sank into the wet fabric as if there was no resistance underneath, no real body casually pouring out its life onto the cheaply upholstered seat of a Renault hatchback.

If only he'd listened to her. Why did nobody ever do what she told them to?

"Wake up, Adrian!" Bridge shouted. He was slipping in and out of consciousness, occasionally regaining enough sense to whimper quietly as the jeep's iron-hard suspension bounced him around while they sped through the night.

When she was young, Izzy had fallen off a low wall in the street, landing on her head. The doctor had attended her at home and said she would be fine except for bruising, but warned their mother not to let Izzy fall asleep for at least six hours, otherwise she might be concussed…or was it that she might slip into a coma… It was so long ago. Bridge thought of her sister lying on the couch, prodded awake by their mother every time she closed her eyes. She shouted at Fred again and threw the jeep down a gear. *The engine complained, high revs whining like a lawnmower, but the vehicle grudgingly accelerated, bouncing over the terrain, and Bridge's laugh was carried away on the desert wind. She hoped he wouldn't remember that, if he lived.*

When he lived. He was going to live. He was not going to die. Not this one.

Not this time.

Fuel. How much fuel did she have? She glanced down, cursing herself for not checking before. Half full. Enough to get to the hospital. More than the jeep, only a quarter full even before the Russians shot a hole in it. Choking its last north of the settlement, dying without drama and leaving Bridge alone in the cold night.

Not this time.

Her foot tried to push the accelerator through the floor, across two lanes and into the hospital entrance. She eased off twenty metres from the emergency admissions door, standing on the brakes, grinding the Renault's offside wing against a parked ambulance. She stumbled out and pulled open the passenger door, trying to haul Fred out of the car. Her hands fumbled on his arm and shoulders, slippery with his blood and her sweat. "Come on, you bastard," she grunted, and then someone was pulling her away, back, as the ambulance staff reached over her to lift him out, shouting and running, and Bridge let herself fall to the pavement, whispering, "*Je vais bien, aidez-le,*" to the men crowding over her, and then he was gone, inside to safety, and there was nothing more she could do for Adrian.

Not Adrian. Fred. Fréderic had been with her in the jeep — *no, not the jeep, the car* — next to her, blood spreading from the wound in his stomach, Adrian's useless hands red and slick — *no, Fred's hands* — fading in and out as they drove through the night, no, the day, *not the desert, not Syria...*

Bridge doubled over and vomited into the gutter. She gasped for breath and wiped her mouth with the back of her hand, her mind clear for the first time in years. She remembered.

She *remembered.*

She vomited again.

64

Adrian's back was turned when the second guard ran in.

Bridge saw him, but she couldn't move. Like a nightmare where her body wouldn't respond, she wanted to draw her gun, eliminate the threat, sweep for follow-up, as all her training had conditioned her to do. But she couldn't open her mouth to shout a warning, much less fire a gun. Less than a minute ago she'd witnessed her first live kill, and now her body was shutting down, trying to make sense of it all. She pushed against it, summoning every ounce of will she could dig out from the depths of her consciousness, struggling to move, to act, to save her partner's life.

The guard looked past her — just a woman — to Adrian, the big man he'd heard shouting in English, and raised his rifle. Perhaps the guard made a sound, something in the air that was imperceptible to Bridge, but that Adrian's experience allowed him to hear. Or maybe he was just turning to shout at her again.

Whatever the reason, turning saved his life. The guard's bullet — single shot fire, not spray, not here in a room full of computers — hit Adrian in his lower side, rather than full in the chest where he'd been aiming. Classic gut shot, Bridge immediately thought. He'll live.

And now her body was working again. The Zastava CZ 99 was in her hands, muzzle raised, sighted at the second guard, who was turning his rifle on her as a third Russian ran in behind him. She squeezed, felt the pistol kick, squeezed again without re-sighting. She could almost see Hard Man watching over her shoulder, nodding approval as the guard dropped to the ground, double tap in the chest and shoulder. The third guard fumbled for his own rifle, but Bridge had the advantage, with her pistol already raised and ready to fire. She adjusted, re-sighted, fired. Missed, but stone chips ricocheted off the wall by the guard's head, and he flinched, and then a single shot from behind Bridge made the guard's nose explode.

She turned to see Adrian on the floor, propped against the base of a server rack, gun in one hand, the other pressed against his body. Blood spread through the fingers. "Fucked that up, didn't we?" he grunted, using the barrel of his CZ 99 as leverage against the ground, forcing himself to stand. Bridge holstered her own pistol and helped him up, dropping his arm across her shoulders. Except for a short pre-teen phase when she first shot past her friends, Bridge had never been self-conscious about being tall. Now she was positively thankful she didn't collapse under Adrian's weight. "Wait," he said, "in case of emergency..."

She reached inside his jacket, found Adrian's backup grenades, their carbon surfaces slick with his blood. "Two for now; keep one back," she said, and took them out. She threw one to the far side of the room with the pin still inside, to cover a wide zone, then pulled the pin of the other and prepared to drop it. She took Adrian by the hand and looked him in the eye. "You're sure you can run."

"It's only a flesh wound," he said, and winked.

Bridge tossed the grenade on the floor and ran, back through the stale air of the stone corridors, pulling Adrian behind her, ignoring his grunts of pain and not thinking about the blood pouring out of his abdomen.

She shot the jeep guard while Adrian followed, using all his energy to stay silent.

They drove the stolen jeep into the desert night together.

The windscreen exploded, showering them both with glass.

Adrian passed her his last ICE grenade in the settlement, and she used it to take out the Russians chasing them.

Bridge laughed. "We're going to make it. We're bloody well going to make it! I mean, Giles is going to bollock us for blowing up the server farm, but we had no choice, right? It was better guarded than we were expecting, and then once reinforcements showed up the job was a bust anyway, so we had to get out of there."

Adrian said nothing.

"Look, don't get shirty with me. I told you they probably had cameras in there, but you wouldn't listen. Now you're going to have a month in hospital to think about that, and maybe if you apologise I'll bring you a bunch of grapes."

Adrian said nothing.

Bridge had done enough club all-nighters on speed to recognise she was hyped, that the adrenaline coursing through her body was making her a blabbermouth. That was fine. It didn't matter. It was good to be alive. They'd got out, and they were going to make it.

Adrian said nothing.

Bridge howled at the night, drowned out by the sound of the jeep, crying for the dead man beside her.

When the fuel gauge hit rock bottom and the jeep sputtered its last, she had no tears left to cry. The Russians hadn't just shot out the jeep's rear fender, they'd hit the fuel tank as well, and Bridge had never been so alone in her life. Just her, the cold black desert, and a Serbian pistol with half a dozen bullets left in the clip.

She began to walk.

Bridge wiped her mouth, tasting vomit on the back of her tongue, and looked up through her fringe as two police cars, lights blazing and bright even at this time of the morning, screeched to a halt outside the hospital. *About time*, she thought, and collapsed in the road.

65

"My name is Bridget Short. I'm a British civil servant. I was visiting a friend when a madman took us hostage. I want to call the British embassy in Paris."

"Your French is impeccable. So let me say this clearly: *bullshit*."

"My name is Bridget Short. I'm a British civil servant. I was visiting a friend..."

Bridge lost count after the fourth *gendarme* interrogator. It didn't matter how many they sent. The first rule of being interrogated, whether by police or security services, was remarkably simple. *No matter what you think they might know, no matter what they claim to have on you, say nothing and demand a lawyer.* Simple, but surprisingly difficult to follow. Interrogators were practised at bluffing, stretching the truth, sensing weakness and giving the impression they already knew what had happened, they just needed to hear it in your own words, and telling all now would make things so much easier later... But in fact, most of the time they knew very little. They relied on educated guesswork, knowledge of the criminal mind, and outright lies to convince prisoners their situation was hopeless and confession was inevitable.

Bridge knew how that felt. She'd screwed up so much, she was just about ready to throw in the towel anyway. Killing Montgomery had forced her to go on the run; fleeing to Izzy had brought Novak to them, and endangered her sister's family; killing Novak had exposed her to the authorities, and blew whatever cover she still had left. And she still didn't know how bad the Exphoria leak was, or what Montgomery had actually stolen.

She had one thing to do before returning to London, but then she was done. Giles had been wrong about her. She should never have gone OIT in the first place. Not three years ago, not now. All she did was screw everything up.

And then François Voclaine walked in the door, smiled at her, and lit a cigarette.

Memories, images, and fragments of conversation flooded Bridge's mind. A carefully placed word here, a cautious silence there, his interrogation, the moment when he defiantly destroyed his phone. And his disappearance from police custody, which Bridge had all but forgotten about in the frantic, violent madness that followed.

"Oh, balls," she sighed, making sense of it all. "You're DGSI." The *Direction Générale de la Sécurité Intérieure* was France's internal partner to the *Extérieure* DGSE, just like MI5 to SIS, or the FBI to the CIA. And they'd sent their own mole hunter to Agenbeux. "Why didn't you tell us? For God's sake, we could have worked together."

Voclaine reached over to unlock Bridge's handcuffs, and snorted. "I could say the same to you. A British spy, operating in France without our knowledge or consent? Naughty, naughty."

"So now what?" said Bridge, rubbing her newly freed wrists.

Voclaine handed her his cigarette. "Now you come with me, and smoke this instead of talking."

He led her out of the station, past *gendarmes* whose eyes held nothing but hatred and suspicion. One senior officer looked like he might try to prevent them leaving, but Voclaine fixed him with a defiant stare and the man backed off. Outside, Voclaine opened the passenger door of a blue Peugeot, and made sure Bridge saw the gun holstered under his coat as he closed the door. The message was clear: *don't even think about running.*

In the three seconds it took him to walk round to the driver's side, Bridge ran through many of the possibilities ahead of her. Voclaine was taking her to his bosses at DGSI HQ in Paris, who would place her under extrajudicial arrest at Château d'If (oh, the irony) and return her to England only in return for political favours. Or he would take her to Henri Mourad, with an offer to cover up the two murders Bridge had recently committed on French soil in return for everything the British had regarding Exphoria. Or perhaps he was simply going to drive to a quiet spot in the woods and shoot her in the back of the head.

What she didn't expect was for him to climb in the driver's seat, reach into a briefcase on the back seat, and hand her a new passport. "Novak was carrying your 'Catherine Pritchard' backup when you killed him. It's ruined. Use this instead." It featured the same picture as her Bridget Short passport, but now she was called 'Fleur Simpson'. Voclaine pulled the car away, nodding at the glove compartment as they approached the main road. She opened it to find, among the log books and driving gloves, a roll of cash held tight by an elastic band. "One thousand euros. You'll use it to buy a flight to London; no paper trail. Once you're back in England, you're not my problem any more."

"Am I your problem now?"

"Too fucking right you are." Voclaine lit two cigarettes, and passed one to her. "Mourad is busy elsewhere, according to your boss Dunston."

Bridge didn't correct him. Voclaine was trying to demonstrate he was in command, that he had enough knowledge about the situation that she shouldn't question him. So let him believe she worked for Emily. The more he thought he knew everything, the more he might talk. "Only myself and two senior officers know who you are, and what you're doing here. The faster you leave France, the easier it will be to keep it that way. Understand?"

Bridge nodded. "How are you going to explain Novak's death? Won't the *gendarmerie* want revenge?" Voclaine gave her a quizzical look, and Bridge swore quietly as she realised how many assumptions she'd made in the heat of the moment. She'd been a bloody idiot. "Oh — Novak wasn't police at all, was he? It was just a disguise. It was you who sent those *gendarmes* to my guest house in Agenbeux, not him."

Voclaine looked at her with surprise. "You were there?"

"Watching from afar." She neglected to mention the officer who'd stopped her, but let her go. It would only annoy Voclaine more. The memory led her to think of the farmhouse, and she gasped. "The hospital —"

"Your family is fine," grumbled Voclaine. "Fréderic Baudin has been stabilised, his family is with him, and the doctor says he'll pull through. Mainly because you got him to the hospital in time, so at least you did one thing right."

Bridge relaxed. Knowing Fréderic would be safe was some comfort. But now she had another thought. "François… I need to do something before I go back to London."

Voclaine shook his head. "I don't care."

"You will. I'm going to make you an offer you can't refuse."

He looked sideways at her. "My cover story was just that, you know. I'm happily married."

"And you're not my type," she laughed. "You're too…French."

"So what are you offering?"

"Take me back to the farmhouse."

"No chance. It's a crime scene, and the *gendarmes* are crawling all over it."

"Fair enough," she said, "I suppose it's fine if the local cops find out about Exphoria, anyway."

Voclaine hit the brakes, hard, and the car juddered to a halt. He turned on Bridge, suspicious. "What are you talking about? We have your laptop and phone already. We found them at the guest house."

Bridge noted he didn't say they'd cracked the security, which pleased her a little. Not that it would matter much if they had, because: "Everything on them is from before I confirmed Montgomery as the mole. But at his apartment I figured out how he was doing it, and retrieved some of the data. I'm sure the *gendarmerie* will find it fascinating."

Voclaine seethed quietly. For a second, Bridge thought he might actually hit her in frustration. Instead he punched the steering wheel, spat out "*Merde*," and pulled a U-turn before speeding back towards *La Ferme Baudin*.

66

Lacking official ID, Bridge let Voclaine do the talking. He told the *gendarmerie* his name was Serge Tolbert, and presented himself officially as DGSI, but she suspected that was no more his real name than 'François Voclaine'.

Whatever his name, she was grateful for his authority. He stopped the police from bagging Fred's HP laptop, and ordered them all out of the room. Bridge opened the lid and was presented with a login screen. Voclaine (she couldn't think of him as 'Tolbert') groaned in frustration. But Bridge had watched Fred log in the night before, and while she hadn't specifically followed his typing, it was a simple enough password that she'd caught it without meaning to. She entered:

```
s-t-e-p-h-a-n-i-e-1-2-3
```

And the login screen was replaced by the desktop. The frontmost window was the DOS shell she'd used to run the recover process. She scanned down to the last message before the prompt.

```
> Session complete: 435 files recovered
```

Bridge opened the SD card directory, and where it had been empty the day before, now it was full of photographs. She could tell just from the thumbnails that these were what they'd all been looking for, but she opened half a dozen at full size to confirm it for Voclaine. Photographs of a computer screen inside the Agenbeux facility.

Voclaine almost choked. "That's my desk," he said in disbelief. "Why are there photos of my desk?"

"Not your desk," said Bridge, "your screen…and the Exphoria code." She scrolled through the photos, to show the pages and pages of code on the screen. "This card was in a mini-tablet Montgomery carried, rather than his phone. I'm guessing he took these while you were out of the room, probably during smoke breaks."

"We didn't find a tablet at his apartment."

"Because I took it with me, and pulled this SD card out last night. You're lucky I managed to recover these photos, to be honest. Novak almost destroyed the entire tablet when he attacked me."

Voclaine shook his head. "You knew this was how James leaked the code?"

"I had a hunch," Bridge shrugged, "but until now I wasn't completely sure. Hell, until now I wasn't completely sure Montgomery was the mole."

"Are you telling me you killed him without proof? Are you completely insane?"

"Hey, it was self defence. I was looking for proof at his apartment when he attacked me, and now we have it. I just wish we knew who he was working for."

"Russia."

"How do you know?"

Voclaine nodded out toward the courtyard, where a coroner's tent had been erected around Marko Novak's body. "His real name is Grigori Pushkin, and the DGSE has a file on him. Ex-FSB, freelance for the past twenty years, but does plenty of work for Putin's boys. We found hidden cameras watching Montgomery's apartment, and there was even a Russian go-bag on the bed, ready and packed. Rubles, fake passport, the works."

"I thought you were DGSI."

"This isn't England, *mademoiselle*. Our departments don't keep secrets from each other."

Bridge sighed. So it seemed Russia really was still up to military espionage, after all. "Do you have a USB stick?"

Voclaine reached inside his jacket and pulled out a small blue flash drive. "Always. You never know."

Bridge plugged it in, and started copying the photographs across. They both watched in silence as the progress bar inched up the screen, until all the data had transferred. Then she removed the drive, closed the HP, replaced it in the bag, and handed it to Voclaine. "The laptop, and the card in it, go straight to London. If Médecins Sans Frontières want it back, they'll have to take it up with SIS."

Voclaine was confused. "Why not take them yourself?"

"Because I'm not going to back to London."

"Now hang on a second."

Bridge tucked the USB stick into Voclaine's coat pocket. "How ever did the DGSI get that data? I suppose the *gendarmes* made a copy before they handed over the laptop. Maybe only I know for sure, but seeing as I escaped your custody and hopped on a plane, you can't ask me."

Voclaine grumbled, but reached into another pocket and produced a small Ziploc bag. It contained a micro camera, bugging equipment, a tiny flashlight, and a roll of US dollars. "You'll want this, I expect. I requisitioned it from the station when I picked you up."

Bridge took her emergency SIS bag and smiled. "Thank you. Now, what's the smallest local airport that can get me to Greece?"

67

Finding a boat to take her from Cyprus to the Syrian coast with no questions asked was easy. Even getting to Homs wasn't too hard, just a matter of offering a few dollars to drivers heading there anyway. But finding someone in the city willing to drive her into the desert was difficult. In fact, finding anyone who would even talk to Bridge was proving to be a challenge.

Picking her way through the ruined streets, shocked at the sheer scale of destruction from the bombings, it was hard to be surprised. Language wasn't the problem, as almost everyone here spoke either French or English. It was that she was an outsider, a Westerner, one of the many who'd abandoned the people here to die, and that created a default state of hostility she'd never encountered before.

She eventually found a man who collected and stockpiled military equipment, lost or abandoned by both government and rebels during the city's long siege. His compound was the shell of an old building that might once have been a centre of local administration, but it was impossible to say for sure. Remove a building's windows, decor, and signage, and replace them with shrapnel scars, shell craters, and fallen rubble, and pretty soon they all look the same.

Getting in to see the collector required bribe upon bribe to various levels of armed guards, and when she finally reached his inner sanctum Bridge's stockpile of cash had a serious dent. A couple of American dollars here was a small fortune. She could only imagine the chaos if she had to ask armed gangsters to break a fifty.

As the complex hierarchy of guards gatekeeping their boss led her through the black-market compound, she glimpsed the stockpile. A stack of assault rifles here, a row of grenade launchers there, mortars and grenades arranged for viewing, and handguns laid out by size and calibre. Was all of this really from the streets of Homs, looted from the bodies of soldiers or abandoned by retreating forces? Or was some of it smuggled in through the old Iraqi supply lines, the very place Bridge wanted to go? Worse still, could some items have been bought from Europe's own black-market traders? She wasn't naive enough to think she could trust anyone here, but could this trader really give her what she needed? More importantly, would he?

Then they crossed a central courtyard, and she saw the rows of vehicles. Land rovers, troop trucks, jeeps (rear-mounted M60 machine gun optional), a US-style humvee, all in differing states of repair.

To his credit, the trader didn't seem surprised to see this pale Western woman, all in black except for the hair-covering *keffiyeh* she'd bought in Latakia, on mysterious business at what was once the epicentre of Syrian violence. Instead he merely asked, in perfect French, what he could do for her.

Bridge told the trader where she wanted to go, and asked for one of his men to drive her there and back. He lost his composure, and laughed in her face. So she offered instead to buy one of his jeeps, and drive herself. He laughed again, but this time more politely. He asked how much money she had. Bridge offered him a fifth of what she was carrying. If they frisked her, they'd find double that. The remainder was inside her underwear, and if things went that far Bridge would happily use the loaded Grach she'd also tucked in there. Perhaps it was detecting that attitude, a dead-eyed fatalism betraying no fear, which made the trader think twice.

They eventually settled on just under half of her 'visible' cash for a fully-fuelled jeep, one of the better models, plus a desert blanket and two canisters of extra petrol. Bridge wasn't sure that would leave her with enough cash to return home, but right now she wasn't thinking that far ahead. If she made it out of the desert in one piece, maybe she could sell the jeep in Tartus — albeit for a fraction of what she'd just paid — and bum around Egypt for a while. Perhaps then she'd finally tell Giles where she was, and he could formally fire her over the phone. But not before she'd found what she was looking for.

One of the collector's guards tried to feel her up as she walked to the jeep, but she broke his shin with a swift kick, disarmed him, and stripped his pistol while the other guards hooted with laughter.

* * *

Night fell as she reached the desert, but Bridge switched on the headlamps and kept driving. The closer she got, the less anxious she became, as if she was returning to a familiar place that she knew well. Still, night driving in the desert was risky, and lacked peripheral vision. Anyone could come at you from the sides or rear and you wouldn't know it until they were on top of you. Or shot out the windscreen.

Around midnight, she parked in the shadow of a rock formation, using her matchstick flashlight to see. She climbed into the back of the jeep, placed the Grach within easy reach, pulled her *keffiyeh* tight, and swaddled herself in the blanket. The stars out here were bright and beautiful, and she fell asleep with their after-image dancing inside her eyelids.

* * *

She awoke to the sound of something knocking against the body of the jeep. She jerked upright with the Grach in hand — and recoiled at the overwhelming smell of dung. A curious gazelle had come to investigate the jeep, and after evacuating itself next to a rear wheel it was rubbing its horns against the metal in curiosity.

After shooing the animal off she made her own ablutions at the foot of the rock formation, emptied a fuel canister into the tank, and resumed driving. Hunger pangs cramped her stomach, and she remembered she hadn't eaten since late afternoon the day before. But while she had water, she hadn't brought food. She didn't intend to be out here more than half a day.

East by southeast, straight as a die except when she had to skirt hills or rocks. After two hours, she slowed and began to pay more attention to the landscape. Nothing looked familiar, and for the first time in three days her emotions threatened to overwhelm her. What had she been thinking? Of course nothing looked familiar. Even if she'd set off from the site of the old Allied base, she'd never find it. The base site itself would have been cleared and lost to the desert long ago. Worse, she didn't follow the same path on her return drive, escaping the Russians and driving through pitch dark. After she abandoned the jeep, it took her another day to get close enough to the base to be spotted by an American patrol, a friendly bunch who kept calling her "real hardcore." When they discovered the British were coming to whisk her away, they gave her a stars-and-stripes patch. Bridge still had it, but it was stuffed at the back of a drawer she never used, so she didn't have to look at it.

Light glinted off metal to the east. Steel girders, reaching for the sun from behind a group of low hills. Bridge let out an involuntary cry of surprise, and turned the wheel.

Was it the same place? The same abandoned settlement she'd driven through that night three years ago, trying to escape the Russians? It looked the same, but it had been so dark, and there were so few identifying features. She stopped the jeep and got out, looking around. Wherever this was, nobody had lived here for a long time. Sand drifts leaned against the breezeblock walls and buried the bases of girders. She walked between the half-finished buildings, pulling the *keffiyeh* over her face as air currents whipped around hard corners, filling the air with sand and dust.

There. To the north, twisted metal visible against the sky. She walked faster, turned a corner, and looked up a street on the perimeter of the settlement. Close to her, an outer wall with a row of bricks knocked out, the same height as a jeep tailgate. And there, further up the street, under the shadow of the twisted girders — rubble and wreckage, half-buried by shifting sands and shattered breezeblocks. Here and there were bones, gnawed clean by scavengers. Mangled steel jutted from the ground, pools of rubber melted and reformed under the desert sun, reflecting off shards of blasted glass.

Bridge took a dozen pictures with the solid state micro camera, then climbed back in the jeep and drove north, following what she hoped was the same path she'd taken that night. After the settlement, the jeep had lasted no more than a quarter of an hour before a bullet hole emptied the fuel tank, and she abandoned it to continue on foot. Fifteen minutes' drive wasn't that far. It had to be around here somewhere.

68

Eighteen hours into the surveillance tapes, Steve Wicker was starting to regret asking Patel if he could liaise with Five on Andrea Thomson's case.

Their visit to SignalAir, and the startup's possible link to drone technology, had seemed an obvious lead at the time. If Nigel Marsh and his company were some kind of front, as Andrea had suspected, then the possibility they could be connected to the ID theft drone purchases had stirred in Steve's gut. It wasn't enough to arrest anyone, but it was more than enough for him to start investigating.

With MI5's help, it had taken two days to acquire all the CCTV footage he could from the locations where the package pick-ups had been made. Four didn't have CCTV, and the ones that did could only narrow down the collection times to a morning or afternoon. Steve cursed poor design and wondered aloud who on Earth would design a system, in this age of ubiquitous barcodes, that didn't automatically track packages and log a time? The response was usually a don't-ask-me-I'm-on-a-zero-hours-contract shrug, and after the first few exasperated enquiries he stopped asking.

But now, a day into scanning the various feeds at x8, he wondered if his gut had simply been wrong. There were mail sorting office collection points, private package holders, newsagents that ran a click-and-collect service on the side, and more. The clientele for all of them ran the gamut, from businessmen to PAs to shift workers to tube drivers to, yes, some very dodgy-looking types. From the ostentatious bling of a dealer or heavy, to the threadbare leisurewear of a street chancer, more than half the people who used these services didn't want to be recognised for one reason or another.

Steve yawned and thought about lunch, as on the screen a bored sorting office clerk in Slough checked his text messages for the hundredth time. A new sushi place had opened in town the week before, and Steve wanted to try it out before it inevitably shut down in three months, drowned out like everything else by the ubiquitous coffee shops. It was a shame, really…

There. Stop. Scan back thirty secs. Pause. Check the records.

Gwendolyne Hartwell, 57 years old. She wasn't even aware of the theft until Slough police made enquiries with her, after Steve called them. She'd checked her MasterCard statement and saw the anomaly. Steve could only wonder how she'd missed an unauthorised purchase for just shy of three hundred pounds, but he was more concerned that the bank hadn't flagged the purchase as suspicious, despite Mrs Hartwell's usual credit card purchases coming to less than a hundred pounds per month.

Either way, that wasn't Mrs Hartwell on the surveillance footage, entering the sorting office and showing the clerk a receipt. The man never showed the camera his full face, and he was dressed very differently. But there was no mistaking that sandy beard Steve had first seen in Shoreditch.

Three weeks ago, Nigel Marsh had travelled all the way to Slough to collect a package that just happened to be the right size for a personal quadcopter drone. Steve isolated an image from the footage and dialled Andrea Thomson's direct number.

69

Wherever it was, she couldn't find it.

Bridge had covered every inch of ground within fifteen minutes' drive north of the settlement. Then she tried to the west, and to the east. She even drove south, doubling back toward the Russian site where it had all gone so wrong, the place from which she'd escaped.

They place from which *they'd* escaped. Together. She knew that now.

Late in the afternoon, something glinted on the horizon and she sped towards it, leaving a thirty-foot dust cloud in her wake. It wasn't a mirage; she knew what those looked like. It was something metal, something here in the desert, and it was in more or less the right place, though further west than she'd expected. It would give her answers, maybe a bizarre sense of closure.

But it didn't, because it wasn't the jeep. It was something like a section of fuselage, blackened and twisted by violence. She almost cried, then, to come so close only to be frustrated again. Instead she let out a wordless shout, pulled the Grach, and fired two angry bullets into the fuselage. The vast sound was lost in the desert's emptiness, emphasising her isolation. It was enough to motivate her to get back in the drivers' seat and resume driving.

But now, as the sun slowly descended to the horizon, the jeep coughed to a halt. Only one canister of fuel left, enough to get her back to Homs if she was lucky. If she was unlucky…

She kicked the side of the jeep, cursing her stupidity, her naivety, her failure.

"Did you honestly think I'd still be here?"

Adrian sat on the tailgate, relaxed and casual, in his fatigues.

"Maybe," she said. "The Russian jeep's still there, just about."

He smirked. Just like the real Adrian had, three years ago. "They got blown up. Whereas you abandoned me sitting upright in a more-or-less working jeep."

"I didn't abandon you. I had no choice, you were already dead."

"Tell me about it. Doubt I was out here a week before someone nicked the jeep and left me to the scavengers. Or burned me to the bone."

Bridge sighed. "No, don't sugar-coat it, tell me straight."

"Look who's talking, BB." He winked. "Anyway, what were you going to do if you found me? Collect the bones and take them home? *'Anything to declare, Miss?' 'Only a three-year-old half-eaten corpse, Mr Customs Officer.'*"

Bridge slid to the ground, her back against the jeep's rear wheel. He, that is to say her own subconscious, was right. Had she been seeking some kind of validation? She'd found and killed the mole. Neutralised his handler, too. MI5 would mop up at home, Exphoria would be scrapped. Her mission was, all in all, a success. And not a single person would thank her for any of it.

"Aw, diddums," said Adrian, now sitting beside her in the dirt. "Did you want a medal? Tea at the Palace?"

"How about my own brain not playing tricks on me? Or is that unrealistic, too?"

They watched the sunset in silence for a while. Then Adrian said, "At least you got the bastard who killed Ten."

"I'd rather have Ten still alive," said Bridge.

"Well, that makes two of us. Fuck it, why not make it three? It'll be days before Giles sends anyone to look for you, months before they find you. Drive back to the breezeblocks, hide the jeep in there, then eat the Grach, and they may never find you at all. We can both be out here, lost forever in the desert. You and me together, BB. Comrades in fuckedsville."

She took out the gun and turned it over in her hands. What was it all for, anyway? What was the point? If it wasn't the Russians, it would be someone else. If it wasn't Exphoria, it would be something else. Ciaran's game of whack-a-mole, never-ending and ultimately futile. They might win a battle here and there, but the war would never be over.

"Might as well press the big red button and have a nuclear war," said Adrian. "Start all over again. Couldn't be much worse, could it?"

"That's not what I was thinking, and you of all people know it."

"Don't know why you bothered fighting Novak, really. Izzy and the kids will all die eventually, anyway."

"Yeah, yeah. You've made your point."

"In a hundred years we'll all be dust, right? Everything we've done will be forgotten, lost to history. People won't even know we existed."

"Will you shut up?"

"Probably should have just shot Izzy yourself while you had the chance, spared her the angst."

"Fuck off!" Bridge raised the pistol at Adrian's head. But he wasn't there. She looked around for him through tear-blurred vision, but saw only the horizon devouring the sun, darkness swallowing light, unstoppable and inevitable; a universal truth.

That was why she'd come here. To prove she didn't need her mind to hide things from her, to mask the pain, to make things hurt a little less with lies and deceit. To own her failures, and press on anyway, because while nature was inevitable, people weren't. People could change.

And that was the truth.

70

The building manager unlocked the door and stood aside, watching open-mouthed as a dozen black-geared Armed Response officers swarmed into the lobby. Four remained there, rifles trained on the elevator doors, while the others executed a perfect cover-and-climb procedure up the stairwell.

Andrea Thomson waited in a car parked on the street, listening to command status on an earpiece. The stairwell wasn't visible from outside, but she'd seen enough raids like this to know how the officers would move. Four muzzles aimed upward, allowing the other four officers to climb under their protection. Then they'd stop, take up their own firing positions, and the first four would climb under their cover, like a joyless, lethal game of leapfrog. Slow and laborious, but effective and foolproof.

Ninety seconds in she heard the magic words, *"Target on visual. Prepare for breach."* This was the critical moment, where her own reputation was now in the hands of eight police officers with heavy-duty weaponry.

Scenario one: the breach and infil were clean. Nigel Marsh, and his colleagues Andy and Charlie, were caught unawares and surrendered immediately. Everyone's a hero.

Scenario two: the breach and infil were clean, but Marsh and his colleagues were ready for them. Hostile contact ensued, resulting in one or more deaths. Acceptable, but not optimal. Andrea would face an enquiry, and the armed response officers would undergo counselling, but ultimately it would be written up as a success.

Scenario three: the breach and infil were clean, but one or more of the three targets wasn't present. Those inside were captured, but the remaining target would still be in the wind. A good start, but too early for celebration.

Scenario four: the breach and infil were messy, potentially booby-trapped. There were enough AR boys that the ultimate result would likely match scenario two, but with additional casualties. Andrea would be hauled over the coals, and there might be a public enquiry. Nobody wanted that.

Wrinkles in each scenario brought the contingency count close to a dozen, but these four main scenarios were the ones Andrea had discussed with the Armed Response unit that morning. Through the earpiece, she heard the sound of the SignalAir door being smashed open with a battering ram, and the officers shouting, *"Armed police! Lie down on the ground!"* as they marched into the office. More shouting, a few calls of *"Clear!"* here and there. No shots fired. That was good.

Then silence, and a hissed whisper of "Fuck." Not so good.

"Location secure, tango negative," said the commanding officer to everyone listening in. *"I repeat, location secure, tango negative. Ma'am, there's nothing here. Looks like the place has been cleaned out."*

Andrea was already out of the car, striding toward the building entrance, with two of her Five colleagues behind her. Nobody there? Cleaned out? What the hell could that mean? The rear door of an unmarked van parked close to the entrance opened, and the co-ordinating AR officer looked out. "Tell them to bloody well stay where they are," Andrea barked at him, and entered the lobby. The officers in the lobby stood down as she passed, heading for the stairwell. "Three foxtrot approaching by stairs," said one into a radio, alerting the officers on the third floor. She took the stairs at a jog with her colleagues following, careful not to overtake her.

After three flights she marched into the SignalAir office, and stared at nothing. Nigel Marsh and his colleagues — alleged colleagues, Andrea corrected herself, quickly realising there was no evidence beyond Marsh's word that they existed — were not only absent from the office, but so was everything else. The desks were empty, the bookshelves bare of the few binders they had, the filing and storage cabinets devoid of everything except stationery. Even the grimy kitchenette area had finally been cleaned, and very well, no doubt to reduce the chance of DNA collection.

All that remained of SignalAir was the inkjet mockery of a company plaque on the wall outside. 'Nigel Marsh', or whatever his real name was, had done a runner. Had he known they were coming? Or had her visit with Steve Wicker tipped him off somehow, and he'd cleared out as soon as they left? Andrea kicked herself for not putting Marsh or the company under observation, but at the time, it would have been difficult to justify.

Hell, it still was. All they really had Marsh on was ID theft, receipt of fraudulently obtained goods, and drinking with a man they now knew was former FSB — and whom Brigitte Sharp believed was connected to the Exphoria leak, but couldn't confirm because she'd killed both the suspected leak and the Russian, before apparently losing the plot and going AWOL. Andrea still hadn't decided if Sharp was a paranoid nut or a genius, and that particular jury would be out until this whole case was closed.

But the only way to achieve closure now relied on finding Marsh. If he really was involved, then as far as they knew he was the last surviving link in a chain of international espionage and potential terrorism. But there could be dozens more behind him, supporting and financing him.

On the other hand, he might not be involved at all, and Sharp's instincts were simply wrong. Giles trusted her, but how much of that was departmental loyalty? What did he say behind closed doors? Did he even know where his golden girl was?

Andrea waved her hands to shoo everyone out of the office. “Nobody comes in until SOCO have been over this place with a dozen fine toothcombs,” she said, exiting with them. “If that smug posh bastard left a fleck of dandruff here, I want it bagged.”

71

"I don't think anything here warrants aborting the demonstration, much less the whole project. Really, Finlay, is this all you have?"

Giles looked up from his briefing file and raised an eyebrow across the table at Air Vice-Marshal Sir Terence Cavendish. He'd expected resistance, but not outright dismissal. "Perhaps I didn't explain things well enough, sir. The evidence we have in hand, including our officer's first-hand account, suggests the entire source code of Exphoria may have leaked."

"Suggests is all very well," said Devon Chisholme, positioned at the head of the table, "but there seems a distinct lack of proof. Sharp made rather a mess over there, including two deaths and a rather annoyed DGSI, and all you have to show for it are some photos of computer screens."

"With respect, Devon, that's the proof," said Emily Dunston, next to Giles. "One of her kills was the mole himself…"

"So you assume," Chisholme interrupted. "But once again, we appear to be rather short on supporting evidence."

Giles forced himself not to sigh or raise his voice. "This isn't a court room. Montgomery had the photographs in his possession when he attacked her, and the *gendarmes* later found a go-bag prepped for Moscow in his bedroom. In our book, that's open and shut."

"And those photos are how the information was leaked, without ever needing to actually conduct a computer hack," said Emily.

"Modern cameras afford extremely high resolution, as the sensors on autonomous vehicles like Exphoria itself demonstrate. What was cutting edge five years ago is now on sale in Argos."

Sir Terence snorted. "Even assuming any code was extracted, I still don't see how it justifies cancelling the demonstration. We assume Moscow has insight on our hardware initiatives anyway. If they now also have some knowledge of the software, surely it's in our interest to demonstrate it quickly, before they can do anything with it themselves."

"Yes, like hack into it," said Giles, running out of patience.

"Is that likely?" asked Chisholme.

"Highly. If we had access to equivalent Russian software, our people would be working around the clock to dismantle it."

"And how long would it take them?" asked Sir Terence.

"How long is a piece of string, or indeed, computer code? Hours, days, weeks, months, it's impossible to speculate."

"And yet, speculation is all you've presented this morning. Months, indeed. What you mean is, it might never happen. Or maybe they'll just take a photograph of it, would that constitute a danger?" Sir Terence closed his briefing file, and his aide quickly scooped it into her briefcase. "In the face of a multi-billion euro project, I find your proposal to be a gross overreaction. Bring me real evidence, or drop it. And thank God we discussed this amongst ourselves before taking it to the French." He stood, and turned on his heel. "Exphoria will proceed as scheduled, and that's my final word on the matter. Good day, everyone."

After Sir Terence and his aide left, Chisholme and his assistants followed, with an apologetic shrug but no offer of help. Giles and Emily remained, seething with shared anger.

Emily spoke first. "He's after Lord Bloody Cavendish, isn't he? Knighthood's not enough for him."

"Come on," said Giles, "we have a lot of speculating to do."

72

"How do you feel, now that you know the truth?"

Six hours ago, Bridge had been cooling off in a Heathrow detention room, thanks to the immigration officer who called security when she tried to enter the country. After three days in Syria she looked nothing like Fleur Simpson's passport photo, but it wouldn't have mattered if she had.

Two hours ago, three SIS juniors came to collect her, and said the passport was red-flagged the moment she went AWOL. They didn't say a whole lot more, and she knew better than to ask. The only real surprise of the journey was that they drove directly to Vauxhall. She half-expected to be tossed in a secure compound.

Ninety minutes ago, she'd delivered a debrief to Buchanan, one of Giles' deputies, down in the 'fishbowl', a basement interrogation room that earned its nickname because it was fully wired for sound and vision from a dozen different angles. She'd watched sessions in there herself from the comfort of a nearby viewing room, and wondered who was watching this time, as she related why she'd gone to Syria and what she now remembered about Doorkicker. She skipped the part where she'd contemplated blowing her own brains out in the desert.

Five minutes ago, she was brought to Dr Nayar's corner office. The doctor had evidently watched the debrief, and now she wanted to know how her patient felt.

Bridge looked out over the Thames, and said, "It's complicated."

Dr Nayar smiled and replied in her gentle voice, "It always is. The mind often protects itself with false memories, trying to shield us from trauma."

"I don't see how thinking I'd abandoned him in the bunker was less traumatic than knowing I'd at least tried to save him." She tapped the side of her head. "Aren't you supposed to know how this works?"

"I'm afraid we're still at the 'more art than science' stage. We can't write lines of code for our minds. Not yet, anyway." Dr Nayar smiled again. "And you now know there was nothing more you could have done. From what you've described, I believe you did more than most people would have in the same situation."

Bridge shrugged. "But we're not most people, are we? We're supposed to be better trained, think more clearly, act more quickly."

"You eliminated several enemy combatants, destroyed the facility, extracted your partner, then outran and escaped your pursuers. What more could you have done?"

"Saved Adrian's life," Bridge said. "Or is that not as important as the mission?"

"You saved your brother-in-law. Surely you can give yourself credit for that."

Bridge snorted. "What, for making sure my sister probably never speaks to me again? If I hadn't gone running to her, Fred would never have been in danger to start with. Buchanan said they've all had to sign the official secrets act, for God's sake."

"But you saved them. You killed their attacker, and eliminated the mole to boot." Dr Nayar put down her notepad, and leaned forward. "I've spent a lot of time talking to officers like you, Brigitte. I've never met one whose mission didn't run into problems. Mistaken identity, hesitation, errors of judgement… I mean, at least you didn't jump into bed with anyone inappropriate, that's always a bonus." Bridge snorted a laugh despite herself. "We're all human, and none of us is perfect. None of *you* are perfect. Do you think you're the only OIT to doubt whether you did a good job? Who thinks they screwed everything up, had to improvise, and only scraped through by a stroke of good luck? Because believe me, all those conversations have proven one thing: there are good officers, and there are bad officers, but there is no such thing as a lucky officer."

"It doesn't matter, anyway," Bridge sighed. "This was the last time."

Dr Nayar frowned. "After all this, are you seriously asking to be taken off the OIT list again?"

Bridge laughed. "Off the list? No, no. I'm quitting SIS."

* * *

"Don't be absurd. You can't resign."

"This isn't the *cosa nostra*, you can't force me to stay here."

Giles Finlay raised an eyebrow. Not for the first time, Bridge wondered if SIS kept blackmail files on its officers in case coercion became necessary. "You misunderstand. You can't resign because your mission isn't complete."

Bridge threw up her hands. "What more do I have to do? I found the mole, I *killed* the mole for God's sake, and by the way, I took out his handler, too."

"Now you're starting to talk like a real OIT," said Giles, and smiled. Bridge scowled in response, and he quickly continued, "Look, you did very well, a commendable A-minus. But we still have a problem. Actually, two problems."

"And why are they my problems?"

"Because I said so. First, Nigel Marsh is in the wind."

"Who?"

"The man Marko Novak met in Islington, the night we lost Novak on the Eurostar. Andrea Thomson and Steve Wicker from GCHQ checked him out, and he claimed to be running a tech startup in Shoreditch. But about the same time you decided to take a holiday in Syria — for which I have run *monumental* interference in Whitehall this week, and you can thank me later — back here at home, Wicker connected Marsh to a series of recent identity fraud purchases of drone units."

"You think that's his connection to Exphoria? So what's he been doing since Novak went dark?"

"That's the problem. Following Wicker's discovery, Five raided the startup and found the whole place cleaned out. Everyone and everything, gone without a trace. So all we know for sure about the Exphoria leaks is what you found on that SD card. Thank you for sending it back in your absence, by the way."

"It was the least I could do."

"Wasn't it just. Now, the second problem is rather more political. You see, Exphoria is still going ahead."

Bridge tried to reply, but all she could manage were wordless, incredulous sounds of disbelief.

Giles raised his hands in resignation, and related the events of his meeting with Sir Terence and the others. "Basically, all they see are a few photos. They can't, or won't, understand the implications."

"Isn't that precisely why they have intelligence agencies in the first place?"

Giles gave her a lopsided smile. "Sometimes I wonder. By the way, Archives found this. You should see it." He handed Bridge a file from his desk. She opened it to see a recent photo of James Montgomery, and several word-processed reports of activity monitoring and financial checks.

"What's this from? Are you saying you knew Montgomery was dirty when you sent me in?"

"Not at all. We only came across this after you'd uncovered him. Turns out there was a watch on Montgomery a few years ago, when he was a departmental advisor at the MoD. There were rumours one of the bidding contractors on a defence job was owned by a conglomerate of Russian oligarchs, through shells of course, and they were trying to buy the contract with bribes."

"Montgomery was working for them?"

"All we had was speculation, so we kept an eye on him throughout. In the end the contract went to a different firm anyway. The file was closed, the flags removed. We didn't make the connection until we found out the Russians were behind the Exphoria leak."

"Are we sure they are behind it, though?"

Giles looked surprised, then frowned. "Explain."

"Well, I'm not a hundred per cent myself, but..."

"Bridge, it's your own evidence that points to Moscow in the first place. Spit it out."

She took a deep breath, still not entirely sure of her theory. But it was the best she had. "Something Voclaine said after he picked me up from the police. He said they found a go-bag waiting on the bed in Montgomery's apartment, with a Russian passport, currency, the usual."

"Correct, and that confirms who his handlers were."

"But I was in Montgomery's bedroom directly before he attacked me, and there was no bag. So who put it there? I didn't. He certainly didn't."

"Then it must have been Novak, after he — *oh*." Giles rubbed his beard. "Yes, now you mention it, that is strange. Why prepare an agent's bag, when you can see with your own eyes that the agent is dead?"

Bridge smiled. "Unless, of course, you want the police to assume he was leaving for Russia." She was growing in confidence. Explaining the theory out loud made it sound more real, more plausible, than when it was locked in her head. "And then there was the gun, a Russian-issue Grach that I'm positive Novak gave to Montgomery."

"Why?"

"Because Novak seemed to know it wasn't loaded before he picked it up. As if it had never been loaded, and he knew that precisely because it was his gun."

Giles leaned back and gazed at the ceiling. "It fits, I'll give you that. But it's not much to go on."

"It makes sense combined with other things that occurred to me in Syria, though. Lots of time to think, out there in the desert, and I realised how old-fashioned this has all been. A traditional code cipher, sent over a part of the internet hardly anyone uses any more. Photographing computer screens, instead of just hacking into the servers. Handing off the photos, rather than a secure online transfer. And Novak himself was old school. He tracked me down with old-fashioned tradecraft rather than electronic surveillance, and he fought like a relic of the Cold War. He couldn't have been any more Russian if he'd had Stalin's face tattooed on his forehead."

"It is all rather outdated, true," mused Giles. "The modern FSB is a hive of tech and wizardry, even in theatre. God knows, it's one of the reasons I set up the CTA in the first place."

"Exactly. But Novak might as well have been flying the hammer and sickle over Agenbeux. So," she took one final breath, "I think this was a false flag operation, to make us think Russia was behind it."

"But Novak was definitely ex-FSB. We've had that confirmed by multiple agencies."

"*Ex*- being the operative word, right? He's been freelancing. Who's to say he wasn't hired by someone else precisely because he was so unmistakeably Russian? And told to blackmail Montgomery, a man we already suspected of taking bribes from Moscow?"

"Who else would run a mole inside Exphoria?"

Bridge shrugged. "Who wouldn't want to get their hands on next-gen battlefield drone technology? North Korea, China, India, Argentina, Egypt, the Saudis... Hell, I wouldn't put it past America, or Mossad. The only people we can definitely rule out are us and France."

Giles' phone buzzed. He swiped the notification away, and stood. "Then it sounds like you've got plenty on your plate. One way or another, we need to know who's behind this, and fast. The Exphoria launch is in two days, big ceremony at an airfield in Lincolnshire. Five is liaising with the MoD to enhance security, naturally, but if we can work out who we're up against, we stand a better chance of guessing their plan. I want a report of everything you know by tomorrow am."

Bridge was halfway to her desk before she remembered she'd gone in there to resign. She sighed and figured she'd see this through, then leave. If nothing else, she wanted to make sure everyone involved in Ten's murder got what they deserved.

73

Bridge never saw Century House, SIS' old headquarters. She was recruited after the service moved to the purpose-built premises at Vauxhall, a furiously modern building that acquired the nickname 'Legoland' even before it was completed. Some of the veteran officers and staff assured her she should be glad; despite the mythology surrounding it, Century House was a cold, damp, crumbling shambles of a building by the time they left. Still, she couldn't help but think of it again as she entered Thames House with Giles, admiring the traditional classic London façade of the place. Five had moved in here the same year SIS moved to Vauxhall, but it was somehow fitting that SIS should move on, into a building of the future, while the home service came to a place that looked like it was constructed a thousand years ago.

Her expectations of leather-backed chairs and wood-panelled corridors, however, were quickly dashed after they passed lobby security. The second security check was more like an airport, the corridors began to lose their classical charm, and when they were finally escorted into the headquarters proper, Bridge thought they might as well have been visiting an accountancy firm in Docklands. Grey carpet, grey aluminium-legged desks, Aeron chairs, gridded strip lights, stale air conditioning, and the omnipresent hum of computers. The air was recycled, thin and stale. Aside from the colour scheme, it wasn't so different to SIS' place over the river, and Bridge felt an inexplicable disappointment.

Andrea Thomson's office was a little bigger than Giles', which Bridge guessed probably annoyed him endlessly, though it was just as tidy and organised. Andrea received them with a smile, dismissed their escorting officer, and closed the door behind them as they took seats at her desk. "I'll get straight to it," she said. "We got DNA from the startup offices."

Giles, languid until now, perked up. "Nigel Marsh?"

"We assume so, although we're going from old photographs." A large screen was fixed to one wall, and after a few mouse clicks Andrea's computer desktop appeared on it. She pulled up a file that had been scanned from an old analogue record. An old photograph of a young boy with a mop of tousled blond hair, against a tropical background. Underneath, a name: *Bowman, Daniel Christopher*.

"You think that's him? Where did this record originate?"

"The Hong Kong archives, would you believe. Now look at this." She opened another photograph, and Bridge recognised Marko Novak sitting at the bar of a pub. Novak was talking to a thin man about Bridge's age, with a sandy beard. "This was taken at the Islington rendezvous, the one you decoded while you were in France. Pretty close, don't you agree, Bridge?"

"Yeah, that could be him," agreed Bridge, noting the resemblance between the boy and the man. "Why Hong Kong?"

"Because that's where Daniel Bowman was born and raised. His father was a minor civil servant for the FCO, hence there's a record of him, and his family. And unlike most of our people over there, they chose to stay on after the handover to the Chinese."

"Where are they now?" Giles asked.

"That's a very good question, and one we haven't been able to answer. Post-handover there's almost no record of them for a couple of years, and nothing at all after that. We're hoping your lot might have more luck, because we're pretty sure they're not here in the UK."

Bridge frowned. "Are you sure? We didn't know Daniel Bowman was here until now."

"True, but we have much more comprehensive domestic records on his parents, and they'd be in their late sixties by now. Bowman Senior retired from the civil service the day before the handover and became a hairdresser."

Giles was taken aback. "Come again?"

"Well, his wife held the scissors. But he started and owned their hairdressing business in Hong Kong, which lasted a couple of years before folding. Like I said, after that we have nothing."

Bridge looked from Giles to Andrea. "So they must have been spies, right? I mean, hairdressers? Really?"

Giles shook his head. "If they were, it wasn't for us. I've never heard of the Bowmans, and I wouldn't forget a cover story like that."

"You should check your files anyway," said Andrea. Giles opened his mouth to object to the obvious, but Andrea continued before he could speak. "But yes, you're probably right. From the few records we could dig up, the Foreign Office assumed they were 'Peking Ducks', spying for the Chinese. But there was no evidence, it was all a very long time ago, and they're probably dead anyway. Before this week, the last time anyone accessed their files was over a decade ago."

Bridge groaned. "And there's your false flag. If Marsh's — sorry, Bowman's — parents were spies for Beijing, it's a safe bet he is too. He would have grown up surrounded by Maoist propaganda, completely indoctrinated and taught to hide it from an early age. A native English boy, loyal to the red state."

"That would be quite an asset," agreed Giles, "but it still doesn't explain why he's doing this, or on whose orders. Would Beijing really need us to think the Russians are behind this?"

"Maybe they're just playing for time, hoping to misdirect us long enough for Bowman to complete his mission. Once it's done, they won't care if we know it was them, because the only evidence is Bowman himself."

"And he'll be completely deniable," said Giles, rubbing his beard. Bridge wondered if Andrea would appreciate the scent of hazelnuts. "Then it's down to Five to locate him before he acts, and fast. You're focusing around the airfield, I assume?"

"Yes, although we're not ruling out Bowman remaining in London and using an agent in Lincolnshire for the attack. Patel's team at GCHQ is all over it, and trying to find this bloody radioactive material too. How's your lad getting on in France?"

Giles stood and offered Andrea his hand. "Nothing yet. You'll be the first to know."

Andrea shook his hand and smiled sceptically. "Don't fib to me, Giles. Second or third will do just fine."

Bridge waited until they were escorted back through the layers of security and out of the building before asking, "Radioactive material? What's Henri doing in France?"

Giles was confused, then gasped like a man remembering he'd left his car lights on. "Sorry, this all happened after you left Agenbeux. There's the small matter of a suspected dirty bomb attack. The material was shipped out of Saint-Malo, and Mourad is trying to track down the men who transported it to find out where it was headed."

"We could contact Voclaine, ask the DGSI to help."

"Who? Oh, you mean Tolbert."

Bridge laughed. "So that was his real name, after all?"

"Well, it's the one they gave us. But no, I think we rather need to keep this on the QT for now. Besides, Mourad told Ems that he's close."

74

By some miracle it wasn't raining, so instead of taking refuge in a café Henri Mourad found an unoccupied bench in a small square of Toulouse's pink city to wait for Marcel. The southern nights were now almost as warm as the northern days, and a group of weathered old men threw *pétanque* on the far side of the square, oblivious to the fading light. Henri's view of the game was poor, but the players' reactions and taunts were enough to tell him one side was handily beating the other, and delighting in their impending victory.

The game distracted him enough that he didn't clock Marcel until after the Frenchman had entered the park. He tried to approach discreetly but failed miserably thanks to a hoarse, chesty cough. Henri expected him to sit on the bench, but instead Marcel walked close by, whispering, "Follow me."

Henri fell in beside him, and they walked toward a park exit. "Have you found them?"

Marcel jerked his head around, checking nobody was within earshot. "Yes. And it won't be long before someone else here does, too. The whole city is jumping, ready to beat them to a pulp."

"Your forger Benoît must have been well-liked."

Marcel shrugged. "He was a skilled forger, and he never cheated. More importantly, he was one of us. Two strangers walk into town, take advantage of our hospitality, and respond by killing one of our own. What would you do?"

Henri couldn't answer that. He also couldn't answer the biggest question of all; why hadn't the Portuguese smugglers used the forged passports? Marcel had summoned him because the Toulouse underground believed the men had returned to the city, despite the obvious danger. Why? Why hadn't they gone with the shipment to England, as must surely have been the plan?

Marcel was so preoccupied with the smugglers' offences toward Toulouse that the question didn't come up, and after switching cabs three times they finally took a ride out of the old town, toward an industrial district that didn't look much newer. The cabbie was reluctant to take them too far in, and from the broken windows and rusting barbed wire Henri glimpsed from the car, he wasn't surprised. Modern Toulouse was a thriving hub of modern industry and technology, but every city had its black spots, and this was clearly theirs.

He followed Marcel, squeezing through a gap in a wire fence, climbing over a gate where the barbed wire had been snipped away, and finally entering a long-abandoned factory building. They picked their way over fallen roof tiles, broken flooring, and discarded raw materials long rusted in the rain. Henri used the LED flash on his phone to see, while Marcel had been prepared and brought a flashlight. They made their way up to the first floor, and as they climbed the concrete stairs, Henri heard an involuntary sniffle from up ahead.

Marcel heard it too, and called out. "It's me, Marcel. I've brought you food." To Henri's surprise, it was true. Marcel reached into his coat pocket and pulled out two sandwiches wrapped in cling film, holding them up so they could be seen in the beam of his flashlight. "I'm coming in."

They were hiding in a former supervisor's office, overlooking what would once have been part of the factory floor. Two men, huddled against the far wall, flinching in the sudden light, sobbing with pain and misery. Or rather, one of them was. As he drew closer, Henri saw that the crying smuggler was holding onto the other with the desperate grief of recent loss. Both had greying, sallow skin, but only one was silent and unmoving.

Henri took one of the sandwiches from Marcel, unwrapped it, and offered it to the sobbing smuggler. He recalled Old Philippe saying how ill both men had looked, that one of them seemed ready to keel over at any moment. "Your friend was already very ill when you reached Saint-Malo, wasn't he? Is that why you didn't travel to England?" The smuggler took the sandwich with one hand and bit into it with furious hunger, nodding in silent reply as he chewed. "And you thought you could make it back to Portugal instead, find a friend who could help you." Another nod. "Did you know what you were carrying? Did the client tell you?"

The smuggler nodded again, but Henri said nothing, waiting for more. The man swallowed too quickly, coughed three times, swallowed again, then said, "But he told us it was sealed. That if we didn't open the package, we were safe."

"Why tell you at all?" Marcel asked. "Isn't is always safer for the courier not to know what he's carrying?"

"That's terrorism for you," said Henri. "People like that, they want everyone to know. Even if these guys had been caught in Saint-Malo, as soon as they said 'radioactive' the place would be sealed off, news cameras everywhere, lots of publicity and people saying *'My God, they came so close, we could have all died.'* It's a textbook play." Marcel shrugged with disdain, and lit a cigarette. "Give him one," said Henri. Marcel was about to protest, but sighed and handed his cigarette to the smuggler. He lit another for himself, and stepped outside the room.

"You're doing very well," Henri said. "Just a couple more things. First, what address was on the package? Where was it going in England? Do you have it written down?"

The smuggler pulled on the cigarette and shook his head, then coughed for ten seconds straight. Henri took out his phone and pulled up the photo of Novak and Marsh from the bar. "What about the client? How were you contacted, how were you paid? Did you see either of these men?"

Before the smuggler could answer, Marcel ran into the room. "We've got company," he hissed, "I told you it wouldn't take long for them to find him." Henri heard distant angry shouts. They didn't have much time before the Toulouse underground would be here to take revenge on the smugglers, assuming they weren't both dead before the mob arrived. The smuggler was coughing incessantly now, and threw the cigarette away. Henri tried to help the man to his feet but he bent over, coughing and wheezing, too weak to stand. "Strange English-looking man," he gasped between coughs, "found us in Sines…"

Henri propped the man up against his own knee, holding the phone screen to his face. "Why was he strange? Did he look like this? Like one of these?"

The smuggler lifted a finger toward the screen, but couldn't hold it long enough to point at anyone in the photo. "On his mobile," whispered the smuggler, "sounded like Chinese…" The man's body softened, as if the tension held within his chest had dissolved into air, and he was gone.

Henri and Marcel left, taking a different route to avoid the mob. As they clambered out of a broken ground-floor window, the angry shouts of criminals denied vengeance echoed through the concrete and steel.

75

Giles was talking about Nigel Marsh/Daniel Bowman, about the radioactive material, about drones and targets. Bridge was listening attentively, hearing every word, but distracted by an insistent, incessant thought at the back of her mind. Something just didn't add up.

She'd spent most of the night failing to find sleep, tossing and turning long after the sleep timer had silenced the almost inaudible Radio 3 feed on her iPhone. The confirmation from Mourad that Daniel Bowman had commissioned the *matériel chaud* smuggling operation — and on a shoestring, by the sounds of it — had begun a flurry of secure phone calls, encrypted emails, records searches, plus warrant applications on both sides of the river and across it, as SIS and Five argued about who had jurisdiction and primacy over whatever was about to happen.

That it was connected to Bowman's interest in drones seemed obvious. A dirty bomb flown into central London by consumer drone to explode somewhere like Oxford Circus would be devastating to the population, to transport, to the economy, to the government. But if that was the plan, why bother installing a mole on the Exphoria project? He didn't need that to buy and control remote drones. And what was the startup in Shoreditch all about? Had 'Marsh' made up that rubbish about quantum state information in wifi signals just to get Andrea and Steve off his back? Steve had filled Bridge in when she returned to London, and her guess was that Bowman knew all along they weren't from a local business bureau. Otherwise, why clear out so fast after their visit? Perhaps he wasn't some genius physicist working on an impossible technology. Perhaps he was doing something much simpler with existing signal technology, which explained the routers and signal units Steve saw on Bowman's workbench. If you were going to run a drone attack on the Exphoria demo, you'd need range extenders and signal boosters in order to maintain a signal across the security perimeter. You'd want to place them in advance, test their reception.

But security around the Lincolnshire airfield had been triple-A for weeks. Bowman would have had to infiltrate the location before Andrea and Steve paid him a visit. Nevertheless, it wasn't impossible. Bridge, having given up on sleep, added a bullet point to the long email she was composing to Giles and everyone else involved. Then she went for a pre-dawn run round Highgate Wood, showered, and headed into Vauxhall.

She arrived to find a response from Steve Wicker at GCHQ, supplying the dump of ICR records from the Shoreditch startup office she'd requested. Internet Connection Records were often maddeningly vague, being only a list of top-level URLs visited, and she didn't expect Bowman to have used the office connection much anyway. But it was a start, and when Ciaran and Monica arrived, she asked for their help to scan through them.

They'd barely begun when Giles stepped into the CTA unit to address the situation and explain the plan. "Everyone seems to be moving in the same direction with regard to method," he said, "so our joint assumption is that Bowman plans to make a radiological dispersal device using the smuggled material, and deliver it using a small domestic drone of some kind. Where we all differ is on target, motive, and solution."

"Just shoot anything that looks like a drone within a mile of the airfield," said Monica. "How is that hard?"

"It's hard precisely because domestic drones are so small they're practically invisible to radar, and to the naked eye once they're airborne above two hundred and fifty metres," said Ciaran. "You'd need a thousand people watching ten thousand cameras to cover every possible angle."

"You're also assuming the airfield is the target," said Bridge.

"But where else?" asked Giles.

"I don't know. I'm still trying to understand why he bothered to infiltrate Exphoria in the first place. GCHQ has sent us the SignalAir ICRs I requested, so maybe we'll find something in there."

"Or maybe he only used the office connection for porn, and all his real comms were done over the cell network," said Monica. "This guy's supposed to be a technical whizzkid, right?"

Bridge shrugged. "It's the current assumption, yeah. I know it's a long shot, but it has to be worth trying. There's something off about all this, and I can't put my finger on it."

"Then you have approximately four hours to get your finger in gear, so to speak, before that demo takes place in Lincolnshire," said Giles as he left. "Keep me informed."

"I can't believe they're going ahead with the demo," said Ciaran. "Do they think we make this shit up for the craic?"

Bridge shook her head. "Worse. They assume we're stupid, and have it wrong."

"No offence, Bridge, but maybe we do," said Monica.

"Honestly, I kind of hope so. But I doubt it."

76

The drone rushed toward them over the airfield, buzzing like an angry wasp.

Air Vice-Marshal Sir Terence Cavendish was pleased to note there were no theatrics this time. He'd had a quiet word with the drone controllers (much as he appreciated their skill with the technology, he refused to call them *pilots*) after the previous demonstration, and made it clear that spooking the crowd was both unacceptable and unnecessary. Everyone watching had seen regular drone flights a hundred times before, and knew what they were capable of with a skilled human controller. What they wanted to see from Exphoria was how it flew without that human control.

The project had faced its share of obstacles. He wasn't directly involved at the funding stage, but he'd seen from afar the difficulty of convincing some of his colleagues that the project was achievable. Having to co-finance it with the French, of all people, was testament enough to that. Then there had been the arguments over where the main project headquarters should be. Sir Terence argued for England, of course. Somewhere like this very airfield in rural Lincolnshire would have been perfect. But the French were putting up a significant amount of money, and had a lot of computer programmers ready to go. What finally won Sir Terence over had been the argument that nobody would think to look for a next-generation military software project in French wine country.

But somebody had. The final hurdle, a bloody mole of all things, sent by...well, they'd originally said Russia, which had surprised Sir Terence not one jot, but yesterday Devon Chisholme had said they now thought it was the Chinese, possibly a lone actor, perhaps intending to sell to the highest bidder. *Thought, possibly, perhaps*; typical hedging from the Service, never willing to commit. But Sir Terence had committed, to this project and this launch date, and nipped any suggestion of delay in the bud. The mole had been identified and eliminated, as had his handler, and they'd even recovered some of the leaked data, which to his eye didn't look like much at all anyway. The only loose end was a computer chap here in England, who they said might have access to radioactive material. But Sir Terence had served in Hong Kong before the handover, and knew a thing or two about Beijing. For one thing, if this computer nerd spy had any sense he'd be lying low in Bucharest or Minsk, to avoid paying the price of losing his mole. Or perhaps the Chinese had already extracted him, and he was on his way to a Nanjing jail cell. As for the possibility of an RDD, that was outside his purview. But a state action of that magnitude, by China or anyone else, would focus on civilian population in an urban environment, not ministers and grandees in a field in the middle of nowhere. What would be the point of that?

Finally, of course, this was all supposition. The man might just be a freelancer, after all. In which case he was undoubtedly long gone, with a new identity in another country, working to concoct a new hare-brained scheme the Services could worry about anew.

All told, there was no reason to suspect the demonstration was in jeopardy, and Sir Terence had firmly insisted it go ahead. Security had been increased further, and everyone was on high alert, but that would suffice. Only a suicidal fool would try to infiltrate this location.

Today's demonstration was more complex than the last, designed to show off the Exphoria system's capabilities to its fullest now that phase one of the software was considered complete. The airfield was filled with obstacles, armaments, and targets, presenting the UAV with a gauntlet ten times as difficult to complete as the comparatively simple demonstration the crowd watched two months before. Several regular drones were brought out first, to attempt the exercises with a human pilot and standard software, and as each was damaged or failed, a replacement was substituted to pick up where it left off. In all, six drones were rendered inoperable by simulated enemy fire or surface collisions before the X-4 was launched. What followed was a flawless display of autonomous and self-correcting flight, targeting acquisition and compensation, and evasive manoeuvres that only the digital reflexes of a computer system could achieve. Twenty minutes after the demonstration had begun every countermissile was spent, every obstacle cleared, every target destroyed.

When the smoke cleared the gathered ministers, dignitaries, buyers, and dealers in the viewing stands stood and applauded, before filing out into the marquee for champagne and vol-au-vents. Later, Sir Terence and his French counterpart made short speeches to thank the attendees for their support, and reminded them of the official launch reception tomorrow evening in London. Then they all departed, car by car, to their offices, homes, or hotels.

Everything had gone perfectly, and Exphoria was set to be a roaring success. As his driver returned him to his home in Hampshire, Sir Terence dared to wonder if there might be a peerage in it for him.

77

"I don't understand. Why didn't he try anything?"

Ciaran and Monica were shutting down, ready to leave. The CTA unit, along with Giles and several other departments, had all stayed at Vauxhall throughout the Exphoria demonstration. Even after the main event, while the drinks reception took place, they kept searching through all the data they could, and waited for word that something, anything, was kicking off.

But nothing did. Finally the attending MI5 liaison phoned Andrea Thomson, to inform her that everyone except security and maintenance personnel had left the airfield without incident. Andrea called Giles, who called Emily Dunston and C, before walking into the CTA office and telling the team himself. Bowman hadn't tried anything, and the demonstration had gone without a hitch.

"Maybe he's cut his losses and scarpered while he can," said Monica, shrugging on her jacket. "Whatever; it doesn't matter. The demo went fine, the drone software works, everyone's happy."

Ciaran buttoned up his own coat and came to lean against Bridge's desk. "She's right," he said.

"Wow, are you feeling OK?" Monica laughed. "Can you say that again while I record it?"

Ciaran ignored her. "There's nothing more for him to do, Bridge. If your man got enough of the software, he'll turn up on the black market trying to sell it, and then we can send an OIT after him. If he didn't get enough, which, to be honest, is my guess, then he's gone to ground and we'll never hear from him again. Either way you're grand, and you should go home and relax for once."

Bridge chewed on her lightsaber pen and mumbled goodbye as they left, still staring unfocused at her screen and turning things over in her mind. Something still wasn't right, and she couldn't shake the notion she was missing an obvious connection.

Giles poked his head round the door, saw she was the only one left, and sighed. "Go home, Bridge. In fact, take tomorrow off. You of all people could do with the extra sleep." She glared at him in silence until he backed out of the door.

But twenty minutes later, on the northbound Victoria line, she resigned herself to the wisdom of her colleagues. She really did need some sleep, and the Exphoria demo really had gone off without a hitch, let alone an attack. Bowman hadn't hacked anything, hadn't planted a bomb, hadn't sabotaged the drone. He hadn't done anything at all, despite the fact that he almost certainly had multiple state-of-the-art prosumer drones and a packet of radioactive material at his disposal.

Why bother, if he wasn't planning to use them? Why go to the trouble of the ID thefts, the smuggling, the secret purchases? It didn't make sense that they could be a red herring. The point of a distraction was to be so big and noticeable that people couldn't ignore it, yet Bowman had worked hard to cover his tracks every step of the way. If the Exphoria demonstration wasn't the target, what else could be in his sights? Was Bowman running two completely separate missions at once, and their only connection just happened to be drones? In a way it seemed the most likely answer, but Bridge couldn't swallow it. If she'd learned one thing in the past eight years at SIS, it was the alarming lack of true coincidences in the world.

Two hours later she was still thinking about it, while she shovelled ready-meal vegetable pasta into her mouth with zero enthusiasm. She reconsidered everything she knew about Bowman, and now realised it was entirely second-hand. Steve Wicker had found the ID fraud; Andrea Thomson had followed him from the meet with Novak; they'd visited 'Nigel Marsh' at the Shoreditch office together; and now the only tangible record they had of that office was a dump of network traffic, most of which was completely uninteresting and useless because Bowman's technology efforts had all been centred around wifi, both the real stuff and his physics-breaking 'quantum state' rubbish.

At three in the morning, as *Through the Night* played quietly on her iPhone, something from Bridge's insomniac episode two nights ago kept scratching at the gates of her mind. But she couldn't find the key.

* * *

She slept until one the next afternoon, and while she woke still tired, it was just her normal state of perpetual tiredness rather than the exhaustion of the past two days. She brushed her teeth, showered, put an old Year of No Light CD in the stereo — her computer was full of MP3s, but she'd never got round to hooking it up to her hifi speakers — and poured herself a late bowl of cornflakes while the kettle boiled. It was the first time in weeks she'd sat down to eat breakfast without the deadline of her imminent commute to work, or a shopping trip into town, or a hangover from clubbing the night before. Given time to actually take in the state of her flat as she mechanically crunched cereal, she now realised she hadn't cleaned it since before going to Agenbeux.

Chaos was Bridge's default mode for living, but the flat was getting beyond the norm. Boot socks tossed over the arm of the sofa, two pairs of tights and a bra over the back, a tangle of t-shirts and leggings on the floor, three used dinner plates in danger of growing legs and walking themselves to the washing-up bowl, a half-finished mug of coffee that could have been there a few days or a few weeks… Even her desk was messier than normal, covered in parts of a failed old tower Compaq from which she was trying to rescue the hard drive, and the various tools she'd been using to take it apart.

Something itched at the back of her brain. Taking apart. Computer parts. Tools.

Andrea's report on the Shoreditch office. A line, innocuous: *'A workbench appeared to be in heavy use, covered in broken-down computer parts. GCHQ liaison advises these consisted mostly of wifi chips and antennae, likely to build signal transceivers and range extenders.'*

Steve Wicker wasn't officially named in the report for security reasons, but Bridge guessed he was the 'GCHQ liaison' in question. And Steve knew his hardware. If he said Marsh/Bowman had been taking apart and building range extenders, that was good enough for her.

Range extenders. Wifi-controlled drones. Fissile material that you'd want to unleash in a crowded environment, an urban gathering, some kind of party…

Bridge spilled milk from her cornflakes as she scrambled for her HP, memories of Agenbeux racing through her mind. Montgomery, vain and egotistical, desperate for recognition and reward. Preening at the thought of Whitehall noticing what a good job he was doing, convinced they were throwing a party just for him, to sing *For He's a Jolly Good Fellow* and pat him on the back.

She opened the laptop, established a secure connection to the office, and started typing. Three hours later she still hadn't had any coffee, but she did have a theory.

78

GROUP: france.misc.binaries-random

FROM: zero@null

SUBJECT: new art

```
      hmxmTNa7Tl!YQzvc7zUmuy2I$06OQecKEVPLKT9JvM@3w0s0iQDM!kKPvPHUiakH0cNd
     xoHwW2mdL9lz5gMmMjIc*Au1U1r+/8coxRns/.$/x+nsYhkL7KO!3xhyhmzafahyhvnh4my
    sCgsTFN9b!-//oD2y3IUxQs5sUulax$hxh!A  Vo£y#c0yhd!!o:-=x0._.\x-of][hhyssg8
   ØFVcBzo-Ø++!WN//FpofY+++sO0oWVqwj3          @dpøsyhYGAExLbFuv!./ssD2yhso+x/+o
  HdEc5ICldkxd^.:+-ØsnOjs6:j86Ts.amrz          zFKOHB8o48LTjRg786q9RHCX8I9RiMbG6m
  ZK2oOyxh3]b[so+UmOuxLDGVqCe^-/+o@5ys         [yXPyVh6/o@so/+xH/CemV3U8Cgh##dUqj
  3x]Ffys?syhmd[h]Wrw3s-:+s_o+O0ouE6Ez/=   5yXPh3sEu2Xx2RXD!yhuwIY4e9HV41`:oswb
  Th5i3Wbt1PZIWtv5e7v:-$!.//+s3                    Mso@xEthYUjF6IMnxqF1NRe5o/-!'.
  djt9G8s36d0sosqc65aYq9fB@d[ovdrido++rmpmyo@-Øsso//+OPI7co+msjcdzb+/:+sYF$x/+o
   o36ss6B  2P45OAsyyf]ioD!dIdoopDm2lwpme5nq1KWfHlsXq-peo0bO0/:-6  JNHbGc5UcKK
    T6NaI  Du1ju692o@s#egxhjbywlo##ysO0oEEgDNhdxh3!/-$-shFdhyso@+xH  +d56sq3L
     y6Npzc0hYRKGXBKBOh@hpenyo-+osD2o^x^/:-pLKd8$-XyMNXddylWcp!o1su6b6K2yhy5
      $-sd0sxy?XPCghoslV7osyo@-Ø6B8yhx)h%yomcwo@yhso+o--o/+shDdstzd0sh42ug=
mwmoypJuvU-`*-:AX\+-6yys++o@+o+/::/+ooyvlunvs:'rmqW1pCHUZvEMgWn++X/A:/otvWB2+/
xwqcheydly 4n2f       opghqx7fcmvipkgxARK6YATUVq6Wf9Ey]Ffys!mIeA5-Ø+/:--nxBoS.
dASGDmmx^o  hndV     piarkxHi8X4S-+sO0orq6Ln/oHd:hMXS0FHE!yn   8@od+hmhs+X:/om
xnzdpø+/-: O0-Ø      o@oy+/:X+yh+zXSeRhmd+/oyo/;osdpøo+4B+/    :/ +oD2o@+xHo+X
+shyhYd34o wqXW      i/jzT3RlfC6/oso^x^     +O03W429HhXMrys      $ /.$'4?/+XH+/
./af5Ekwm  /e:         +sahrlq\ghqxsyhd      0MBy35so:!AtsBc        /-jwiw$kaosz
++/+s6B8esasho          @ssci%zm++osyA          #0iqhrh*/+O0o        36gvjypo@sgW
bqjvzeshho/!:          ^"%*./sA#H/!.oLhy        +--syh$:s5vnh        Fs-*.+yhesYY
1sy/`.-o@sylA         h##+-^.-/s##kyyyyys      5ss..y+sd0+  o.     mdhyAHep0mdsqr
RqV+/X+sssd0          +/^r-HKiqyh4so@+yg8yyhhso+!A#Hyscdo7y  s5  xh3haPX0KsoGZeW
e./AD+  oy#o!C    gszORGqJ9lP39sc   V2DJA$5m5iB  NEs:^I:o+  +  osyXPs-Ø+o@7B$U
i7OhM?  h]oAR8   FdXHhQis+O0o+o          sYdQIsH    Smpc1xZ%MJByb  Z[f^.:+shhs-tx
xS#kyqL  $       w8oe4K4laspy!           :/+0ggh      sWMb7adxiqzT S3ss+oCgyso/+dm
$gcys+o  C      +PY+di!hmOVhazec  -Øshybschl8xT     -/++oso:-:  o/::/oyS+d'h4so
@ycpZemdu   92GDdpeVUhhyo@o+xBtdw7(y%XPAgDy$D:/jTlPeH4!x60Dy58 #  Sm:Sdy2yXPhd
dRu6T1LBdhjhysO0 oxnz+++og3xu5H4Y?6MB-os+/+!WN/:zO0omwmAX\ntC      GJTSnZyO0Scj
s18-:ofRxJ2XY/-  ?$+osyhmdOaDekS:dA#Hydpø+8:/o+O0soD2Uz24U8B    Mjr!1:oys+4uWx
OTD&uzxKKJoZCeS  d%(huifjVo/+o@xnzØEz0rN2OxD4+n/+o@sy]kgycw   +N!N/:;/sy)h%!3x
atCHwsm8hfo*xZc plCbhVD5oo9AEtS  (s4:/og8yo+/:yu  xGgTU9Nd[  #]hhyysCgyho+o@/+
-Øox95NtNxnz+B7v HJP$.kl+syhyo                          mqcZ2Q   +oyf][hrVo*2jMzlx
JrEymJ"HbIxNy9U5 2X74  6WR-EMCJSuxex              y081MX77k9e  UvjyIjyGVF$ae1E7Ke5
A5G\dyO2/UJcfj6ae 2Hvc  rzMYx=R8#iGdf2zD4p0eDdE#!rSE4SpD   Q3Iy38??neo4j6gSQUX
K!UVH$BnDZnyJzsbg   LpB xmk+)ueIDFy6!Vddr[TnSeqy1k$es8\   JRlyO24vbskxLss4RuvC
YEuz[rjIkaNSj5SE    OAG67/Mcv=OTson%hqOKM&*Uf1028I3Vw4l   ptAjRCfG?bNA2Fyw7RTL
xa$QnvJh+diagF    VNdv0o58B$5kgcT/r85SkVxn84s!zhDenxmESxv  5teFA94IF89UWb531lQ
VhMa=4IY5#s7TR    7e2eP$t9FRik%n4bJASP$lg\fbqTWK!4g04w]cA5   EXN!PnL*07265A21D
```

79

The post from Novak was unexpected, but Bowman had learned very quickly the Russian was full of surprises. That was why he'd been hired, after all.

But it could wait till after mission end. Novak had already missed the previous week's deadline for final code leaks, and nothing he could offer now would help anyway. He probably just wanted more money. Bowman's own deadline had been yesterday, leaving today for debugging only. Too late to incorporate any more information from Exphoria, and there didn't seem much more to learn. His own work, combined with the leaked code he'd seen, would suffice. He did miss the Shoreditch office, and wished he could have stayed there to see out the mission, but comfort was for the weak. Only completion mattered. This place in Rotherhithe was fine, and he was glad of the foresight to take out a cash rental on it months ago, as a backup. But it was further out from the target than Shoreditch, and freezing cold.

More than anything, it was England's cold he'd been unprepared for. Even during the summer, it was merely clement compared to the heat he was used to.

Thinking of home was a mistake. He struggled to shut down such thoughts. Memories of his parents, unbidden and unwanted, scratching at the edges of his awareness. Trying to overwhelm him. His mother, hanging in silence, her arms stiff and lifeless by her side. She opened her eyes to stare at him, asking without speaking, *How could you let this happen, Daniel?* He turned away, shaking. He had no answer.

All he had was now, this moment, this vengeance. Here, in London, not Hong Kong.

Get a grip, lad. His father, invisible and deafening. *We didn't raise you to be soft.*

He took a deep breath, chanted a mantra, and cleared his mind. He was focused. He was in the moment. He got a grip.

The first wave, five quadcopters of varying design, rose quietly into the air at his command, fingers dancing over the keyboard of his Acer laptop, manipulating with practised ease the control program he'd spent so long perfecting. Each drone was different, but they were all fitted with identical low-slung cargo attachments. He let them hover at eye level and walked among the mismatched flock, triple-checking their cargo and flying condition. Get a grip.

The second wave consisted of four identical drones, with enclosed blades and sound bafflers that rendered them almost silent in flight. He'd removed all identifying marks from their exterior, leaving a jet-black body that would be invisible in the night sky. They sat patiently on the concrete floor, in formation and ready to rise at his command. To deliver the killing blow.

The endgame had begun, and Daniel Bowman smiled in the certain knowledge that as he spent the last weeks of his life in agony, the man from the market wouldn't even know he was playing.

80

"Ms Sharp has a theory. You're going to want to hear it."

Bridge's call had caught Giles as he left a budget meeting, irritable and short on patience. When she arrived at Vauxhall, he was waiting in the CTA office with Ciaran and Monica. She explained her thought process, and showed them what she'd found that afternoon. They spent the next two hours checking her findings, and digging further into the records, while Giles arranged an end-of-day meeting with everyone concerned.

Now they were in Broom Two, the second-largest briefing room in the building. Andrea Thomson and Sunny Patel were on video link, Henri Mourad was on speakerphone, and in the room were Emily Dunston, Giles, Ciaran, Monica, and several assistants — including one from C's office.

Bridge had her lightsaber pen in one hand, impatiently clicking and un-clicking the top. She realised with some surprise that she was nervous, and eager to get this right. Maybe she wasn't ready to quit, after all — assuming she didn't fuck it up completely and get fired instead. She took a deep breath and said, "I think we were focused on the wrong target. Bowman never intended to attack yesterday's Exphoria demonstration. There's a project launch party tonight, here in London, with all the bigwigs present. I think he's going to hit that instead."

"We're aware of that party," said Andrea. "The Prime Minister is scheduled to drop by for ten minutes of handshakes, so Five sent a team to work with the police for security. What makes you think it's Bowman's target?"

"When you went to check out the fake startup — actually, Mr Patel, could we call Steve Wicker in on this? — you described a bench full of range extenders, wifi antenna, and so on, all in various states of being built or dismantled. And Bowman said he was working on a breakthrough in wifi technology."

"Yeah, but I read that file, and it's nonsense," said Sunny. "There's no 'quantum state information' in radio signals, he was feeding you a load of bollocks."

"I know that," said Bridge, reassuring him. "But what if he came up with that story so people wouldn't ask why he was building wifi transceivers?"

"Hiding the truth in plain sight," said Giles, elaborating for the room. "Go on, Bridge."

She took a breath to calm herself. "Bowman still has the radioactive material. Naturally, we assume he intends to use it. But if you're going to set off a dirty bomb, where's the best place for it? Not a wide-open space like an airfield. You want a populated, crowded, urban area."

"So why not a shopping centre, or a football match?" asked Mourad, on the phone. "Why a party in Whitehall?"

"First, because if Bowman's mission is to sabotage Exphoria, all the higher-ups dying in a terror attack would put a big black mark on the project's reputation. Plus the mole himself, James Montgomery, was scheduled to be at this party. What better way for Bowman to tie up a loose end than by killing the mole, while making it look like he wasn't the target?"

Emily Dunston nodded. "That makes sense. But Montgomery is dead, so why bother going ahead with the attack?"

"Because I don't think he was the *prime* target. Getting him would have just been a nice bonus, but the principal target is the head of the Exphoria project, Sir Terence Cavendish." She paused to let everyone take this in, before turning to the speakerphone. "As for the second thing, Henri…the party isn't in Whitehall. It's halfway up the Shard."

A murmur rippled through the room. Any attack on the Shard, the country's tallest building and a symbol of modern London, would make headlines and instil fear; the aim of any serious terrorist.

"The CTA unit has been looking into this," said Giles, and Bridge half-smiled at his determination to ensure everyone knew his brainchild was leading the way. "We've found compelling evidence, much of which was simply a matter of connecting dots we hadn't previously looked for. But in light of Bowman's identification, they became clear. Ciaran?"

Ciaran cleared his throat. "We went through the ICRs — that's Internet Connection Records, all the traffic at a given IP address — from the Shoreditch startup office. Bowman didn't use it much, as we assume he was on a cellular signal most of the time, and without the device he used we can't trace that traffic. But what he did use the hard connection for was interesting. He looked up a lot of details and biographies of Sir Terence, for example, over the course of several weeks."

"That doesn't prove anything," said Emily. "Sir Terence is a public figure. If Bowman knew of the project's existence at all, it would make sense he'd also know the Air Vice-Marshal is in charge."

"But he's going to be at the party," said Ciaran, as if that explained everything.

"We think —" Bridge began, then corrected herself. "You know what, I shouldn't hide behind the unit, here. I think that this is personal, something between Bowman and Sir Terence. Otherwise, why keep looking him up? And those searches ceased immediately after Andrea visited the Shoreditch office, as if he suddenly assumed the connection was being monitored."

"Are you implying Sir Terence is in league with Bowman?" asked Andrea.

"No, no," said Bridge, "there's no suggestion he's involved with the leak, or being blackmailed. But I think he was always the principal target, for personal reasons."

"Why go to such trouble over an RAF officer?"

Monica spoke for the first time. "You said the FCO suspected Bowman's parents of being spies for Beijing. 'Peking Ducks', which by the way is so incredibly offensive, I can't even. Well, guess who first raised that suspicion with the former British Governor, while serving at RAF Sek Kong?"

Emily Dunston groaned in frustration. "Oh, bloody hell. Sir Terence Cavendish."

"Squadron Leader Cavendish, as he was then," said Giles. "We assume this is also why we have no record of the Bowmans past a couple of years after handover. Beijing has never liked loose ends, and if they found out the family's cover was blown…well, I wouldn't fancy their chances."

"But young Daniel Bowman survived somehow, and now he wants revenge on the man who effectively killed his parents," Bridge added.

Andrea sighed. "How did we miss this before?"

"To be fair, we didn't even know who Bowman was until you found his DNA. And Sir Terence is hardly the only RAF officer who served in Hong Kong."

"He also returned several times as a civilian, after the handover," said Monica. "Again, not unusual for someone with his record, but at a certain point there are so many coincidences, they start to look more like a pattern."

"Assume you're right, and Bowman's going to set off an RDD

at the party," said Andrea. "How? Like I said, we have officers co-ordinating with police, and they're already on alert because of the PM's visit. How's he going to get in the venue?"

"Who says he has to be anywhere near it?" Bridge turned to the GCHQ video feed, where Steve Wicker had quietly slid into view beside Patel. "He's been buying up drones for testing, and now he has the means to control them at a distance. Right, Steve?"

He nodded. "Afraid so. If he's been working on signal range extenders and custom transceivers, he could be half a kilometre from the place, maybe more. And without knowing where he's likely to be, isolating and tracing his signal will be tricky. A dirtbox would grab every signal around, but how would we know which one was him?"

"Hang on, before we get too technical," Giles interrupted, and checked his watch. "Can't we just cancel the party, or move the venue? It doesn't start for thirty minutes."

"I don't think that's a good idea," said Bridge. "This is our chance to draw Bowman out. If we evacuate, he'll know we're onto him and vanish back into the shadows, complete with his radioactive material and drone collection."

Giles nodded. "Replacing an attack we're expecting with a future one that's completely unknown to us."

"He may not wait long," said Henri over the phone. "The smugglers both succumbed to radiation poisoning, and they only had the material for three weeks, tops."

"Bowman's surely better prepared to handle it," said Bridge, "but point taken. And it reinforces our theory. He timed the material's arrival so he wouldn't have to store it for long before using it."

"I was going to suggest a sniper team around the building to shoot the drone down," said Andrea, "but if the drone itself is carrying a bomb…"

Ciaran said, "Steve's right, locating the signal will be tricky. But if we can, then we could swamp the source. No signal; no flying instructions. Most drones will default to hovering in place, or safely descend to earth, when there's no signal or a low battery."

"Perhaps I should have emphasised the difficulty more," said Steve. "If he's using multiple extenders and transceivers, combined with the hundreds of active wifi signals at any given location in London, this is like half a needle in ten haystacks. We'd have to get down there, figure out which local signal might be Bowman, then hack and piggyback it to trace to source, and finally hope we'd picked the right one to start with. And on top of all that, we have to assume he's built redundancy into the system."

"We also couldn't begin isolating until the drone was in range, because we have no idea where Bowman himself is," added Ciaran. "It's not enough time."

"So just cut them all off," said Monica. "Use a jambox to shut down everything around the venue."

Bridge shook her head. "Too many legit signals that might get shut down. Guy's Hospital, London Bridge station, God knows how many internal signals to keep the Shard itself operating. Jamboxes are chainsaws, when what we need is a scalpel to attack only the drone signal…" She stopped herself, an idea forming.

Giles saw the change and raised an eyebrow. "I can almost hear gears turning. Bridge?"

"Ciaran's right, we don't know where Bowman is. But we do know where the drone will be, and that means we can lay a trap, so long as I can get to the venue in time. As soon as the drone comes within range, boom."

"I'm on my way there as soon as I get off this call," said Andrea. "I can swing by and pick you up. But what kind of trap do you mean? Something to catch a drone?"

"Something like that. It's called *MaXrIoT*."

81

At any other time, Bridge would have enjoyed watching Andrea's driver break enough traffic laws to get his licence revoked every hundred metres. Instead she was focused on her HP laptop, running a custom signal scanner and packet sniffing software. As Steve had said, the streets of London were saturated with hundreds of wifi signals and gigabytes of online traffic at every moment. Bridge knew the signal she was looking for wouldn't be in range yet, as they raced toward the Shard, but it was better to get the software up and running early. Andrea was in the front passenger seat, Giles in the back with Bridge. Both were talking non-stop into their phones, taking reports and issuing clipped instructions.

"Three minutes," said the driver as he ran a red traffic light and leaned hard on the wheel, to weave between the opposite lane of traffic and an illegally-parked white van. Bridge held the HP tight as she and Giles slid across the back seat.

Andrea turned to them and said, "No sign of anything airborne at the venue, according to our people. Even in the dark, you'd expect them to see something out of the window, right?"

"Maybe, but only if it was on a similar plane," said Bridge. "If he flies really high, or really low, they wouldn't see it. And then he could quickly drop or ascend to the venue floor, and they'd only have seconds to spot it. What you really need is something like proximity sensors on the outside of the building to warn against this sort of thing."

"I somehow doubt they had things like this in mind when they designed the place. It's all a bit sci-fi."

"iPhones were sci-fi until suddenly they weren't," said Bridge. "In the meantime, we've just got to cope. Tell them to keep looking, while I keep scanning." Andrea returned to her phone, shouting instructions.

"One minute," said the driver, squeezing between taxicabs bound for London Bridge station. The car's passenger side wing scraped lightly against one of the taxis, and Bridge wondered if the cabbie would be able to get compensation from MI5. How would he know?

They were close enough for the sniffer software to pick up every signal around the building, and Bridge filtered them out as quickly as she could. Ciaran, Monica, and Steve Wicker were in a secure VOIP chatroom connected to a Jawbone bluetooth mic wrapped around her ear, but up till now all she'd heard from it was the sound of keyboards clacking. She pressed Talk on the headset and said, "Shitloads of signals, as expected, but I'm not seeing anything that looks likely. None of the transit delay patterns look like obvious remote control packets."

"Maybe the drone isn't there yet," said Ciaran. "The party's scheduled to last ninety minutes, you could be in for a long wait."

"Sudden thought," said Steve, "Bridge, how granular is your frequency selector? Is it default?"

"No, replacement upgrade," she replied. "Point-oh-one gigahertz increments. What are you thinking?"

"If he's building his own extenders, he might have them fixed on a non-regular frequency. For this usage, we'd normally assume low frequency would be best, right? Drone control is low data bandwidth, and low frequency is more reliable over distance."

"Here," said the driver as they stopped in front of the Shard, and the three passenger doors automatically popped open.

Andrea and Giles de-bussed with practised efficiency, and Andrea immediately shouted at the police to turn off their flashing lights. Bridge, meanwhile, struggled to climb out without accidentally closing her laptop, and found herself surrounded by police officers and vehicles on the narrow road. The MI5 driver showed no sign of going anywhere, so she used his car roof as a makeshift desk for the HP and began adjusting the scanner software's frequency.

"All right, let's see if he's broadcasting on an unusually high frequency. Kind of crappy over long distance, but if he's packed the area with custom transceivers, there could be one right next door."

"It's what I'd do," said Steve. "Not sure what that says about me, but —"

"What it says is you're a bloody genius," said Bridge as the software lit up. "I reckon I've found him. There's an ultra-high frequency signal, just idling in this area."

"What do you mean, idling?" asked Giles.

"I mean it's just sitting there, like in a standby mode. All it's doing is broadcasting itself as ready, tiny packets, but nothing's actually happening."

"Definitely sounds like our guy," said Ciaran. "And if it's idle, that means the drone isn't in range yet."

"If we're right about the plan, and if this is the right signal," said Bridge. "Lot of *ifs*." Nobody replied. They were all thinking the same thing, but were too polite to say it out loud. *What if Bridge's theory is a load of rubbish?*

"I've started a traceroute," said Steve. "You never know, we might get lucky."

Giles had been watching in silence over Bridge's shoulder, letting her work, while Andrea talked to the police officers surrounding the building. Now she returned, wearing a radio earpiece, and stood on her tiptoes to peer at the laptop screen. "Did I hear that right? You've found it?"

"We think so," said Giles. "Won't know for certain until he attacks."

"Oh, that's very comforting. I do love standing around, waiting for something to happen."

"If I'm right, we won't have too long to wait," said Bridge.

"If you're right," repeated Andrea, with emphasis. "We had a word for people like you in the Forces; *Quasis*."

Bridge tried to figure out what the nickname could mean. "Quasi-skilled? Quasi-normal?" She shrugged in defeat.

Andrea smirked. "*Quasimodo*, you big daft. 'Cos you've always got a hunch."

"Bit harsh," Giles snorted.

"I didn't know you were a soldier," said Bridge, looking down at Andrea. "I thought…well, I mean…"

Andrea gave her a withering look. "No height requirement in the army, Ms Sharp. So long as I can kill you with one hand, it's all good."

Bridge looked to Giles for help. "Can't tell if she's joking."

"Best tread carefully, just in case," Giles said with a smile. "And be fair, Andrea. This isn't some vague gut feeling. You saw the CTA's evidence, and you know what Bridge found in Agenbeux."

"Hang on, she's read my reports?"

Giles shrugged. "More like an oral summary."

Text scrolled up the side of a window on the laptop screen. "Activity," said Bridge. "Here we go. Ultra-high frequency, RC-style packets. Hang on, though…there's a side stream of really high-bandwidth, low-latency traffic, funnelled from multiple destinations. It's like he's watching Netflix on half a dozen monitors at once, or — shit, it's multiple units. He's not flying one drone, he's got a bloody fleet of them."

"The high traffic streams are probably mounted camera feeds," said Monica through the headset. "Which suggests they're being controlled directly, not following a pre-programmed route. That's probably good for us."

"Multiple drones?" said Andrea. "So which one has the material?"

Bridge frowned. "No idea. Maybe all of them."

"Fucking hell. Right, I'm going in." Andrea marched toward the entrance, shouting into her earpiece. "Move everyone away from the windows. Fast as you can, but be subtle. They may have cameras watching." Bridge wasn't sure how an entire party retreating could be in any way subtle, but that was Andrea's problem. The Scot pointed at a police sergeant as she passed, and shouted, "You, get that woman with the laptop whatever she needs and stay with her till I say otherwise." Then she ran into the building.

The sergeant jogged over. "What can I get for you, ma'am?"

"You can stop calling me *ma'am* for a start. It's Bridge." She turned to Giles. "We should probably get the fire service down here. And I guess a hazmat team might not be a bad idea, just in case."

"Biohazard and CBRN fire already en route," said Giles, "I called them from the car. Are you OK for power, connectivity, all that?"

"Yes, fine." She turned back to the sergeant. "I don't suppose I could get a cup of tea from somewhere?"

The policeman chuckled. "Absolutely, ma'am. You too, sir?"

"I should bloody coco," said Giles. "Bridge, what are our chances? Is this hacking app of yours going to work?"

"All I can say is, it's our best chance. Do you really think I want to be standing here at potential ground zero?"

"Not much would surprise me this evening," said Giles, craning his neck to stare up at the towering glass edifice.

"I think I've got him," Steve shouted in the chatroom. "Location's in Rotherhithe, hang on… I can get you within a hundred metres, but you're on your own from there. Stand by, I'll ping you the location."

"Steve's found Bowman," Bridge said to Giles. "He's just east, in Rotherhithe."

Giles copied the location from her screen, then leaned close to the bluetooth mic and said, "Well done, Steve. We're on our way." He turned to Andrea's driver, who had remained ready in the driver's seat. "Mind if I commandeer you?"

"My pleasure, sir."

"Bridge, stay here and keep on those drones," said Giles. "I'll try to cut him off at source with an AR squad. Get the copper to find you a table," and he slid into the back seat. Bridge lifted the HP off the car roof as it sped away with Giles inside.

The sergeant approached Bridge. "Tea's brewing in the van, ma'am. Is he…?"

"Changed his mind," said Bridge. "Now, can you find me somewhere to put this bloody computer down?" The sergeant led her to his car, fitted with a driver's laptop stand over the gearshift median. He disconnected his own computer and tossed it on the empty passenger seat, then beckoned for Bridge to climb inside. As she swung the stand towards her and sat the HP on it, a constable appeared carrying two polystyrene cups of tea.

The sergeant took them, handing Bridge her cup and keeping the one intended for Giles. "Have a feeling I might need this."

"Hold that thought," said Bridge, as a background window on the screen lit up. "*MaXrIoT*'s locked on the signal," she said to the chatroom. "Here we go."

She punched *Execute*.

The 'IoT' in *MaXrIoT* stood for 'Internet of Things', the world of so-called 'smart devices' that had become so pervasive. Smart door locks, smart thermostats, smart kettles, smart TVs, smart dog bowls, you name it. The majority of these devices had security so laughable, it might as well not be there — passwords like *123456* that, once entered, put the device into 'engineer mode' where it could be made to do almost anything. And not all were housebound, domestic devices. Small business CCTV setups, car entertainment systems, even smart pedometers were the same. On many of these devices the password was permanently hardcoded into the firmware. Still others had literally no security at all, not even a simple password. If you knew where to look online there were archives listing default passwords and entry methods of entire product categories, just waiting to be hacked. Or you could download a 'black hat' package like *MaXrIoT* that did all the hard work for you. Point it at an online target destination, and the app would use that password archive to automatically hack as many smart devices as it could find around the world, making them part of an enormous 'botnet' that could be turned against the target.

Many people didn't understand this as a real threat. What good was hacking a smart TV, anyway? What damage could it do? But it wasn't the smart devices' own capabilities that programs like *MaXrIoT* were interested in. It was their internet connections. Every smart device had a connection to the online world, which meant every one of them could be made to send a request to any other internet-connected device via its Internet Protocol address, or IP. A single request, for a webpage or network ping, might not seem like much. But when millions of devices all sent simultaneous requests, and continued sending them at the rate of a thousand every second, the traffic could overwhelm the target's bandwidth and knock out huge data centres in what was called a Distributed Denial of Service attack, or DDoS.

But while programs like *MaXrIoT* existed for one sole purpose — to conduct DDoS attacks — and governments around the world had been trying to figure out a way to outlaw them for years, strictly speaking they remained legal. Not that the hackers who used them cared either way. These packages were developed and distributed underground, found only in the dark, secret, unlinked places of the internet, destinations only the best (or best-funded) hackers knew existed. There was a hunger for DDoS resources, and if one was somehow eliminated, ten more would take its place within hours.

Steve Wicker had been right. Trying to trace the wifi signal back to Bowman's location would be difficult, and take time they didn't have. Bridge could tell from the traffic that he was anonymising his origin, bouncing between servers around the world, and satellites above it, to obfuscate his IP address. But Bridge wasn't trying to attack Bowman. She was attacking the drones.

Because the drones weren't anonymised. Their IPs were child's play to isolate. And once they were in its sights, *MaXrIoT* threw everything it had at them.

Bridge watched the counter rise as the package travelled the globe, recruiting smart devices to its botnet; from zero to a hundred in five seconds, then three hundred, seven hundred, a thousand, five thousand, and up and up it went. The DDoS immediately began filling the drone signal traffic with garbage, a torrent of meaningless requests and pings. Bridge exhaled slowly, trying to relax. It was going to work. Everything would be fine.

A couple of hundred metres above her, windows shattered as a bomb exploded.

82

The first explosion blasted glass into Andrea's back and left her deaf in one ear.

She'd just arrived at the party. Her officers, along with the members of Special Branch in attendance, had done as they were told and begun moving people away from the windows without causing a fuss. But some of the partygoers were stubborn, demanding to know why the police were getting uppity and insisting they be told what was going on before they would move.

Andrea was arguing with one of them, a senior civil servant, when the first drone hit. The explosion took out several windows and blasted glass into the room. She'd been standing between the civil servant and the windows, and absorbed most of the impact with her back. But the civil servant took a faceful of glass, and when Andrea pushed herself upright she found him lying on the floor, shivering in silent shock. She grabbed his arms and started to drag him backwards to safety, until a burly Five officer ran over and scooped the civil servant up, dropping the man over his shoulder in a fireman's lift.

"Evacuate, now!" shouted Andrea, struggling to be heard above the cries, screams, and roaring wind.

The officer opened his mouth to respond, and the second drone exploded.

83

"What the hell do you mean, explosions?" Giles shouted into his phone.

"Two so far," said Bridge on the other end of the line. "The software's going as fast as it can, we're at over a hundred thousand botnet agents now. That has to be enough to stop it." She sounded more hopeful than sure, to Giles' ears.

"Casualties?"

"No report from the party, yet. None down on the ground, but we're probably all coated with caesium."

"Thirty seconds," said the driver, accelerating out of a hard corner.

"Just keep at it, Bridge. We're nearing the source, but we don't know how many more of those things Bowman might have up his sleeve. If he gets wind of us, he might send them all crashing in at once." The car stopped. Giles leapt out, narrowly missing a collision with the police assault van he'd summoned during the journey as it screeched to a halt. He faced a row of shops, with single-storey flats over them. "Shit. Can Steve narrow it down? Looks like the target's in a flat above some shops, but there's a dozen of them."

He heard Bridge relay the question, then say, "No, sorry. We're dealing with wireless signals here, not a fixed line. Area radius is as good as it gets."

"Then where the bloody hell are you, Bowman?" mused Giles,

looking at the row of buildings. The shops were closed, dark except for the odd soft glow of a security nightlight, while most of the flats above had lights on behind drawn curtains. "He had to move here fast, possibly at short notice. Maybe he's squatting in a flat?"

"Not if it was a planned contingency," said Bridge. "He's been smart so far. We can probably assume he had a backup on standby. Can we check occupant records?"

"It'll take too long. And once we breach, the game's up. Like you said, he's smart, and he'll have an escape route. Something hidden..." He trailed off, noticing something different about one particular shop front. The windows were papered over, the business closed, but there was no 'To Let' sign above the frontage. And a dim interior light illuminated the newspapers covering the glass. "Stand by, we may have him. Sergeant," he waved to the officer in charge of the waiting armed police, "that closed-up store. Breach immediately."

Giles stood back as the police took positions, broke down the shop door, and charged inside with flashlights blazing, making enough noise to wake the entire street.

After thirty seconds the sergeant called out that it was clear, and Giles approached. He hadn't heard any shots fired or shattered glass, and everyone had stopped shouting. That meant either Bowman was incapacitated and silenced...or that his hunch had been wrong.

It wasn't wrong. An Acer laptop sat open on a trestle table, running specialised software, with video feeds of aerial cameras playing in small windows. Empty packaging boxes of expensive consumer drones, the models from the ID fraud purchases, were stacked neatly in a corner. Several units lay around the edges of the shop interior, many partly dismantled.

But Bowman was gone.

84

Bridge sipped her tea as Giles explained what they'd found. Since they'd last spoken there had been one more explosion, before the *MaXrIoT* package finally succeeded and disabled the two remaining drones. They hovered in default mode less than a hundred metres from the Shard windows, while the firemen who'd arrived after Giles departed raised ladder platforms to reach them.

It felt like a pyrrhic victory. She'd prevented two more explosions, and Andrea assured her that while there were some nasty injuries, there had been no fatalities. But three drones had still exploded, and that meant Bridge, Andrea, everyone at the party, all the gathered police and firemen, and probably everyone in the building would all have to be decontaminated of fallout. It was possible they were beyond saving, but Bridge was oddly calm about that. She was more concerned that the whole area might be off-limits for years, potentially decades to come. They might even have to pull the Shard down and dispose of it, but in light of events, that wasn't necessarily a bad thing. Otherwise it would become a constant reminder, an empty symbol of terror with its shattered windows.

The windows. Something about that bothered her. Why had each of the bombs flown into a separate window, rather than flying in through the first breach?

There was definitely an element of terror to Bowman's

operation, and shattering the windows high up in a skyscraper had obvious connotations that would scare people. But radiation aside, nobody had been killed by the actual explosions. Half the material would have been directed outward with the blast in any case, and as each explosive took out the drone carrying it, they couldn't somehow 'inject' the radiation through each broken window after it smashed.

It was wasteful, inefficient, and left a lot to chance. And that didn't seem right. Bridge had never met Bowman, but so far he'd been smart and careful. To put in so much work for such a low percentage of success in the final attack was out of character for any terrorist, and especially one who'd gone to so much trouble. According to Giles, Bowman hadn't stuck around to see if he'd been successful. But then, he'd find that out in tomorrow's papers. All he had to do tonight was set the drones off on a course and leave them to it, on a prearranged course.

But Monica had said the patterns indicated he was controlling them directly. Both things couldn't be true.

"Shit," Bridge cried out, making the police sergeant look in. She shooed him away, typing furiously. "It's not over," she said to the chatroom. "Hang on, I'm scanning again now…there, four of them." Four more signal destinations on the same ultra-high frequency, this time with no high bandwidth side-stream of data. "I think those first drones were regular explosives, not the RDDs. Their job was to blow out the windows, and make holes for this second wave to fly through. These are the drones with the radioactive material."

"But how are they flying?" asked Steve. "Giles shut down Bowman's laptop. And if they're autonomous, how could he be sure they'd make it through the broken windows?"

"Because that's what this was about all along. They're autonomous, self-guiding, error-correcting. They compensate for obstacles, re-target accordingly…this is the Exphoria code in action."

The chatroom fell silent as everyone digested the implications. Then Ciaran said, "Isolate and add them to the target list. The package will swamp them, too."

"The botnet's not big enough," said Monica. "It'll distribute agent resources equally, and we saw how long it took to shut down the first drones."

"Monica's right," said Bridge. "I'm going to redirect the whole botnet away from the first wave. Hit this second wave head on, with the full force."

"Whoa, there," said Steve, "we don't know what the first drones will do when you let them loose. They might continue straight into the building and explode."

"Or they might just drop on my head and explode," muttered Bridge, "but that's got to be better than letting an RDD through, right?"

"What if you're wrong? What if that first wave was carrying the dirty bombs, after all, and you have two unexploded RDDs above your head?"

Bridge took a deep breath. "I know it's a hunch, but this is a classic setup. You set off a small bomb to get everyone's attention, and then you set off a big one in the same place to take out all the people who come running to look. This has to be Bowman's plan. It just…it has to be." She imagined Andrea's voice whispering "*Quasi,*" and realised she was trying to convince herself as much as the others, because there was no time for second-guessing. She couldn't see or hear the new drones overhead, but it was now thirty seconds since they'd appeared in range. If they were designed to catch the party while people were still reeling from the explosions, they could hit the Shard at any moment.

She half-stepped out of the police car, and called to the fire watch commander. Of the three fire engines that had attended the scene, one crew had entered the building after the first explosion, while the police began evacuating everyone inside. The firemen who'd remained outside were now raising ladders to reach the hovering drones. Bridge craned her neck to see, but couldn't make them out against the night sky.

The watch commander jogged over, followed by the police sergeant. "Right old mess, this, ma'am," said the policeman. "What can we do for you?"

She turned to the fireman. "How close are your ladder men?"

"We're getting there, ma'am," he said. Every man here was willing to follow Bridge's orders, but not a single one would stop calling her *ma'am*. "Rotation positioning is delicate when you get that high up. But we'll get them down safely, so long as they don't fall first."

"That's exactly the problem," said Bridge. "They might be about to do just that. How long?" The watch commander nodded and held a brief radio conversation with each of the fire squads operating and climbing the rotating ladders. The consensus was about two minutes. "Too long," said Bridge. "You've got thirty seconds, and then you'd better be ready to catch them."

Bridge climbed back inside the car and started typing. "Diverting in thirty seconds," she said to the chatroom. "Cross every digit and limb you've got."

The police sergeant leaned in. "Dare I ask?"

"Best not," Bridge shrugged. "Then you can tell everyone you had no idea what the mad woman who blew up London was doing."

"Oh," he said, looking up at the fire ladders. "Happy days, then."

She entered the command to turn the *MaXrIoT* botnet on the new drones, and hit Enter.

One second later, three million requests hit the second wave of drones. Bridge crossed her fingers and waited.

Five seconds later, she heard a fireman call out, "Ladder one, capture achieved. Returning now."

Seven seconds later, the remaining first wave drone careered into the Shard ten floors down from the party venue and exploded on impact, showering more glass over the road. Bridge strained to see the fireman up ladder two, who'd been closest. He was still there, and she hoped he was OK.

Ten seconds later, straining her neck to see up, she thought she saw a couple of dark spots move across the sky, toward the windows.

Thirteen seconds later, Andrea called her phone and said, "What the hell just happened? The last drones dropped out of the sky, and now there's a new bunch hovering twenty metres outside the windows up here. What did you do?"

Bridge laughed with relief. The botnet had neutralised the second wave before it reached the target. "I think," she said carefully, "that we won. But the firemen might need some fishing nets."

She climbed out of the police car to stretch her limbs, and massaged the back of her neck. It was cool to the touch.

* * *

When Giles returned to the Shard, the clean-up was in full flow. Andrea was co-ordinating debriefings from the back of an ambulance, assigning officers to watch over certain attendees, and making sure Sir Terence Cavendish went directly to a secure hotel suite where his family would be brought to him. The firemen were busy snagging the hovering second-wave drones, with a hazmat team ready to oversee their safe transport and disposal.

The surviving drone from the first wave had been checked with a Geiger counter and the hazmat team had confirmed they contained only explosives; no radioactive material.

Bridge stood on the edge of the activity, smoking one of her last cigarettes and gazing up at the building.

"I thought you quit," said Giles as he stepped out of Andrea's car.

Bridge looked at the cigarette as if seeing it for the first time, and threw it into the road. "Old habits die hard," she said. Giles looked as if he was about to say something, but didn't. Bridge shrugged. "We stopped the drones, and Andrea said there are some injuries from the explosions, but no fatalities. We have to call that a win, don't we?"

Giles grimaced. "Not while Bowman's in the wind. Either he knew we were coming for him, or he abandoned the broadcasting unit immediately after commencing the operation. Hell, the whole thing could have been on a timer and he's in Timbuktu by now."

"He might," Bridge nodded, "but I reckon he's still around."

"And why is that?"

Bridge smiled. "Fancy a lunchtime walk tomorrow?"

85

5 Across: Newcastle

21 Down: Intransigent

The lunchtime crowds in Whitehall Gardens had thinned out, leaving only tourists, executives, freelancers, and the unemployed — those without offices waiting for them to return. Bowman glared at them all from behind his sunglasses. He'd spent the previous evening shaving his sandy beard and cropping his hair, and now wore a driver's cap, light blazer, trousers and brogues. Nobody would recognise the modern hipster he'd been a few hours before. Even Novak might walk straight past without knowing him.

Bowman had always planned to change his appearance before returning home, but the night's events had forced him to move up his timetable. The Rotherhithe unit was raided, preventing him from monitoring the mission through completion. But according to the morning's papers, the command code he'd written for the second wave of drones had been enough. The attack on the Shard was the lead story in every rag he could see, and while details were sparse, that would change as the day went on. Mainly, he was waiting for word of Sir Terence Cavendish. Had he died in one of the first wave explosions? Or was he now merely cursed to die an excruciating, agonising death by radiation poisoning? Bowman hoped the latter, but either would suffice.

July 28 - 1400 - Tyndale

A tall, dark-haired woman, all in black, walked to the bench facing the statue of William Tyndale and sat at the far end from Bowman, reading something on her phone. He turned away slightly, hoping she'd leave before Novak arrived, and that the Russian wouldn't be late. It was Novak who'd arranged the rendezvous, after all. Bowman was ready to leave the country, having arranged no-questions-asked passage on a private jet to Tripoli. From there he could use any one of a dozen fake passports to hop his way back to Hong Kong, and pay tribute at his parents' shrine. Now they could truly rest in peace.

"Have you seen this? It's amazing," said the woman. Bowman assumed she was making a phone call, then realised she was talking to him while looking at something on her phone.

"Not really interested, thank you," he said, as curtly as he dared without causing a fuss, and looked away.

"Oh no, you really have to see this, Daniel. It's quite special."

She held up the phone to show him the screen. On it was a photograph of a concrete floor somewhere, arranged on which were four black, unmarked drones. His drones.

He grabbed for the woman's arm, but she was ready. As his fingers closed around her arm she unleashed a can of pepper spray, hidden in her other hand, at his eyes. He screamed, reflexively releasing her and staggering to his feet. He fumbled for the pistol tucked inside his blazer, but the pain was incredible, even with his eyes closed. Almost as painful as the impact when someone heavy tackled him from behind, and his head struck the ground.

Somewhere, through the sound of his own screaming rage, he heard the woman laugh.

86

Bridge cradled a cup of coffee and looked out across the river. This was her favourite chill-out space in the Vauxhall building; a low, wide room with a Thames view, cushioned sofas, and machines for tea and coffee. The tea was awful, and the coffee wasn't much better, but the view made up for them both.

She heard the door open behind her, and the scent of hazelnut reached her nose. "How's Bowman?" she asked.

"Still sitting pretty in Belmarsh," said Giles, taking a seat next to her. "He's convinced we captured Novak and tortured the rendezvous code out of him."

"Hubris is a powerful thing. I was relying on that when I posted the fake ASCII."

Giles frowned. "I wish you'd told me about that before we all went running off to Rotherhithe."

"Didn't want to give you false hope. He might have known it was a trap." Bridge sipped her coffee. "What about Sir Terence?"

Giles sighed, and Bridge knew what was coming next. Bowman had confirmed that Air Vice-Marshal Sir Terence Cavendish was his real target, and why. Then-Squadron Leader Terry Cavendish had an affair with Bowman's mother while he was stationed in Sek Kong. After the handover he'd continued to fly over there from time to time, under pretence of a holiday, and see her in secret. But Sir Terence came to realise the Bowmans had been turned by the Chinese, and were in fact preparing to blackmail him to use as their own double agent. After all, if the British government discovered one of their soldiers was sleeping with a Chinese spy…

To save his own skin, Sir Terence instead reported his suspicions about the Bowmans to the Foreign Office, claiming the reason he'd slept with Mrs Bowman in the first place was to discover if she was a spy. The FCO believed him, and simply made it known to Beijing that the family's cover was blown. When the National Security Guard Bureau arrived to remove the source of embarrassment, the 'Pandas' made sure Daniel, then just a child, knew exactly how his parents had failed to honour the glorious people's republic. And throughout his subsequent upbringing by the state, they never let him forget.

Now it was Sir Terence's word against Bowman's. A knight of the realm versus a confirmed terrorist and Chinese spy, one highly motivated to smear the decorated military officer in charge of the project he'd just infiltrated, and whom SIS had since linked to four prior Chinese espionage attacks in the past decade.

"Cavendish is going to get away with a slap on the wrist, isn't he?" said Bridge. More of a statement than a question.

"Not even that. Exphoria looks set for success, and a little birdy told me he'll retire as Lord Cavendish in the new year. No public interest in making a fuss."

She turned back to the river. "So they boot him upstairs with a peerage, to get him out of the way. Lovely."

"And what about you? Are you all packed and ready? Got everything you need?"

"It's only Ireland, Giles. I'm not going camping in the Andes."

He stood. "All the same. I hope you, um, well, not exactly have a good time, but you know what I mean, I think?"

She did.

87

GROUP: uk.london.gothic-netizens

FROM: ponty@top-emails.net

SUBJECT: the death of shadows [Tenebrae_Z RIP]

sad news. our friend and fellow goffik netizen Tenebrae_Z recently passed away. tonight we raise a snakebite and black to the stubborn old bastard, and find ourselves wishing for just one more tale of automotive tomfoolery.

goodbye, my friend. you⊡ll never know what you did for me, and so many others.

[in accordance with his family⊡s wishes, no more details will be forthcoming]

--

ponty

// a wind of promise in an empty house //

Less than twenty-four hours later the thread was 143 posts strong, but Bridge had muted it immediately after posting. She had no idea what his family's wishes actually were, but the Government's were explicit. It would be impossible to go into any details of Declan O'Riordan's death without revealing confidential information about Exphoria. O'Riordan's family had been told he suffered a massive heart attack while walking by the Thames one evening, and simply fell into the river. The coroner's report was 'adjusted' accordingly, and his body sealed from family viewing under the pretence of extreme damage and disfigurement from the water. All they received were his personal effects.

Bridge had never been to Ireland before. Driving across the country from Dublin, she marvelled at how beautiful the landscape was. Completely different to France, especially the Lyon of her childhood, but every bit as lovely, and extraordinarily green. Ten had never spoken about his childhood. Until his death, she hadn't even known he was Irish.

The cemetery was atop a hill outside the town where Ten's widowed mother now lived, after returning here from Dublin following her husband's death. That's what the records said, anyway. Bridge wasn't insensitive enough to call on the family and introduce herself.

The old graves stood in front of the church, nearest the car park, weathered and beaten by the centuries. Names and dates faded to impressions so faint, only the ghosts could read them now. Crumbling angels clung to broken crosses, praying with their half-eroded hands. One reached for the sky as if struggling to return to heaven, to escape the climbing, winding plants that bound it to the earth.

Ten's grave was behind the church, in the modern section where headstones were thick, sharp-cornered, and whole. A fierce wind swirled around the hill, and Bridge was glad of her long woollen overcoat. This coat had seen many a graveyard over the years, mostly at two in the morning with a bottle in her hand, and she imagined Ten would approve of the way its hem pooled on the ground when she crouched to place a deep crimson rose in his vase.

Standing, she had an urge to say something, anything; to apologise. He may have known Bridge worked for SIS, but when he arranged a meeting by the Thames with Marko Novak, he had no idea what he was getting into. What Bridge had unwittingly got him into.

But even here, in a cemetery atop a wind-blown hill in the green divinity of western Ireland, she couldn't bring herself to speak to a spirit she knew didn't exist. Seeing Adrian in Syria was an effect of her subconscious coping with trauma, nothing more. His body was out there somewhere in the desert, while Ten's was here in the ground, and both were nothing more than that.

Bridge saw movement at the edge of her vision, and looked over her shoulder. Two women turned the corner of the church, heading this way. She had to get back to Dublin for the ferry, anyway. She took a breath, said a silent, sad farewell to the headstone, and walked back.

The cemetery pathways were narrow, so she cut sideways between two headstones to make way for the women, whom she took to be a middle-aged daughter helping her elderly mother along the narrow strip of grass. Bridge saw a hint of disapproval in the middle-aged woman's expression, and supposed it was because taking the shortcut risked stepping on a grave. Then she recognised the woman's necklace, and quickly turned away.

Halfway back to Dublin she pulled over to the side of the road, lit a cigarette, and cried.

88

"You wanted to see me?"

"I should coco. Come in, have a seat."

"Which one?"

"Oh, take your pick. I'll get you a coffee."

Giles Finlay's new office was twice the size of his old one, and occupied a coveted corner spot in the labyrinthine Vauxhall corridors. In addition to the usual chairs opposite his desk it also had a small leather sofa and a kitchen stool at the back of the room, by the kitchenette counter where Giles now made a fancy coffee from a fancy machine. The view faced directly north, but today the autumn rain was coming down like stair rods and Bridge could barely see Lambeth Bridge, let alone Parliament.

She chose the sofa. It creaked as she sat down, then again when she leaned forward to take the coffee from Giles, then again when she leaned back, and she decided in future to maybe stick to the Aeron in front of his desk. "You've done well out of this one," she said, genuinely impressed at Giles' ability to turn any victory, no matter how pyrrhic, into a promotion.

"I had some help," he said, raising his coffee to her as he sat down. "And now I need it again."

Bridge sipped her coffee, waiting. She had no idea what this was about, and knew better than to jabber to fill the silence.

Giles placed his coffee down and picked up a file on his desk.

"First, congratulations, you're now indefinite OIT. Everything finally ticked and approved."

She raised an eyebrow. "Indefinite, not permanent?"

"Nobody's permanent," Giles shrugged. "You know how quickly things change."

Bridge said nothing.

"I was in a meeting yesterday at Number Ten, whole lot of generals and the like. Terry Cavendish was there, too." Bridge groaned at the mention of his name, but Giles held up a hand before she could speak. "And in his defence, he put his weight behind a suggestion from the MoD that I think you could help me with."

Bridge remained sceptical. "If you try to put me on his staff, I'll be out that door before you can open my resignation envelope."

"Good heavens, no," said Giles. "They've asked me to draft a proposal for a new task force. Cross-departmental, collaborative, relatively high-autonomy. One of the conclusions of the Exphoria business is that we're all rather too compartmentalised. If us, Five, GCHQ, and the MoD had all spoken to one another and shared information more consistently, it might never have got out of hand. And you, I might add, wouldn't have been placed in harm's way."

"I'm touched by your concern," she said sarcastically, "but what do you need my help for? Do you want me to research potential operatives?"

Giles laughed softly. "Bridge, I want you to *be* one of the operatives. In fact, I rather think you should lead it. And yes, that will mean helping to figure out who else we should recruit."

She fought not to show reaction in her expression, as a multitude of emotions collided inside her. Mostly there was surprise, but also pride, and even a certain amount of optimism. "Definitely worth giving it a try," she said, deliberately understated. "Count me in."

"Don't get too excited," said Giles, half-smiling. "It's only draft stage, no guarantees. There's a whole circus of flaming hoops to jump through for approval, not to mention trying to scrape together funding from somewhere. But what do you think?"

Bridge looked around at Giles' palatial new office and thought the funding part wouldn't be a problem.

* * *

After dinner, she logged into the chat server at Telehouse and purged the entire machine, running a seven-pass overwrite to ensure nothing could possibly be retrieved from the hard drive. When it finished two hours later she installed a basic NT profile, infected it with a weak trojan, then deleted the admin login and cleaned all trace of it from her own computer.

Bridge made a cup of tea, took the laptop to her bedroom, and unmuted the Tenebrae_Z memorial thread.